PROMISE BRIDES

THREE-IN-ONE COLLECTION

S. DIONNE MOORE

ISBN 978-1-61626-473-4

All scripture quotations are taken from the King James Version of the Bible.

Cover Design: Kirk DouPonce, DogEared Design

Published by Barbour Publishing, Inc., P.O. Box 719, Uhrichsville, Ohio 44683, www.barbourbooks.com

Our mission is to publish and distribute inspirational products offering exceptional value and biblical encouragement to the masses.

Printed in the United States of America.

Dear Readers,

It has been my pleasure to write the stories you are reading. I can only hope that I have done justice to those times in history, so filled with turmoil and tragedy, and that the characters reflect emotions becoming to such experiences. History is full of heroes. Not those we read about in text books or see in the media, but those who live quiet lives determined to reach out to someone else who might have greater need than themselves. And those who determine to overcome obstacles of sin in their lives with the help and grace of God, so they might be better prepared to help others along the way. These are the true heroes of time.

It has brought me such joy to read your responses to the stories within this book. Please know that the time you take to fill out and send in the tear-off sheets is not unappreciated. I grow from your comments and sometimes even glean a fresh idea for another book! And to those of you who have written to me—beautiful letters and cards that give me a glimpse of your hearts and struggles—your notes have become some of my most precious treasures. Whenever I lack inspiration or wrestle with a particularly hard subject, or if I'm just feeling lonely, I often take out those notes and think of the time and heart you put into penning those words.

From the bottom of my heart, I thank you.
S. Dionne Moore

PROMISE OF TIME

Dedication

In loving memory of Jacalyn Wilcoxon,
pastor's wife, friend, mentor. I miss you.

Chapter 1

Gettysburg, Pennsylvania, 1863

The prayer of the reverend, standing on a raised platform for all to see and hear, droned in Ellie's ears. She saw him but did not see him. Her heart and eyes focused more on the huge arch designating the entrance to Evergreen Cemetery and the rising fog that still clung over the raw mounds of dirt, marking the fresh graves in the new burial site of Gettysburg, about to be officially dedicated.

Reverend Stockton got louder, his prayer building, the words plucking at the taut chords of her heart. ". . .because Thou hast called us, that Thy blessings await us, and that Thy designs. . ."

Blessings!

Witnessing the terror of her friends and family during those terrible days of intense battle between the North and South. This was a blessing? What of the mourning Wade family, grieved over the loss of Genny, their young daughter, killed by a stray bullet as she made bread? The stench of death, still a powerful memory in her mind, when bodies lay in the fields bloated and rotting. Ellie's breath choked and she pressed her hand against her mouth. What of the *blessing* of a husband of less than two years lying in a grave in hated Southern soil, lost and forgotten except by the one person who had loved him?

". . .in reverence of Thy ways, and in accordance with Thy word, we love and magnify the infinite perfections. . ."

Ellie pressed her hand tighter to her lips. A touch on her elbow made her turn toward her friend.

"Ellie?"

She could hear the concern in Rose's voice.

"You need to rest. Why don't we go home?"

Ellie took a deep breath. She couldn't allow her own grief to pull her friend away from this very important program, not with the president set to speak. Besides, at some point she needed to distance herself from her grief if she was to be of any use to Rose. Her quiet friend's swelling body and pale face showed signs of her own private torment, what with the impending birth of her first child and the continued report of her husband missing in action.

Ellie led her friend through the crowd, mostly women. Some reached out to her, widows themselves. She felt their isolation in a physical way that pinched her vision to a narrow tunnel, and at the end of that tunnel was the cold stone of a grave marker.

Sunshine broke through the haze that marked the beginning of the day and shone down on her head, yet she felt it from a distance, the warmth unable to penetrate the shell of her grief.

"I believe we will see some sunshine today after all," Rose murmured, resting a hand on her stomach. "It will be good to feel warm again."

"Yes. It would feel good," Ellie said, more to placate her friend than from any feeling of conviction. How long had it been since she'd felt the lulling warmth of peace? Seven long months. Ever since the news came that Martin had died.

"You don't have to stay for me," Rose said.

Ellie closed her eyes and swallowed. Forced a smile. "You wanted to hear Mr. Everett. We should stay." Mr. Edward Everett's speech would be long. She knew the man's reputation, and she was unsure what reserve of strength she would draw from to survive what was surely to be a long day of even longer speeches. "And Mr. Lincoln, of course. What a treasure to have him come and speak on our behalf." She again pressed her hand to her lips, recalling the president's own recent grief. To lose a child so young. She chided herself for being selfish. Others knew grief and still functioned. She must as well. "I—I think I'll take a stroll."

She felt Rose's eyes on her, and when her friend held out a handkerchief, Ellie took it without comment. That Rose knew where Ellie's stroll would take her didn't surprise her. The sight of row upon row of neatly placed graves tore at her. She rolled with the wave of fresh grief, shocked anew by the bitter taste of despair that sucked away what fleeting strength she had tried to cloak herself with.

She stopped at the edge of the field of graves. Disbelief swirling. All of this was a mistake. It had to be. Martin should be here, in Gettysburg, not buried haphazardly in some Southern field. She closed her eyes and went to her knees in the damp soil, uncaring of those who might be staring. No, they would have their attention fastened upon the speaker, she comforted herself. She shifted, grinding dirt into her skirts, dimly aware that the long prayer had ended and music played. She made use of Rose's handkerchief until it became a saturated mass.

The music went quiet, and a man's rich voice began the slow rise that marked the beginning of a speech. Everett. Rose must be entranced. Having heard so much of the orator and his absolute support of the Union's cause, her friend had been excited to hear him talk. Ellie caught only bits and pieces of the man's speech as she walked along the perimeter of the crowd, too restless to sit, too grieved to stand still.

Her legs had begun to ache when a smattering of applause broke her reverie. Ellie headed back toward the place where she had parted from Rose. Thousands of people crowded around the raised platform. When Ellie could not discern the familiar shape of her friend, panic plucked at her. Rose wouldn't leave her. She was sure of it. Her throat closed. Maybe something terrible had happened. Dread squeezed her chest. She would be alone. Again.

Ellie took in the smear of pale faces staring her way. One moved in her direction and touched her arm. "Are you all right, ma'am?"

She did not recognize the man, nor the woman beside him. A couple. She squeezed her eyes shut and shook her head.

"Ellie?"

Rose!

She turned, and Rose's small form hurried toward her. "I was keeping an eye out for you." Concern etched Rose's expression and dimmed the twinkle in her eyes. "You've been crying."

"I'm fine."

Ellie could see the protest form on Rose's lips, but she turned her attention back to the speaker, steeling herself. She did her best to concentrate on the speech, but only when President Lincoln stood did she feel anything close to anticipation. Here was the man—black crepe around his top hat in honor of the death of his own son—who understood death in a personal way. President Lincoln's presence injected a measure of life into the corner of her heart that the news of Martin's death had withered.

Papers in hand, his higher-pitched voice strong with conviction, Lincoln began. "Fourscore and seven years ago. . ."

☙

Theodore watched from the shadows of Rupp's Tannery as a group of men on horseback cantered down Baltimore Street, passed him, then eased onto Emmitsburg Road. He pressed his back to the building that squatted parallel to Baltimore Street and prayed the moonlight would not reveal him. He withdrew to the back of the building, crossed the yard, forded a small stream, and passed through several yards before he reached Breckinridge Street. He stared at the house in front of him. It was the one he remembered from the day of his cousin's marriage. His cousins's bride's house, left to her by her mother. The place Theo hoped to find her.

His tension eased when he realized the windows of the brick house were dark. A wide oak tree blocked the front of the house from view, but his cousin's letters had described the clever entry to a cellar at one end of the porch and how his wife worked hard at putting up vegetables and storing various canned goods in the cool space. It was the place he hoped to call home for the night.

Theo rested against the cold brick and dared to close his eyes. His feet burned with rawness, a torture worsened with every passing day but endured out of necessity. He dared not loose the bloody strips of cloth he had tied on to relieve the pain in his bare feet.

In slow degrees, his body relaxed, but he jerked alert in the next breath. Exhaustion would be his downfall. He pushed himself away from the brick wall and went to his hands and knees. With ears keen from nights spent discerning the difference between the sounds of humans or animals approaching, Theo absorbed the atmosphere. Where his vision might fail, his ears would not.

Satisfied that nothing out of the ordinary moved, he stood and hastened toward the house. Sweat broke out on his upper lip as the porch came into view. He squeezed himself up close to the brick wall of his cousin's house and slithered toward the porch. In the darkness, he felt for the hinges of the cellar door and found the ring used to pull the door open.

Theo spit into his hand and smeared the wetness on first the top hinge then the lower one and prayed the added moisture would work as a lubricant and keep the door from squeaking. With trepidation, he eased the door toward him, drawing a breath only when the opening became large enough for him to slip through.

With the door firmly shut behind him, he felt his way along with his hands, a damp, cool wall of stone greeting his fingertips and scrubbing his palms. For a moment he stood perplexed. The porch ran the length of the house, a good ten feet by his estimate, yet he guessed that he had come only five feet. This stone wall must be to support the middle section to avoid sag. Sure his assessment must be correct, he followed the wall into a room that smelled of apples, with undertones of dust and mildew. But the scent refreshed him. He longed for a light to see by but dared not risk giving himself away, even if he had possessed a lantern.

His fingers skimmed the jars of produce and rough gunnysacks of apples and potatoes. Food. His hand closed around the smooth skin of an apple, and he sank his teeth into the fruit, surprised by the tart bite of the tender flesh. He munched as quietly as he could then began on a potato and finished with another apple.

A dull thud brought him up straight. His hands went clammy and he lowered the apple and cocked his head to listen harder.

The sound did not repeat. He took another bite, quieter this time. It must be someone in the house turning over in bed or falling out. If Martin's wife, Ellie, was not alone, or if she had relatives living with her in the wake of her grief, his chances of being identified increased. The thought congealed the contents of his stomach into a heaving mass.

He put the apple aside and stretched out on the dirt floor, his body demanding rest. With his fist, he made a pillow of a small sack of apples. He closed his eyes and tried to plan how he would introduce himself into the household.

What would Ellie Lester be like in person? He had read so much about her in Martin's letters that Theo felt as if he knew her. But among Martin's personal effects, he never located a picture. Not everyone, he supposed, had the benefit of such a treasure to remember a loved one by, but he had hoped to remind himself what she looked like before coming face-to-face with her. His cousin's wedding to the woman had been a long time ago, and though Theo recalled the day, the faces had receded a bit as the horrors of war had driven the pleasant memories into hiding.

Something tickled along Theo's arm, and he slapped at the place, feeling the crush of a tiny body. A spider, no doubt. With a weary sigh, he rolled to his side and fell into a deep sleep.

Chapter 2

Ellie tied a dark handkerchief over her golden hair. She crossed to the table and tested the knot of the dishcloth, in which she had tied a loaf of bread and cold salt meat from her lone supper. Rose had invited her to stay and eat with her, but Ellie had made the decision to seclude herself after the dedication ceremony to rest for the evening duties she needed to perform. Though she made sure to remind Rose to call her should her labor begin.

"You know I will."

"The minute your pain starts," Ellie pressed.

Rose had given her a wan smile. "The very minute."

Her friend's pale complexion had concerned Ellie, but she knew little of babies and birthing. She would be the one to go fetch Martha, the black woman who had attended more births than Ellie could count.

Ellie leaned forward and tested the weight of the food within the dishcloth. Too heavy and she would have a hard time slipping quickly down the cellar stairs. She peered out her darkened kitchen window and waited, her ears attuned to the ticking clock and the chimes to mark two o'clock in the morning. It would be soon, she knew. She moved back to the table and sat, her hands cupping the package of food. She inhaled the familiar scents of fresh linen combined with that of fried salt pork that still lingered.

She loved her home, left to her—along with the family farm on the outskirts of Gettysburg—upon the death of her mother. Her only regret—that she could not have shared it with Martin for more than the few months they had been together. Her mother's death, followed so closely by Martin's, compounded her sadness. Still, she had a home, and her mother's words echoed in her head. *"A woman should have a place of her own, Ellie, and there's no place like your birthplace."*

Ellie couldn't help the smile. Her mother might have been gentle and kind, but she also had a backbone made of brick. After her death, Ellie had moved back into town, renting the farmhouse to a young couple and the land to a farmer to work.

This house suited her better than the farm. She loved the uniqueness of the building—two separate homes under one roof, the front porch shared by both—and having Rose so close by. She had been thrilled when Martin agreed to stay in town versus moving out to the farm, especially when talk of war had started to brew.

Oh, Martin.

The clock began to chime the hour, and Ellie snapped from her memories and got to her feet. She hefted the dishcloth of food and stepped out into the night. She was careful to watch where she placed her feet, the ends of the boards less squeaky than the centers. But too close to the edge and a warped board might groan a protest. She breathed more easily when she cleared the porch and made her way to the cellar as fast as she could.

She hesitated when the cool air of the cellar whooshed across her face and neck. Something didn't seem quite right. She held the door and squinted into the darkness. As far as she could see, the stone wall in front of her remained intact, so no worries there. That's when it came to her. The door. Of course. She wiggled the door back and forth and realized it hadn't uttered its normal whine of protest. Perhaps the wood had dried a bit in the low humidity and shrunk enough to solve the problem.

Ellie shrugged off the matter and descended the cellar steps until she stood in front of the stone wall that supported the porch in the middle. She began to work at the loose stones with her bare fingers then searched in her apron pocket for the slender knife she carried for such purposes. Removing the first stone was always the most difficult. With the aid of the knife, she wedged the tip between a gap and withdrew the first stone. The smell of unwashed bodies hit her full in the face. When five stones were removed, she set the dishcloth on the ledge, turned her back on the hole, and marched up the steps to the yard where she shrank beneath a tree.

In the dim light, the man and two women moved from the cover of the cellar toward the back of the house.

As fast as she could, Ellie returned to the cellar and replaced the stones. In the stillness of the night, she could see nothing moving. She didn't know where the runaways escaped to. It was safer that way.

"Lord, go with them," she whispered.

☙

Theo's heart rate slowed with each passing minute of silence. Again, his ears had not failed him even though his body lay suspended in near unconsciousness. At first his instinct had been to rise and run, but the darkness of the cellar had registered in his mind and assured him that whoever he was hearing could not see him.

He had gone to his knees and crawled from his corner toward the doorway. Sounds of scratching and stabbing against a rough surface made him hold his breath. He heard more scraping then light steps retreating. He weighed whether he should retreat to the tree in the front yard or stay put.

But as he debated, more noises came to his ears. This time a lower murmur—a grunt. A low sniff. A pair of footsteps on the stairs, then another, and another, the tread of the last heavier than the first two. A wave of fetid, warm air assaulted Theo's nose. He stood to his feet, biting down on a gasp as his tender feet were reintroduced to his full weight.

Dim light streamed through the open cellar door, and he could just make out the hole in the stone wall before the rustle of material forced him to retreat a step. He dared not take the path back to his corner in the dark, lest he knock something over or disturb a jar. He stood, stock still, fear of discovery pressing down on his spine.

He heard the rush of breathing and the scraping of the stones. When he inched his head around the corner, he saw the outline of a woman, her dark clothes making her nearly invisible, only the soft sounds of the stones giving away her presence.

Ellie? He wanted to say the name but knew he must bide his time. Whatever she was doing, he must not startle her.

When the scraping of stones stopped, the woman retreated up the steps and lowered the cellar doors, leaving him encased in blackness once again.

Chapter 3

Theo lay still, wide awake yet confused. He longed for a watch of some sort to tell the time and free him from the prison of not knowing how long he slept or whether it was day or night. He rubbed his head and scratched his chest. A bath would be nice. A real bath. Not a little bit of water on an already filthy rag, but one with warm water and a bar of soap.

Theo groaned and lay back on the earthen floor of the cellar, feeling very much a prisoner of a different sort than the ones the army demanded. He grinned and reached under his head for the sack and withdrew an apple. At least he would not go hungry, surrounded as he was by the store of vegetables.

His first bite of the fruit did nothing to alleviate his ever-darkening mood. Mushy on his tongue, the apple was one best used for sauces or apple butter than for snacking. Eating presented another problem as his system awakened to the presence of food. He finished off the apple and sank back against the sack. He would go mad in this darkness.

With renewed determination, he got to his feet and felt his way to the doorway. Each step brought him closer to the place where the cellar began. It took a minute for him to realize the blackness had receded somewhat and that he could vaguely make out the stone wall he had seen the previous night. When he turned his head in the direction of the cellar stairs, he saw the strips of daylight through the cracks in the doors.

His heart rejoiced at the prospect of sunlight and fresh air. Of an outhouse. He had to do something and knew he would be able to judge by the place of the sun in the sky what time of day it was.

Before he could climb the first step, something scraped against the outside of the doors. As fast as his sore feet would allow, he hobbled back to his spot and realized his first duty should have been to find a way to hide himself rather than to feed his stomach.

The doors swung open and streams of light bounced off the stone wall. He stood stock still, unsure what to do or what to say, for surely the woman was not returning to release more runaway slaves from their hiding place. Not at this time of day. If it was a woman, she would scream upon seeing him, and he couldn't afford that.

Able to see the interior of the room now, Theo crouched near the doorway. The whooshing of skirts and petticoats confirming the gender of his visitor.

He picked up a potato lying in a neat pile and gripped it in his fist. When he figured the woman would be ready to round the corner, he rolled the potato along the floor in her path, hoping to divert her attention and give himself time to come up behind her.

Her gasp and squeal let him know the ruse had worked. He poked his head around the corner. Her face was turned in the direction of the potato. In an instant he was behind her and pressing his palm over her mouth.

She tensed.

"Don't scream. Please. I can explain, and I'm not going to hurt you."

He hated the fear he was generating and continued to speak in a soothing voice even as his nerves burned. If she got away, if he let go without securing her promise, he knew the consequences he would face.

"My name is Theodore Lester. We've met before. At your wedding. I'm the Southern cousin whose idea it was to hang your wedding bed from the rafters." He gulped and felt the heat creep into his cheeks, but his candor was rewarded and the terror in her expression melted into wariness.

She nodded.

He held his breath as he released his grip on her mouth and backed up two steps to give her room and a measure of reassurance that his intentions were noble. He grimaced at the irony of the thought. As noble as the intentions of a man hiding in a cellar could be.

"The name is familiar." Her words were guarded. "Martin's cousin."

"You're Ellie."

Her voice came out strained. "What are you doing here? And why didn't you come to the house instead of. . ."

He saw the moment the enormity of his problem sunk into her consciousness.

"You're a—a soldier."

Theo nodded. "Confederate, and they'll likely kill me if they find me."

☙

Ellie studied the man closely, afraid to believe he was who he said he was and afraid not to believe it. The man was admitting to being a deserter. And kin. But he was also the enemy, and she would not soon forget the conceited and bullying ways in which the Confederates had strutted about Gettysburg during its occupation. Horror stories whirled in her head, not to mention the rumors of the way the men had raided other towns for food, with little thought for the people from whom they had taken.

Yet his lean face and painfully thin frame lent credence to his story. If he had run away, he had been running for a long time. Her gaze swept the length of him, and she frowned at his feet and the sight of blood that saturated the rags that bound them.

When she raised her face to his, a horrible dread swept over her. She had come down to the cellar yesterday morning for potatoes, and last night, too, though she had not entered the cellar, just the hallway long enough to—

The thought exploded in her mind. If he had been here last night, surely he would have seen what she had been up to. She willed herself to remain calm. Not to jump to conclusions. He could have found the cellar at any time in the predawn. But the question remained. "Why here? What do you want? Why shouldn't I turn you over to the authorities?"

He drew air into his lungs, seeming to draw on some deep-seated reserve of strength.

When his gaze caressed her face then fell to the ground, her senses knotted, and for a moment she felt the first stirrings of sympathy. But his words, when he finally spoke, crushed the soft feeling beneath its heel.

"Because being a Southern gentleman, I would mightily despise telling others what your nighttime occupation involves."

Chapter 4

Ellie shifted her arm so the jar of preserves nestled more firmly against the crook of her elbow. She spewed a stream of air at the still dangling strand of hair tickling her right eye, cast an eye over the cellar doors to make sure they were shut, and marched toward the house with a million thoughts ricocheting around her brain.

The memory of her wedding day was sharp in her mind. Martin's crooked grin when he saw her, the light in his eyes when he leaned in to kiss her, their late supper together, both too nervous to eat much of anything. But the faces of the guests were hazier. She remembered Theodore more because of Martin's talk of his letters and their childhood together. And of course, the bed incident. She would make sure to take a light with her next time. She wanted to see him and make sure the man was not an imposter bent on wickedness.

Instead of heading into her side of the house, she went to the door on the other side of the long porch and gave a light knock before entering. Laid out as a mirror image to her home, Ellie had no problem finding the kitchen where Rose stirred up a panful of gravy.

"It's a beautiful morning," Ellie said, making an effort to quell her nerves and force a note of cheer that she did not feel.

"You brought the preserves?" Rose gave a glance over her shoulder, a smile lighting her hazel eyes.

"Don't I always bring something?" She bit down on her tongue. The question sounded harsh, even to her own ears. "I mean,"—she forced a light tone—"what kind of neighbor would I be if I didn't bring something to add to the meals you so kindly invite me to?"

Rose patted her hands into a mound of flour and began kneading a trough of dough. "You're always welcome."

She set the preserves on the counter at Rose's elbow.

"Peach will go well with the sourdough," Rose said.

"I need to get down in the cellar and do some organizing before next year's harvest creates more confusion. It's full of cobwebs, too, and needs a good cleaning."

"True enough." Rose's eyes twinkled. "You always come over with some manner of dust or dirt clinging to you." Her friend's eyes were on her hair, and

Ellie touched the spot that held Rose's attention. She pulled out the clinging remnants of a cobweb.

"Once I get this bread to rising, we'll eat and I'll help you tackle that cellar."

"No!" She almost choked on that syllable. She forced calmness into her tone and tilted her head to indicate Rose's swollen stomach. "You shouldn't be going up and down those steps in your condition."

Rose laughed and the paleness of her complexion benefited from the exercise, bringing spots of color to her cheeks. She smoothed a hand over her midsection, a soft smile curving her pink lips. "I'm feeling fine. Never better."

"Then work on the nursery or that blanket you've been so furiously knitting. Going up and down the stairs is best left to those of us who can see our feet."

Her friend gave a mock grimace. "But look at what I'll have to show for it." Her eyes flashed to Ellie's and she gasped. "Oh, Ellie, I didn't mean for it to sound like that."

It was a fact that no children would be in her future now that Martin lay dead somewhere in the South. Maybe never. She sent her friend a smile. "I'll simply enjoy spoiling your girl."

"Boy," Rose corrected.

Ellie laughed. "Twins."

Rose chuckled and dug deeper into the dough, turning it and pushing outward. "I'll make sure to have a good dinner waiting for you when you're done down there."

"I'll set the table."

Rose swept her hands together and loosed a white cloud of flour into the air. "While you're doing that, I'll slice the ham."

Ellie did her best to put her heart into the breakfast conversation. It was times like this, when the deeds of the night before seemed to hang heavy in her mind—along with the fear that Rose might have seen or heard something—that Ellie felt most tense. And now she had yet another secret to shield from her friend.

When she finally excused herself and got the cleaning rags and broom from her own house along with a lantern, she dragged everything through the yard and around to the front of the house that faced the street, alert for prying eyes of curious neighbors. At the cellar, she put the broom against the wall and the lantern on the ground and pulled open the cellar door. She skirted down the steps of the cellar, making a racket as she went. When she reached the landing, she set the things aside and went back up the steps to retrieve the rest. When she finally pulled the doors closed behind her, darkness engulfed her and a shiver went up her spine.

ᴄᴙ

Theo heard the telltale rattle of the cellar doors and swept to his feet as icy dread suffused him. He lunged toward the doorway and picked up a potato, bent on distracting the person as he had done with Ellie. His only option—to give himself time to escape.

Lord, please let it be Ellie.

When he thought the person close, he rolled the potato through the doorway and bit his lip.

"Do you honestly think I'd fall for that again?"

Ellie. Relief flooded him, and he staggered backward and collapsed. She appeared with all manner of things in her arms. Though he wished to rise and help her, he knew his legs would not hold him.

"Theo?" Concern etched her tone. He heard the strike of a match and watched as she lit the wick of a lantern then lowered the chimney.

Shadows fell back and still he felt the weakness, ashamed of it. "You scared me."

She held the lantern up and crossed to him. In the light he could make out her features. The same woman he had seen right before the war. Martin's bride. Then she had been flushed with life and hope for her future. Now the blue of her eyes held shadows, and her expression seemed weighted by the cares and horrors she had experienced in the interim.

"We'll need to set up a signal of some sort so that you'll know when it's me coming."

Her words brought him a measure of relief. "Are you ill?" She placed the lantern on a low ledge and sunk down beside him. Her cool hand pressed against his forehead.

He tried to form an answer but could not. He jerked his head away from her touch and closed his eyes. "Nothing food wouldn't solve. I'm sick of apples and raw potatoes."

For a golden moment, her laugh encased him in a bubble of warmth. "I didn't think to bring anything from the last meal." She paused and her brow creased. "I'll have to figure something out."

He knew the question he was about to ask seemed pathetic, but he had to ask it for his own sanity. "You won't tell on me?"

Her lips firmed and her gaze met his, unflinching. "If you promise not to reveal what you saw."

Theo nodded, content in their stalemate. He had made the threat of telling about her night occupations out of desperation. He could never do something so terrible to a lady, and especially not to the wife of his cousin, but she didn't know that. Let her think him a cad. He had little choice. "Do you keep them every night?" he asked.

She sat back on her heels, her skirts puffed slightly around her. A lone minute passed as her eyes seemed to focus on the bandages on his feet. She reached out her hand as if to touch the soiled rags. "No. There was a problem and they had to come here. For that reason, I was thinking it would be a good place for you." She raised her head. "Before you decide to move on."

He recognized the steel that had inserted itself into her tone. He was not to let himself get too comfortable in her home and think he could stay.

"I'll bring some salve for your feet and bind them with clean linen." In a smooth action, she got to her feet and brushed at the dirt on her skirts. "For now, I've work to do."

She moved about the room, rag in hand, kicking up a cloud of dust that tickled his throat. He did his best to keep his eyes elsewhere but would inevitably find himself drawn to her form.

Bits and pieces of his cousin's wedding day came into focus. Martin's laughter that precluded his usual tendency toward stoicism. It had not been hard to see that Ellie's good-natured personality had drawn Martin out of his shell. Theo recalled, again, the way Martin had talked of her in his letters, with pride and love.

He wanted to tell her what he had seen. Of Martin's last moments. Such knowledge would ease her grief but generate a very different pain. That of betrayal. Now that he had seen her, he wondered if telling her the truth was merely his excuse to fly toward freedom or his misplaced sense of duty toward his cousin. If he told her all he knew and handed over the mementos he had secured, there would be no lasting reason for him to stay, and he would be on the run again.

He closed his eyes and licked his lips. He wanted so much to rest. To be strong again, whole and happy. Unhindered by war and death, friendships cut short by shrapnel or balls or bullets.

Just a little while. I'll rest. Then I'll tell her all I know and move on.

Chapter 5

It galled Ellie to see him lie there, unresponsive and uncaring, while she was working so hard to clean the cellar. Martin would have certainly asked by now, and even if she had turned down his offer of help, he would have done something else to ease her burden. It was the kind of man her husband had been.

When Ellie sneaked another peek at Theo, she was again struck by the evidence of his weariness. The same telltale marks that she'd seen in the soldiers she'd helped nurse back to health in the wake of the Battle of Gettysburg. Dark circles. Paleness. A strange sensitivity. She'd heard stories from Union soldiers of Rebels stealing boots off dead bodies. Of their strange screeching yell that invaded their nightmares.

Yet she had tended Confederate soldiers as well and knew that they suffered just as much as the ones they called their enemies. Perhaps more so. Most were more poorly dressed than the Union soldiers. And when they would ask for the result of the battle and learned of Lee's retreat, a fierceness seemed to overtake them. Or complete resignation.

Theo's feet, bound in bloody, old rags, seemed to speak to her of horrors she could not comprehend. Was it so bad that he had to escape? She had no doubt that he had walked hundreds of miles, spent nights hiding in the woods, and it struck her that the runaways she aided probably had it better than a deserter.

Martin's letters spoke of scanty provisions and long marches, but the letters he wrote did not often linger on the atrocities of war. He might allude to something, but he would always smooth it over by sharing something funny or personal, a dream he had for them when they were reunited or the memory of a private moment that never failed to draw a smile from her.

Seeing Theo's face had assured her he was who he said he was, though he was slimmer and the boyish curves of his face had matured into angular planes since their last meeting. His eyes were the same. As soon as the lantern light revealed his silver-gray eyes, it pulled up a clear memory from her wedding day. That of Martin's cousin standing in the doorway of the barn with the bed dangling high above his head. Those eyes shining bright with mischief as Martin howled with laughter.

She placed her rag over the bristles of the broom and lifted it to clear a cobweb in the corner of the room. As she continued working, she knew that

Martin would want her to help Theo, even to hide him.

Her arms grew weary of the dusting, and she stopped to survey her work, satisfied with what she saw. She turned when a low groan issued from behind her.

Theo writhed on the floor like a man in deep pain.

She went to him and pressed her hand to his cheek. He jerked and the motion startled her back on her heels. She grabbed his shirt to gain leverage, but the thin material rent beneath her touch. She sat down hard on the dirt floor as Theo came up to a sitting position, blinking awake.

Stunned, Ellie could only stare.

In a slow movement that betrayed the depth of the slumber she'd woken him from, Theo braced his hand against the floor and stood. If his feet caused pain, his face did not show it. "I'm sorry. Let me help you up." The slow drawl of his words marked him as Southern more than his appearance.

"You were groaning terribly. I thought. . ." His hand touched her elbow and guided her upward. Her thoughts scrambled in the second that he steadied her, and she felt the intense desire to draw close to him, even if for a moment. Just to feel once again the comfort of a man's embrace. She drew in a breath and gave herself a mental shake.

His hands grasped her upper arms and set her away from him. "I sometimes have nightmares," he explained.

She turned away, confused and saddened.

☙

Theo didn't know what to do. Everything in Ellie's demeanor communicated stress. He wondered if she had been hurt in her tumble but didn't know how to ask. Ignoring the discomfort in his feet, he took up the broom she had left in the corner and began sweeping the dirt floor.

Her delicate cough caught his attention.

He stopped and looked at her through a haze of dirt.

She gave him a small smile. "You're kicking up quite a cloud of dust. You can't sweep a dirt floor like you do a wood one."

"Oh." He stared at the broom as if it alone had been the offender. "I'd offer to fetch you a cup of water, but I. . ."

"I'll get some. And some food, too." She moved to untie the apron at her waist. "You can help yourself to the peach preserves." Her gaze dipped to the tear in his shirt that revealed some skin beneath. "And a clean shirt."

He swallowed. "I need to. . ." How did a gentleman ask such a thing of a lady?

"You need to. . .what?"

"I could use a trip outside. . .to the. . .uh. . ."

Whatever she felt, it was not horror or embarrassment. Instead, her eyes crinkled at the corners and he thought he saw her nostrils flare.

"I assure you it is no laughing matter, ma'am."

This time she did laugh. "I'm sorry." He could see the effort it took for her to get serious, and the sight lightened his guilt. If she could chuckle, even at his expense, it meant she must not be hurt. "It's really dangerous for you to be out during the day. It's around back, you see, and Rose, my friend, uses that entrance far more than she uses the front. So it's a matter of timing."

"I'll do whatever it takes to keep you safe."

She went still. Her lips pressed together, and she averted her face.

He reviewed what he had said, realized the intimate suggestion of his words, and ran a hand over the back of his neck. "What I meant—"

Her gaze snapped to his. "I'll think of something. First, I'll get the food and some clothes, maybe a bucket and some soap?" Her eyes dropped to his feet. "And some salve for those feet."

She lifted her skirts and passed through the doorway and up the cellar stairs before he could make sense of anything.

Her reaction didn't seem reasonable. But having grown up with three brothers and no sisters, he doubted he would ever understand women. Down South, before war had left things in shambles, he had admired women for their beauty and poise. But he had never found a woman who could fire his mind and match his desire for conversation that did not revolve around the latest ball or beau or gossip.

Theo sat on the dirt floor and crossed his legs. No matter, he had enough muddying the waters of his life without worrying about the intricacies of a woman's mind. It might be better for him to simply tell her the terrible truth of her husband's death and move on.

Chapter 6

Ellie stroked the material of Martin's shirt against her face. In searching for something that would fit Theodore, she had been unprepared for the clutch of emotion fingering Martin's shirts stirred. She could imagine the scent of him rising from the smooth fibers. When she closed her eyes, she tried to picture him at his shaving stand, hair not yet combed from the rumpled mass sleep produced, donning the shirt and working the buttons.

She yanked the shirt away from her face and balled it up. Why had he left her? Why hadn't he written to her those last months? She didn't want to be alone. A widow.

Ellie eyed the bed and debated about draping herself across it and having a good cry, but the image of Theo surfaced, his torn shirt and dirty face. His feet. He needed this shirt. She closed her eyes. How could she give something so precious to the enemy?

"Ellie?"

She turned toward the door of the bedroom and moved out onto the narrow landing. "I'm here, Rose."

"You've got mail."

Where at one time those words had struck a thrill into her heart, now she descended the stairs with more dread than hope.

Rose stood silhouetted in the kitchen, checking Ellie's bread supply then pushing into the bread box what looked to be a fresh loaf. "You need to eat more for lunch."

"I'm fine, Rose. Really."

"You hardly eat a thing, and I've held my tongue on the matter long enough." Rose's gaze sagged downward.

Ellie followed her line of vision. With a jolt, she realized she still held Martin's crumpled shirt. "I was sorting some things out to give away." Satisfied at the truth of those words, Ellie gave the shirt a sharp snap and draped it across the back of the chair. "It's time, I think."

Rose made quick work of pulling some cold ham and cheese from a basket she must have brought and laying it across slices of bread. She held the sandwich out to Ellie. "Now eat."

In order to avoid fuss, Ellie accepted the offering and set the plate on the table. "With you feeding me such a huge breakfast, there's not room left for lunch."

"I'm sure you'd like me to believe that." Rose picked up her basket. "Now I've set you up with a fresh loaf of bread. Tomorrow I'll be making some apple cinnamon bread to use up some of those apples in that cellar of yours. Be sure and bring some up before supper, and I'll set to work peeling them."

Rose went through the door and grabbed the post to brace herself as she went down the single step. She stretched her back and turned her face to the sun. "It's a good day to put hay over the carrots and parsnips."

Ellie knew how much her friend loved gardening. "I had better not catch you out there on your hands and knees thinning the spinach."

Rose gave her a mischievous grin. "Now you wouldn't expect me to make a promise I can't keep."

Ellie flinched and straightened, a new idea stirring around in her head. "I'm thinking of hiring a man to help out with hauling in the last of the garden and making repairs around the house and farm. I'm sure he would be willing to work the soil for next year."

"It's a good idea."

Energized by the solution to Theo's presence amidst two women, Ellie could barely stand still. "He can get started today. . . ."

Rose's head tilted, and she climbed back up the step that led to the back of her side of the house. "Sounds like you already have someone in mind."

Her friend's keen observation took the wind from Ellie's sails. She would have to be careful with what she said. She changed the subject. "When I come over tonight, I'll be good and hungry."

"Well, that's nice to hear." Rose paused and stared at Ellie through the screen of her door. "Try to eat your lunch before you read the mail. I think one of the letters is from your uncle."

Ellie brushed back a stray strand of hair and tightened the strings of her apron before she headed back inside. A quick glance over the names on the two envelopes proved Rose was right. Uncle Ross, her mother's brother, would once again be suggesting that she, a woman, might need help maintaining the properties since Martin's death.

The three-hundred-acre farm on the outskirts of Gettysburg had taken serious damage to the barn in the three-day battle, but the other buildings had remained mostly unscathed.

Ignoring the letter, Ellie wrapped the sandwich and loaf of fresh bread in a linen towel and placed them into a cloth-lined basket along with a ceramic jar of salve, another linen cloth, and a cake of soap. She filled a bucket with fresh water, then another, hoping anyone seeing her would think the water strictly for cleaning.

She cast an eye over all she had collected and went back upstairs. In the corner of the room, a pair of Martin's boots, almost new, collected dust. She picked them up and used her apron to clean off the dust. In a drawer, she rooted around for socks and found two pairs. She stuck them into the tops of the boots and went downstairs, satisfied that she now had everything Theo needed.

☙

Theo couldn't believe all the things Ellie had gathered in the short time she had been gone. It was the sight of the ham and cheese sandwich that brought him the greatest pleasure. He sank his teeth into the salty meat and smooth cheese and munched quietly as Ellie spread out her supplies.

"If you change quickly, I'll take you around back. Rose is probably taking her afternoon nap. She tires easily because she's expecting her first child any day. The tree shields you from the road, but wearing these clothes and agreeing to help us with some repairs and the garden would make your presence legitimate."

"Slow down there." He eyed the shirt she held up. "Won't those who meet me recognize Martin's clothes?"

She lowered her arms. It was obvious by the distress in her face that she had not anticipated such a problem, but then she held the shirt out to him. "It won't matter. I just told Rose I was going to give clothes away. It makes sense I might give the hired man first pick."

She bent over the box she had brought down. "And here." She held up a pair of fine boots. "You can probably fit into these, and I brought one of Martin's hats to keep you from being easily described to anyone who might be hunting you. Can you limp?"

He took a great gulp of the cold water she had smuggled down in the basket. "Limp," he said in a flat tone. "You want me to limp?"

"People might wonder why you haven't volunteered or been conscripted."

He eyed the boots she held out to him, the thought of stuffing his sore feet into the confines of them enough to make him think limping would not be too hard a ruse to keep up, especially if they were too small. He wolfed down the rest of the sandwich and tried one of the boots on. His foot got stuck halfway down. He pushed harder, feeling something soft. Pulling it off, he ran his hand down inside and pulled out a pair of socks.

Ellie rolled her eyes. "I forgot. I put a pair of socks in each one."

Theo tried again; this time his foot slid easily into the fine leather. They were a little bigger than he needed, but with the socks they would be almost perfect.

"We should get some salve on those feet first."

He acquiesced and pulled the boot off. He worked the bandages off slowly, wincing as the loosened scabs bled. He set about bathing his feet as Ellie continued wielding the broom over the walls.

"When I'm done, I'll leave these things down here and you can. . ."

He saw the heat of a blush in her cheeks and caught the direction of her thoughts. He needed a bath, and they both knew it. He stroked his hand over the soft wool of the shirt he held. "I can't thank you enough for the clothes."

Her chin came up. "They're Martin's. He would want you to have them."

"But you didn't have to give them to me."

"They'll keep you warm while you're here. You're probably not used to the cold."

Her tone conveyed a coolness that he found strange.

"There's a pump out back near the outhouse and tools in the building beside the garden plot."

Theo nodded, his mind spinning with all she was telling him.

"I'll leave the salve here for later, after you've plowed. I eat with Rose, but I'm sure if you take good care of her garden, she'd be delighted to offer you something to eat." She turned on her heel and snapped up the rag and broom. "It'll take me about half an hour to clean up the other room."

Other room? He thought she might be leaving until he heard the scraping sound of the previous evening and realized she was taking stones from the wall. *That* room. Theo understood that her declaration of how long it would take her was a warning for his sake as well as hers.

He made good use of the water and soap Ellie had brought down. He donned his cousin's clothes, grateful for the warmth and the cleanness of the material. Though Martin had been shorter than he by an inch and wider in the chest, they still fit well enough.

His belly full and feeling cleaner than he had in weeks, he peeked around the corner of the room and out onto the landing. Five stones had been removed to make a hole in the wall just large enough for a medium-build person to push through. He cleared his throat.

"I'm not finished yet, but we need to get you started on some work if you're to earn something to eat." He heard her skirts swishing closer and wondered how she had ever hauled herself up into that hole. She must be stronger than she looked.

When Ellie's head popped out of the hole, he held out his hand, offering help.

She shook her head. "If you'll just turn around. . ."

He presented his back and listened until he heard her land lightly on the dirt floor. "Is it safe?"

"Yes." She lifted a stone and slid it into place.

Theo followed her lead, brushing aside her help, his fingers swiping against hers. She yanked away. He finished the task, and when he glanced at her, she averted her gaze and rushed up the steps to shove open the cellar doors. She popped out of the cellar and held up her hand to indicate he should wait.

It took a minute before she came back. "Hurry, or someone might think it. . .unseemly that we were down there together." She darted into the inner room and lifted the chimney to blow out the lantern. She brushed by him, motioning for him to follow.

He emerged as fast as he could and together they shut the doors of the cellar, a low creak screeching a protest. "My first repair," he said.

She nodded and allowed him to come abreast of her. She began to recite a short list of tasks that needed to be completed on the house, but her words slid away as he breathed the chill November air.

His shirt offered warmth. Emerging from the darkness and doing work around the place would be a welcome diversion. It was more than he could have asked for, though he knew he would have to be careful.

"Don't forget to limp," she encouraged.

"Maybe if I ball up a pair of those socks that'll help me remember."

She pursed her lips and nodded.

A wagon rattled down the road and Ellie raised her hand in response to the wagon driver's wave. Theo did the same. No time like the present to try to fit into the community.

From his scan of the area, he could see that the large oak tree in the front yard screened the front porch with its gnarled, nearly bare branches. The side of the house had a lone evergreen of some sort that provided only a brief screen when one walked from the back to the front. A small road entered the property after the tree and led to the back of the house. There he saw the remnants of the past year's harvest.

Ellie pointed to a building on the opposite side of the yard, near a gate that marked the end of the property and the beginning of the next. "Tools are in the shed. If you could turn out the horses while you're in there. . ."

He crossed the lawn, the grass brown and crunching under his feet. The smell of horseflesh came familiar and strong to him. A dappled gray and a bay mare came to see who had entered their domain. He admired the strong lines of the smaller horse and the beauty of the gray's markings.

After releasing them, he inspected the interior. A rusty hoe, a well-used shovel, a leather harness, a sidesaddle, a plow, and numerous other tools were neatly lined up along one wall. He chose what he thought he would need to get started, wishing Ellie had at least told him more about the things grown in the garden.

"Here."

He jerked at the sound of Ellie's terse command.

She shoved a hat at him. "You should wear this. It'll help keep you from being recognized."

He nodded and put the hat on.

She stared at him, her expression unreadable. "I'll be down in the cellar if you need me."

Theo smiled into her eyes. "Am I going to get hired hand wages?"

He could tell by the stricken look on her face that she hadn't considered such a thing.

"I'll expect a good price," he poked fun at her.

Something in her expression faded, and she went pale. He thought he caught a sheen of tears in her eyes, but she hurried away before he could think of anything to say.

Chapter 7

Ellie pressed her back against the cool rocks of the cellar wall and let the tears fall, her first glimpse of Theo in Martin's clothes uppermost in her mind. When she had held the material of Martin's shirt to her cheek in the bedroom, she had felt the loneliness of his death, but seeing Theo in that same shirt gripped her with another emotion. One that beckoned her to move on. It had unnerved her almost as much as when his fingers grazed against hers, and when she'd seen him in Martin's boots. The clean scent of him and the way his too long hair curled on his neck brought a longing squeeze to her heart.

She shuddered, warming away the chill by rubbing her upper arms. To move on meant to betray the love she held for Martin, and she could not, would not, do that. She had forgone widow's black after two months, too depressed by the idea of continuing to wear the solemn color for six months or even a year. But she had never thought flippantly of moving on in her life and of loving again. She still loved Martin.

She touched the wetness on her cheek and pressed her fist against a heart that dared generate such traitorous thoughts. Tears streamed down her cheeks for all the tomorrows she would not have as a wife, a woman, a mother. Of bridal white scorched away by the black of mourning and of a noble man cut down with so much life still in him to be lived.

She gripped the broom and willed herself to move. With fervor fueled by anger at herself, she ferreted out the dark places she knew spiders were wont to hide in hopes of destroying their nests.

☙

Theo turned at the sound of the woman's voice, his hand tilting the hat forward more, placing his face deeper in shadow.

"Ellie works fast. You must be the man she hired to help her."

The slender-framed, obviously pregnant woman in front of him could be none other than the friend Ellie had mentioned. "Reckon that's so, ma'am."

Something flickered in the woman's eyes and suspended them in time as they assessed each other. Too late, Theo realized that his deep drawl had lent itself to that knowing spark in Rose's eyes.

"Well, my name is Rose Selingrove, and you're welcome to have some supper with Ellie and me. You have a place around here?"

A direct question. He cast about for a way to answer that would not raise more questions. "Yes, in Ellie's cellar," was out of the question. Yet he could not truthfully say he had a place in town, which also troubled him because to say less than that would surely raise more questions and perhaps get her suspicions aroused. He shrugged. "I manage fine."

"Which probably means you don't eat very well. Men don't often eat well unless they have a woman to cook for them." She pressed a hand against her rounded belly.

"No, ma'am, I guess we don't." There he went again, answering with the drawl that would peg him as Southern. He swallowed, hoping the woman might not have noticed.

Rose's smile was soft, and she took a step closer to him and stared him straight in the eyes. "With that heavy Southern accent, you're better off staying quiet. If people hear you talking like that, you just might find yourself facing a firing squad." Without missing a beat, she pointed at a row of the garden. "This row needs a smattering of hay to insulate it against the cold."

And with not another word, she spun on her heel and marched back to the house. A collision of dread roiled his stomach, mixed with a healthy dose of respect for the woman's verve. That she hadn't reacted with horror and hysterics over the realization that he was a Southerner gave him courage. Perhaps she would be a woman he could trust. If she ran slaves, as Ellie did, wouldn't that mean she would be sympathetic by nature? And might not some of that sympathy be reserved for men like him? Even if the enemy?

She was his enemy as well, he sought to remind himself. Harboring slaves, the rightful property of their owners. He could not believe his cousin's wife would be engaged in such a practice, but what did he really expect? The North was staunch in its support of freedom for slaves, despite the expense the Southern plantation holders paid to purchase the blacks as workers.

Theo picked up a handful of straw and let it fall through his fingers. It twisted and spun its way to the ground, insulating the row as Rose had requested. He just hoped it was enough, though he was certain she would let him know if it wasn't. In the South, no one had to insulate anything against the cold. Though he'd become used to the cooler temperatures in the four months since his desertion, the winds stung him the deepest. Harsh and icy cold, they had left him a shivering mass on many nights during his journey north. But it had been a small price to pay to be free of the war. Or as free as he could be as a deserter.

He frowned down at the row of straw he had placed. Deserter seemed such an unkind word, the punishment for deserting so harsh in light of the horrors each man was made to suffer and endure. His familiar nightmares tried to niggle at him. If only he could sleep through one night without tasting the terror anew, or hearing the screams. . . .

Theo pivoted, his heel grinding into the soft dirt. He stooped to collect the tools, determined not to let the horrors of it all destroy what he had at this moment. A trembling began along his arms and into his hands. He leaned the tools against the wall of the barn and stared at his shaking, sweaty palms.

He tried to think of the list Ellie had given him, anything to block the tormenting images. *Lord, please help me.* He took a deep breath, then another, forcing his mind to the horses and the pleasure of riding one over the fields and down the roads. . . .

His hands stilled, and when he shut the door to the shed, he realized the sun skimmed the horizon in the west. He lifted his nose to the air and sniffed. It smelled of rain and something frying, and he guessed supper must not be far off. He wasn't sure if he should return to the cellar or knock on Rose's door. *Rose.*

He needed to talk to Ellie. Tell of his meeting with Rose. If Ellie deemed her friend trustworthy, he would be safe. If not. . .

He didn't want to consider it.

Chapter 8

Ellie thought fear must smell much like the long, narrow room on the other side of the stone wall in the cellar. As those people given into her care left the small enclosure, it seemed the odor clung to them as it had all the room's previous occupants. She hated that they had to live like this. To hide and endure the stress of being found out or of putting those who cared for them into danger.

Ellie figured it must be early evening. Her stomach twisted with hunger and she realized, too late, that her ham and cheese sandwich had gone untouched. At least by her. If Rose asked her about lunch she would have to change the subject quickly to avoid telling a lie.

She put a hand to her back and bent backward to ease the ache lodged tight against her spine. In short order, she had gathered all the things she'd brought down to the cellar and emptied the buckets of the dirty water.

She needed to settle Theo into a comfortable corner of the barn. Tonight would be as good a time as any to move him there. Should Rose get brave enough to negotiate the steps, she would wonder why the stranger stayed hunkered in a dark, damp cellar. She would then be forced to tell her friend all about Theo's background, a risk she really didn't want to take.

She worried over the idea as she gathered her skirts and peeked out through the hole and toward the cellar doors. No one was there. She sat and slid her left foot out first, searching with her toes for the floor of the landing before she shifted her weight, ducked her head, and pulled out of the hole. Before her toes could find the solid promise of the dirt floor, she felt a hand on her arm and gasped.

"You really should come out headfirst. It's dangerous to do it this way. Anyone could sneak up on you."

Ellie pulled her leg back up, embarrassed at exposing the naked length. She pulled herself upright and into the secret room. Theo's head popped through the opening, his grin bringing a rush of heat to her face. "Wh–where did you come from?"

"Right there." He pointed to the inner room of the cellar.

"A gentleman would never have spied on me."

His grin only widened. "Wasn't spying. I thought it best to show you the danger." His head disappeared. "I'll turn my back."

The amusement in his voice nettled her. She had known her exit was not the best way, but it was the only way she could think of, and now she had this smirking Rebel exposing her fear and ogling what she never intended to be ogled.

She knelt and stared out the hole. True to his word, he stood with his back to her. As quick as she could, she went through the hole.

"You finished? I'm getting hungry, and the smell coming from Rose's house is tantalizing."

He faced Ellie as the words spilled over her, stilling the beat of her heart. He must have read the startled question in her eyes.

"She came out and introduced herself. I'm invited to eat with the family."

"Rose?"

"Her, too."

"No. I mean Rose invited you. . . ." She was babbling and she knew it. She drew air into her lungs and tried to settle herself. "She came out and saw you?"

"Recognized my accent, too."

Ellie berated herself for that. Why hadn't she considered that his accent would be a sure giveaway? She pursed her lips and met his gaze. Why, for that matter, hadn't *he* realized the danger of talking in front of enemies? It was his hide after all.

But she must remember how much Theo meant to Martin. The two had grown up together, until his uncle had bought a small farm in the South and moved his family. She still remembered Martin's immense satisfaction when Theo had written to say he would be traveling north to attend their wedding. While she had her head wrapped around last-minute details, Theo had spirited away Martin.

"Don't you realize how dangerous it is for people to know you're from the South?"

He shrugged.

She folded her arms. "You want me to risk my life hiding you, yet you're not caring one wit to help conceal the fact that you're a deserter from the South?"

He frowned. "I do care. I just don't know how to talk any other way."

True enough. What could she expect? His years in the South had erased whatever Northern accent he'd had as a youth. "Can't you try?"

"I could try."

There now. His words held as much Northern-ness as hers. She relaxed, the tension in her shoulders melting away. "Say something else."

"You're looking quite lovely this evening, ma'am."

His thick Southern accent caressed every syllable, and the twinkle in his eyes baited her to protest. "You're insufferable."

"No, Martin was insufferable. I'm charming."

Hearing Martin's name crushed the lighthearted moment. She ran her finger over her face to find a stray hair that tickled at her cheek, groping for something to say. "I'm moving you into the toolshed."

"The barn?"

She glared up at him. Why was he being so difficult? "Barn, toolshed, whatever you want to call it."

"The garden work will be done tomorrow. I hope you have a list of other things that need tending, else it's going to look mighty suspicious my being out there with a hoe when there's snow on the ground."

"I gave you a list earlier."

He shrugged. "Can't remember half of what you said."

She huffed. "I'll write it down tonight."

His eyes twinkled. "Good. Now let's go eat. It smells like fried chicken."

ʗɜ

If he'd hoped to bring some humor back to the conversation, he failed abysmally. It had been the mention of Martin that had sparked the remoteness in her. He must remember that she was a grieving widow, touched by the war in a way that could never be recompensed.

Though she had mentioned the need to finish up, she remained stock still, her eyes on some distant point that would remain forever a blur to him unless he asked.

He wondered what she would do if he went to his satchel and removed all the things Martin had given to him. How his death must be shattering her. Every day a new crack and another chunk of her spirit broke off, never to be restored. She would hold the things he gave her as precious and dear. . .as she should.

His mind calculated the number of steps it would take for him to reach his pack and retrieve his secrets to share with her. He swallowed. Perhaps it was time. "Ellie."

Her gaze flickered to him, waiting, expectant.

The longing to take the shadows from those eyes pinched at him. He pressed his lips together and held up a finger to indicate that she should give him a minute. But as Theo crossed to his small bag and knelt before it, he realized the danger this revelation would bring to him. Should she demand answers from the Union army, they would in turn want to know where and by whom she had acquired the information.

From a deserter.

A Southern deserter.

His hand closed over the packet of letters.

Behind him, he heard Ellie gasp. He turned as he rose to his feet, surprised to see her disappearing around the corner. "I'm here, Rose."

Theo half turned and toed his sack behind a barrel of potatoes. He reviewed what he could say to account for his presence in the cellar with a grieving widow woman.

Ellie darted back into the room, cheeks flushed. "I think Rose's labor has begun. I'm going to check. You stay here and finish the cleaning."

Chapter 9

Ellie found Rose in the middle of the porch, face ashen, her hand pressed against her protruding stomach.

"It woke me up."

Ellie nodded. "How long have you had pain?"

"I was frying chicken and thought it was because I'd been on my feet for too long. I lay down and must have fallen asleep."

She wheeled her friend around as gently as possible and guided her into the house. "Let's get you settled, and I'll go fetch the doctor."

"Send your man," Rose squeezed out before she stopped on their way up the step and sank against the wall.

"I've got to go ask him," Ellie responded when she felt the tension leaving Rose's body.

The pain passed and Rose straightened. "I want to lie down."

Ellie did her best to get as much ready for the impending birth as she could. She set a kettle of water to boil and tried to get Rose to sip tea, but her friend refused it, and when she stiffened up to ride the crest of another pain, Ellie held her hand and prayed for strength. Whether for herself or for Rose, she couldn't be certain.

When Rose relaxed again, Ellie stood. "Let me go ask Theo to fetch Martha." She could sure use her help right now. She hurried down the stairs, out the door, and across the side yard to the cellar door. It took a moment for her eyes to adjust to the dimness of the cellar. "Theo?"

He sat cross-legged, with his back to her, his head raising at her voice. "How is Rose?"

"Holding her own." She studied him. A small book lay open on his lap, the lantern turned up beside him. "Could you fetch someone from the doctor's office on the corner? Tell them I sent you."

Theo nodded and followed her up the steps. She turned to him as he lowered the cellar doors. In the waning light of day, his eyes were a pale silver. "Please don't forget your accent. And your limp."

☙

Theo stared into Ellie's face and wondered if he would have to scrub himself clean of everything remotely Southern in order to survive up here. But it was unfair of him to feel so aggrieved at the thought. It had not been Ellie's idea that he should come north, nor Martin's. He had done so because of his mounting anger over the conditions war imposed, then the desire that the truth be known—an irony now that he realized how much he risked by being in enemy territory.

As Ellie went around the house to go inside, he went through the front gate to the street and toward the corner building that, upon nearing, clearly showed the sign for a Dr. Selingrove. No doubt the man would be elderly, what with most of the younger men fighting the war.

Theo opened the door, a slow heat taking the chill from his skin. The office seemed still, as if frozen in time. Dust tickled his nose. Instruments gleamed behind the glass of a locked cabinet with a gleaming glass front. A small desk in the corner of the room seemed too neat for that of a busy doctor's office.

A light shuffle alerted him, and Theo turned, rehearsing Ellie's list—limp and talk like a Yankee. Footsteps indicated someone's approach. Something strange accompanied the sounds of the steps, a rustling, but before his mind could process the sound, the person appeared.

Bright, dark eyes stared at him with a cool reserve and a proud tilt to the head. An unmistakable, though silent, challenge.

Whatever Theo expected, it had not been this. He felt raked by the piercing dark eyes of the black woman. "I'm looking for Dr. Selingrove."

"He's not here. It's just me."

Theo's mind stumbled over that. Hadn't Ellie said to come here, to the doctor's office on the corner? "You mean, he's out on a call?"

The woman's direct gaze didn't waver. "No."

He chafed at the delay. "I was told to fetch the doctor."

The woman's chin inclined another inch. "You sent by Miss Ellie?" But the question apparently didn't require an answer because she was already moving, picking up a black bag that rested in the vacant chair behind the desk.

He flinched as the realization pricked that the woman was intent upon leaving with him to help Rose. "I was told to fetch the doctor," he parroted his earlier statement, unable to process this black woman's role in a doctor's office. Or at least, what she supposed her role to be.

As the woman bore down on him, he held up his hand, palm out.

She stopped, her eyes no more downcast than a white man's.

Not something Theo was used to seeing, though he knew the Northern blacks had far superior opinions of themselves. "We'll wait for Dr. Selingrove."

He thought he detected a sparkle in her eyes, but her words were without humor. "You awful young to be waiting on the doctor."

The words didn't make sense to him. Was it her attempt at humor? "How long before he'll be back?"

"Mighty long time."

Theo didn't know what to do. Ellie wanted the doctor, yet this woman seemed determined not to produce more than the merest of replies, and she certainly didn't seem inclined to fetch the man he sought. "Could you send him when he returns?"

Her nod was stiff, almost imperceptible, but he took it as her promise to fulfill his request. He had little choice but to return to Ellie with the disappointing news and the nervous unease that in the absence of a doctor he might somehow be called upon to help.

His return trip to Ellie's home seemed interminable. When he knocked on the front door, he immediately realized the futility of the effort. Ellie would be with Rose upstairs. He let himself into the house, expecting to hear an earth-rending scream from upstairs.

The kitchen seemed serene. Towels folded into a neat stack upon the smooth wood of the kitchen table. Water simmered in a pot on the back of the stove, and a low fire worked its magic to take the chill off the room.

Silence stretched long and worked to soothe Theo's frayed nerves as he sat at the table, unable to conceive what he could do to help, let alone whether he should leave or stay put. His debate over ferreting out Ellie's advice on another doctor or letting her approach him when Dr. Selingrove did not appear upstairs left him befuddled. He did nothing.

When an hour rolled by, he began to pace, saved from wearing a path in the wood floor only by the hollow taps on the stairs that indicated Ellie's patience with the doctor's absence must be thin.

Theo waited for her appearance, nerves stretched taut. His first glimpse of her rooted him to the spot.

She smiled his direction and lifted the stack of towels, eyes shining more than he thought acceptable for a woman facing an impending birth with no help. "Thank you for fetching Martha for us. Rose is doing quite well."

Chapter 10

Ellie made as if to turn then realized Theo looked at her with slack-jawed amazement. Fear shot through her as she wondered if he was having a bout with some strange illness.

"Dr. Selingrove is here?"

Ellie lowered the stack of towels to the table. "Why no, of course not. We don't know where Robert is, to be truthful."

"Robert?"

Ellie shifted her weight, frustrated at the delay explaining would force. "Robert Selingrove is Rose's husband. He joined the Northern army some time ago. It's been months since Rose has heard from him, and he's believed to be missing in action, dead, or a prisoner."

"Then who is up there? With Rose?"

"You mean Martha?"

"Martha?"

She nodded. "She's Robert's midwife, but she knows more than most doctors."

"But she—I mean, how. . ."

A muffled scream rent the air.

Ellie clutched the towels tighter to her chest and spun on her heel, heart slamming against her ribs. It was hard enough for Rose to endure the unknown of Robert's whereabouts, but to have his child with that knowledge. . . Her throat closed over that grief.

☙

Theodore could endure no more. The muted moans and occasional cries jangled his nerves and sent him fleeing from the kitchen and to the sanctity of the cellar. Chills held him captive as he dropped to the floor.

In his ears he heard not the moans of a woman in labor but of his comrades, his friends, shot full of shrapnel, falling to the ground and writhing in pain. The spot vacated by his fallen friend was replaced by another familiar face and together they advanced. In his head, the cacophony of war set his skull to throbbing. He heard a blast, heard yet another scream, and watched the man beside him go to his knees then fall face forward, hand clutching his midsection, blood streaming through his fingers.

Theodore sucked air into his lungs and tried to block the deluge of painful memories. It seemed the further he got from the war the more the memories plagued him. Was it his own guilty conscience? He had left his friends to warn Ellie out of disgust for the deed and respect and love for his cousin. No matter what, it seemed he was a coward.

Coward. The single word seemed to explode in his mind, and he felt the weight of the label pull at him, demanding penance. Images of fallen comrades, of Martin as he tried to halt his execution, bit at his soul, and he fell into a restless sleep full of blood and screams.

The earth below him seemed to shake, and someone grabbed his arm to pull him forward. He didn't want to advance. Not into the enemy's line, but the hand would not let go.

"Theo!" The voice came close to his ear, pitched low, yet higher in tone. "Theo, wake up."

He could feel the hand tug at him and realized it was not a dream at all. When he opened his eyes, Ellie stared down into his face with watchful eyes and sober concern.

"Settle down. You were screaming so loud I feared you were hurt."

He blinked and relaxed. Her words sunk in slowly as his mind returned to the present. No war. No men surrounding him, running. No shots. Just Ellie and the smells of dirt and overripe apples.

He covered his face with his hands to staunch the sob of relief and cover the emotion that flooded his senses. He shuddered.

"You were dreaming," Ellie stated, her tone sympathetic.

No, he wanted to correct her. Dreams are light things, not terror-riddled images of men so real he could see their faces, hear their voices, and taste their fear.

Her eyes shifted over his face, and her expression softened. The sight of her empathy made him turn his face away. He gasped to staunch the tears then felt something soft press into the palm of his hand. He stared down at her hand nestled in his.

"Martin came home only once. He had nightmares, too." Her voice became a whisper. "It must have been terrible."

He wanted to explain the horror, but words failed him. Instead, he pulled his hand from hers and pushed into a sitting position. "I'm sorry."

Her compassionate expression rolled over him, and he found himself wanting nothing more than to pull her into his embrace and feel the comforting warmth of another human. Someone alive and real and unmarred from the war. Again he forced the urge back. She would not welcome the advance and would never understand the frailty he felt or the security her presence offered.

She tugged on her skirts and rose to her knees, her smile more relaxed. "It's a boy."

The words seemed strange, yet it jarred his mind to a world far from that of his nightmares. Rose. Of course. "A boy?" He forced a smile.

"I thought the cries were from him, but the sounds weren't those of an infant."

He squeezed his eyes shut. "I'm sorry," was all he could think to offer.

The muscles in his neck loosened as the last events of his wakefulness slid into sharp focus. Rose. Dr. Selingrove. The mysterious Martha. He blinked and wondered at the beauty of new life. One untouched by such things as he had known in the war. He forced his mind away from that thought, knowing it would only pull him down.

"You never got supper. You must be starved, and you were right. There's a whole platter of fried chicken upstairs."

He didn't like the way she was looking at him. Maybe he'd smudged something on his face in the midst of his restless sleep, but the thought of food woke his appetite. Perhaps eating would calm him.

"He's the cutest little thing," Ellie said then held out her hand. "Stay here and let me make sure the coast is clear."

His eyes followed her as she disappeared. He could hear the doors opening and her light steps on the wooden planks of the stairs.

He inhaled a slow, long breath, closed his eyes, and rested his head against the wall at his back. A low-level pain pinched at the top of his neck. He shrugged and rolled his head to relieve the tension.

"Come on up," Ellie's voice whispered down to him. As he emerged, she continued her scan of the area. With a flick of her hand, she motioned him forward. "There are some things that need fixing on the house itself, starting with the porch."

A lone horseman trotted up toward the drive and guided the horse toward Ellie's house. Ellie stiffened then relaxed and lifted her voice. "There are some supports on the front porch that need straightening."

Puzzled by her words, he cast her a sidelong glance. She lifted a hand to point to a sagging section of the porch. He caught on to the ploy she was using and played along with his role as a handyman being shown what needed to be done.

"The fence needs a good whitewash, though it might be best to wait on that since cold weather will hit in full force at any time." She waved toward the man dismounting from a black mare, a uniform of blue covering his slender form.

Theo's spine went ramrod straight. In a reflexive action, his hand went for his Colt, but as the man neared, Theo realized the folly of his actions and relaxed. He was not in battle. Far away from the fields that had honed his instinct, not so much to kill the enemy, but for survival.

In the growing dusk, the stranger stroked along his horse's neck and lifted his broad-brimmed hat from his head, revealing wiry gray hair to match his beard.

Beside him, Ellie grew still, her mouth firmed into a hard line.

He didn't like what he was seeing in her expression and wondered if the man's presence meant trouble. "Ellie?"

She turned her gaze on him. "It's all right," came her whispered reply. Ellie took a step toward the newcomer.

Theo remained where he was.

As she drew closer to the man, he turned from his horse and gave her a hug that seemed awkward for both of them. They exchanged words too low for his ears.

Theo stepped forward at Ellie's encouragement. "This is the help I just hired. We were just talking about the work that. . ." Her voice faded.

Horror edged up Theo's spine as his gaze locked with the man. The hair. Those eyes. That beard. He'd seen that profile once before.

Ellie's voice, oblivious to his sudden tension, continued, "I'd like you to meet Theo."

Chapter 11

Theo left her alone with her uncle but returned in time to eat with them. Several times Ellie caught him casting sidelong glances at Uncle Ross. And in turn, when Theo wasn't looking, her uncle's expression would become questioning as he took in the hired man. That Theo knew her uncle was obvious, though she wasn't sure if her uncle merely picked up on Theo's hard stares or if he had seen Theo before but couldn't place him. Other than her wedding, which her uncle didn't attend, she couldn't recollect one time when the two would have met over a family event.

The meal she offered provided more of the same behavior between the two, though Theo kept his head down most of the time and remained quiet unless directly addressed. If she hadn't already invited him for fried chicken, she would have suggested he use the time to settle in the barn and allow her to bring him a plate. She forked a bite of chicken and slipped it into her mouth.

"You're quiet, Ellie. Have you been alone so long that you've forgotten how to be social?"

Though her uncle's comment seemed harmless, and there was a twinkle in his eyes, the chunk of meat she'd been chewing seemed suddenly flavorless and dry. She washed it down with water and pasted on a smile. "There's been a lot going on. Rose had her baby right before you arrived."

"Ah. That would be your neighbor?"

"Her husband hasn't returned from the war, and she hasn't heard from him in months."

"Most unfortunate. What regiment?"

"The 28th Pennsylvania, I believe. As surgeon."

"Generals Lee and McClellan agreed to grant surgeons neutral status, so even if captured by the Southerners, they wouldn't be imprisoned."

"That's a comfort."

There was a long pause in which Ellie struggled to find something civil to say to her uncle. She knew all too well that his visit wasn't a simple social call. "I expect you came here seeking my answer to your proposition."

Her uncle made good use of his napkin then shoved his nearly empty plate back. "You're as forthright as ever, Ellie, my dear. Yes, I wondered why I never received an answer. But then mail service isn't always reliable. I was in the area." He paused and seemed to collect his thoughts. "You must agree, Ellie, that your newfound widowhood would be much less taxing if you allowed me to help."

She cast a glance at Theo. He caught her eye and pushed back from the table. "I'd better turn in for the night."

"You're not going to stay for Rose's pie?"

"I expect you two have business to discuss," he said in a perfect Yankee accent. "I wouldn't want to hinder."

Ellie stood up, tense at the thought of his leaving her with her uncle. "At least stay for pie."

His presence offered her a modicum of protection against what would certainly be her uncle's long diatribe on the reasons why a woman should not be hindered by "business." Since Martin's death she'd received several letters from her uncle Ross inquiring if he could help.

She didn't know if it was her tone or Theo's hunger or simply an act of kindness on his part, but he nodded and lowered himself back down onto the chair.

As she crossed the room to slice the pie, Uncle Ross wasted no time in peppering Theo with questions about his heritage and upbringing. Subjects that had her holding her breath and straining for his answers. She sliced two large pieces and a smaller one for herself.

Theo's answers were vague. He'd grown up in the North. Happy childhood. Normal boyish pranks. No lies in anything he'd revealed so far, but she wondered if her uncle would ask the ultimate question. "Why aren't you fighting?"

She hurried to get the plates to the table and plunked one down in front of Uncle Ross before further questions could slip from his mouth. He frowned up at her then down at the plate. How was it her once lighthearted, fun-loving uncle had become such an uptight old man since her mother's death? Whatever the reason, she didn't like the change.

He lifted his fork and dug in. "Your mother's pies were unbeatable. I still remember her making me a cherry pie when she was sixteen."

Ellie set the other wedge in front of Theo. "It's apple."

Theo nodded and clipped off a small wedge of pie with the edge of his fork.

"Reminds me of the old days," Uncle Ross said, his lips smacking. He shoved another generous bite into his mouth. His head bobbed in rhythm to his chewing. "Really good, Ellie."

"Thank you." She caught Theo's glance and nodded, hoping he might understand the words to mean far more than a trite answer to her uncle's appreciation for pie.

As soon as she sat across from her uncle, he crammed the last bite into his mouth and shoved his plate away.

Her mind shuffled for something to say to distract him from further questions of Theo, and she decided to take the offensive. "I received your latest letter earlier today, so you can imagine how surprised I am at this visit."

"You haven't answered any—"

Ellie held up her hand. "I didn't answer, Uncle, because the answer has not changed. I am not selling the farm. There are too many memories, and it was my mother's legacy to me."

Uncle Ross's nostrils flared, and his eyes narrowed. "Don't you think it might be too much for you to handle, my dear? You could sell it to me at a good profit and leave all the fuss of renting it out and the lands—"

"No." The word slipped out on a rising wave of frustration. She popped a bite of pie into her mouth to buy her time to think.

A storm rose in her uncle's dark eyes. He glanced over at Theo then back at her. She could see that he wondered about the relationship between them.

In an effort to cut off the inquiry sure to come, she turned to Theo. "Before you leave this evening, we need to make a list of the things you'll be working on in addition to what we've already discussed."

Theo inclined his head. "A sound idea, Mrs. Lester."

"I'll be staying the night, Ellie. I assume the guest room is available? I'd like to turn in early."

She would not rise to the bait he laid, chagrined at the suggestion behind his question. "The linens are fresh, though the room may be a bit dusty from disuse."

There, let him chew on that for a while. But if she hoped to dissuade her uncle from further debate on any subject, he disappointed her.

"We'll speak more of this tomorrow. I'd like to look the property over if you don't mind. For old times' sake, you understand."

Chapter 12

My foot."

Theo suppressed the chuckle that threatened to erupt as Ellie's words, spoken in a whisper after her uncle left the room, showed exactly what she thought of the older man's idea.

"What farm is he speaking of?"

Ellie met his gaze. "Ever since Martin's death was made public knowledge, he has wanted to buy the farm Mother left to me."

"A farm?" He cocked his head, absorbing the fact she had just shared and what it meant in relation to what he had witnessed. "If it's yours, why do you live here?"

Ellie lowered her eyes. "She left me this house as well."

So Ellie Lester was a rich woman. If Uncle Ross was the man Theo thought him to be. . . Theo rubbed a finger over the bridge of his nose and scratched down the growing stubble along his jaw. He had no proof. There were hundreds of thousands of bearded men fighting in the war. The sight of Ross's beard and general physique seemed similar, but his position wasn't such that he could easily point a finger at any man, Union or Confederate.

"Are you not feeling well?"

He clenched his teeth for a second. "I'm fine."

"You should get settled in the stable. At least the air there might be better than. . ." She gave him a huge smile and laughed. He caught on to the turn of her thoughts.

"Fresher?" he suggested.

"Well, maybe not that."

They laughed, their gazes locking. Theo enjoyed the sound of her laughter and the way her curls brushed against her shoulders with the tilt of her head. What they shared felt a little bit like camaraderie, and the warmth of the emotion bit hard into his soul. He was here to deliver a message—to let a grieving widow know that her husband's death had been anything but accidental, that he was not a casualty of war. Yet here he sat, beguiled by her laughter in a way that was not what he had expected.

She blinked and the fringe of her lashes shadowed her cheek for a slow second. She looked away. "I need to check on Rose. I'll probably stay the night with her."

He rose when she did, watching as she quietly gathered a shawl from a peg on the wall and slipped open the back door.

He followed her onto the back porch. The yard was dark, though the moon shimmied along a gossamer cloud, trying to shine its light. "I'll stay until you're inside."

She turned toward him. "There's no need. Really."

Theo looked out over the yard toward the garden.

Beside him he heard Ellie give a gasp.

He jerked to face her. "What is it?"

Her eyes flicked to his face. "I thought I saw something. Probably a rabbit."

He didn't believe her. The way she hugged herself, her direct gaze seemed forced, as if her eyes wanted to look elsewhere. But she didn't give him time to press her. She shrugged around him and hastened to Rose's back door, giving him a little wave and shutting the door firmly.

Theo scanned the yard, seeing nothing out of the ordinary. Frustrated by Ellie's swift departure, he whipped around, restless at the idea of retreating to the barn so early. With no choice, he crossed to the stable, glad he'd brought his knapsack and the lantern up from the cellar after Ellie's uncle's arrival.

He touched a match to the wick and allowed the flame to catch before lowering the chimney. Between the straw and the old, dry barn boards, he would have to be careful with the lantern or the whole place would go up in flames. He searched through the tools for a nail, found a hammer, and pounded the spike into a solid support post then hung the lantern from it.

He tugged around a few bales of hay and stacked them to form a low wall. One swipe of a rather dull-edged knife on the tool bench and the strings of another bale broke. He spread the hay around, pushing it into a thick mound for use as a mattress. Then, with nothing else to do, he stretched out and tucked his arms beneath his head.

A dark spot on the beamed ceiling tugged a grimace from him. Evidence of a leaky spot. Right above his head. With a grunt he got to his feet and studied the ceiling. Only the place where he had been lying showed signs of previous leaks, so he swept his pile of hay to the other side of his little space. Satisfied he had thwarted being watered like a tree should it rain, he stretched out again and closed his eyes.

Within seconds he sat up, nerves stretched taut. It worried him that he would have another bad dream. He didn't want to remember. He did his best to focus on the things around him, the tools and what he planned to accomplish the next day, but his mind stumbled when he thought of Ellie. How she might look holding the new baby. The straggle of cobwebs clinging to her blond hair when she'd been cleaning the cellar. Her long lashes and flashing blue eyes. . .

Theo reached out and pulled his knapsack closer. He needed a distraction, but thinking of Ellie only churned emotions he thought best left alone. She was a widow, and he was a deserter with nothing to offer. He dug around a bit and extracted the small Bible he carried. Its cool leather and the familiar cracks in the cover brought a measure of comfort. And he needed comfort.

ᘓ

Ellie held the baby close as Rose made herself comfortable in bed. "Thank you, Ellie. I can take him now."

"Have you thought of a name?"

Rose's features pinched. "Colin was Robert's choice. Colin Daniel."

Ellie wrapped the blanket more snugly and placed the child into his mother's arms. "A strong name for a strong boy." She straightened, trying to hide her anxiousness to be outside again.

She hated outright lying to Theo, but the sight of the open gate, coupled with the face of her normal contact person, a black man named Saul, had so startled her that she knew the black man was showing himself for only one reason. And it was important. His very presence communicated that she should be on the alert, even if his overalls and the casual way he stood against the open gate said nothing more than a man out for a late evening stroll to others.

"If there's nothing else you need right now, I'll go back and fetch a plate for you. Food will help you get your strength back."

Rose made a face and adjusted the baby's position.

"Martha told me to make you eat something. She worries that you're too thin."

Rose sighed. "If I must."

Relieved to have an excuse to leave, she paced her steps so her footfalls wouldn't seem rushed to Rose's ears. Rose's needs had taken over an hour to tend to. She wondered what Saul's message might be. . .and dreaded finding out.

The first thing Ellie noted upon being outside was the light flickering from the stable onto a patch of grass only a few feet away from the still-open gate. She'd never realized how dangerous Theo's presence would be to her and the contacts that helped her get runaways to safety. That he knew about her dealings in the Underground Railroad did little to quell her fears. He was a Southerner, after all.

She saw no sign of Saul now and didn't expect to. Staying risked people getting suspicious of his lingering presence at the gate.

Ellie moved into the circle of light bleeding from the barn window onto the brown grass where her backyard joined with that of her neighbor's. Her stomach heaved with dread. With a deep breath to steady her nerves, she moved closer to the garden gate.

From there she could see the worn path that snaked behind the next three houses and down to the offices of Dr. Selingrove, Rose's husband. It was the same path Saul would have taken earlier.

She skimmed over her neighbor's garden to her left, a dark, eerie place of twisted trees and gnarled old roses, then to the stand of evergreens to the right of the path.

Something moved among the evergreens. She blinked, unable to penetrate the darkness or make out the form of anyone. Maybe it was a dog. Still, her stomach clenched in fear. What if it was a trap? A stranger sniffing around for his runaway slaves who had discovered her part in the operation.

She shivered. In that moment of uncertainty, she retreated a few steps closer to where the light from the lantern offered her some security. For surely if she cried out, Theo would come to her rescue.

"Miss Lester?" The whisper caught Ellie's attention, and the form of the slender black midwife emerged from the path, her black bag gripped in her hand.

Ellie bit back a response. The woman had left Rose only two hours previous. She would not return unless asked, which meant. . .

"I'm glad you came." Ellie nodded and swung the gate shut behind Martha.

Martha said nothing but followed Ellie into Rose's kitchen. When she turned, Martha sat at the table, her black gaze hard on her. "He came to me."

Saul.

Of course. Ellie turned the logic of it over in her mind. He must have heard about Rose's delivery and known Martha would be a logical choice to deliver his news.

"There is a husband and wife who could not move. The woman is ill and expecting. I done what I could for her, but they needin' a place to go for the night 'fore they move on."

It would be risky to direct the woman and her husband to the cellar with Uncle Ross's room not far above. Ellie shook her head. "I can't do anything with my uncle here."

"If she gives birth, she will need to be far away. You have a farm?"

The farm! Her mind tripped over possibilities. Her renters stayed in the main house and had a garden on the acre directly surrounding, but the springhouse, barn, and summer kitchen were all possibilities. "I can't take them tonight."

Martha gave a slight nod.

Ellie didn't want to ask where they would stay that night. A pregnant woman ready to give birth would be a huge risk factor. "When I'm ready for them at the farm, I'll show our signal and expect them after dark."

"I hoping to get them to Philadelphia as soon as possible. Pray for an easy birth."

She led the way up the steps to Rose's room where the young mother was just finishing nursing her son. "Martha came to check on you," Ellie said quietly, running a finger over the baby's head.

Rose lifted an eyebrow. "Really?"

"You make good and sure the mother gets her rest and is eating as she should."

Rose gave Ellie a sheepish look. "I guess Ellie has been telling on me, but I was going to eat."

Ellie just smiled.

Martha turned to her, a slight twinkle in her eyes. "You get some food."

"I feel fine, Martha." She stared down at the bundle in her arms. "But I worry about. . ."

Ellie left them alone, her mind already considering and rejecting a hundred scenarios on how to transport the slaves such a distance without being seen. She put together a tray of toast and peach preserves for Rose and delivered it to the room. Martha, she had no doubt, would make sure the young mother ate.

She went back to worrying over the problem of transporting the slaves without being seen. And the frequency of the trips might lead someone to grow suspicious. And how would she care for the runaways when they were so far away? She couldn't leave Rose.

The solution presented itself as she stepped onto the back porch and laid eyes on the light still glowing from the stable.

Chapter 13

Theo had been startled at the sound of Ellie's voice asking if she could talk to him, but, his eyes weary from reading and his mind still unable to sleep, he had welcomed the company. She scooted around the bales of hay and sat down at his invitation. He sat across from her, noting her grave expression. "Horses aren't much company." He tilted his head to indicate the bay mare and the gray. "A one-sided conversation isn't very appealing."

Her face lost some of the tightness and a small smile curved her lips. "No, I don't expect Libby and Mina are much company." She twisted on the bale to stroke the nose of the mare who hung her head over the stable door to get attention.

For the long minute she petted the horse, he admired her silhouette—the curve of light along her cheekbones and the slender hands that moved from the horse's muzzle to her ears. Her beauty stirred in him a hunger for companionship. Human contact. Home-cooked meals and fresh linens. A cozy fireplace and the soft touch of Ellie's lips on his at the end of a long day working. . . .

He shook himself and straightened, realizing his image had been that of Ellie as his wife, not as that of a widow grieving for her husband. What would Martin say if he knew Theo's thoughts had stirred in the direction of becoming his replacement in Ellie's life? The idea held him suspended in horror for a moment, until it occurred to him that Martin would be pleased.

Ellie's hands fell to her sides and she sighed, turning to face him. "I came to both ask a favor and offer a solution."

He shook the thoughts from his head. "I'm listening."

"I don't know how long Uncle Ross will be staying, and I know it's not comfortable for you in the cellar, or even in here. You see. . ." She clasped her hands together and bit her lip.

He wasn't sure where she was headed with it all and decided to remain quiet.

"I thought it might be nice for you to have a place over at our family farm. All to yourself. For however long you want or need to stay. But there will be certain responsibilities." She wiped her hands on her skirts.

He sensed her frustration and waited patiently for her to continue.

She met his gaze for a second before glancing away then released a sigh. "I'll just come out and say it. You know what I'm doing, and I know what you are. I need your secrecy just as much as you need mine. Hanging around here posing as my handyman is a good idea, but it puts you at risk as well. At the farm you'll be away from curious eyes. But I need help." Her blue eyes on him were imploring. "I have a young couple. The woman is pregnant, due to give birth any day, and I need a way to get them out to the farm. I was thinking of the wagon. Maybe you could put in a false bottom? I've heard of others using that method to transport—" She shrugged. "You know what I mean."

He scanned the stable, his gaze landing on the wagon itself. "I would need wood and tools."

"There are repairs that need to be done on the buildings at the farm. I had some repairs made to the farmhouse before the renters moved in, so you don't need to disturb them. But there is plenty of other work to keep you busy. There's a lot of old wood there. You could take Libby over before sunrise with the wagon, and as long as you're done with the false bottom by evening tomorrow—"

"Evening?"

"That's when we're going to make the transfer. If Uncle is here and demands to go out with us again, for whatever reason, at least he won't see the people. And it'll put distance between you and him."

He stroked his hand down his face, wanting to ask for a razor.

"Would you like to shave?"

The way she read his thoughts. . . Her need to put distance between her uncle and him made him suspect his covert glances at Ross had not gone undetected. He would have to be more careful to guard his expressions.

"Do you know my uncle?"

There it was. The question he had asked himself a hundred times. "I thought I did, but there are so many gray-headed men with beards. . . ."

She seemed content with his answer. She leaned forward, expression tense. "You'll help me then?"

Theo saw hope flicker in her eyes. Just her asking him to engage in the transfer of slaves was a risk. She had no way of knowing he wouldn't turn her in or take the slaves himself and return them to the South. Other than the fact that she knew his secret as well.

What beckoned him to say yes the most was the prospect of that farm. No cramped cellar. No pitch blackness. Even less chance of being caught. He could go back and forth to her house to make the repairs she had asked to be done there or to help with the garden. He'd be free to move around at whim.

It struck him then that his plans were stretching toward long term. Theo swallowed hard over the constriction in his throat. What kept him here? Why didn't he just tell Ellie the terrible news and all that he suspected, give her the letters, and leave?

Ellie hung suspended, breathless, waiting for Theo to answer the simple question. She knew he must be guessing how desperate she was to ask him, what with all he would risk helping her. What she didn't prepare herself for was the intensity of his stare. She felt pinned by that pewter gaze, as if he was searching for a hidden motive. A vulnerability she hadn't expected to see. Did he really think she would lure him to help her then turn him in? "You know I won't betray you, Theo. I could never do that."

Something shifted in his expression, heightened.

She tried to draw a breath, confused at her inability to move beneath that commanding stare. "You're. . .you're Martin's favorite cousin."

He inhaled sharply and scratched his jaw, turning away. "Yes. Of course. Tomorrow evening will work fine."

He stood and she did the same. She'd never seen this side of him. Stealthy. Curious. Fearful. Again, his gaze searched her face, until he shouldered his way past her and out into the night, leaving her to contemplate the rear end of the dappled gray. Why were men so complicated? Correction. Man, not men.

Martin she had understood all too well. From the time they started courting he had been easygoing and kind, though quiet. She had loved to hear his laughter. But this man confused her. He garbled her senses and made her wonder what it would be like to have a husband again. To love and be loved.

Guilt washed over her. How could she forget so easily all that she'd lost on that battlefield? So much more than a husband, but a companion and friend, a way of life. Theo was only Martin's cousin, and though he must surely struggle with being forced to trust the enemy—her—didn't he realize she was making the same sacrifice by asking for his help?

Libby swished her tail and broke the reverie of Ellie's thoughts. At one time she might have prayed for guidance, but God had seemed far away since Martin's death. What she needed was sleep. With her uncle Ross so close, she knew taking care of Rose, sparring with Uncle Ross, and the "cargo" left in her care would tax her more than normal.

She swept open the door of the stable and stepped into the night. She waited a moment, allowing her eyes to adjust to the dimness, and swept the yard for signs that Theo might be nearby. Still puzzled over his reaction yet buoyed by his commitment to help, she crossed the yard. Maybe all he needed was a good night's sleep, too.

She was about to close the door behind her when his voice came to her. "Good night, Ellie."

Startled, she scanned the yard, still unable to pinpoint his location. "Good night," she whispered, unsure if he would even hear her reply.

Chapter 14

Theo had watched from the shadow of the tree as Ellie closed the door after his "Good night." When he saw a light flicker upstairs, he finally pushed away from the trunk and wandered back to the barn. He bedded down, hoping sleep would claim him quickly, before he had to rise for his predawn escape to the farm. But he lay there, unable to get the images of Ellie out of his mind.

He pulled into a sitting position, draping one arm across a bent knee, and lowered his head to work kinks out of the muscles in his shoulders. He forced himself to think beyond the stable and the farm and the runaway slaves he would be working to help. He would help Ellie out, give her the letters, and leave. West would probably be a good direction to follow, and the thought of owning a ranch, or even working as a ranch hand, appealed to him.

What he couldn't allow was the feelings Ellie stirred. Just sitting across from her in the barn, their knees inches apart, her blue gaze running the gamut of emotions. Seeing her profile and aching to touch her cheek or hold her hand had gnawed at him. Then, as she was asking him about her uncle and if he would help, he had been certain he could trust her. He had even given consideration to the rising thought that she might be able to love him back, but when she had implied she would keep his secret, not out of any emotion for him but because he was Martin's cousin, he'd felt like she'd punched him in the gut.

It would do him well to remember the reason he was here. Not to fall in love, but to tell her about Martin and deliver the letters. If he didn't make his escape soon, he might fall in love with her, and that would make leaving impossible. But he couldn't let that happen. Ellie was a woman who deserved a man with something to offer, not a Rebel deserter on the run and in fear, doing odd jobs to make a little money.

He vowed to make the repairs as quickly as possible and get out of there. It was the only solution.

☙

Uncle Ross's note both perplexed and relieved Ellie. That he had "early morning business to attend to" meant she would be free to help Rose and even make a trip to the farm to check on Theo's progress. His "won't be home until very late" was also something to be cherished. Still, why come visit her only to go off for an entire day? Maybe he was hoping she would soften in his absence. And with his return sometime "very late" she worried he might get back just as they prepared to load the couple.

She went straight over to Rose's house and scrambled an egg for her friend, poached one for herself, and took the toast from the top of the cookstove.

Rose blinked her eyes open, and Ellie saw right away the signs that her friend got little sleep. In the swirl of last-minute plans, she'd forgotten her promise to stay with Rose.

"I must look a sight. I couldn't relax then thought I would roll on him." She gave a sigh. "It was a terrible night."

"I should have stayed. I'm sorry." Ellie waited for Rose to maneuver herself up in bed before she placed the tray in front of her friend and slid the plate onto the surface. "I'll hold pumpkin."

Rose laughed. "I didn't think I would be hungry, but I am." She winced. "Sore, too."

Ellie bent to pull the bundled babe close to her. "Baby Colin," she breathed the name in awe. "He's so perfect."

"A miracle."

A quiver in Rose's voice made Ellie raise her head. Her friend's eyes were squeezed shut, and her face flushed from the effort to hold her tears at bay. She scooted onto the bed beside the woman and put her free arm around her shoulders. Rose immediately broke down, her sobs tearing from her chest, wringing tears from Ellie as well.

Through the entire ordeal Rose had been brave and hopeful that her husband would return. In Ellie's darkest hour, her friend had been there for her, offering a shoulder to cry on and doing kind deeds. Together they had fought their own war, and Rose's war still raged.

Ellie wiped her tears and pulled the baby closer as he began to squirm, no doubt troubled by all the noise. His face reddened.

When his mewing began in earnest, Rose sniffed one last time and reached for him.

Ellie stroked her hair back as her friend nuzzled the baby's cheek and encouraged him to nurse. "You really must eat something," she encouraged.

"I will. I promise." Rose raised her swollen eyes to Ellie. "You've been such a comfort to me, Ellie."

"We have been to each other."

"Yes, God does know what we need in the midst of sorrow."

"You have hope that as a doctor Robert will be safe. And now you have baby Colin to bring you comfort." Her throat closed. The unspoken lay between. Ellie's lip quivered, and she bit it and pushed to her feet. "I've got other things to tend to. Uncle Ross isn't home until late tonight and there's laundry to be done and an afternoon meal to be cooked."

"And God to run away from."

She spun toward Rose. "That's not fair!"

Her friend's gaze held a distinct challenge. "Isn't it?"

"You haven't lost your husband. How could you understand?"

"Why does a departure from God need to be understood? It is what it is, Ellie. Nothing should separate you from God. He's the comfort you lack now. Isn't that what you were just saying? I have hope Robert will return and now I have little Colin, and you have nothing?"

Ellie pressed her knees against the edge of the mattress and bowed her head. She should have known Rose would see through her.

"You think I don't see your frustration over what you perceive to be God taking Martin from you?"

"I don't feel that way." Yet she could not deny the evidence. She'd laid down excuse after excuse for avoiding any form of church function, and her Bible, once sampled from daily with great delight, lay on a shelf in her room, coated with dust. She squeezed her eyes shut. "It's so hard."

The bed creaked and sheets rustled. She felt Rose's arms stretch around her back and her head nestled against her waist. "Would Martin want this for you?"

"How do I know what he would want? He's not here."

"You would know in your heart."

Her heart. It had become a cold, hard thing. Frozen by the absence of love promised to her in vows breathed by a smiling Martin on their wedding day. It all seemed such a long-ago dream.

Though she had managed to get through the hot summer days by concentrating on the garden and helping Rose put up vegetables, the hollow nights of winter nipped at her heels. Work would be centered around tasks that could be done inside where the walls echoed the roar of silence. She knew it waited for her, just as it did in the long, restless nights before sleep gave her relief.

"Ellie, why don't you talk to someone? The pastor's wife?"

"Because all it does is stir the thoughts of forever without him."

Rose squeezed her hand. "I know there's no words that will take away your pain. But there is a promise in the Bible. . ."

Fragments of scripture after scripture flitted through Ellie's mind. She could think of many that offered hope and encouragement, but nothing seemed able to penetrate the deep, dark spot where death had suffocated her joy.

"God promises that time will heal our hurts, Ellie." Rose tugged on her hand until Ellie met her gaze. "Do you believe that? *Can* you believe that?"

She didn't have an answer. Oh, she wanted to believe, to feel the security she once felt and believe that even this, the death of her husband, could be for her good. But even the thought of it seemed incongruous.

Still, Rose wanted an answer. Expected it. "I'll try. That's all—" Her voice broke, and she pressed a hand to her lips.

She rushed from the room, stopping on the landing and pushing her fists into her eyes to staunch tears. *I don't know how to heal. How to believe through this that You still love me. . .*

Chapter 15

In the swelling light of the rising sun, a haze of rainbow hue colored the underbelly of the low clouds. Theo shivered in the cold and huddled deeper into the flannel shirt. With the wagon safely out of sight and the horse contentedly munching oats, he surveyed the expanse of farmland stretching before him. He had passed the farmhouse a quarter mile down the road, well hidden from the barn tucked behind a tall privet hedge, assuring him privacy, and the slaves as well when they made their journey to the springhouse later that night.

It had been a walk down memory lane for him. He clearly remembered the wedding in the backyard of the farmhouse, then the laughter and quiet stealth required of him and his other cousins hiking the bridal bed to the ceiling. Such good memories gave him confidence, even if the damage done by the Battle of Gettysburg to the structures dimmed the reality somewhat. The work would be good for him.

He began by inspecting the wagon then the boards stuffed into a corner of the barn. Building the false bottom would not take as long as he had first thought. Since the wagon bed was solid, he need only place a strip of wood around the perimeter of the sides then secure boards together and lay them on top. As Ellie suggested, the barn held all types of tools to get the job done.

He stroked his chin, clean shaven now, the razor waiting for him just inside the barn door when he woke. She'd left it for him without a sound. Perhaps he slept and she didn't wish to wake him.

He raised his face to the meager warmth the morning sun provided, its feeble heat welcome on the smooth skin of his jaw. He recalled a similar morning, surrounded by his comrades, hot sun beating down on them. Those happy times that knit together a group of men who otherwise would have never known each other. Chad's smiling face and bright red hair. Tom's limp, a result of a still-healing ankle. Bud's solemn eyes and tense smile, his expression the embodiment of everyone's fears for the next day, the next battle.

The vision shifted and Theo tried to shut out what he knew would be a darker memory. He pushed up the sleeves on his shirt and began sorting through the pile of boards. In his mind, he heard Bud's voice. His proclamation the night before they would engage in battle at Chancellorsville.

"It's gonna happen."

Theo's hands began to shake. He pushed at the thought and lifted another board, anything to block the stream of memories he had unleashed.

War. Fighting. Blood.

He gulped air, and the board he held fell to the ground.

Bud.

He saw the boy's face in his mind, a tanned face. A Georgia boy who had signed up because he believed war was an adventure. The many skirmishes soon taught Bud otherwise, as it had taught them all. That night Bud had slept fitfully.

Theo's skin crawled, and he sank to the ground, cradling his head, recalling the muffled sound of Bud's tears.

"What's the matter, Bud?" But Theo had already known the boy's fear. He placed his hand on the slim shoulders of the boy-man and shook him gently.

Bud's crying ceased, but he didn't open his eyes.

Theo retreated to his own blanket, pulling it up high to ward off the chill of that May evening as much as to quell nerves stretched taut by Bud's strange dreams and bold proclamations that always seemed to come true.

He had learned to console Bud with his voice. Would often break out into hymns when Bud seemed bothered or anxious, inevitably the night before they took on the enemy.

Hymns.

In the barn, Theo forced himself to stand and raised his voice to full volume to push against the memories. The hymn he remembered best. "Rock of Ages." And as he sang, he picked up the board he had abandoned earlier. He forced out the next verse of the song, feeling the steadiness of his mind returning.

By noon he had installed the lip on which the false bottom would rest and still he sang. Song after song. His voice growing weaker from the strain. When he could sing no longer, he led Libby out to the small pasture and let her loose then returned to the barn where he continued to measure boards and cut them to size.

He stretched his arms above his head and worked his head from side to side. Some sound brought his mind to full alert, and he turned toward the doorway of the barn where he'd left the doors open just wide enough to allow natural light to permeate his work area. A horse buzzed its lips, and Theo's mind tripped over one excuse after another to make plausible to a visitor his presence in a barn that he didn't own.

A hand appeared along the edge of the barn door. "Theo?"

Tension ebbed from him as he recognized Ellie's voice. And not her voice. "Yeah."

When she pulled the door open a little more and appeared in that opening, sunlight washed her in its bright rays. "I wondered if there was anything you needed." She wore a fresh gown of lemon yellow.

As she neared him, he cleared his throat and added another reason to the list of why he needed to leave. Ellie Lester did not need a man haunted by visions of his past. She needed someone who could shrug off the war instead of allowing it to become a ball and chain to his emotions.

But even as she closed the distance between them, he knew the truth. He had not escaped soon enough. His heart galloped at the sight of her, and his head filled with the sight of a stray strand of her hair dangling against her neck and of her clear skin. And when she got close enough, he smelled a hint of jasmine.

She stopped in front of him, a question in her blue eyes. He felt her gaze skim along his clean-shaven jaw and saw the small smile of approval that belied the telltale signs of redness rimming her eyes.

"You've been crying." It accounted for the strangeness of her voice and the slight puffiness around her eyes.

"You weren't supposed to notice."

He gave her a small smile and lowered his voice. "A gentleman should always take notice of a woman in distress."

Something akin to panic flashed in the blue depths before she lowered her eyes to the dirt floor.

He cleared his throat again, his voice gravelly from his singing. He was scaring her. Even if he was ready to admit what he could no longer deny, she wouldn't understand. He forced his voice to come out strong. "Nothing has gone wrong, has it?" Yet even as he asked the question, he knew the answer. If she had somehow been discovered or a problem had come up, she would have been more anxious, even fearful.

"Everything is fine."

He could deny those words and pry for the truth, but he had no right to do such a thing, unless. . . "You won't even tell your cousin what's bothering you?"

Her lips settled into a grim line. "Just missing Martin, I suppose. Maybe feeling sorry for myself."

The willingness with which she shared startled him. No coquettish holding out or games meant to wrap a man in knots as big as the hooped skirts the young Southern belles wore. Still, her grief built a wall of restraint in him. She needed time, not a declaration of love. "He was a good man."

Her stiff nod told him she kept her emotions in check. "Why don't I just look over what you've done and get out of your way?" She did not wait for an answer but stepped around him and to the wagon.

He watched as she inspected his work. If he were to make his escape, he needed to seize the moment and tell her everything. Now was the time. Knowing about Martin's death would bring her a measure of comfort. He could reduce her grief by giving his account. But the truth smacked the face of her trust in him. He was a Confederate. And a deserter. And his accusation would be against a captain in the Union she held so dear, and who perhaps was her uncle.

Theodore licked his lips and shifted his weight, his eyes on her as she ran a hand along the rough wood of the wagon. As she stretched an arm to reach inside and touch the lip of wood he had just installed, he swallowed over the dryness in his throat. As her hair fell about her shoulders in riotous curls and her profile revealed not only the puffiness of her eyes but the grace with which she held herself, Theo closed his eyes tight. Here was a woman whose determination to help others without thought of her own safety and reputation was something he could not only admire but a quality in direct contrast to his own inability to perform. The strength with which she endured losing someone she loved, her desire to help *him*, and her devotion to Rose showed a noble spirit he could not hope to match.

He had waited too long to show her the truth. She would suspect his motive now, and rightly so. But not telling her made him more of a coward than he already was, and he risked losing everything. He would be forced to leave and head west.

Ellie returned to him, her soft smile and a light of appreciation in her eyes squeezing his heart. "You're doing a wonderful job. I can see exactly what you're planning and think the stack of lumber in here would make a good cover for. . ." A line appeared between her brows. "Theo?"

She touched his arm, and the heat of her fingers added to the torture of his guilty secret. Time seemed to slow in that moment when he stared down at her small hand on his forearm. Her eyes grew wide, and he brought his other hand to cover hers. She tried to draw away, and he could see that she didn't understand. But how could she? He steeled himself against weakness and held her gaze.

"There is something I need to tell you, Ellie. Something I should have said the day you found me."

༄

As Theo walked away from her, toward the stall that held Libby, Ellie stilled herself. She could see by the slump of his shoulders and his hesitant steps that he was bothered. What would he have to tell her? Her mind considered and rejected a thousand things, but nothing made sense.

He knelt at the front edge of the stable and dug into the small knapsack she had seen in the cellar. His hand withdrew a packet of white papers then dug down again to withdraw three loose sheets of paper. He folded them with the other stack and rose, his back to her, head down, the tail of his flannel shirt hanging loose from his trousers. "I met Martin."

She heard his words but didn't understand what he meant. Of course he had met Martin before. Many times because Martin. . .

"Before Chancellorsville. I knew his regiment. We saw each other across the field as they were retreating from us." He turned toward her, and her eyes went to his face, stiff and paler than normal. "We managed to work out a time to meet in an old, abandoned house that was already torn apart from a battle a week before."

"But. . .how? You're a. . ."

"There was a widow woman who helped tend the sick on the battlefield. I got a message to her and told her who to deliver it to. She said she would try. I didn't hear anything for a few days until. . ."

She waited, not knowing what to say.

She startled when Theo sank to the dirt floor, as if his knees could no longer hold his weight. He draped his arms over his bent knees and let his head sink down, shielding his face. The packet lay on his lap.

She knelt beside him, afraid to touch him. "Theo? I don't understand. How?" She shook her head, wondering if she was hearing correctly, concerned by Theo's demeanor and what it might mean. "You're scaring me."

When he lifted his head, his expression was wistful. "Don't mean to. It's just. . ." A shudder swept through him. "There was a young boy. His name was Bud. He was always saying something was going to happen to this one or that one. And it always did." He paused and rubbed his cheek. "I could usually calm him down if I sang to him, but the night before nothing seemed to work. He was convinced his time had come and that something would happen to him that day in battle. And it did." His jaw clenched, his eyes fixed on a distant spot. "I found him facedown. I carried him back. 'Twas the widow woman who found me on the edge of the field. Guess I lost my head a little bit. I don't remember much, except her taking me aside later on and pressing something into my hand."

"Martin?"

"Yes. He wanted to meet on the edge of their camp. Said his captain had a fitful temper for anyone caught sneaking around." He paused and straightened one leg.

"What about Bud?"

Theo chuckled, a dry, humorless sound. "I sat next to him through the night. He was dead before daylight."

"So you didn't meet Martin?"

"We fought all that day. At least I think I did. I remembered shooting and moving and hunkering down in a trench. I wondered what it all meant, and then I didn't care anymore."

His voice caught, and she saw the struggle it took for him to retain his composure. Part of her wanted to reach out to him and tell him it was fine to cry. During his one furlough, Martin had spoken of the horrors he'd seen, but she had also sensed a pocket of emotion that remained untapped.

"I wanted out. Thought of nothing else all that night and up to the time I met Martin. I imagined a bullet in my back at any minute as I crept out of camp that night. Kept hoping it would come." He shook his head. "When I met Martin, he was thin, painful thin. He was writing by the light of the moon filtering through a hole in the ceiling and wall. No lights because light meant we'd be detected. We talked for a long time."

Theo lifted his head and stared her straight in the eye. "Seemed I wasn't alone in wanting to desert. Martin said most everyone he knew had thought of it at one time or another. Even him. He even invited me to visit after the war was over. Said no matter if I was a fool Confederate, I'd still be welcome in his home." Theo's smile melted away as quickly as it appeared. "We agreed to meet again the next night, provided we were still engaged. I slipped off from the cabin first, but then I heard something behind me and hunkered down in some bushes. I saw Martin leave the cabin and heard footsteps right at my ear. A man passed by and then. . .I don't know. There was a shot. And somehow I knew it was Martin that shot was meant for. The same man went by me again, and I caught a glimpse of him. I heard a low moan and knew it was Martin. When I went to him, he was already gone, Ellie. I promise you. There was nothing I could have done."

Stunned by what he was implicating, Ellie raised her hands to her face, processing the information over and over. "He was murdered?"

"That's not all. The man I heard, I saw. Just a glimpse, but I—" He put a hand to his brow and massaged the spot between his eyes.

Ellie chafed at the delay in what he was going to say. She opened her mouth to prompt him when he dropped his hand to his lap and met her gaze.

"The man looked a lot like your uncle Ross."

Chapter 16

Ellie pressed her fingertips to her lips as the tension built in her neck and shoulders.

"I have no proof," she heard Theo's voice. "But when I saw him the other night, my impression was that I'd seen him before."

Uncle Ross? Shoot Martin for no reason? A curl of doubt wound its way through her mind. It had been Uncle Ross who had delivered the news of Martin's death. His letter assured her that he would oversee the burial. Even in her reply, asking that he bring Martin's body back to Gettysburg, Uncle Ross had indicated it could not be done, and she had accepted his word as a certainty. She drew air into her lungs, determined to hear whatever else Theo had to say before drawing a conclusion. "You. . .went to him."

Theo nodded. "As soon as I could. I knew his effects would be sent home to you under normal circumstances, but I feared the man would come back. Or that Martin's body would be overlooked. I didn't know what to do, so I took what I could." His long fingers wrapped around the packet and held them out to her. "Papers. Letters and the one he was working on in the dark when I arrived. There are a few coins and a bit of money from his pockets, but nothing else."

She accepted the papers, hands trembling. Her mind reeled from all she had heard and from the familiarity of the simple script on those three pages that had no envelope. Martin's last words to her.

Theo got to his feet and moved away. She followed his movement with her eyes, knowing he was putting distance between them to give her privacy.

She ran her fingertip over the small stack of papers in her lap, almost afraid to see what Martin had written to her. He had been a well-spoken man, and his letters were full of details about the men rather than their maneuvers and upcoming plans for battle. As it should be. But she'd stopped receiving letters from him about a month before news of his death. She realized she now held those letters. He hadn't stopped writing her but must have been holding the letters until he could post them.

She picked up the three sheets of loosely folded paper and her hands trembled. As she gently unfolded them, her eyes fell on the familiar handwriting, and she once again heard his voice and saw his smile in her mind's eye.

My Dearest Ellie,

How I long to be home again. I am more convinced with each passing day that war is more terror and fear than victory and valor. It will take every day of my life to forget memories etched in my mind. I fear only heaven can take away the horror of this living hell. Your softness of spirit and carefree laughter keep me sane yet bring such a terrible longing for home that I fear I have, more than once, been tempted to leave without regard for punishment.

I hate the pitting of man against man. We are given little to eat and made to walk miles, under the extra weight of our packs. My bones ache with a tiredness I cannot name. Only when I see your smile or hear your laughter does my heart rest from it all, if only briefly.

I hope with the next letter you will send a likeness of yourself, so that your face won't go blurry in my mind's eye. I fear it will. Some days I think it already has and that the woman I perceive is only that of a long-ago memory, an angel who is there but just out of reach.

Tears welled in her eyes and she blinked, releasing them to stream down her cheeks. *Oh, Martin.*

☙

Theodore saw it coming. He had known the letter would stir her grief, but he wasn't prepared for the heart-wrenching whimpers that emanated from her lone figure.

Unable to witness her grief without trying his best to quell it, he went out to the pasture to bring Libby back in. When Ellie didn't react to their movements, Theo knew her world was narrowing to that spot of sorrow that no human could touch. How many times had he himself held a fallen comrade and felt that same isolating grief?

Her whimpers turned to something more. Deeper. As if her soul was shattering. He turned back to the board he had been sawing to fit against the others, but he was unable to block out her need. When he could stand it no longer, he laid the saw aside, bumping the sack of nails. They spilled at his feet, but he ignored them.

In a modicum of strides, he covered the distance separating them. "Ellie." The shivering whimpers were building in volume. He cupped her elbows. "Ellie?"

For the time it took him to exhale, she quieted, her gaze focusing on his face. All the pain in her heart reflected in the stormy blue of her eyes. "He's all gone," she whispered, her voice soft and sad, like a small child whose beloved toy had been smashed to bits. Her eyes closed again, and she began to shake her head.

He felt drawn to her grief. Connected in a way he understood all too well, and not at all. His hands slid up her arms, and he pulled her toward him, tucking her head beneath his chin. Her hands clenched the folds of his shirt, and her tears flowed freely. He cupped the back of her head and rocked her gently within his embrace. Her breath coming in gasps, punctuated by mewls that turned him inside out and left him ragged with hurt.

Gradually her sobs gave way to gasping breaths then sniffles. He stroked her hair and felt her shift, releasing his shirt and running a hand under her nose. When she pulled back, he let her go, and an immediate chill filled the space she had occupied.

To give her time to further collect herself, he leaned to pick up the scattered sheets and envelopes and worked them back into a neat pile. He held them out to her, wishing he could see her face then felt the hand of guilt press against his conscience.

"I should have told you sooner. I. . ." He didn't know what more to say. "Ellie. . ."

She hugged herself and lifted her gaze to his. A wan smile played on her lips. "I need to get back."

"Let me go with you."

Her smile became more brilliant. "That's kind of you, but I need time. To think." She took a step toward the barn door and turned. "I'll expect you whenever you've finished."

"I'll be another couple of hours." What else could he say? As much as he wanted to go after her, to erase the pain, he knew his presence was a reminder of what she no longer had.

But there was one thing he could give her. As he watched her disappear from his line of vision, he fully understood the folly of what he felt and the risk of expressing it now, while she still grieved for Martin.

He crossed to the doorway, the words on his tongue as he watched her mount the dappled gray from a boulder. His throat filled as he watched her leave. The lane was empty, and the evergreens blocked his view of the road. In the silence left by her departure, he breathed out what he had dared not say out loud. "I'm loving you, Ellie."

Chapter 17

Rose said little as Ellie slid the plate onto the tray in front of her friend. Really, Rose had said little for the hour she'd been working on doing laundry and sprucing up her room.

And it suited Ellie fine. The last thing she wanted or needed was to be forced to carry on a conversation she didn't have a heart for. She moved about in a comfortable haze of spent emotional exhaustion, doing the few tasks she knew needed to be done for Rose and baby Colin, in a rush to get back to her place for the evening.

Martha came by in the late afternoon to check on Rose.

When she came back down to the silent kitchen, Ellie made the statement they used as code. "Do you have to go out of town tonight?"

Martha didn't smile, her sharp eyes acknowledging the secret message. "Got to work spreading my garden after sunset. No babies to deliver tonight."

Ellie nodded and walked with Martha to the door, her tension over the slave transfer ebbed at the black woman's reassuring message. "How is Rose, Martha?"

"She fine if she'll stay put. Most want to get up and jump around right away, but you tell her to stay put." Martha placed her hand on the garden gate and paused. "Any news from Dr. Selingrove?"

Ellie knew how much Rose's husband meant to the black woman. "Not yet."

If Martha felt disappointment, her expression did not show it. She merely gave a stiff nod and headed down the pathway.

Ellie headed inside to check on Rose one last time before leaving for the evening. Though she couldn't see through Rose's kitchen window if Uncle Ross's horse was in the stable, she could see that the pasture was empty, and she hoped it meant he still had not returned. She opened the back door and cocked her head to listen for sounds that he had returned. Nothing.

In her kitchen, she checked the roasting chicken for doneness. Juices from the bird's breast ran clear, and she returned it to the still-warm oven. Maybe she would have an appetite later but not now. Not even the jar of her favorite tomato chutney coaxed her appetite.

She snugged the dishcloth tighter around the bread and, with the mundane tasks finished, sat down at the table, only then letting her mind wander. She conjured the image of Martin at the table laughing over some inanity, but when she tried to bring his face into focus, it wouldn't come and a new wave of sadness washed over her.

With leaden feet, she dragged herself up the stairs to the sanctity of their room. Her room. As it had been for the past seven months. Scooping up the stack of letters she had left on the bed earlier, she unfolded the three sheets and read again Martin's last words to her. It would be so easy to discount Theo. She wanted to reject it, the idea of Martin being murdered. . .and by her uncle. So repelling. But what reason would Theo have to lie? Though he had deserted, the emotion he had expressed over the loss of Bud showed the mental strain the fighting had taken on him. Even Martin showed signs of that strain. And Uncle Ross. . .

Everything swirled in her mind. Deliberately, she ripped the end of one of the other envelopes, needing to know what else Martin had to say. The date was one week before the letter he had been working on the night he'd met Theo. She opened the other two envelopes, each dated a week previous to the other. She smiled. He had told her while on furlough that it sometimes took him a week to finish one letter, then he would send three or four of them all at once.

She found the one dated in April, three weeks before his reported death. As she read, she noticed that the tone matched that of the last one she had received. He was worried and tired. Though he tried to keep his tone light, his agitation showed. The next letter revealed the source of his frustration.

Your uncle Ross isn't well liked, darling. He is cold to the men's needs and seldom hesitates in carrying out extreme punishment for the mildest infraction.

He made no other mention of Uncle Ross. Ellie wondered if his assessment of punishment was from personal experience or what he had witnessed. The next letter seemed more desperate.

Punishment is ramping up. Talk of desertion is more common as are rumors that the captain is drinking. Most know my relationship to the man and withdraw from me. Yet Ross seems to show mercy to no man, regardless of relationship.

Most nights I lie awake thinking of you and our home. Perhaps we should think of moving out to the farm. The peace of that place speaks to my soul even now.

Ellie lay down and rested her head on her arms. Martin's unhappiness colored his death in shades of cold gray, just as the idea of his being shot burned into her mind like a great black ball. She fought the weariness that pulled at her and closed her eyes with the promise that it would be for only a minute. Just enough time to pull herself together before Uncle Ross returned or Theo brought the wagon in.

☙

Theo leaned his head against the wall of the barn. He flexed his fingers, noting the bluish tint to the skin from where he had pinched them between two of the boards as he stacked the wagon full to conceal the new wood of the false bottom. At least his fingers weren't broken, though the first joint on his middle finger was tighter and more painful than the others. Now all he had to do was get over to Ellie's.

As the breeze filtered through the thick branches of the evergreens that screened him from the main house, he closed his eyes to drink in the solitude. Working with his hands had felt good. Even hearing Libby's happy munching from the stall as he finished his project had given him a sense of home. How long had it been now? A year? Two? He'd requested a furlough several times, always denied.

But he didn't want to think about the war, knowing what thin ice he treaded by allowing his thoughts to shift that direction. What was wrong with him? He didn't understand his nightmares or why his hands shook so badly sometimes. And least of all, he couldn't understand why it was so difficult for him to control the memories.

Frustrated, Theo pushed away from the barn wall and decided to walk around the property. Ellie had a jewel here, though the buildings, as she had suggested, showed some damage.

Where had he been during the battle in Gettysburg? Hunkered down in the woods of West Virgina most likely. Waiting. Biding his time. He'd known the general plan for the South to push north, and his desertion and plans to find Ellie made his position particularly precarious. He'd waited for almost a month to make a move, even finding work on a farm where the people had never asked him questions. Maybe when he left he would return there instead of going west.

The fields surrounding Ellie's property remained unplowed for next year's crops, and he wondered at the losses the farmers had endured. In the distance, he spotted a small building beside a pond. The springhouse. It would be the place Ellie planned to hide the runaways.

He was headed in that direction when movement caught his peripheral vision. He turned his head toward the fields on his left, expecting to see a bright-colored bird, but it was a man. Probably out looking for trinkets left behind by the warring troops. But the suddenness with which the man had appeared, unobserved by him, shook him, and he lost his desire to explore further.

With the sun dipping in the west, he turned back to the barn. His gaze went over the loaded wagon. Libby stuck her head out of her stall and whinnied at him. He stroked the animal's nose. A bittersweet longing rose in him to be the young man he had been before the war. The carefree fellow who delighted in playing tricks on his newly wedded cousin and loved nothing more than breaking horses for the wealthier plantation owners to use as carriage horses. He'd known as soon as the war started and the destruction of the South began that things would never be the same.

Weariness pulled at him, but he resisted. Instead, he hitched Libby to the wagon. He turned the wagon and headed out the drive and out onto the road leading back to Gettysburg.

He forced himself to concentrate on the bright red blotch flying through the air, a cardinal, and its less gloriously colored mate. A rabbit hopped off the road and into the field. Libby's harness added a pleasant jangle to the air, and Theo pursed his lips to whistle a tune to match the rhythm of the horse's hooves.

As Libby leaned harder into the harness to get up a gentle hill, Theo's tune died. In the midst of another rise to his right, covered by trees, he could see at its edge a wagon. Two black men worked with shovels. Whether they dug around a knickknack they'd found or a body yet uninterred, Theo didn't really want to know. He turned his head away and slapped the reins against Libby's back to hurry her along.

He pulled up to Ellie's as the sun skimmed the western horizon. Everything seemed still and quiet. He set the hand brake on the wagon and slipped to the ground. Libby knickered softly and arched her head, and he reached to run his hand over her velvet neck. Pain shot up his arm. He winced and studied the fingers of his right hand. The middle finger had swollen to twice its size, and the bluish bruise across his other fingers had become a ragged purple mark.

"Theo?"

He lifted his head, seeing Ellie standing on the back porch. He heard her repeat his name and the note of concern, and then, before he could focus again, he felt her hand on his arm.

"Why are you standing here?"

He stared into her eyes, concern pinching the place between her brows, and held out his hand for her inspection.

☙

Ellie felt a stab of anxiousness when she saw his fingers. "Oh!"

She couldn't believe the mottled mess he'd made of his fingers. "Come over to the porch and sit down so I can look at them." Ellie made sure he followed her then pointed to the place where he should sit and perched next to him. She gently lifted his hand, aware of the weight of it against hers and the rough feel of his palm flush with hers. She traced the length of his middle finger. She watched his expression for signs of pain. When she placed pressure on the upper half of his middle finger, his face paled and he tried to pull away.

"It might be broken," she said. "What did you do?"

He sat up straight, a little color flushing back into his cheeks. "I was stacking wood into the bed, and my fingers got smashed between two pieces. It'll be fine. I got here without a problem."

She frowned. "Anyone can guide a horse with one hand. I bet you used your left."

He shrugged, realizing his arguments would fall on deaf ears. He tried to pull away again.

She pulled back. "Stop it. You're acting like a child."

For the first time, he raised his gaze to meet hers. His gray eyes held a solemnity that caught her breath. And something else loomed there. . . . "You don't make me feel like a child."

Her breath caught in her throat, and she released his hand and pushed to her feet. "I've got to get some bandages." Realizing how abrupt she sounded, she tried to soften her tone. "You sit still. I'll be back."

Chapter 18

Ellie's thoughts swirled as she searched for an old sheet to rip into strips to bind Theo's fingers. She couldn't be sure that middle finger wasn't broken. She would have to have Martha look at it. Maybe Theo would let her touch it.

Her face grew hot when she recalled the roughness of his palms and the luminescent light firing his eyes before his last statement, asking something she didn't quite understand. Or maybe she did. She closed her eyes and released a sigh.

When she reached for the tin of cloves, she realized how much easier Theo's injury made their job. Taking him to see Martha wouldn't be questionable at all. The only danger left would be his lone drive out to the farm. But, she reasoned, if anyone questioned him or her, the fact that he was doing repairs at the farm for her would be a solid excuse for his presence there.

She mashed the cloves and chickweed then made a paste and hurried out the door. He still sat where she left him, his wide shoulders slumped. For a second, she felt sorry for him. He had done so much. Sacrificed himself for her. Brought her evidence of the truth, however unpalatable she found it. But was she ready to believe him over her uncle Ross?

Ellie touched his shoulder to let him know she was there. He raised his head as she sat next to him and collected his right hand. "Spread your fingers out."

He rested his hand on his thigh and spread his fingers.

Her face flamed. She wished she wouldn't have to be quite so personal in order to wrap his finger. She debated leaving the job for Martha, but the injury must hurt, and he had done it while trying to help her.

"What's the paste for?" He lifted his hand from his thigh and held it out.

Relief spread through her at his action. She dabbed the dark paste onto his middle finger then the others. "A mixture of cloves and chickweed to bring down the swelling."

"You know herbs?"

When she tied the last knot, she shook her head. "Not really. Martha knows many, though. It's part of the reason why Dr. Selingrove, Rose's husband, finds Martha's help so invaluable."

"She didn't seem too talkative when I went to get her that night."

"She's shy."

Theodore spit out a laugh. "That's not the impression I got."

She crossed her arms and frowned. "Martha is a kindhearted woman with a real gift for healing, even if she hasn't had formal training." She regretted her defensive tone when all the lightheartedness left his expression.

"I meant no offense."

She shifted away from him and stared out at the dead garden. "No. I—I overreacted. It's been. . .quite a day."

A wagon rattled up the road, and they paused to watch its passage. The traffic on Breckinridge Street grew less as the day melted into evening.

Ellie felt a sickening dread in her stomach when she thought about Uncle Ross's inevitable return. He would be on horseback and they would be able to see him before he saw them, but it was the conversation she dreaded. How could she pretend she didn't know a thing? Yet Theo had said he wasn't sure it was Uncle Ross, just that the man looked a lot like him. Uncle Ross would never shoot someone in cold blood. Was it Martin's punishment for leaving camp? Cavorting with the enemy?

Theo's voice cut into her thoughts. "When I saw her at that doctor's office, I thought she was a servant or something."

Ellie dragged herself back to the conversation. "And acting too good for a woman with black skin?"

Surprise lit his features. "Well, yes. I guess this Southern boy has a lot to learn. I worked with black men. Breaking horses for the rich."

"Did you pay them?"

"Never crossed my mind. We were friends, though, and they often spoke of horrors their kin endured at the hands of their owners."

"If you give the blacks a chance, you can learn a lot about laughter, perseverance, and God."

"God?"

Ellie warmed to her subject, weighing each word against her own untouchable sorrow. "I've seen so many of them come through here, their clothes little more than rags, scars on their backs, arms, even their faces. One slave had a brand mark on his cheek because he'd run away once before and gotten caught. The brand was his punishment, but it didn't stop him from trying again. One older man said the reason their skin was so black was because they'd been through a sight more fires than white folk, and though they got scorched, the good Lord never let them get burned up."

And if they could persevere through such pain, I should be able to as well.

ଓ

Theo took note of her tender smile as she recounted the story. "You've done a lot to help them. That shows a great deal of spirit on your part. I think the Lord would be pleased with you."

Ellie's eyes darted to his face then away. "Maybe."

"You've stayed true to something you believe in."

"Martin always believed that everyone had a gift. He was the one that first saw Martha's talent for herbs."

"But you don't do this for him. You do it for yourself."

She nodded and squinted into the setting sun. "I suppose I do. It's always been hard for me to see people hurt. Even during the battle here, Rose and I did our best to help the wounded. We went to the hospital every day. It was terrible."

How well he knew. The one time a bullet had grazed his scalp, his visit to the field hospital had been frightening. The sourness of infection, the moaning, the bugs. . . Those men did not have the gentle touch of a woman or the thoughtful care of clean bandages and homemade poultices. He let his gaze slide over Ellie's profile, and his chest tightened. And they most certainly didn't have the beauty to help them forget their wounds and ease the long, lonely days of recovery.

She faced him then, her gaze searching his. "You're feeling better."

He could only nod as emotion clutched him. "Yes, I am."

"I listened to many war stories from the men as they recovered." Her gaze skittered away from his face. "Martin told me a few." He saw the way her lips quivered and knew she struggled for composure.

"He told you about the things he saw?"

"Some."

He straightened his back, working out the kinks, and rubbed his bandaged hand. "If I were married, I think it would be hard for me to talk about everything. It would be the one place the war couldn't touch unless I let it in, so I'd try and keep the door shut as long as possible."

A lone tear slipped down her cheek, and she swiped it away like an errant fly. "But I wanted to help by sharing his burden."

She was showing him a part of her hurt that he could only hope to soothe in some small way. He wasn't sure he knew how, though. How could he wrap up the torment of watching his friends and fellow soldiers die and the patriotism that tore at him to stay and fight? And then there were the other complications. Leaving meant death. But if not killed, then forever walking in a cloud of shame. Or struggling with not being able to endure when others did. Martin had been the same haggard, war-torn man he himself was. The difference was Martin had stayed and died, and he had left and was dying in a very different way.

Ellie's hand on his arm brought him alert. Her fingers dug into his forearm. Following the line of her gaze, he saw the lone horseman and heard Ellie's whisper. "It's Uncle Ross."

Chapter 19

Uncle Ross took his time dismounting. He acknowledged Ellie and Theo by an upraised hand but seemed otherwise relaxed to Theo's eye.

Theo studied the man more closely as Ross led the horse into the barn, trying to remember. But he feared the passage of time and his own dislike for Ross had biased him.

"We should leave." Ellie jerked her head to indicate his bandaged hand. "I'll help you get Libby hitched up. Just stay calm."

"Sure." He grinned down at her.

"What?"

"I'm calm. And Libby never got unhitched." His eyes slid down to where her hand grasped his arm then back to her. His smile grew.

She shook her head. "Yes, I guess she is." He saw the sudden shift in her mood when she glanced at the barn. Tension squared her shoulders, and her voice came to him low and terse. "Are you sure, Theo?"

It took him a minute to understand the change in subject and absorb the real meaning of her question. Her eyes never left her uncle as he reappeared briefly then turned his back to close the barn doors. "All I can tell"—he pitched his voice low—"is that he looks familiar."

Uncle Ross strode up to them.

Ellie stood.

Theo remained where he was.

"Ellie, my dear, I'm bushed. I'll probably eat something then head straight to bed. We can talk tomorrow."

"I'm sorry, Uncle. Theo's finger looks broken. We—we were just getting ready to hitch up Libby and take him to see the doctor."

Uncle Ross slid a look over at Libby. "I see." His gaze met Ellie's, brows raised. "And I thought Dr. Selingrove was fighting."

She gaped and pink suffused her cheeks. Theo had never seen her quite so rattled. "Yes, that's right. He is fighting, but he's not the only doctor in Gettysburg."

Ross's eyes flicked to Theo, his expression cold.

Theo raised his hand to prove to the man that the need was legitimate. "I think I broke something." He was proud of himself for maintaining the Yankee pronunciation.

Ross looked away. "Then I suppose I'll make myself at home."

"Your business went well, I hope?" Ellie asked.

"It did. Thank you. I'm in an even better position than I thought possible."

To Theo's eye, Ross's answer caused even greater strain to Ellie, evidenced by the stiffening of her back and the worry line between her eyes.

"Went by the farm today." Ross's expression became gentle. "It's looking a little run down. If you'd let me, I could hire someone to take care of the repairs."

"I've already hired someone."

Ross's nostrils flared, and his hard gaze flicked to Theo. "I see."

It was that stare, the set of the jaw, and the way the fading light of day hit the planes of his face that brought a flash of certainty to Theo. It had been Ross that night. He would stake his life on it.

Ellie pulled her skirts up slightly and motioned to Theo to follow her before setting off toward Libby. "I'll see you tomorrow morning, Uncle."

"Tomorrow morning? I wonder what Martin would say about your being out that late."

Ellie spun on her heel. "What is that supposed to mean?"

Theo felt the weight of Ross's gaze but he kept his own eyes on Ellie.

Ellie's eyes blazed hot. "Martin is dead, and Theo is my hired help."

Ross opened his mouth, not looking the least bit cowed.

Ellie cut him off. "Nothing more, *Uncle*. And I resent the implications of your statement. It might be best for you to find somewhere else to stay for the remainder of your visit. Snyder's Wagon Hotel is just down the street."

Ross held out his hands toward Ellie. "Now, Ellie. You misunderstood me. Let's talk about this."

"As you suggested, *Uncle*, morning would be a better time to talk." She didn't wait for a reply, and Theo could only admire the steel reserve of the woman as he followed her to the wagon.

When he helped her into the wagon then settled in beside her, he glanced at her profile. She seemed oblivious to everything. Her arms were wrapped around herself. "He was a little too sure of himself," she murmured.

"Is he normally suspicious like that?"

"What if he knows about you, Theo?" Her blue eyes clouded, her words came fast. "You could take a vow to the U.S. Government, then we'll have nothing to fear."

He guided Libby with his good hand. Ellie's statement made it sound so simple, yet he knew a simple vow would not be the end to the turmoil and memories that plagued him. He glanced at Ellie's profile, not having missed the "we" in her last statement. He wondered if she cared. Would she offer the solution if she didn't? He couldn't help a little grin of satisfaction.

The wagon squeaked and moaned down the road, the sounds loud in the stillness. "I thank you for defending me, ma'am," he drawled, hoping to tease her into relaxing.

"It's none of his business who I'm with. And you're my cousin anyway."

He turned toward her. "Really?"

"By marriage."

"Oh."

She put a hand down to brace herself on the seat and frowned up at him. "What do you mean, 'Oh'?"

"Just. . .oh." He pulled back on the reins to slow Libby for the turn into the narrow road beside the doctor's office and wondered if what she'd said meant she would never think of him beyond cousin status.

"Pull over toward the garden and stop."

He tried to see the garden area in the dark. There was no sign of movement. He wondered if the slaves even knew of his arrival. Ellie leaned close to him, and he felt her warm breath against his ear. "They've already been instructed what to do. Don't worry. By the time we're done here, they'll be in place. Don't let on that anything is different."

He dared to turn toward her before she had a chance to lean away from him. Her eyes flew to his in surprise. He gave her a lazy smile. "Thanks, cuz."

Chapter 20

Ellie watched as Martha examined Theo's fingers, knowing that as she sat there the runaways were crawling into the wagon as pre-instructed by Martha. From the code Martha had given the previous night, Ellie had known the baby hadn't been born yet and where to place the wagon, but the impending birth would cause the woman great discomfort in the bumpy ride to the farm. Still, it couldn't be helped. At least there would be less likelihood of discovery if she gave birth out at the farm than if she were in the cellar of Dr. Selingrove's offices—provided her uncle didn't decide to pay the farm another visit. That he had been on the property at all, without her permission, irritated her.

Ellie found herself transfixed by the placid expression on Theo's face as Martha probed his fingers. She confirmed that the middle one was broken, the pressure of her fingers on the joint and the wince of pain on Theo's face lending credit to her diagnosis. Without informing Theo of her intentions, Martha's strong fingers cupped around his middle finger and yanked.

Theo released a grunt then inhaled sharply.

Martha didn't even glance his way but set about putting herbs in a mortar and pestle. Ellie watched as she ground the herbs, noting that Theo remained quiet though collected.

She wished she could read his thoughts. Was he considering her suggestion? Was it because of what he had revealed about Uncle Ross that she felt such a need to protect him? Or was it because protecting him meant protecting her own secret?

For a fleeting moment, in the wagon, she had thought he might kiss her. When he had only smiled and commented about being her cousin, her disappointment had been palpable. Worse, she'd felt every bit the fool for thinking such thoughts.

When Theo turned his head and caught her staring at him, another flush of heat went through her. After tonight she wouldn't see him as much. Returning to the mundane tasks of living and taking care of Rose would make things easier. She could grieve uninterrupted.

If Theo stayed out at the farm, there would be plenty of work for him to do for a couple of weeks. Then, instead of having him do the necessary repairs on her house, she would pay him and encourage him to leave. Thank him for all he had done and release him. If he didn't take the vow, he would continue his journey, running from his responsibility.

Embers of anger stirred over that thought. How could he look at himself knowing he had deserted the cause for which Bud and all his other friends fought? If only it had been Martin to come back to her instead of Theo. . .

☙

At the farm, Theo backed the wagon to the barn and left it there as Ellie had instructed him. He would stay in the stable for two nights, then the springhouse would be his until he finished the repairs. According to Ellie's racing monologue on the way back to her house, she would then pay him and he could leave. His services no longer needed. And the whole time Ellie spouted the litany of instructions, she hadn't once looked him full in the face.

He worked the straps to unhitch Libby. "Some oats should help ease the workload you had today, huh, girl?" If only his own load could be erased so easily. He led the horse into the barn and closed the doors, leaving the runaways to do whatever it was they'd been instructed to do.

He didn't begin to understand Ellie's strange withdrawal from him but attributed it to the lateness of the hour and everything he had shared with her that day. She would need some time and space to process everything. The farm and the work would keep his mind off her. Maybe she would change her mind and ask him to stay, but he had to be prepared if she didn't. Could be she realized having him around was too big a risk to her own safety.

Libby pawed the ground when she saw the bag of oats he was preparing. The horse's happy crunching didn't cover the low mewling that came to his ears. He stilled. The runaways must be making their move through the field to the springhouse.

If prayer changed things, he prayed for freedom for the couple and their baby to come. He'd often given thought to the things he and his friends held dear and the way of life that called upon them to fight to preserve what was familiar. Many of his unit struggled between the knowledge that they fought for the entire South, even as their homes and hometowns struggled to survive.

Thoughts of home brought an ache and anger, but he let them go. Had to. Did he have a right to be angry at the destruction when he had deserted? He hadn't fought so much for his home state's right to have slaves as much as his right to have a home unsullied by war.

Theo spread a layer of hay in the stall next to Libby's and stretched out. A piece jabbed him in the cheek as he turned his head to get comfortable and raised his arms to pillow his head. His muscles relaxed, but his mind raced with problems, and every problem seemed to lead to Ellie's image burned in his mind, beautiful and kindhearted. And alone.

Like him.

At some point in the night, he was startled awake. He rubbed a hand over his eyes and blinked into the darkness. Used to a nightmare waking him, he recalled nothing remotely frightening tearing away his sleep. On the edge of his awareness, though, he recalled something.

He rose to his knees then to his feet, moving quietly lest he miss whatever sound woke him. Libby remained quiet in her stable, a lone ear pricked in his direction as he moved through the barn.

He pushed the wooden bar back and swung the door out enough to slide through the opening. Cold swept over him, stealing his breath. Stars shone brightly from the heavens. Everything seemed still and in its place.

Theo turned in the direction of the springhouse. Though he couldn't see it from the barn, he wondered if the runaways were doing well. Maybe the woman had given birth and the sound of the baby had woken him. He frowned. No, that didn't seem quite right.

Frustrated, he ducked back inside and settled down in the hay, still warm from his body.

Chapter 21

Ellie woke with a headache and a vague feeling of unease. She pulled herself up in bed and squinted into the blush of light coming through the eastern bedroom window. Everything rushed back to her in a flood. Martin's letters. Uncle Ross's persistence. Theo's suspicions about her uncle. And thoughts of Theo brought other memories. The intensity of his gray gaze on her. The way he had said she didn't make him feel like a child. His silly grin down at his arm where she had clutched it while insisting that Libby needed hitched. How her breath caught at the sight of him.

Infatuation. He was a man. She was a woman. And she was alone.

Confused by what it all meant, Ellie leaned to grab the letters on the table beside her bed. She fingered the paper, its stiffness and smooth texture, but it was Martin's bold script that mesmerized her. She expected the sting of sorrow at the sight, surprised when the emotional tidal wave did not come. She sifted through each of the letters, sad that she would never be able to say good-bye to Martin and that she would never hear his booming laughter again.

She went over the passages that referred to Uncle Ross, puzzled by the changes in her uncle. He had been by her mother's side as the months had drained away her strength. Yet Ellie couldn't deny that even her mother seemed unsure of Uncle Ross before she died.

One occasion in particular rose from dusty memories. About a week before her mother had slipped into unconsciousness, Uncle Ross had stayed with her the entire day. Ellie never knew what they talked about, but she did know that her mother was troubled. "He is not the brother I once had," had been the simple comment.

At the time Ellie hadn't thought much of her mother's observation, but now, in light of Martin's letters and Theo's revelation, she recalled other things. Her mother's agitation. Her desire to see Alex Reeves, her attorney. The general exhaustion in her mother's face and the red-rimmed eyes. Perhaps the most telling element of all was that Uncle Ross never returned to see her mother again, even avoiding the funeral with a wire that he was up north.

Muddled with all the problems on her plate, Ellie determined to get up and moving. She would check on Rose and baby Colin, then. . .

What?

Theo's face flashed in her mind, and she wondered if he would have everything he needed for repairs. Even if he did, it might be a good thing to check on the runaways. If the woman had given birth, she might need some things, though she doubted Martha would have allowed the woman to leave her ever-watchful eye without supplying her with the basic needs.

Her thoughts toiled and tumbled over each other as she washed and dressed. She scrambled eggs, and the yellow and white mass matched her mindset. She sat to eat and bit her lip when she thought of Martin sitting in the chair across from her all those months ago. Then Theo's presence. She shook away the images and hurried through her breakfast. After finishing, she prepared a fresh mound of eggs and a slice of ham for Rose to eat.

When she slipped into Rose's kitchen, though, her friend was busy at the stove, the smell of bacon and coffee hanging in the air.

"You're up!"

Rose turned, her house dress swirling around her legs. Her eyes were bright and her smile relaxed. "I was so tired of being in bed I thought it best to get up and move around. And I was hungry."

Ellie raised the covered plate. "I brought you scrambled eggs and a nice slice of ham."

Rose's laughter trilled across the room and she pointed to the plate beside her on the counter. It held a mound of eggs and four strips of bacon. "I'll probably eat both plates."

Happy to see her friend in such good spirits, Ellie picked up baby Colin from his cradle while Rose, true to her word, polished off both meals. "If I continue to eat like this, I'll be twice the size as when Robert left."

Ellie rubbed her finger down the soft cheek of Colin's face. "Robert would be so glad to see you, he wouldn't care."

"He might if he has to buy me a wardrobe of new dresses."

There was a hope in Rose's words that had been missing lately. "Have you had news?"

Rose leaned forward to gather Colin into her arms. "No. But I've prayed and felt such a peace over it all that I'm certain he'll be home."

Ellie had felt the same way for so long. Then the news of Martin's death had shaken her. Hard.

"Where's Theo?"

"Out at the farm doing some repairs."

"Are you going out to see him? He's probably hungry. Take a plate for him."

Ellie thought Rose's tone had a suggestive lilt, but when she glanced at her friend, she was busy rearranging the blanket around Colin. "I had thought about making sure he had all he needed for the repairs." Food hadn't occurred to her for a minute. She would make a number of sandwiches and take some apples over to him. After that he would have to fend for himself.

"Are you still thinking of selling to your uncle?" Rose lifted the baby to her shoulder and patted his back.

"Why, no, of course not. I've never given it serious thought. It's only that Uncle Ross is so stubborn that he won't take no for an answer."

"Why do you suppose that is?"

"I wish I knew."

"Does Theo like it out there?"

Ellie thought it a strange question. "I don't know."

"It's safer for him at the farm."

She had to concur.

"You're lonely without him."

Ellie sucked in a breath and met her friend's steady gaze. "Rose," she breathed, "I'm a widow."

Her friend's lips curved into a soft smile. "You're a woman first, Ellie. And Martin would want you to love again."

"I could never think of Theo in that way. He's my cousin."

Rose's smile grew wider. "Only by marriage, and I think you've been thinking of him that way since he arrived."

Ellie gulped air and shot to her feet. "How could you say such a thing?"

Rose pulled Colin from her shoulder, looking not the least bit flustered by Ellie's protest. "Because I'm a woman, and I've seen him look at you that same way."

"Rose!" was all she could say in protest.

Her friend widened her eyes mockingly. "Ellie!"

"I don't believe this. I made a vow to Martin to love him and honor him. How could you think. . . ?"

Rose was nodding. "It's true. You've kept your vows."

Ellie stilled, mollified.

Rose's smile was back. "But you forgot a very important detail."

A protest rose to Ellie's lips.

"Till death do you part. He's gone, Ellie."

All the air left Ellie's lungs, and she flopped back in the chair, shaken by her friend's words. She loved Martin. Theo could never take his place, but Rose's other suggestion niggled at her. Did Theo really look at her in that way? Beyond admiring his eyes and admitting how much nicer he looked clean shaven, had she thought about him in *that* way?

She stiffened, appalled at the plunge her thoughts had taken.

"Martin would want you to move on and be happy again. I can't think of anyone better than his best friend."

Ellie spat a sigh. "What are you trying to do?" Her eyes sheened over. "How can I just—"

She jerked to her feet.

Rose stood as well, a stricken expression on her face.

Ellie shrugged past her friend and out the back door. The sobs built in her throat. She hurried across the porch to her door and slammed it open, the first tormented cry ripping from her throat.

ଔ

The knock on the door grew louder, and Ellie wondered at her visitor's determination. Uncle Ross could knock until he fell over; she wouldn't answer. It couldn't be Rose since she was on her feet and obviously feeling better.

She rolled onto her back and stared up at the ceiling in her bedroom as another knock echoed up the stairs. It must be serious. Maybe Rose had taken sick. Or Colin. Unable to stand it another minute, Ellie hurried down the stairs and to the back door, throwing it open.

Martha stood there, her black face tense, her eyes solemn. "How's that man's finger doing?"

She hardly had time to stand aside before the woman pushed by her. This was not like Martha. Something was going on and she was using Theo's broken finger as a diversion in case she had visitors. Ellie gave the door a shove and faced her friend. "It's safe. Uncle Ross is not here."

Martha nodded. "One of the conductors was caught. Most of the people got away. They were sent here, but there's no room for them."

"Theo is at the farm, and Uncle Ross is staying elsewhere tonight. The cellar would work."

But Martha was shaking her head. "You don't understand. There's great risk. These people were almost caught and might still be followed. It's dangerous to have them in town."

"The farm?"

"It's what I hoped you might be offerin'. There's eight of them."

"Eight!" Panic edged up Ellie's spine. They would never be able to get eight people into the concealed part of the wagon.

"They'll do what needs done. You know that."

She did know that. She had heard stories of blacks huddled in crates, enduring all manner of rocky roads and dusty trails, not to mention stifling heat, freezing cold, and awkward positions, if it meant gaining their freedom. "When?"

"Not tonight but tomorrow. We'll use the usual signal. Do you think that man will help us, and can he be trusted?"

"Theo?" Ellie realized with a sinking heart that the situation was dire. Even if she didn't want to see him again and rebelled at the idea of taking food over in light of Rose's observations, the decision to see him was being taken out of her hands. She would have to make the trip now. To trust him for help and secrecy. Why did that make her afraid? Ellie ran her hands down the front of her dress then raised her chin. "Yes. I'll talk to him, and I'll leave the signal tonight if all is well."

Martha's dark eyes snapped to a point beyond Ellie's shoulder.

Ellie's flesh raised, and a cold chill breathed against her skin.

Martha's words came out slow and distinct. "You change his bandage and apply the poultice." Though Martha spoke of Theo's fingers, her eyes signaled caution to Ellie. The woman mimed for her to open the door as she continued. "You checked on Miss Rose?"

Ellie nodded that she understood and put her hand on the doorknob. "She was up and about at breakfast. She said she felt good, and Colin seemed content."

Martha dug her hand into an apron pocket and held out a small package. "I made up some more poultice for his fingers." She pressed it into Ellie's hands and gestured for her to open the door.

Ellie realized with a sinking feeling that the door had not caught when she went to shut it, but the greater horror gripped her as she swung the door inward to reveal her uncle Ross standing on the porch, his stony gaze broken suddenly by a huge smile. "Good evening, Ellie."

Chapter 22

"I was just leaving, Uncle Ross," Ellie blurted. His smile didn't wilt a bit, and that in itself heightened Ellie's nerves. Steeling herself, she turned to Martha and floundered for the direction of the conversation before she had opened the door to Uncle Ross.

Martha pointed to the small parcel. "Listen good, now. Apply it to his fingers and wrap them tight." She pushed forward and Uncle Ross fell back a couple of steps to let Martha by, acknowledging her with the merest nod.

Ellie dreaded what it was he might have heard. She dared to pray that God would protect their deeds from Uncle Ross.

"I'm so sorry to interrupt." His smile seemed forced now. "I wasn't sure you would be home, though I'm glad you are. Is Rose doing well?"

Ellie struggled with how to react. Should she show her irritation at his interruption, or would that anger him? Yet she couldn't quite find the strength to be the dutiful niece. "Rose is fine," was all she could manage.

"If you would invite me in, I would like to talk to you."

She tried a smile to match his own. "As I said, I was just leaving."

"But your wagon isn't here. I checked."

The knowledge angered her. "I'm sorry, but I don't see what right you have to be in my barn."

His smile fell into a firm line. "I was looking to assure myself that you might be in. When I didn't see your wagon, I assumed you weren't. I'm certainly glad I didn't leave right away." He took one step closer to her. "I think I must have offended you somehow. In my diligence to offer my services to help you at this terribly hard time in your life, I overstepped myself and made it appear I thought you incapable of managing."

The farm. It was always about the farm. Staring into his face, she saw vestiges of the kindhearted man she'd known since a child, and the slightest doubt crept in that Theo might have been wrong.

"You're a very capable young woman, just as your mother was quite capable. The truth is, my dear—" He paused and glanced around, as if embarrassed. For the briefest moment his eyes landed on Martha as she cleared the gate that led back to her home. "I have a very fond place for the old farm. I would like to manage the rents for it and, if you would consider it, perhaps carve out a couple of acres for myself. It would please me greatly to be close to family again. You are all that I have left."

Ellie hesitated at the earnestness in his eyes. Touched by his sincerity, she reminded herself that he was all she had left as well. In the lines around his face, she could see the family resemblance. Her mother's cleft was her uncle's as well as her own. And living at the farm had been her dream when the promise of children had been alive. Martin's death changed all that. Other than her own memories of the place, there was no longer a reason to hold on to the land. The crops had been ruined from the battle. She could notify the farmers that rented the land that it was being sold.

But still Ellie hesitated. She couldn't bring herself to say the words. She couldn't totally dismiss Theo's story. Martin had been Theo's cousin and best friend. What would be the point of his making up such a thing? Her stomach twisted with stress. Who did she believe? If she told her uncle Theo's story, would he simply laugh and deny the charge, or would those dark eyes become murderous?

She wrapped her arms around herself to mask the shudder of fear.

Uncle Ross shifted his weight and placed his forearm against the door frame. "It is a chilly night. Look, I can see that you need some time. It just so happens that I'll be here a little longer than I thought. Why don't I come by tomorrow evening and we'll discuss more of the details."

Her stomach tightened. She wondered if he had heard the conversation between her and Martha. Wondered if the extension of his time in Gettysburg was connected somehow to what he'd heard if he'd been listening at the door.

But he wouldn't know about her activities. How could he? Besides, he was a Northerner. Surely he would sympathize with what she was doing. If he had heard, they still had no choice but to go forward with their plans. With the number of blacks needing to be hidden there was no way they could use the cellar. Martha would know that as well. It had to be the farm. Uncle Ross wouldn't harm them.

She met Uncle Ross's dark eyes and wondered why, then, she felt so afraid.

☙

Theo lowered his arms and rested his back. The constant pounding on the loose boards that made up the fence surrounding the barn and house had left his shoulders tense and his back sore. His broken finger throbbed, but he kept on. Without an official list of repairs, he had eyeballed the various buildings and picked the tasks he would undertake based on the tools he had available.

He'd kept an ear cocked toward the springhouse all morning, wondering about the couple. Hoping they had made it into the secret compartment of the wagon and not entirely sure they had. How could they be so quiet? What if they hadn't made it at all? Or if they had arrived late? He had no way of knowing whether they were there or not, and it troubled him.

He'd told himself a million times that he was better off not knowing and not getting involved. Still. . .

Theo gripped the hammer tighter and knelt to fix the lower boards. His stomach growled a protest, and he swallowed a gulp of water he'd fetched from the pond at the springhouse. He needed food, and he would need more nails soon, too. If Ellie wanted the farmhouse siding repaired, he would need planks and paint, and if she wanted stonework on the barn fixed, he would need sand and lime and some hand tools. Maybe if he did a great job, she would relent and let him stay on to help fully restore the buildings. By then he would know if she would be capable of returning his love.

He screamed out in pain as the hammer came down on his thumb. He popped the mashed digit into his mouth and sucked. Served him right for letting his mind wander to business that wasn't his. He sank to the ground and pulled out his thumb. Purple. And swelling. Fast. He grimaced at the sight and twisted around at the sound of a horse clopping closer. When he cupped his hand over his eyes, he could make out the form of a woman in the saddle.

He waited as Ellie came up the dirt lane toward the barn. Her coldness the previous evening left him unsure of how to approach her, or even if he should.

He turned back to the loose board, lifted it into place, and began to sink the nail. In his mind, he traced the path she would take to reach him, if indeed she had come to speak to him. She might have come to collect rent or check on the runaways. But no, she wouldn't have come down the dirt lane toward the barn. For rent she would have gone to the house. And for the runaways she could have cut across the field.

He tried to wring her from his thoughts by pounding hard and fast. The nail sunk in three strikes, his broken finger throbbed from clutching the hammer so tight, and his purple thumb on the opposite hand beat its own pained protest. He got to his feet, tempted to look over his shoulder but forcing himself to focus on the fence. He checked the next board and found it stable and firm.

"Theo?"

Despite his desire to remain aloof, the sound of her voice tripped the rhythm of his heart. He took his time straightening and finally turned to face her with a thin smile and a casual, "Howdy, boss."

Chapter 23

Ellie caught Theo's glances as she directed Rose's horse up the dirt lane to the barn. Her stomach tickled with nervousness as she neared him. His back to her, wide as any wall, effectively separating them. She dismounted and took a step closer, stopping when he faced her and ground out his flippant greeting.

The planes of his face were hard, his mouth without the usual good-natured smile. But his eyes were what she didn't understand. The gray light of his gaze was cold. "I—I came to see if there was anything you needed. And to bring you something to eat," she hastened to add.

His eyes raked over her, bold and careless. "Now why would you think I need anything? I'm just a Rebel without responsibility or care."

His flippant attitude stung her, confirming her fears that he could be the liar and her uncle the innocent victim. If he could act like this to her, what made him incapable of being a vicious liar bent on destroying. . . Who? What? Her heart raced, and she couldn't catch her breath. She took a quick step backward, closer to the horse.

He closed the distance between them and grasped her forearm, his fingers a gentle band of iron. "Ellie, forgive me. I. . ." His gaze commanded her attention, gray eyes searching, no longer remote and cold.

"Let me go!"

He did and she slid away from him, closer to the dappled gray. She stroked the horse's neck, her back to him. She had come for some measure of reassurance. Evidence that her trust in him had not been ill placed, and she had gotten coldness. Anger. Why was he angry?

When she finally found the strength to turn, she avoided looking at him on purpose. She moved to the saddlebags and retrieved the food. She set it on the rock and forced herself to say something. Anything. "If you'll give me. . .a list"—the quiver in her voice could not be quelled—"I'll get what you need."

But the other matter pressed on her. She could not leave without asking for his help. She brought air into her lungs in an effort to still her fears. The horse's warmth beckoned to her. She could pull herself into the saddle and leave, but Martha's news meant she needed him. At least until tomorrow night, then she would tell him to leave. Rose had been wrong about him, and the thought brought a hollow ache to Ellie's heart.

She stiffened her spine, finally locking on his face.

ᏋᏋ

Theo allowed her the time to think things through. When she had turned back to him instead of riding off, hope burgeoned that she would be quick to forgive. She didn't immediately say anything, and every throb of his thumb and ache of his broken finger ticked off the seconds of her silence.

When at last she met his gaze, he dared to speak. "I'll get a list together."

Tension seemed to ebb from her shoulders at his simple answer. He chided himself for being so careless with her but acknowledged his own hurt feelings. "Last night. . ." He wondered if she really wanted to hear his explanation but forged ahead. "You were so quiet. Then when you told me I should leave in a couple of. . ."

She bit her lip and stared down at her feet. "I brought more poultice for your finger."

Hadn't she heard a word he'd said? "You really want me to leave, Ellie?"

Her eyes slid shut, and she dug a hand into the pocket at her waist and pulled out a small package. "Why don't you sit down on that rock and let me look at your finger."

Without pushing the issue further, he retreated to the rock and sat. She blinked in the sunlight, seemingly shocked that he had obeyed her request. With growing impatience, he lifted his hand and began work on the bandage, but his injured thumb was too swollen and clumsy. He groaned at the stabbing pain and she was there, by his side.

"What did you do now?"

He grinned up at her, drinking in her concern, the soft curls that framed her face.

As she captured his hand in hers, she sat beside him and began inspecting the swollen, darkening thumb. "How. . . ?"

"Hit it knocking in a board."

"I would think you would learn to be more careful."

"I was being careful, but I got distracted."

She pulled his hand closer, clearly exasperated. "What on earth is there out here to distract you?"

She unwrapped the bandage and laid it aside, her fingers stroking along the edges of his thumb. The sensation of warmth and the tickle of her touch filled his senses. "Nothing."

She leveled a glare on him, eyebrows raised. "Then what?"

"I was thinking about you."

He saw panic rise in the depths of her blue eyes, and she turned her face away. "I'm a married woman, Theo."

"You're a widow," he whispered.

She gave a nervous laugh. "Rose said the same thing."

He lifted his free hand to her chin and brought her face back so he could see into her eyes. Confusion settled in her gaze, and something else. . .fear. He wanted to erase both of those emotions. He would test the waters first. "I can leave in two weeks if you'd like."

A flash of emotion sparked in her eyes, and he wanted to believe it was because her feelings were matching his. She opened her mouth, but no sound came out.

He leaned in, forcing her to pull away or surrender.

"It's too soon, Theo."

"Too soon for what?"

She swallowed hard, her lips trembling. "For this."

"For a conversation?" he teased.

She shook her head, the warm smoothness of her cheek rubbing against his palm.

"For what, then?" He could see evidence of the war within her, the longing to love again and the chains that bound her to the memory of Martin.

"A gentleman would understand and—"

He brushed his thumb over her lips to stop the flow of words. He could feel the pulse in her neck that matched his own racing heart. He lowered his head and smiled into her eyes, whispering the words. "I'm a Rebel, remember?"

Her soft exhale blew warm against his face, and he closed the distance between them. Her lips, so soft. Her hair silky beneath his hand. And when he pulled away and she opened her eyes, he saw the beginning of something new shining there.

Chapter 24

So many emotions crashed around in Ellie's mind. Anger at herself. Fear of letting Martin go. Terror at the desire that propelled her to want Theo to kiss her. But his lips smoothed all the knots of her distress. The feel of his fingertips along her jaw and the innate gentleness of his lips, only when he pulled back did she breathe and float back to reality. His eyes held mischief, and his lips pursed in a knowing little grin that brought a rush of heat to her cheeks. She would have turned away, but his hand still cupped her face.

"I didn't come here to fall in love, Ellie." His gaze, steady now, all humor gone, sucked her in.

She closed her eyes and bit her lower lip. "What about Martin?"

Theo's deep chuckle surprised her. When she opened her eyes, his were luminous. "You love the memories you made together, the love you shared, and you make sure there's room in your heart for me." He leaned away from her and winced.

She remembered his broken finger, the poultice, and Martha. "Here." She reclaimed his hand with the swollen thumb in her own, trying to absorb all that had happened in the last few minutes and figure a way to shift the conversation to the runaways.

"Yes, boss," he ribbed.

They shared a laugh.

"Ellie?"

"Hmm?" She rubbed the poultice over his thumb.

"When did you find out about Martin?"

"About a month before the Confederates arrived here."

"So you were still helping the runaways despite your own hurt."

"Yes. I wanted to help them. After I found out about Martin. . ." The pang his name invoked was dull. Guilt stabbed momentarily at the kiss she'd just shared with a man other than her husband.

Rose's admonition tugged at her. *But you forgot a very important detail—till death do us part. He's gone. . . .*

"Ellie?"

She focused on him. This man. Her lips still warm from his kiss. She realized for the first time in a long time that maybe God hadn't abandoned her. Her own stubbornness and, yes, bitterness, had robbed her of hope. Her gaze went to the sky. He was there. Waiting.

I am so sorry.

Theo's hand moved in hers, and she felt the touch of his fingers along her cheek. "I didn't mean to make you cry."

She shook her head. "No, no. It's just. . . I realized something important."

His eyes searched hers, a question there, but he didn't ask.

She looked away.

"You were saying about your work with the blacks."

He was giving her some space, and she was grateful. "Martha talked to me about it. She and I grew up together, and I couldn't imagine a world in which black people were treated as, well, as property. She told me stories of her kin in the South. Then one night she needed help and asked me if she could use my cellar. I've helped ever since." She shifted away from him and scooped some of the poultice from the wrapping. She felt the hard calluses of his hands and tried to remember what Martin's hands had felt like. She couldn't. "I read Martin's letters."

"It must have been hard to see his writing after so long."

She gave him a quick smile and concentrated on wrapping his finger. "Yes. Very hard, but it was. . .I don't know. . .healing somehow. But that's not what I wanted to tell you." She raised her gaze to his. "Martin mentions Uncle Ross several times. I get the impression that he was careful how he said things, probably because he knew Ross was my uncle, but his last letter indicated that Uncle Ross was acting strangely."

Theo inclined his head. "Go on."

"There wasn't much else. He went on to express his disgust with the war and how much he just wanted to come home." The telling and Theo's closeness made her waver from her earlier conviction that Uncle Ross might be the victim. Or was the kiss distracting her from seeing the truth? How was it Uncle Ross could be innocent? How could she doubt Theo? He'd risked so much to get to her.

"Most of the men just want to go home, Ellie."

ꟽ

"You did?" Her gaze held no guile, but the question begged more than a pat answer. It wasn't hard for him to find the words.

"You feel trapped. You're expected to kill on a daily basis at the whim of a man you only hear about." He firmed his jaw, the old anger coming back. "You march for miles with little food then sleep in a tent if you're lucky enough to have one."

He watched her tie a small knot in the fresh bandage. She waggled her fingers, indicating he should let her look at his other hand. She unwrapped and examined the broken finger and began to rub fresh poultice over it. He wanted to tell her it didn't hurt as much but figured there was no reason to, being that he enjoyed her closeness. Her touch.

"Then there are actual battles, where men you've become friends with die right beside you, blown to bits or shot up so bad. . ." His mouth went dry, and he felt the now-familiar chill of nerves. "You can't imagine what it's like."

"I think I can." Then softer, "Why did you leave?"

Hadn't his explanation made it obvious?

"I mean, why did you risk everything to come here to tell me about Martin when you could have gone west and written it out in a letter?"

Theo stared down as she finished wrapping his finger. "It was the only place I could think to go, and I knew if the roles were reversed, if Martin had lived and I had died, I would have wanted him to be there for my wife."

She lifted his hand and twined her fingers in his, an unexpected gesture that should have sent a warning signal that the next question might rattle his world. "What if you're caught?"

He tilted his face toward the sun, stretching the muscles in his neck and squeezing her hand, knowing the answer to the question and suspecting she did as well. "I'll be shot."

They sat side by side for a long time before she released his hand and began wrapping up the rest of the poultice. "Uncle Ross came to me this morning."

"About this place?"

She stared at the fields stretched out to their right. He followed her gaze where, in the distance, a lone man and a small boy walked, probably looking for relics. It was the same man he'd seen before, probably explaining to his grandson the reason why his father wasn't coming home.

"He confused me."

Theo waited. There was more, he was sure.

"It made me doubt your intentions and wonder if Uncle Ross might be innocent." She patted the pocket wherein lay the package of poultice. "I got so mixed up."

"What changed that?"

"I don't know."

But he suspected her reaction to *him*, their kiss, had confused matters in her mind.

"Before he arrived, Martha was with me. There's a group of runaways. Some of them were caught and the others escaped. They're scared, and Martha needs a place large enough for them all. I offered the farm."

It flitted through his mind that the kiss was just her way of getting him to help her, but he rejected the suspicious idea before it had a chance to take root.

"Martha began to act strangely, and we discovered that the door hadn't been closed all the way. When I went to open it—"

"Your uncle was on the other side."

Her eyes went huge. "How did you know?"

"Guessed. Where is he now?"

She stood, and he slipped off the rock as well and followed. She moved her eyes along the fence he had repaired, running her hand against the now-straight line of boards. "I told him I would have a decision for him, and he's coming back tomorrow evening."

"When do we need to transfer the runaways?"

"Tomorrow evening. Late. Martha will give me the signal if all is well, and I'm supposed to let her know tonight whether we're clear to use the farm."

"You mean whether or not I agreed to help."

She sent him a brief, sheepish smile. "Well, yes."

He had to know. "Didn't you just say you were afraid to trust me?" He had thought he glimpsed emotion in her eyes after their kiss, but if she couldn't trust him now, with all he had risked for her, he wondered if she ever could. Or maybe he was being unfair to expect so much. Maybe the better question was did he want to risk his heart to a woman who might not return it to him whole?

Chapter 25

Ellie waited as Theo made a list of things he needed for the work on the buildings around the farm. She tried hard not to admire his profile or the way his hair curled on his neck or the remembered touch of his hand on her jaw or the look in his clear, gray eyes after he had kissed her. She hugged herself, more pleased than she could have imagined, refusing, for this moment, to let the doubts assail her.

Theo, leaning against the rock and using the surface to write on, caught her movement and sent her a wink that made her catch her breath. "Think we're almost done here."

She walked to Rose's dappled gray and stroked the horse's neck to take her mind off the man. She couldn't help but see the irony of her situation. To feel such things for another man so soon after Martin's death. . . Yet it had been seven months. A year total, she realized, since his furlough late in 1862. The last time she had held him. Was it right to feel so strongly about someone else so soon, or was she fickle? She tried to imagine Rose's response and knew her friend would tell her to embrace the moment. She would point out the fact that Mrs. Emma Bradley and Mrs. Louise Shevring had both remarried since the death of their husbands at Gettysburg. True, Mrs. Bradley had remarried a man much older than herself, but Mrs. Shevring, now Mrs. Nelson, had married a Union soldier who had hidden in her home at one point in the Gettysburg battle. Did every widow feel such a sense of guilt about moving on?

"Ellie?"

She started, Theo's hand on her arm steadying her.

"I didn't mean to scare you." His eyes crinkled at the corners, and his smile was lazy.

"I didn't expect you to be done so soon."

"It was harder to write, but I managed." He held out the paper.

She accepted the sheet with trembling fingers and turned to collect the reins of the gray. Without her mounting block she would need to find a surface high enough from which to mount. She clicked for the gray to follow her and led him toward the rock she'd used previously.

"Need a hand?" Theo appeared beside her. "You need only ask, my lady."

Ellie glanced between the rock and Theo and wondered if she could stand being so close to him again. Would he press her for another kiss or could she escape. Did she want to?

Without waiting for an answer, Theo took the reins from her hand and brought the horse in closer to the rock. He grasped her waist and swung her up to the rock and climbed up beside her.

She arched a brow. "You could have just given me a leg up."

"Naw, this is much more fun."

Heart pounding, she made sure the horse was in position. He waited for her to arrange her skirts then pulled her closer where they stood inches apart. Before she had a chance to draw another breath, his hands went to her waist and he picked her up.

She gasped. "Theo!"

He set her down on the sidesaddle. "There now, you're ready to ride. Except one thing."

Head swirling, she shot him a look and shifted to settle herself, looping her leg around the pommel.

He leaned toward her, creating a shadow over her face, and planted a tender kiss on her forehead.

Words jammed into her throat, waiting to be spoken. She gulped air and groped for something else to say. "You'll go into town tonight to pick up the supplies?"

His grin was crooked. "Yes, boss."

ঙ

Theo watched her wheel the horse around. She glanced over her shoulder at him then tapped the horse's flank with the crop.

He'd been tempted to plant that last kiss on her lips but thought it might be pushing her too hard. If she'd known the intensity of his feelings, no doubt she would have run and hidden. Even he hadn't known how much she had gotten under his skin until he had seen the light in her eyes upon pulling away from their kiss.

Lord, keep me strong.

He picked up his hammer and returned to driving new nails into the board fence or pounding the loose ones in. It was boring work. Lonely. He'd welcomed the lonesomeness after leaving camp. Having been surrounded for so long by shouting men, the sounds of cannon and gunfire, or the bugle corps, solitude appealed to him. But now, with the taste of Ellie's kiss still on his lips, he became aware of a need for something more.

As she had suggested, he could take the oath of the U.S. Government and settle down to farming. If not in Gettysburg, maybe Ellie would go west with him.

He worked out his plans as he hammered then added to them as he went into town to fetch the supplies. The south road into town seemed busier than usual. He felt the stares of the older men at the store and knew they wondered who he was and where he'd come from. Keeping his mouth shut as much as possible, he made sure to limp as he loaded the wagon. At last, he turned the wagon and headed north, back to the farm, his heart lighter than he could remember it being for a long time.

Chapter 26

Ellie glanced up at the back of Dr. Selingrove's office in the distance, to the second floor, barely visible, where Martha had a little room. She unlatched the iron gate and swung it wide, latching it so it could not be easily shut, then crossed her backyard to knock on Rose's door. From the security of her second-floor room, Martha would see the signal that all was going as planned.

The kitchen area was empty, though a plate gave evidence that Rose hadn't been down since breakfast. She hurried upstairs, afraid to find Rose in the midst of a raging fever because she'd done too much too soon. The stillness of the little house seemed heavy, eerie. She gave a light knock on Rose's door before peering through the crack and nudging it open.

The bed was empty, but the rocking chair was not and her friend sat, baby Colin close, as she nursed her son, her arm perched on a collection of pillows to support his position.

Rose put a finger to her lips, but her expression held no joy. "We've had. . .a trying afternoon."

In the dim light allowed by the setting sun, Ellie sensed a darkness within her friend, and the only possible reason for it came to her. She hurried across the room and knelt at her friend's feet. "You heard from Robert."

Rose reached over Colin's body and squeezed Ellie's hand. "No. Not from him. From—"

Ellie went up on her knees and hugged her friend as best she could. Rose's shoulders heaved once, twice, before the tears dripped down her cheeks, wetting Ellie's face as well. Baby Colin's snuffles punctuated the moment, the irony of his life in the face of Robert's death not lost on her. She would do all she could to be there for her friend, just as Rose had been there for her all these months.

When her tortured knees could not stand being pressed into the hardwood another minute, she leaned back to give Rose some room to tend Colin. "Tell me about it."

Rose's lips trembled, and she stroked the back of her hand against Colin's cheek. "They think he went out onto the field to a fallen soldier and got caught in cross fire. They said he was still alive when they got to him but died later of infection."

How she hated the war. All it had taken from her. And now Rose, too, would suffer the pain and grief of loss. She stood and lifted baby Colin close to her as Rose went to the basin and splashed water into it. "Why don't you lay down and rest. I can take care of Colin."

Rose wrung out a cloth and pressed it to her face. "I don't think I could sleep, but I would like some time to myself." Her eyes softened when she stared down into her son's face. "He'll be hungry again in an hour or two."

"We'll manage, Rose. I'll take good care of him, and I'll be here tonight for you."

Rose gave Ellie a smile full of shadow and grief and sat down again in the rocking chair. "Thank you, my friend." From the table beside her, she pulled a black book onto her lap, and Ellie retreated with her small bundle, hoping Rose could find the comfort she sought in her Bible.

ଓ

Another crash of cannon. Another scream. A man raced toward Theo, and his gun belched a cloud of dark gray smoke. He watched as the brown-clothed man twisted, face contorted, hand to his gut where oily red liquid already pumped through his fingers. His plunge to the earth was a slow buckling of knees and twisting of the upper body, and Theo watched in morbid fascination.

"Get up! Get up!" his fellow soldier yelled in his ear. "Go! Go!"

He stood, tripped, and went down on one knee. His hand reached out for balance and touched the body of the enemy he'd just shot. The dark eyes stared at him, his lips moved, but Theo could understand nothing. Do nothing. He was the enemy and had to be conquered. The boy's lips continued to move, and his tongue darted out to lick his lips.

"Get up!" He heard the command, yet he was rooted to the spot, to the face of the first soldier he had shot. And as the seconds ticked, he watched the lips still and the man's gaze grow unfocused.

Theo opened his eyes to the stillness of the barn. He shoved himself upright, bent a knee, and rested his forearm across it, massaging his head, touching the sheen of sweat there. The same dream. He would never forget that face. Those staring eyes. The guilt that weighted him. Images of a mother waiting for her son flipped back to that pair of staring eyes. The images collided and repeated, tormenting him.

A waking torrent of war-torn memories. His friends. The smell of fear. Dismembered corpses. Bodies flying into the air upon impact and landing like the lost rag dolls of an errant child. And Bud. Always Bud. His charge forward that day in battle, a shot, then the fading warmth of Bud's hand in his as life seeped from his body. Another casualty. Another friend dead.

Sweat beaded on Theo's forehead, and he leaned forward and cradled his head in his hands. His breathing went rapid. He tugged at his hair, the pain grounding him, pulling him back to reality, even as he felt entrenched in another world where darkness ruled. The images tore at him. Accusing. Building desperation.

He hummed a hymn, but the thoughts battered him. He sang louder, thinking each word before he sang it. After one verse and chorus, the song left him, and he leaned his head back and tried to suck air into his lungs in measured breaths. To blank his mind. *Lord. Lord, help me!*

He forced himself to focus on the bits of scripture he'd heard throughout his life. "'Think on these things.'" What were those things? Peace? Peace, yes. Joy. Love. A sound mind.

God, help me.

"Casting down imaginations, and every high thing that exalteth itself against the knowledge of God." He couldn't remember it all, but the words etched a deep path in his tortured mind. Those things that exalt against God.

God was all powerful. Even in the mind. But peace came only from a clear conscience. Why hadn't he thought to ask forgiveness for his sins? To set them at the Lord's nail-scarred feet.

His chest heaved and his mind groped for the words, but he could not utter them. They twisted and lodged in his throat. Theo doubled over in a ball.

I didn't want to do it, God. I killed him. Oh, God. Oh, God, forgive me. He pressed his hand to his mouth, his mind frenzied now to be free of the burden. His prayer eased him with each syllable, and when he cleared his mind of all the words, his declaration of freedom, the peace did come. Sweet. And pure. And joyous.

Chapter 27

The following day, Ellie finally felt comfortable leaving her grieving friend. Rose had not cried again, and she'd gone about taking care of little Colin and busying herself with laundry. They talked of Robert's clothing, and Ellie urged her not to make too hasty a decision.

"Nonsense, Theo can use the clothes. Robert won't be back anyway."

So she took the clothes, noting that Rose held back a couple of shirts and the tears that flooded her friend's eyes despite her matter-of-fact words.

Rose swiped a hand down her left cheek then turned to face her. "Are you going out there today?" Rose asked later. "You should, you know. He'll miss you."

Ellie bristled. "I don't think so."

"Has he kissed you yet?"

She gasped at her friend's straightforward question. "Why—" The protest was on her tongue before she remembered the look in Theo's eyes and the warmth of his lips.

"Ah. . ." Rose breathed. "Well, good!" Her friend sent her a huge smile and headed out into the second-story hallway. "I thought it might happen soon."

Chagrined at Rose's ability to read her so well, Ellie frowned and followed her down the steps. "Honestly, Rose."

"It's putting the pink into your cheeks and the shine back into your eyes. Why fight what you're feeling?"

Rose moved into the kitchen where a small pile of linens lay on the table. Ellie plucked one up and smoothed the fabric, considering her response. "It makes me feel unfaithful."

"To what? A vow that shattered as soon as Martin drew his last breath?"

Rose's words seemed so harsh. Yet Ellie could no longer deny the truth of them. Martin was not coming back to her. Holding on to his memory was like trying to hold a rainbow in the palm of her hand. Impossible.

"Do you feel that way?" she dared to ask. Boldly assured that Rose wouldn't be able to agree with her own words once they were turned back on her.

A shadow passed over Rose's expression, and she closed her eyes. Ellie didn't know if her friend prayed in that moment or simply made up her mind, but a smile quirked along her lips, and when she opened her eyes, relief shone in her eyes. "Yes," she breathed. "Yes, Ellie, I do."

Ellie flinched.

"You're surprised." Rose lifted a stack of dried linens into her arms, and Ellie did the same with the other stack, following her friend upstairs. "Did you think what I said was somehow easier for you than for myself? I've had these months to consider that Robert might not return, and though I'll miss him and grieve for him, he would want Colin to know a father and for me to love again. I'm not ready for that now, but neither do I believe that God wants us to bog down in our grief. To love and be loved by another is His gift to us."

As Ellie left Rose to rest, she crossed to the stable, considering her friend's words. She stopped at the iron gate and removed the latch that had held it open. Open gate meant all was a go, and Martha would have seen and interpreted the silent message long before now. She would let Theo know it was safe for him to come into town later that night. He would go to Martha's, and should anyone ask, his fingers would be a good excuse. Martha would probably change his bandage just to lend credence to the excuse.

Ellie saddled the dappled gray and mounted, picking up the reins and heading out to the farm to deliver the message and check on Theo's progress. She couldn't stay long, though, for she knew Uncle Ross would be back at some point in the evening, and she didn't want to miss the opportunity to let him know her decision. Between Martin's letters, her uncle's odd behavior, and the risk Theo endured getting to her—not to mention his friendship with Martin—she had chosen to believe his version of the story. Though she still struggled to reconcile the uncle she had known as a youth with that of a man capable of murdering her husband.

Her mind tripped over that part of the revelation. Why would he kill Martin? What did it matter whether Martin lived or died? Was there a private problem between them that Martin couldn't, or wouldn't talk about? And was it wise to confront her uncle with the truth?

Ellie sighed. It seemed a foolish thing to tell her uncle about Theo seeing him kill without some form of protection. Maybe it was best not to mention it at all, but to tell her uncle firmly and with resolve that she was not selling the farm to him and that she did not need him to help her with managing the property, or anything else for that matter. Her mother had not trained her to be coddled and dependent on a man anyway, and she didn't plan on beginning now.

Then there were Rose's words to consider. The deeper truth of what her friend was encouraging her to do. That she needed to move on from her grief for her own well-being.

Even now, she felt that swell of love for Martin, but its edges were blurred by time, like an old friend she hadn't seen for a long time whose face took a few minutes to process before recognition. In her heart, she realized she was letting go. It was the promise that time would heal grief, blur the line, and dull the edge of the pain.

She felt lighter. Free. She smiled at the image of Theo before he had kissed her. Why had she been reluctant? Hadn't she felt a pull toward him since finding him in the cellar? An attraction she tried to outrun at every turn but couldn't.

His desertion troubled her, though. Martin's talk of such things, coupled with Theo's stories, had swelled a sympathetic understanding within her, yet other men endured and even returned to their families honorably. Could she love a man who deserted the ideals he fought for, or had they never really been his in the first place? Did he, like so many, fight because of the conscription or because, like many others, he felt a need to defend his home and family from an idea contrary to his own?

Martin believed that the South should have stayed with the North and not seceded. He believed in the right of a state to govern itself but within the guidelines offered by a government unifying those ideas. Yet he, too, had struggled with the war, the death and fighting. Could she, then, fault Theo? Did his desertion make him a coward?

As she guided the horse onto the road leading to the barn, she struggled with that question the most.

☙

The springhouse squatted at the edge of the woods, a small pool of cool water surrounding it. Inside, Theo found nothing to trace the presence of the runaway couple. He used the chill water to bathe then dressed again, soaking in the peacefulness of the spot and the seclusion the small house offered from the main house and barn, though he could catch the back of that structure through a row of evergreens. The small house was the perfect place for the runaways to hide. It chilled him to think the people moved so quietly as to be untraceable. Like ghosts. He only hoped the woman had borne the move well.

He had decided to stay in the barn, what with another group needing the springhouse that night. But the roof needed a patch, and he intended on working on that and rehanging the door to make it square. He needed the work to keep him busy and his mind occupied and away from the tormenting dreams of the previous night.

Making a mental note of the supplies he would need for the repairs, he returned to the barn to gather everything, feeling refreshed in body. He would have to purchase a washbasin and stand soon. Not that he'd be here that long. . .or would he?

One day at a time.

He worked on the springhouse until he deemed himself far enough along in the repairs that he deserved a break. The air had picked up a deep chill, and Theo wished for a coat of some sort. He ran his fingers through his hair and took one more look around the springhouse, satisfied at what he had accomplished.

He swung the springhouse door shut behind him and it groaned a protest. The latch didn't set right. Theo gave the door a good wiggle to set the latch in place then froze. He thought he'd heard a branch snap and turned to stare behind him. Nothing moved. Probably a deer or some other animal wandering the woods.

Another snapping sound and he jerked his head to follow the direction from which it came. He could see nothing, but waited, still, his heartbeat racing. When his stomach clenched in panic and his mind flashed a panicked message to run, Theo steeled himself to calm. He clenched his jaw hard. When the silence stretched long, he relaxed his muscles and breathed deeply, praying for strength and peace. He had no need to be so tense over an animal.

As he started out on the path that led back to the barn, he paused when he thought he heard a horse blow air through its lips, but the sound didn't come again.

Dismissing what he heard as the wind in the trees, he set out down the path again.

Chapter 28

When Theo broke into the clearing before reaching the barn, he spotted the dappled gray nose-to-nose with Libby, the paddock fence separating them. He couldn't help but grin, and when he ducked into the barn and saw Ellie sitting on a hay bale, the sight of her stumbled the beat of his heart. "You missed me." He went to where she sat and drew her to her feet, gratified to see the sparkle of humor in her gaze.

"I came to check on my handyman and make sure he was earning his keep."

He cupped her elbows with his hands. "Sure am, boss." He wanted so much to draw her close but knew he needed to bide his time and give her a chance to let go of Martin in order to embrace whatever might develop between them. "I worked on patching that roof on the springhouse. Just need to square the door." He took a deliberate step back.

Was that disappointment in her expression? "Oh."

"Should have it done by tonight."

"Oh." She bent to pluck out a strand of hay and began to weave it through her fingers.

"Is everything a go for tonight?"

Her eyes flicked to his. "Yes. Yes, it is. I'd forgotten about that."

He motioned for her to follow him outside. "You look like you have other things on your mind." There. He'd opened the door for her to share what she was thinking. He congratulated himself for his genius.

"Rose got notice that her husband is dead."

His mind rebelled at the news. "He was a doctor."

"Yes."

He laid hold on a bag of sand and shouldered it, feeling sorrow for yet another war widow. "I'm sorry for her and for her son." His eyes traveled over her face. "And you. It must bring it all back."

She lowered her hands, eyes wide. "That's the amazing part. Rose is doing so much better than I did."

He lowered the sand to the ground and went back for another, brushing his hands together. "Everyone handles things differently."

She began weaving the straw again. "But I. . .Rose is at peace with Robert's death."

"I'm sure she will still have her moments."

"She said she's had all this time to deal with it."

"You seem to be doing fine."

☙

Ellie pursed her lips, frustrated at her inability to express herself. "I thought I was until—" She shot a glance at him, biting down on the rest of her sentence.

He lifted another bag of sand, and she admired the stretch of Martin's shirt across his back.

A blush heated her cheeks, and she looked toward the road, the fields, anywhere but at him.

She heard his grunt as he lowered the bag. "You were saying?"

There was no reason not to let him know. Not if she hoped to move on. She raised her chin and looked him straight in the face where he leaned against the back of the wagon, poised to lift another bag. "Until you came along."

"Oh?" His eyebrows lifted, and his smile showed exactly how pleased he was at her words.

"No need to be so cocky about it."

His laugh flowed as rich and deep as garden soil.

She crossed her arms and frowned.

He laughed harder.

"Honestly, Theo. It's not like I've asked you to court me." She felt the heat of her blush. Why did she have to say it like *that*? And why was he still laughing? She glared.

He caught her expression and cleared his throat. "No, ma'am, you didn't." He allowed his Southern drawl to draw out the words, and the warmth in the accent brought about a shiver of delight. "I would never expect a lady to do a man's job."

He advanced a step, his gaze locking on her, suddenly intense. When he came to stand in front of her, he blocked the low-slung sun.

She shivered again.

"Are you cold?"

She wanted to look away but couldn't. She opened her mouth to say no, but nothing came out. Those gray eyes held her captive. He touched her elbows, with a touch as gentle as butterfly wings. "Would you consider courting, Ellie?"

She was on the precipice. A tug for the old life made her afraid. Yet wasn't it that very fear that kept dragging her away from the promise of a new life? With Theo? She knew that being physically drawn to him wasn't enough, and the old question of his desertion nagged at her. But weighed against what she'd seen of him, his desertion seemed warranted.

Even while dealing with the sick soldiers, she'd come across those who wanted a reason to go home, going so far as to beg the doctor not to send them back. Could she fault Theo for deserting a cause he didn't believe in? After all he had suffered? The mental stress of watching those around him die. She bit her lip. "I need some time."

His gaze didn't waver, though his hands slid to her upper arms then fell away. "Don't wait too long, Ellie. The boss only gave me two weeks."

She thought he might laugh, but his eyes remained sober, and when he turned away, she could only watch as he shouldered the last bag of sand from the wagon. Regret washed over her.

Chapter 29

As he piled the last bag of sand upon the others, he realized Ellie had moved toward the paddock where the dappled gray stood, still saddled.

He bit down on his disappointment and frustration and went to her. As she turned the gray, she gasped when she almost plowed into his chest. Her eyes told the tale of unshed tears, and he felt a fist squeeze in his chest. As hard as her answer was for him to hear, he had to remember this was even harder for her. Her grief a territory she had never navigated before, and he could not push her. He touched her cheek. "Don't cry, Ellie."

"It's just—"

"It's all right."

She leaned her forehead against his chest.

He reached down the length of her arm to where the gray's reins were fisted in her hand. She surrendered them to his grasp.

"Why don't we talk about it later."

"But I want this. I want to—to. . ."

He pulled back slightly and dipped his head to catch her gaze. "Listen to me. You've been through a lot. I shouldn't have pushed so hard." But the words that came from his mouth weren't the ones that burned in his head.

"I didn't mean it about those two weeks, Theo." She tilted her head back. "I didn't. If you'll take your vow here, everything will work out. People would understand better why you. . .left."

Theo closed his eyes, fully understanding her hesitation now. It made sense. He was a deserter. Martin was killed in the line of duty. Or so she had thought. Even though Martin's letters had hinted at his desire to leave his regiment, he hadn't. All that mattered to her was that he look respectable to those not fighting and wondering why he had abandoned that for which he fought. And if he took his vow for the North, honor would force him to return to fight for his new allegiance.

Slow dread ate at his insides. *Lord, I thought I had settled this.*

The horrors of war. Bud. Images spiraled against his senses and flashed through his mind. They tumbled one after another. The man he had shot. Staring. The flash of gunfire. Smoke. So much smoke. It filled his lungs. . . .

Theo released his hold on Ellie and lowered his head, taking deep gulps of air, yet feeling as if all the air was being squeezed from him.

☙

Ellie saw his reaction unfold in front of her. He went pale and squeezed his eyes shut, and she feared he might fall. She pulled the reins from his hand and loosely turned the horse and tied him. When she returned to Theo, his lips moved. "Theo?"

He opened his eyes. His gray eyes were dull, filled with shadows she did not understand. "Why don't you sit down?"

He shook his head.

Ellie pressed her hand against his chest and tried to back him up. "On the wagon."

He pressed his hand over hers. "Give me a minute."

She licked her lips, afraid of what she was seeing and realizing now that she had seen him like this before. "I should get Martha to look at you."

"No." The syllable was emphatic. He squeezed her hand and closed his eyes again. His chest heaved as he took deep breaths.

She waited, helpless, for him to release her or for him to explain. He swayed, and she caught his arm with her other hand to steady him. "Theo, please!" She began pressing at him frantically. "Please sit down."

As if pulled from a daze, he finally turned.

She followed close on his heels to make certain he reached the wagon without falling.

He patted the place next to him, not looking at her, seemingly caught on a plane of thought she couldn't comprehend.

She waited in silence, feeling every breath he took and watching as he wiped the sweat from his brow. It was like he was caught in a nightmare even though he was awake and able to walk. She recalled something else, too: the soldiers in the hospitals.

She'd been assigned to twelve soldiers inside a room at the Foster home, which had been turned into a hospital. Between the festering wounds and the groans of the three men who were closer to death than the others, she had witnessed a young soldier crying, lost in a world of horrors that caused him to break out in a sweat. The doctor called it nervousness. Effects of the war on those with no constitution. Ellie hadn't thought much of it at the time, though she remembered feeling empathy for the young man.

But now, seeing Theo, she knew he suffered, too. She put her hand over his and watched his profile for signs of the distress.

"I thought I was better after last night."

"Last night?" She traced his long fingers with her own.

"I dreamed," he said simply.

"Of what?"

He sucked air into his lungs, chest heaving with the effort. "Memories."

She waited. If he wanted to share, she would listen. If not, she would be patient.

"I killed someone."

The irony of his statement puzzled her. He'd been a soldier. Of course he had killed.

He glanced at her, studying her face, then looked away. "It was my first time. He was young. Like me." He breathed a shuddering breath that showed his struggle for composure.

She picked his hand up and nested it between both of hers. His fingers were chilled to match the cold air, but she had a feeling this coldness emanated from deep within his soul.

"I watched him. . .die."

It came to her lips to tell him she had watched wounded soldiers die and could understand, but she hadn't been the one to shoot any of them. That would be the difference.

His head dipped, and he tugged his hand from hers and put both to his face. "I asked God to forgive me."

If his reaction to shooting one man was so severe, knowing he killed so many must eat at him like a canker. "God is good and forgiving, Theo. It's yourself you need to forgive."

His hunched shoulders curled more. "If I take a vow, they'll want me to go back." She placed her hand along his back, feeling the vibration of his emotion, and the weight of what she had suggested as a solution crashed on her like the trunk of a felled tree. Taking his vow for the North and going back into the war might not kill him physically but it would mentally. Her heart broke for him, for his struggle to do what was expected of him beyond the limits of his endurance.

As his shoulders continued to shudder, she bowed her head and breathed a prayer for a healing that had nothing to do with the body or soul.

Chapter 30

Ellie stayed with him, talking quietly, until the haunting images blurred. On occasion she swiped the hair back from his brow or her expression showed empathy as he talked. She talked, too, about a man she had seen while tending the wounded. And how that man's struggles seemed to fall along the same lines as Theo's.

He didn't feel as alone as before.

He gathered the nails, and she walked with him to the springhouse. She seemed pleased with what he had done and listened as he pointed out how he would square the door.

It was on the walk back that he realized he felt much more settled. He lost himself for a moment in the breath of chill air on his face and the new strength he felt. He raised his hands and stretched the fingers then clenched them. They were steady.

At the paddock, he cupped his hands to receive her foot as she mounted the gray. He felt her gaze heavy on him and assured her he was better. And when she turned the horse, she raised her hand in a simple gesture of good-bye.

The work on the springhouse soothed him, yet the panic that had gripped him in Ellie's presence lessened the peace he had wrapped himself in the night before. Maybe Ellie was right. Maybe God was using her to show him his need to forgive himself. He had done what was expected of him. He'd hated it, but the deed was done.

He finished squaring the door in fifteen minutes then he hitched the horse to the wagon and replaced the false bottom, piling the lumber on top. He would unload some of the wood into Ellie's barn since the porch needed repairs. The rest would do its job concealing its secret.

Theo inhaled the bracing cold air, snuggling deeper into the heavy flannel shirt Ellie had given him. The fields on either side remained stark and brown, a tribute to those who had died. A good place for horses. He could train horses again. Find a place like this and settle down to work with the majestic animals as he had in the South, before the war.

Snow would soon cover the scars of these war-torn fields. One house to his left and in the distance had been burned nearly to the ground. Another farmhouse showed severe damage to the roof. With the reminder of war came the images, but this time he forced himself to pray, and his thoughts turned to Ellie and the danger that lay ahead in transferring the eight runaways out to the farm. Maybe helping to save their lives and get them to freedom would heal him.

☙

As Ellie came from the barn, Uncle Ross was guiding his horse down the road toward her house. Her heart began to pound as she took in his dress uniform and austere demeanor. She wondered how her news would settle with him. Not well, that was sure, but then why did she care? If he had shot Martin, she certainly owed him nothing. He halted his horse and dismounted with regal grace.

Anger-pumped blood pounded into her ears. She forced herself to be calm as he approached, a wide smile curving his lips.

"My dear niece. Let's go inside before the chill turns into a biting cold." He raised his hands to his mouth and cradled one as he blew on a clenched fist, giving imagery to his words. Ellie didn't budge. "My answer is no, Uncle Ross."

His dark eyes snapped, and his lips withered to a cruel line. "That's not the kindhearted niece I recall."

She knew the folly of showing her hand, but the words were out before her mind could snap down on them. "You shot Martin."

Ross's expression revealed nothing. No surprise. No shock. Not even anger. Seconds passed before he raised his eyebrows. "That's quite an accusation, my dear. You know Martin died at the hands of the enemy." But his explanation was too calm.

"Why don't we go inside?" Before she could refuse, he grasped her upper arm and propelled her toward the house. "I'll go over everything I know about Martin's death, but I can't abide this cold another minute. It's the least you can do for your uncle."

She tried to pull out of his grasp, to lock her knees and free herself, but he was moving too fast and his greater weight left her no chance to assert herself. At the step leading to the back porch, she hooked her arm around a log supporting the overhang. Her arm ripped free of his grasp in a painful jarring that forced a groan from her lips. "Get off my property."

Uncle Ross faced her, his face a mask of granite coldness. "I think we should talk, Ellie, or I might just be tempted to let the authorities know about your harboring runaways."

She gasped, too late realizing that her reaction made denying his words futile.

But her uncle wasn't finished. A wan smile brushed his lips. "Perhaps you should ask your hired help about that night. I saw him with Martin."

Ellie processed the implication of what he was revealing.

"They talked for a long time and there was a lot of shouting going on. It was when Martin was leaving that your hired man shot him in the back. His own cousin."

Whatever air she had left in her lungs squeezed out and left her unable to draw another breath.

"I'm surprised you would believe a Rebel over your own flesh and blood. Your mother would be very disappointed in you."

Ellie fisted the material of her dress, glad for the support of the porch post and railing. She felt confused by the twist with which her uncle delivered the sequence of events. Theo pulled the trigger? Then it was all a lie. His journey here to tell her the truth wasn't because he felt such an obligation to her for Martin's sake.

"You should know better than to place your trust so blithely. Which is the very reason I have offered to take over your financial obligations. It is such a stress on a woman without a husband to guide her."

He kept talking. Every word beat at her mind until her thoughts became a jumble of his words mixed with memories. Theo's long journey. His sincerity. The plague that preyed upon his mind that she had suffered with him that afternoon. Their kiss. Martin's letters. His suspicions about Uncle Ross. . .

She weighed it all against what her uncle was posing as truth and realized she believed Theo and Martin more than she did Uncle Ross.

". . .it would be my honor, Ellie, to be near you."

Hadn't she seen the coldness in his eyes? Sensed that beneath the warm exterior he could put on and take off at will, there lurked a dark side? It had been what kept her from yielding to his desire to go inside and have the conversation. She feared him.

Shielding the runaways could get her into trouble, sure, but after tonight she would let Martha know of the danger and another route would be chosen for a period of time.

Her decision made, she stiffened her spine and raised her chin. "I don't need your help, Uncle Ross. My decision is final."

Chapter 31

Uncle Ross took a threatening step forward, and Ellie raised her hands against whatever ill he had in mind.

"You can't talk to me like that, you little tramp. How long has that Rebel trash been hounding you? Wooing you. Don't think I haven't noticed the way you look at him." He grabbed her upper arms in a vise grip.

She cried out and began thrashing to break his hold.

"Let her go, Ross."

His hands left her arms and he spun.

Rose stood there, the black eye of the shotgun an extension of her arm.

Ross snarled and leaped off the porch. In seconds he untied the horse and worked him into a gallop before leaping into the saddle.

Ellie's knees buckled and smacked the hard boards of the porch.

Rose knelt beside her, drawing her cold hands into her own. "Can you stand?"

At first Ellie didn't think she could—the enormity of what she'd just done, the decision she had made, and the heat of Ross's rage drained her of all strength.

"I heard everything, Ellie. I reasoned that he had been badgering you about this for a long time."

She gave a weak nod.

"Just watching his expressions gave me chills, and I knew if it came down to it, I would have to help."

Ellie sighed and reached for her friend. "Thank you, Rose. Now"—she forced a smile—"help me up."

Rose stared at a point beyond Ellie then down at her. "Stay right where you are. I think your hero has arrived. A little late, maybe, but. . ."

Ellie blinked, not understanding until she heard the creak and jangle of a wagon. Theo. "I am not going to let him see me—" She gripped the post to pull herself upward, chagrined at the weakness in her legs. Within seconds she heard footsteps echo on the porch then felt strong hands lifting her from behind.

She was turned in the circle of Theo's arms, and his hand rose to cup the back of her head. "Ellie?"

With a deep sigh, she leaned into him. Maybe Rose was right after all. She inhaled the scent of him, closed her eyes, and let his strength be hers.

ෂ

Theo had been terrified to see her on her knees, instinctively knowing this was not a casual position to share a chat with Rose. Not out in the cold air.

Over Ellie's head, he swept Rose's form to reassure himself she was unhurt, a jolt tripping his heart when he caught sight of the gun she held, partially covered by the gingham of her skirts.

Rose caught the direction of his gaze and lifted it with a little laugh. "Her uncle got demanding. He needed some encouragement when Ellie invited him to leave."

Theo couldn't help a grin. So much for his idea that Rose was a dainty little woman who wouldn't think of harming anyone. The delicate weight in his arms redirected his attention. He bent his head and whispered in Ellie's ear, "Let's get inside."

Rose led the way for them. She set the gun down and put a kettle on.

Ellie pulled from his embrace and took a seat at the small table with a deep sigh.

"I'm going to check on Colin," Rose said. "I'll be back."

Theo watched Rose leave, a gust of wind blowing in from the open doorway as she slipped outside. He slid down into the seat across from Ellie.

A bit of color had flushed back into her cheeks, and she smoothed a hand over her breezed-mussed hair.

"Feeling better?" He chafed at the simple question when all he really wanted to do was gather her close and bury his face in her blond curls.

"He got so angry, Theo. He tried to tell me you had shot Martin, that you were telling me the lies." She lowered her hands from her hair and ran a hand over the smooth surface of the table. "But I knew it couldn't be true. Martin wouldn't lie to me." She searched his face. "And I knew you wouldn't lie to me either."

He gave her a brief smile that did nothing to express the warmth that he felt in that moment. She trusted him. He would hold that trust close and cherish it always.

Silence grew between them.

He raised his arm and reached across the table. She met his hand and held it firmly in her own. "I thank you for your faith in me, ma'am."

"He knows about what I do."

Fear gripped Theo hard. "Can we change the plans?"

"It's too late now. But if he's watching me. . ." She pulled in a breath. "It might be best for you to go alone this time."

He nodded. "I'll do what I can to help."

She dropped her eyes, and when she lifted her face, tears glistened there. "Is now a good time to tell you I think I'm falling in love with you?"

Theo absorbed her words like dry ground soaked in rain, but he couldn't help but tease. "You think?"

She gave him a nervous little laugh. He wouldn't release his hold on her gaze and watched the effects of the moment trace a path of red hot heat up her neck and into her cheeks.

The kettle began to sputter, prelude to a full whistle, and neither of them moved to tend to it.

She brushed her thumb across the tender place on the back of his hand where the thumb and index finger met. The gentle gesture alone expressed more to him than her words.

A knock on the door sounded, and Rose let herself in with a rush of skirts and cold air. "It's really going to be cold tonight." She took off her outerwear and hung it by the door. The kettle gave vent to a full whistle.

Theo sent a wink at Ellie and pulled his hand away. "I think I'll go unload some of the wood into the barn. I could use some cold air."

Rose turned from the stove, kettle in hand, her gaze bouncing between the two of them, a knowing smile on her lips.

Chapter 32

Theo made the trip to Martha's alone. Martha greeted him with the same glint in her eyes that made him wary. "I'll not have you set foot in this house at this hour. If you want me to look at that finger, you hug into that shirt and wait. I doubt a big man like you will freeze to death."

Theo didn't have a chance to reply before she shut the door in his face. "Yes, ma'am," he mocked. "I'll surely do just that." He collapsed in the chair on the porch and wondered, again, at how eight runaways expected to fit into the tiny cavern under the false floor of the wagon.

Martha reappeared with a lantern, her features devoid of emotion. He held out his hand and she began. With two snips of the scissors, she cut away the bandage and examined the injury. "You've been working too much. The swelling will not go down if you continue to use the hand."

He wasn't sure if she expected an answer or not, so he chose to remain silent.

She went back inside, and he examined the broken joint, wondering how he could make repairs for Ellie and rest his hand. He heaved a breath and sat back in the chair, hunching his shoulders against the cold air. He would be a block of ice by the time he reached the farm.

Martha returned with a mortar and pestle, the familiar paste of a poultice within. She lifted her face to where the moon shone down on the town. "It is warmer tonight," she mumbled. He almost laughed out loud. "I was thinking how cold it was."

Martha settled herself into the chair opposite him and set the poultice on a low table that separated them. "It is cold because you are used to heat."

Her words jolted him. Yet when he caught her gaze, her expression revealed nothing. He wondered if Ellie had told Martha he was a Rebel deserter. Or maybe the woman knew by intuition; she seemed the type to be able to figure out such things.

When she finished wrapping his finger back up, she gave him a silent nod and picked up the lantern.

Knowing he was being dismissed, Theo returned to the wagon and pulled himself onto the seat. When Libby started out, he thought he could feel her straining more than normal against the harness, until momentum relieved her of some of the work.

It seemed to take forever to get down the street, turn, and reach the outskirts of town, where the fields and rolling hills dotted with trees rolled south toward Baltimore. He did his best to remain alert and the cold helped. He laughed now at Martha's easy comment, sure the woman didn't care one bit who he was, only that he had a heart to help.

As he pulled onto the lane leading to the barn, he realized that he couldn't remember any of the last twenty minutes of the journey. A strange feeling of lost time. Shaking himself, he set the brake and got down.

The silence of the night was broken by the whinny of a horse. He stared at Libby but knew it hadn't come from her. Alert now, Theo watched Libby. She turned her head, nostrils flared just as a lone rider cantered up the lane. Before Theo could move away from the wagon to put himself between the wagon and rider, he saw the flash of something in the rider's hand.

Everything seemed to happen in slow motion. A pulse of pain and a slow burn that increased in intensity made him cup his shoulder. His hand felt wetness. His mind worked to catch up as the rider flew to the ground.

The pain grew in intensity, and Theo never understood how he came to be on the ground, but he saw a face over him, backlit by moonlight, though the silver hair seemed familiar somehow.

ᢊ

Theo jerked awake, the face of Captain Ross Bradington flooding his mind and bringing everything into sharp focus. The sway of the wagon let him know they were going somewhere. He tried to sit up, but several pieces of wood pinned him down. Theo flexed against the logs and grunted at the pain that radiated along his chest, up his neck, and down his arm. He panted, trying to catch a breath that didn't add to the pain, but every inhalation became tortuous. His head throbbed and his stomach heaved. Darkness tinged the edges of his world, and he closed his eyes to rest.

In seconds, he was alert again. The runaways! Ross was driving the wagon full of runaways. He sucked in air as best he could and braced himself against a log. It fell away, but three others blocked his ability to move.

The jostling of the wagon made his movements awkward. When the next log rolled against the side of the wagon, he could move his arms and see the back of Ross's head, but his feet were stuck beneath another log. He sat up to free his feet of the log that lay diagonally from his left thigh to his right ankle, when the wagon jolted to a stop. Theo caught sight of Ross and the cold eye of the gun aimed at his chest.

"Don't move or I'll kill you. Might kill you anyhow with all the lies you've spread."

Beside Ross sat a black man, but before Theo could process the man's appearance, Ross spit another threat.

"I'm taking this property you're hauling back south." His grin went ugly.

"I imagine someone down there would give me a nice sum for your return as well. Then they can finish you off for me."

Theo's mind clutched for some way to divert Ross's attention. For one second, he gazed into the dark eyes of the black man beside Ross before that one turned away. With Ross's revelation of Theo's loyalty to the South, he knew the black man would be hesitant to help. He clenched his hands and realized the log that captured his feet could be used as a weapon. It wouldn't be easy to lift. Ross's gun could kill him faster than he could free the log.

Ross turned to the black man. "You get down there and pile those logs on him until he can't move an inch. When you're done, I'll check your work." His tone took on a snarl. "That way if you don't do a good job, you can stay up here in the North. Six feet under."

The black man climbed down from the wagon and circled to the back and out of Theo's line of vision. He felt the wagon lurch and knew the man had climbed up into the wagon bed. Theo watched as the black man crouched beside him, his face in profile to Ross. In that time, he pressed his hand against Theo's shoulder, though he never once glanced at him. Theo tried to interpret the man's gesture, cautious hope bringing a surge of strength. When the black man straightened, he hefted the log that had blocked Theo's legs and gouged a toe into Theo's side.

Theo saw the thrust of the big man's arms and heard Ross's cry of pain. Theo leaped to his feet and saw Ross holding his arm, his hand empty of the gun. Theo dove, the wagon seat catching him in his upper thighs, but his weight caught Ross off guard and sheer momentum threw them over the side and to the ground.

Theo's back hit first. He immediately pushed out as Ross's body came hurling toward him. A thrust with his hands and legs and Ross went sailing off to his right. Theo went to his side and kicked hard, landing a blow along Ross's thigh. The older man groaned and writhed.

Theo rolled to his feet and stood above the man. "Get up."

Ross glared up at him. His booted foot shot out to catch Theo behind the knees, but Theo expected such a tactic and flopped his full weight onto Ross's chest, knocking the wind from the man's lungs. Theo pulled back enough to land a blow on Ross's cheek, and the older man's gaze went unfocused. Theo put a hand to the ground, spent, sticky warmth pumping down his shoulder.

A rustle of movement beside him made him tense and turn. The black man stood there, holding the gun. He pointed the gun at Theo then at Ross. "Going north, mister. I ain't going back south again."

Theo raised his hands, grimacing at the pain the effort caused him. He gave a sharp exhale. "I'll take you there, but you're going to have to trust me. I'll need you to keep an eye on him."

The black man didn't answer but slowly, gradually, he pointed the gun away from Theo and straight down at Ross. "You bleedin' bad, mister."

"That's why I'll need your help."

"I'll keep the gun," the black man said.

Theo nodded, finding the man's reasoning agreeable. He knelt beside the still-dazed Ross and dragged him upward, holding his arms. His waning strength sent waves of nausea stirring in his gut. Theo stopped at the edge of the wagon bed. The black man had circled the wagon and moved in on the other side, blocking any attempt Ross might have at escape. Grateful for the support, Theo nudged Ross forward and waited to make sure he was going to listen before he retreated a few steps.

A roar sounded in his ears, and his hand went to his shoulder. He blinked to clear his vision and focused on the wagon seat. With great effort, he placed one foot in front of the other, knowing his strength was seeping away with every beat of his heart. He saw the wagon move but saw no one in the wagon seat. His gaze shifted to the black man, sitting in the bed of the wagon, the gun still trained on Ross.

"You drive." The black man's words penetrated the haze growing in Theo's head.

He grasped the side of the seat and placed his foot on the step. He flexed to pull himself into the wagon and gasped at the waves of pain as he sat. With slow movements, he lifted the reins, grateful now for the cool air. He tucked his chin to stare down at his shirt. A wide stain of blood had soaked a circle around the entire wound. He swayed on the seat. Or maybe that was the rocking of the wagon? He couldn't make sense of it all, and when he closed his eyes, he had no strength to open them again.

Chapter 33

Ellie startled awake. A dream. Only a dream. But vestiges of it lingered like the unseen strands of a cobweb, unnoticeable until one walks through it.

Ellie pushed back the covers and swung her legs over the side. A mild gray glow let her know the sun had not yet risen. She brushed her hand down her long braid, trying to understand what had so startled her. A certainty. Something she needed to know.

She felt each strand of the woven braid as she replayed the confrontation on the porch. Something Uncle Ross had said. . . It eluded her.

Frustration gave her energy, and she attacked the unbraiding and brushing of her hair swiftly. All the while trying to understand what it was she was missing. It had been after his smooth words, when her firm no had ignited his temper and struck fear along her spine.

"You can't talk to me like that, you little tramp."

She'd been so shocked at the change in him. The baseness of his assessment of her character.

"How long has that Rebel trash been hounding you?"

Ellie gasped. Rebel trash! He knew!

Her breathing came in little gasps as she hurried to finish dressing. That was what her subconscious had been trying to warn her of. If Uncle Ross knew Theo was a Rebel, he might try to go after him. Coupled with the fact that she had revealed Theo's memory of Ross shooting Martin, her uncle might find it necessary to dispense with any risk that might get him in trouble with his superiors. Meaning Theo.

Breath squeezed from her in a little moan. She dashed to the barn, urgency driving her movements, her hem collecting the morning's dew as she ran. She saddled the gray as fast as she could, mounted, and snapped her crop against the horse's flanks.

Only when the lane to the barn came into view did she slow the horse. In the bright morning light, everything seemed eerily quiet. Her gaze slid over the wagon and the closed barn doors. When the gray rounded the wagon, her gaze fell to the ground where a wide pool of red made her blood race. She raised her head. "Theo?" She ran to the barn, and grappled a bit with the door. It swung open and she entered. "Theo?"

A lantern flickered at one end of the barn and she ran to it. A black man was standing up and another man lay in the hay, eyes closed. Theo. A wounded sound came from Ellie's throat.

The black man held up a hand. "He is asleep."

Ellie didn't recognize him. "Who are you?"

"He needs a doctor. Bad. I done all I could, but he's got the fever."

Ellie sank to her knees and pressed a hand to Theo's brow. "What happened?"

None of it made sense. The blood on the drive must have been Theo's. Ross had gotten to him. It couldn't have been the black man, or why would he care for Theo afterward?

"Am I in the North?"

Ellie turned to the man. "Yes, you are."

Relief relaxed the black man's lips, and the lines around his eyes faded. "I was afraid I was at the wrong place. The old man in the blue coat came and shot him"—he indicated Theo with his eyes—"then found us in the wagon. He was taking us south, going to get the bounty for us, but the mister here stopped him." The black man stood and motioned for Ellie to follow him.

She plucked at his sleeve, and the black man stopped. "What about the others?" she whispered.

His teeth gleamed in the low light. "Got 'em to the place. I stayed to help the mister."

In the empty stall next to Libby's, her uncle sat on the ground, his legs and wrists bound, a cloth around his mouth. His eyes were bloodshot, and one was swollen and blackened. When he lifted his head to see who had approached, he scowled at Ellie and turned his face away.

Words wouldn't come to Ellie, and Theo's need trumped her desire to hear what her uncle had to say. She spun on her heel. "Can you help me load him in the wagon?"

The black man didn't move. "I'm safe here?"

It would be a natural worry, Ellie understood, but she needed the man's help. "If you want to stay here in Gettysburg, you can work for me. I have a lot of repairs that need to be done."

"My name's Josiah, ma'am, and I'd be grateful to work for you and the mister."

Ellie didn't bother wasting the time to explain Theo's relationship to her, not with the fever pulling strength from his body every minute it raged.

ᘓ

Martha sat on the porch, rocking in her chair, when Josiah pulled the wagon up to the house days later. Ellie allowed Josiah to help her down. Rose followed, with baby Colin bundled tightly.

Josiah turned to Ellie. "Will you be long, ma'am?"

She smiled at him. "I might. Come on in. I'm sure Martha would like to see you."

She delighted in watching the black man's obvious consternation at being found out. For all the times his face masked his emotions, it had been obvious to her from the start that Martha captured his attention. Ellie stared up at Martha who had stood and come to the edge of the porch. Seemed Martha felt the same way about Josiah.

"Josiah, you put that horse away around back. I'm guessing Miss Ellie'll want to put in a good long visit now that he's awake."

Ellie's head came up, and she gasped in surprise.

"Oh, that's wonderful news." Rose gave words to the moment.

Ellie started toward the steps, excitement lifting her spirits. It had been nearly two weeks since Theo had been awake for more than a few minutes, though Martha kept saying those few minutes were a good thing. Still, it had worried her. But now. . . "When?"

Martha led the way through the door and to the back of the house. "Just this morning I went in and noticed him stirring more than usual. About an hour later, he was wide awake and asking for something to eat. Full of questions, he was. Plumb wore me out with all the tongue waggin' he done." She opened the door to his room and rolled her eyes toward the man on the bed. "I'll be out here talkin' with Miss Rose. We needs to decide what to do now that the doctor isn't coming home."

Ellie purposely didn't look right at Theo at first. She had waited for this moment for so long. It was one thing to see him when he was unconscious, but now that he was awake and able to see her, too. . .

"Who are you?"

Her heart plummeted, and she turned toward him.

His face split in a huge smile that told her he was teasing. "I thought maybe I'd grown so ugly you couldn't stand the sight of me."

Ellie took the seat next to the bed where she'd sat for the many days he struggled through the fever then lingered in unconsciousness.

His jaw sported a few days' growth of beard, and his cheeks were hollowed from the weight he'd lost, but his eyes. . . Her breath caught at the light that glowed from his eyes.

A happy light passed over his face and grew in intensity until she felt the heat rising in her cheeks. "Really, Theo."

"I can't help it. You're a beautiful woman."

She pressed her hands to her face. "We're not even courting."

"I hope to be asked as soon as I get back on my feet."

"You lost a lot of blood."

"So I heard."

"Josiah said the only reason he found the barn was because he'd paid close attention to the road Uncle Ross used."

"Josiah?"

"The black man who helped you get back here."

"I must have passed out."

Ellie pulled at the fabric of her skirt so that it settled around her legs more comfortably. "You did. Josiah wasn't sure if he was at the right place or not."

"Your uncle Ross figured he would capture whatever slaves we were hiding then take them down south to collect the bounty. Did he confess to everything?"

Ellie pressed her lips together. "Yes. They put him under arrest."

Theo slid his hand over and waggled his fingers in invitation.

She took it, her heart full because of this man. The rough bandage rubbed against her fingers, and she lifted his bandaged middle finger for examination. "I'm sure your being unconscious has helped this heal."

"It's the least of my hurts right now."

"Still bad?"

Theo raised their clasped hands and placed hers against his chest. "This helps."

"I'm serious."

He widened his eyes. "So am I."

℘

How Theo loved to see her cheeks awash with color. Her blushes always made her eyes bluer. If she truly knew the pain that spiked along his arm and neck every time he moved his hand, she would have never allowed him to even hold her hand. But he didn't care. The pain was worth it.

"Tell me about this black man."

Ellie gave a little laugh that amused him, though he didn't quite understand her mirth. "Ask Martha. She probably knows more about him than anyone."

He couldn't believe it. "Martha? And Josiah?"

Ellie gave an enthusiastic nod. "I think so."

Theo's mind clicked along at the news. But something else troubled him. "Your uncle was spying on us, wasn't he?" He recalled the whinny of the horse he'd heard at the springhouse and when he'd been woken in the night by a sound he couldn't pinpoint. "He must have been watching my movements."

"He'd been watching you, mostly, trying to figure out your connection to me and if it went deeper than merely a hired hand. And of course, he overheard my conversation with Martha and decided to cash in on the moment and take care of you at the same time. After shooting you, he found the slaves in the wagon, got Josiah out, and made him pick you up and put you in the wagon."

"Good thing for me. If it hadn't been for Josiah's help, I don't think things would have worked out quite as nicely." He pulled in a slow breath. "What about the runaways?"

"When Josiah got back to the barn, he told them all to go ahead as planned. They would have been a little bit behind schedule, but being in the North seemed to give them some peace of mind."

He heaved a sigh of relief. "That's good to know."

"You're getting tired."

"No, I'm fine."

"You are not."

"If I fall asleep, will you stay?"

"I have to."

He cracked his eyes open. "You have to?"

"Martha and Rose needed to talk about their plans for the office now that Robert isn't coming home."

Was she deliberately avoiding what he meant? "You sound like you don't want to stay."

Her eyes danced. "I've watched you sleep for the past nine days."

"Did you miss me?"

She tilted her head, a sparkle coming into her eyes. "Not as much as I will when you leave."

"Where am I going?"

"Well, seeing as how I need those repairs done and you're lying in here sleeping, I hired Josiah to take care of things."

"So I don't have a job then."

She shook her head, but the light danced in her eyes. "No."

"I guess I'll be leaving then as soon as I'm able."

"I guess so."

He was going to have to pry it out of her. "That makes you happy?"

She leaned forward, her breath on his cheeks. "It does because I was hoping that you would decide to stay if I offered you a promotion."

He turned his head toward her, all vestiges of sleepiness gone. "A promotion to. . . ?"

"Suitor?"

"Ellie Lester," he breathed, "are you inviting me to come courting?"

When she pressed her lips to his, he knew he had his answer.

Epilogue

Dear Rose,

It has been a wonderful time. The Bedford Springs Resort is lovely, though the ride out here from the train was rough. Theo and I have enjoyed our time together so much. He has been so patient to wait so long before we wed. But I wanted to be sure. I'm sure that makes you laugh, since you were convinced far before I was. I knew I truly loved him when he agreed to risk going south to bring home Martin's body. Still, it troubles me that some view our marriage as a slap to the face, even daring to treat him—us—with such derision. I believe it helps him that Josiah, Martha, and most of the blacks view him as a hero for what he did that night. If only the white people were as convinced, but I must not judge them too harshly, for I can understand how they feel, especially those who lost their husbands and sons.

We leave here in a few days to go out to Council Bluffs, as far as the train will take us, but still plan to return on the agreed date. I hope Josiah asks Martha to marry him soon. Please make sure he gets paid. The money will help ease his mind on the matter.

I hope by now you have found someone to buy our house and that you are getting settled in with Martha. I know she is a comfort to you, just as she was a help to Robert. Give Colin a kiss for me. Tell him his aunt Ellie will bring him a wonderful toy to play with.

Oh, and please let Josiah know that we've decided to take his idea and build a wall in the largest room on the second floor of the farmhouse. We'll need the room should we have children. Not that I'm in the family way yet, but it is one of our dreams to raise a family on the farm where I spent all my growing-up years.

Take care, my dear friend. I'll write again soon.

Love,
Ellie

PROMISE OF YESTERDAY

Dedication

For Lauren, the next writer in the family. You've overcome so much and still retain your sense of humor. It is hard to believe you are the same baby who struggled for life for seventy-five days, and I can only marvel at the young woman you are becoming. *Te quiero.*

Chapter 1

Greencastle, Pennsylvania, 1878

Marylu Biloxi took careful aim with her broom. "You stagger yourself around somewhere else, Zedikiah. We don't take to your drunken binges, and you're a shame to the rest of our young black folk."

Zedikiah blinked hard in the waning sunlight. His dark skin and bloodshot eyes gave evidence of his hearty patronage of anyone who slipped him corn liquor.

Marylu swung the broom at the back of his baggy britches. "Now get. You near mowed down Miss Rosaleigh, and I'll not have you knocking over any more of Miss Jenny's customers."

Miss Jenny McGreary, owner of McGreary's Dress Shop, the best dress shop in Greencastle, Pennsylvania, appeared on the boardwalk beside Marylu. "Let him go. Miss Rosaleigh's fine. Besides, she's got her head so far into the clouds these days, *she* probably ran into *him*."

Marylu leaned on her broom and chuckled, the sun warm on her head. "You sure right about that. Never seen a woman so scatterbrained." Her mirth faded when she turned back to Zedikiah, who swayed on his feet. "His mama, the Lord rest her weary soul, would have his head in that trough for acting the way he does."

An idea popped into her head. Zedikiah stared at her with an unfocused gaze and slack jaw. Marylu crept closer and grabbed the back of his scrawny neck. His slight frame had no chance against her robust figure and greater weight as they took the steps down into the street. If not for her hand on his collar, he would have sprawled face-first into the mud. Marylu stopped him in front of the trough, bent him double, and dunked his head into the warm, horse-slobbered-in water.

"Marylu!" Miss Jenny's voice held horror.

"His mama would do the same. Since Dottie's not here to haunt him into sobriety, I'll take the job."

Miss Jenny pressed her lips together, her eyes on the trough. "Oh, dear. Marylu..."

Seeing her employer's concern, Marylu noted that bubbles were slower in getting to the surface. She pulled the boy upright and gave him a good shake to rattle his brain to wakefulness.

Zedikiah sucked in gulps of air, color flushing back into his cheeks. He started sputtering and spewing.

Marylu let him go, and he promptly slumped at her feet. But as he sat in the dust of the worn road, something tugged hard at her heart. He'd lost his mama near a year ago and him not even fourteen. "Time for you to stop your wild ways," she huffed and bent to help him to his feet.

"You go on over to my house." Jenny touched the boy's arm. "Cooper will get you some dry clothes and warm milk."

But Miss Jenny's words didn't seem to penetrate Zedikiah's stupor. When the boy swayed on his feet, Marylu caught hold of his arm, noticing, again, how large her hand appeared against his scrawny bicep. Drinking himself to death, he was. She would have to keep a closer eye on Zedikiah, else his wild ways were going to land him in a real stew.

Miss Jenny patted the boy's back and turned. "I have to get back to Miss Rosaleigh," she threw over her shoulder.

Marylu frowned at the boy and released his arm. "Zedikiah?" She waited for him to look at her, but his head remained sunk between his shoulders, eyes on the ground. "You do what Miss Jenny just said. Have Cooper get you something to eat." But her words still seemed not to penetrate the fog of the boy's drink-addled mind. With a heavy sigh, she left him in the street, turning back once to see him stumbling down the road. At least he was headed west, toward Miss Jenny's place. She hoped he had understood after all.

Inside the shop, Miss Rosaleigh Branson stood before the dressmaker's model in the corner, inspecting her ivory wedding gown, not seeming the worse for wear from her brush with Zedikiah. Marylu shook her head at the sounds of the young white woman's sighs and giggles, as her hand brushed over every single detail of the gown.

"Let's get you into this," Jenny suggested as she motioned the bride-to-be to a smaller room out of sight of the front door.

Marylu dismissed Zedikiah's binges and the sad state of the thirteen-year-old boy's future and set about her chores. She ducked back outside to draw water to mop the floors, where mud from recent rains mottled the hardwood planks. Wouldn't do a fig to have Miss Jenny's floors so dirty. Not with all the highfalutin clients she served.

The motion of scrubbing the wood floors brought a song to her lips, and she sang low and mournful of a people in Bible days released from slavery of a different kind. She got to the second verse, when the two women emerged from the back room.

Miss Branson gravitated to the large mirror and gave a squeal of delight, punctuated by a little jig.

Marylu couldn't help but laugh.

"Careful there, Miss Branson. Those pins of Miss Jenny's will poke you full of holes."

"I'm getting married!" The young woman sighed as she brushed a hand down the spotless material.

"You sure are." Miss Jenny crossed the room and knelt beside the young bride-to-be. She folded the material at the hem and secured it with a pin. "You'll be a beautiful bride."

Marylu caught the wistfulness in her employer's tone and harrumphed. Jenny paused her pinning and the two exchanged a smile.

It was an old subject. One they had discussed and lamented many times. Marylu believed her employer should get married, to which Miss Jenny would turn the tables and try and convince Marylu to give marriage a chance.

Marylu's answer was the same then as it was now. "No one's going to see me popping over a man like grease in a hot skillet." With that, she leaned forward to resume scrubbing, her knees cracking in protest to the abuse.

As her employer finished up with Miss Rosaleigh, Marylu scrubbed with vigor at the dried mud. She should have done this yesterday when it seemed every dainty-booted foot crossing the threshold held some chunk of muck to be ground underfoot, but she'd been too busy hemming skirts. Now she paid for the neglect by having to scrape extra hard at the crusty filth. Her back ached as she worked the stiff bristled brush. She stopped long enough to allow Miss Rosaleigh to float past and make her exit, doubting the girl even felt the floor beneath her feet.

"You know, Miss Jenny," Marylu stoked the embers of the old argument, "that widower at the mill sure would be a good one for you. Don't you want to be floatin' around like the ones you stitch such fluff for?"

"Sally Worth has her eye on him already."

Marylu recognized the resigned tone. Jenny McGreary was a plain woman, and older than most of marrying age at twenty-five, while Sally was much younger and very pretty. Little by little, Marylu had seen Jenny's girlhood dreams of marriage and family wither.

Before she could gather her thoughts enough to say something comforting, the creak of the door's hinges signaled another customer. The prospect of dainty, dirty boots getting ready to smear her clean floor made Marylu huff and sit back on her heels. She'd make sure this patron wiped her feet. But the form that appeared inside the door was not of feminine persuasion, and the booted feet were neither dainty nor clean.

The black man raised his hat and grinned down at her. His grizzled black hair, touched with gray, seemed to explode from his head, and she wondered how he managed to keep a hat on at all with such a springy mop. It was when her eyes lighted on the thick mud crusting his boots that Marylu's normally stiff knees got some youthful spring back into them.

"Don't know what you're doing, but you're not crossing my floor with those muddy boots."

Miss Jenny headed their way, a dark frown, aimed at discouraging Marylu's tongue, marring her features. Marylu knew if it weren't for the fact she'd cared for the woman from the time she pinned cloth rectangles onto her bottom, and that their relationship had matured into friendship, Miss Jenny would have probably fired her long ago. "Really, Marylu, can't you just greet our visitor?"

Marylu snorted. The man was someone she'd never laid eyes on, to be sure, but any courtesy Jenny's admonition drummed up fled when the man lifted a booted foot and stared straight at her, a challenge in his dark eyes.

"You full of pepper, but you'll land on your backside out this door if you set that dirty boot on my clean floor."

Miss Jenny stopped at the edge of the wet floor to speak. "Can I help you?"

The customer's gaze shifted, and he lowered his booted foot to the dry spot within the front door. He lifted his hands, palms up, then shrugged. His mouth opened then closed.

When he rolled his gaze to Marylu, the realization dawned on her slow and sure. She'd heard of people being deaf and unable to talk, but the man could obviously hear.

Without prompting, he opened his mouth, eyes rounding, a manic, evil gleam sharpening his gaze and turning his eyes almost black.

Miss Jenny gasped and took a step back.

Marylu watched the man closely. "He can't talk," she said for the benefit of her employer. Still, she took a step closer to Jenny to offer the woman her protection should the man be a lunatic after all. Best safe than a name in the *Greencastle Press*'s obituaries.

The man's head bobbed in agreement to Marylu's observation. He returned to his pantomime, hands raised, fingers like talons, the dark, coarse material of his shirt giving them a detached life of their own. The pale palms wrapped around his neck.

Miss Jenny's cold hand grasped Marylu's.

"He's not crazy." Marylu hoped mightily she was on target with that statement. "Watch him close. He's telling his story."

His eyes took on something akin to terror and desperation, as the hands seemed to bend him backward. One released his neck and hovered over his open mouth, making a quick slicing gesture. An awful gagging sound emanated from him.

Miss Jenny didn't loosen her grip until the man's hands went back to his sides and he straightened, his face once again emotionless.

Marylu felt weak at what she'd witnessed. "Your tongue was cut out," she stated in a flat tone.

His nod made her stomach heave at the vileness of such a thing.

His eyes held a twinkle that sparked brighter. His gaze on her felt like hot sunshine after a cold rain.

Marylu felt warmth slide along her arms and across her chest, in a way she had never felt warmed. She broke away from those probing eyes and rubbed her stomach. Probably just indigestion from the plate of eggs she'd gobbled down that morning.

"What can we do for you?" Miss Jenny asked.

"Least you can do is offer up a name," Marylu suggested in a hard, impatient tone.

But despite the hard clip to her voice, his brown eyes never wavered from her. He raised his hands to his chest and patted. His lips moved to shape two syllables.

Marylu watched in spite of herself and caught on right away to what he was trying to express. "Chester. Um-hm. You must be right proud of yourself thinking up a way to tell people that one."

He sent her a melodramatic wink that nevertheless rolled a pleasing sensation through the pit of her stomach. Maybe it wasn't that cold fried egg after all.

Miss Jenny snapped her fingers. "Chester Jones! You're here to pick up the order for Mrs. Lease. She mentioned sending someone over."

Chester's grin went huge, and he nodded, showing a set of bright whites.

"Let me get that for you." Jenny did an about-face and disappeared into the storage area. Chester's attention swung back to Marylu, starting another strange roiling in her stomach. She tried to ignore the intensity of his gaze and focused, instead, on the huge chip on his right front tooth. "Miss McGreary'll get your order right off, but you don't set one foot on this here clean floor."

Chester's lips pressed together in ill-concealed mirth and he lifted his very muddy booted foot, eyes daring her.

Marylu gave him a hard frown.

He took a step forward, eyes locked on her. Then he took another. Crumbles of mud left vague outlines of his boots on the planks.

"You get!" Marylu lunged and yanked up the broom she'd used earlier. She lifted it high and swung it.

Chester put his hands up as the broom came down.

"Marylu!"

She froze, lowered the broom, and waited for her employer to chastise her further.

Chester's eyes were as wide as his smile.

"He's picking up an order for a customer," Miss Jenny reminded in the gentle tone that stirred remembrances of her mother's.

Chester bent and slapped his knee. A coarse sound issued from his throat, the unmistakable garble of laughter.

"I'm sorry, Miss Jenny," Marylu said, all the while her fingers itching to give the man another dose of the broom.

Jenny handed the package over to Chester and walked him to the door.

Mud fell off his boots in chunks now. Clutching his package to his chest, he turned and looked beyond Miss Jenny and straight into Marylu's eyes. He winked at her and left.

When the door closed behind him, Miss Jenny turned and stared at Marylu, a strange look in her pale blue eyes.

Marylu set the broom aside. "What you thinkin' on so hard?"

"I've never seen you act that way before."

"Never had a man so ornery before."

"No, no. I mean, there's a glow about you. . . ." Miss Jenny smirked and crossed her arms. "I think I hear the popping of grease in a hot skillet."

Chapter 2

Marylu rolled to her side. Sleep would not come. Maple syrup eyes and a grin full of vinegar kept invading her thoughts and making her heart beat harder. She sure liked what she'd seen of the man, but Miss Jenny's comment rubbed her wrong. Hot grease indeed!

She squeezed her eyes shut and willed her body to relax. In only a few hours she would need to be at Antrim House, a hotel across the street from Jenny's dress shop, cleaning up the rooms.

Upstairs.

Twelve steps.

Her knees ached just thinking on it.

Her right knee did better than her left, what with the injury that had happened all those years ago. Scrubbing floors always woke up the pain. Shifting positions didn't help ease the hurt neither. She decided to get herself up and start on breakfast. Miss Jenny wasn't a big eater, but the rest of the "family," as Jenny liked to call them, could put away some food. Old Cooper ate like a man condemned to death and scheduled to hang.

Marylu lumbered into the kitchen and worked some firewood into the box of the cookstove. A light shuffling made her jump and spin.

Cooper White stumped his way to the table and sat down.

"Good morning to you too, old man."

Cooper lifted drooping eyes to Marylu. "None of your lip, woman. Why don't you get some coffee going?"

"I ain't your woman."

"Could be."

Marylu crossed her arms, invigorated by the morning word toss. "Not till I'm stiff and cold."

"I don't figure I have long to wait then—you being as cold-hearted as they come."

She flicked open the coffeepot as much to check its contents as to hide the grin erupting. Cooper was ancient. Near to fifty-five by her best guess. If she married him, she wouldn't have to wait long to be a widow. But a year over thirty didn't mean she was desperate, her only regret being she'd probably not see any beautiful black babies of her own. Sobered a bit by the sad thought, she pointed at the empty water bucket. "You scoot yourself and get some water."

Cooper got to his feet, slow as a slug in salt. He returned as she finished grinding the coffee beans and set the full bucket on a stool. "Now can I get some coffee?"

Marylu ladled some water into the coffeepot, added the grounds, and set it to heat. "You'd think you'd have learned yourself some patience by now." She used a linen to protect her hand and opened the firebox to stick in a couple more pieces of wood.

"Too old to be patient. Gotta hurry and get things done before no more time's to be had."

Marylu wiped her hands and sat down across from Cooper. "You still getting your night scares?"

He lifted tired eyes to hers. "I'll never forget that time. Thought that man was gonna shoot us dead. Then when he didn't and he told us we was going south, I wished he would have."

Marylu sat up straighter. "Seeing you all was the hardest thing. . ." The silence stretched long between them. Images of that night fifteen years ago flared to life in Marylu's head.

The wagon had rolled into Greencastle upon the Confederates' retreat from Gettysburg, full of black-skinned strangers with fear in their eyes and guards surrounding them. Marylu remembered watching Miss Jenny's mama and papa taking in the pitiful sight. She also knew, before they ever started whispering, that they were forming a plan to help the blacks, just as they, for years, had helped those who came to them in the night to escape to the North.

"You were a brave woman," Cooper interrupted her thoughts. "When that horse reared up, I thought you was done for, but you just did what it took."

"Except where those hooves snapped on my knee. Still aches."

Cooper nodded. "Reminder of what you done. Brave woman. Still are. Got more sass than most. Guess living with Miss Jenny's family made you feel that brave."

Marylu dropped her hand to the table and speared Cooper with her eyes. "Not brave. I just knew what was right. There'd been enough suffering from them Rebs looting the stores as they came through town the first time. Had all our people runnin' farther up north."

"Those of us still 'round won't ever forget what you done." Cooper's eyes took on a faraway gleam. "When you came out right under that chaplain's nose with Miss Jenny's daddy and that other man. . ." He shook his head.

She wrestled for something to distract Cooper from the subject of that night and the wagon full of slaves she'd help to free. Only God's strength had helped her then, as it helped her now. No matter how the slaves had hailed her as their hero and dubbed her "Queenie," she had only done what had to be done. The fact that she'd lost her heart in the process didn't matter none. Most had forgotten Walter. He was a moon that would never rise again, and Marylu didn't want to think on him. Didn't do any good. Just like taking the reverence to heart of those that she had helped free didn't leave her quite comfortable.

Cooper slapped his leg. "I told the whole story to Chester, and he just smiled and nodded like he does—"

Marylu's back snapped erect. "Chester?"

Cooper chuckled. "That's right. The mute. He wanted to meet you real bad. Said he'd heard the story even way down in South Carolina about a black woman freeing her own."

She ignored that and focused on his apparent familiarity with the black man. "Mute he might be, but he can hear just fine."

"Heard he stomped on your floor and got your temper to flarin' pretty hot." He slapped his leg. "Wished I'd seen that. Not often a man gets one over on you." Cooper loosed a chuckle. "He was right impressed with you and the story of you saving all of us, Queenie."

Marylu frowned. "Don't call me that. I was as scared as you all were that night." She cast an eye toward the coffeepot and used it as an excuse to move from the table.

"And what about them years you worked in the railroad?"

"Miss Jenny's papa did that. Was my job to keep Miss Jenny safe."

"That's not the way Miss Jenny tells it."

"She wasn't even eight when we started. You taking her word over mine?" Marylu poured coffee into two tin cups and set one in front of Cooper. "Don't you have a garden to tend or something?"

Cooper eyed the window and the peek of sunlight lightening the sky more with each passing minute. "Guess so. Good time to work when the heat's not so much."

As the older man sipped on his coffee, Marylu realized her only way to learn more about Chester was to pry it out of Cooper. The trick was to do it without his knowing she wanted to know. "How'd you find out that Chester muddied my floor?"

Cooper's smile showed few signs of teeth. "Told me. Not so much with words as with his hands and face. He's something else."

"Where'd he come from?"

The older man scratched his scantily bearded face. "Jumped him a boxcar and road in. Got himself some kin hereabouts."

"Kin? Up here? What'd he go down south for then?"

Cooper cocked a brow at her. "Why you so interested?"

Marylu puffed up. "Ain't interested a speck. Can't a body make some conversation? He's new in town. Don't that stir the curiosity of most?"

Cooper slapped his leg and spit a laugh.

She snapped a hard look at him, which made him laugh all the harder. "Ain't you got a garden to hoe?"

Cooper got himself vertical in a painful unfolding that took a full minute to happen. He'd been worked hard in the fields all those years before escaping north. It made him seem older than he really was. But he didn't complain. His eyes took on a gleam as he looped a finger through his coffee mug. "I'll let Chester know you're wanting to know about him."

"You best not, Cooper White."

The sound of his laughter dimmed only when the door shut behind him.

ঙ

Chester Jones shook the water from his head and buried his face in the towel. The water felt good to his skin. It was a welcome contrast to the warm pond water in the South where he used to do all his bathing under the mammoth branches of an ancient oak, streaming with moss.

He eyed himself in the mirror of the washstand. No matter how much he dabbed his face with water, he'd never be able to wash away the redness brimming his eyes. He shivered as the sounds of his dream twisted and taunted his mind. A familiar dream that by turns kept him awake or shattered a sound sleep.

Lord, help me. Cleanse me of these scares. Clean me up.

Clean like the days before he'd left home seeking a life apart from his mama and siblings. No use sticking around when they had all those mouths to feed. He'd made himself believe that was his only reason for leaving. Truth had come with maturity and suffering. Reality being he'd left because he was nine parts rebellious and one part wanting to scratch the itch to travel.

He'd been a fool to leave the only security he'd known all his life, all the promise that his yesterdays and his youth had held. Staying north would have saved him the stripes on his back and the long hours in the fields, but he hadn't listened to his mama. Hadn't allowed himself to soften at her crestfallen expression when he'd announced his decision to leave home. In his head, he could still see the hurt in her eyes. The fear. All for him. If he had expected tears at his announcement, he should have known better, for his mama was too strong a woman to spill salt all over the place, no matter the depth of the heartache.

I failed her, too, didn't I?

He filled his lungs and released the breath in a long, measured exhale. Was no use talking to God. No use talking at all anymore. But he'd come to this state to see his mama and sister, the only kin he knew of, the rest scattered by his father's sudden death. His family's noble sacrifice for the North that his father loved, fought, and died for as part of the 54th Massachusetts Volunteer Regiment.

He died a braver man than me.

Chester straightened and tried to shake off the gloom that permeated his mind. He had to put the past behind him and figure out a better way to get people to understand him. Some understood him better than others. Like the fine woman he'd seen in the dress shop. Surely she had sass aplenty. He'd heard many stories of how she'd set free a wagon full of slaves captured in Gettysburg. Even on the run he'd heard the stories. Among blacks, stories of heroism were transferred from one wagging tongue to another, faster than any mail service.

He had delayed heading west to Mercersburg, where his mama and sister lived, in order to meet Marylu Biloxi. Chance had brought him face-to-face with Cooper the day he'd gotten off the train. It had taken Chester a week to discover that the man knew Marylu. He even lived in a little house out back of the one Marylu lived in with her friend and employer, Jenny McGreary. As soon as Cooper discovered his passion for building furniture and such, the old man had taken him straight to the owner of Antrim House and got him a job. Mr. Shillito's recent purchase of the hotel, and his plans to renovate, meant job security.

Chester shifted his weight and squinted out the window of his little room on the first floor of Antrim House. He reviewed his meeting with Marylu. He had been surprised at her beauty. High cheekbones. Moonlit-night skin that set off the glow in her eyes, the color of a golden pancake. But her sass had brought his smile out of hiding, and once he felt the grin on his lips, it seemed he couldn't stop smiling. His spirits had lifted and soared. A feeling he'd not felt for a long time.

He blinked and reached for his worn shirt, buttoning it on as he crossed the room. He needed to get started on the tables and chairs Mr. Shillito had requested. He finished the last buttonhole and swung the door wide.

A woman stood in the hallway, her back to him, but Chester's heart slammed against his chest as Marylu Biloxi threw a questioning glance over her shoulder. When their eyes met, she turned and put a hand to her chest. "What you doing here?"

Chapter 3

Marylu dropped her hand. "You 'bout made my heart stop."

Chester took note of her bright blue dress and crisp white apron, not to mention the curves filling out the clothing in all the right places. He wondered if her statement meant his presence stirred something in her or if he'd spooked her. He donned an imaginary hat and gave her a deep bow.

"Mr. Shillito didn't tell me you were the one he'd hired."

Chester pressed his lips together and let the sparkle shine in his eyes, then punctuated the moment with a quick shrug.

"You best be knowing how to work real hard."

His mind drifted to the many scars across his back, not that he'd been afraid of work or ever caught shirking the rows in the fields down south. No, the lashes had been a matter of pleasing a very unpleasable master. He must have let the melancholy slip into his expression, because Marylu's eyes grew softer.

"I'm right sure you know all there is to know about hard work."

To this he bobbed his head. He knew about running, too. Running hard and long and trying to outpace howling dogs on four legs. He knew the racing heart and the prickle of cold sweat and the twist of dread that clinched the gut tighter as each howl got closer and the voices of his pursuers louder.

She put a hand on his arm, and he gave himself a mental shake.

"Make a list of what you need to make room five right again. Drunk man smashed it up pretty bad, and Mr. Shillito wants it put right."

Chester stood straight as a stick, stuck out his chest, and saluted.

She frowned and mocked anger. "Don't you be forgettin' it either, or I'll have your hide."

He watched her go, aware of her in a way that was sure to bring him trouble. How could he think for a minute to pin his hopes of settling down on a woman whose soul showed more bravery and courage than he could ever hope to muster?

☙

The man was haunted, to be sure. Marylu knew the interpretation of the expression on Chester's face. She'd seen it a thousand times as she'd helped Miss Jenny's father feed the slaves that came to them on those dark nights, long ago. Pain and suffering. Fear so deep it cut her to witness it.

Something else tweaked at her mind. The sight of the faint red around his eyes. She knew what that meant, too. Had seen it too many times in Cooper after he'd spent a long, sleepless night, rocked by his nightmares of the days he'd spent down south.

She pushed the broom she held into the corners of room three and chased a spider away in the process. After Marylu finished cleaning the first four rooms and entered room five, she was amazed to find most of the repairs already taken care of.

Chester hunched over a broken chair, his thick fingers assessing the smoothness of the new chair leg he was sanding. He placed the chair on the floor and braced his hands on corners diagonal from each other and rocked the piece to see if it wobbled. Marylu grinned when she saw that it remained stable and level. Face lit with satisfaction, Chester got to his feet and smoothed down his spiking hair.

"You need a shearing," she observed.

His eyes glowed, and he ran a hand over his hair and stirred it into a wild fan around his head.

Marylu shook her head at his antics, reached out, and pressed it back down. The springy feel of his hair startled her somehow and stirred her to a heightened awareness of the intimacy of the gesture. She snatched her hand away and swallowed over the sudden ache in her throat. "You get on over to the McGrearys' tonight, and I'll sharpen my shears and fix you up."

His eyes rounded, and took on the look of an excited puppy. He rubbed a hand over his midsection.

"I'm guessing I can find something to feed you as well." With all his hand-waving, even if born of necessity, he must work up an appetite. But how did he eat without a tongue? She wondered, too, if he got tired of trying to communicate everything with his hands and gestures. To have to be quick to act out everything he wanted to say, not to mention patient enough to wait for the person he talked with to interpret what he meant. It must make him feel very isolated. "Cooper says he knows you, that you got kin 'round here."

His nod came slow, and the sadness returned to pull his face into a frown.

She wondered why he hadn't moved on to see his family already. "You not here to raise trouble, are you?"

He shook his head.

"See that you don't. We don't like rabble-rousers. We got ourselves a church. You do church, don't you?"

His eyes went round and dull for a fleeting minute but lightened into a gentle glow, accompanied by an enthusiastic nod. He spread his arms wide as if to take in the whole room then pointed to the chair he had been working on. His puppy eyes locked on hers, and he raised his brows.

"You did a fine job, Chester." She folded her arms and grunted. "But if you ever dare to walk across any floor of mine with your muddy boots again, I'll pluck you bald one hair at a time."

Chester gave a look of mock horror and covered his head with his hands.

Marylu bit down hard, but a single laugh squeezed through. Chester's laughter joined hers, until both of them were gasping for breath.

That bit of merrymaking sustained Marylu through the long morning. Chester, too, seemed lighter of spirit when she left to go to McGreary's Dress Shop in the afternoon. Announcing herself as she opened the back door of Miss Jenny's shop, Marylu hadn't moved three full paces through the back door when Miss Jenny stuck her head out of the nearby storage area.

Jenny's huge grin mirrored the look she had given Marylu the previous day when making her hot grease comment. "I don't guess I have to ask what has you so cheery looking. I heard Levitt Burns's wife whispering something about the 'mute,' as she called him."

"That's full nonsense."

"The 'mute' part or that Mrs. Burns was whispering?"

Marylu sent her a look.

Her friend's smile spread from ear to ear. "Mrs. Burns will be in later today to drop off some mending and order some new dresses. I'll let her know you said she was full of nonsense."

"Wouldn't do you good to open your mouth at all. She wouldn't let you drop one word before she trampled you 'neath a mouthful of her own."

Miss Jenny juggled two bolts of cloth. "So you didn't see him?"

"I saw him."

"It's good to see you so happy."

"Ain't no happier than usual."

Miss Jenny giggled in response, clearly unconvinced, and passed the bolts of cloth to Marylu. "These need to go out on the table, and then the hem needs to be put in Miss Rosaleigh's wedding dress."

Glad for a change in topic, Marylu plucked the bolts from her employer's arms. "You finished her bonnet?"

"It came together nicely this morning. Good thing, too, because I've got to start on Mrs. Carl's order."

"You're working awful hard."

Jenny paused in pinning a pattern to smooth blue cotton. "It helps fill the hours. If not for you and Cooper, I don't know what I'd do for company." She smoothed the wrinkles in the paper and continued pinning.

"You could give Aaron a chance. That Sally is a little too flighty for him. Pay him some attention, and he'll be sure to notice."

Scissors appeared in Miss Jenny's hand. She gave a practice *snip-snip* then set to work cutting around the edges of the pattern. Marylu waited for a response, surprised when none came, not even a blatant denial of the suggestion.

They worked at their respective tasks for more than an hour, interrupted when Mrs. Burns entered the store, cheeks flushed and hair slipping down from the combs, forming ringlets around her face.

"Good afternoon, Mrs. Burns." Marylu watched Miss Jenny welcome the woman. They conferred on materials for a good ten minutes before Jenny faced her. "Could you lay out some patterns for Mrs. Burns, Marylu? I've got to get this dress basted."

Marylu did as instructed, laying out the patterns on the long display case, as Mrs. Burns expressed interest.

"It's good to see you so well, Marylu," Mrs. Burns commented.

"Thank ya, ma'am."

The woman drew in a great breath, and Marylu braced herself for the verbal flood headed her way, wishing she was Moses and could part the waters before the flood drowned her.

"I was just telling Jenny the other day how lucky she was to have such a faithful and devoted servant in you. I know how much comfort you and Cooper bring to her. It's a shame she can't find a suitable companion. Of course, I did hear that Aaron down at the mill was looking her way, until Sally Worth wore that azure dress last Sunday and sashayed around him until he finally asked her to the church picnic. Though I'm sure you wouldn't have known about that since you have your own church. You should be having a new member, too. Mr. Shillito hired that mute man who came into town. You seen him?"

Marylu didn't even bother molding her tongue around a reply.

"I'm sure you did," Mrs. Burns answered her own question. "He's a quiet one to be sure, but I guess that's because of his tongue being cut. Not all of it from what I hear, but enough to make it impossible for him to form most letters. A shame, I'm sure, but right punishment for a murderer, don't you think?"

Chapter 4

It can't be true." Miss Jenny's mouth pursed. She gave the scissors a snip into the air to punctuate the statement. "He doesn't look the type."

"Since when are you one to judge on looks?" Marylu unfolded the large section of material her employer was set to begin cutting.

"Oh, I don't. He just seems so"—she bent over the table, her brows creased—"gentle."

Marylu didn't answer. Couldn't answer, truth be told, because it was the exact word she would have used to describe Chester Jones's appearance. Sure, he got sassy with her, but his eyes held a quietness that seemed to show an inner strength. Her skin tightened, and gooseflesh rose along her arms. But that description could fit a lot of men. And she had been wrong before. Maybe Chester wasn't gentle. Those red-rimmed eyes might hide a deeper problem, and she herself had felt he looked tormented at least once during their morning exchange.

She sighed. No use fussin' around with thoughts of him anyhow. What with Miss Jenny pinning on the pattern, there was work to be done. Marylu smoothed her hand over the fabric, and she recalled the impulsive touch of her hand upon his hair earlier.

"You're blushing, Marylu." Jenny's eyes sparkled with pure mischief.

Miffed at having been caught woolgathering about the man, again, she opened her mouth then closed it with a snap.

"You look like a fish!" Jenny's laughter tinkled across the table that separated them.

Heat rose up Marylu's neck and fanned into her cheeks. She pressed her hands to the warmth and averted her face.

Jenny's mirth stuttered to a stop. "I'm sorry. It's just that I don't ever get to see you so flustered, and I, well, I couldn't resist."

Marylu felt her friend's light touch on her shoulder and raised her head.

"There's something about him, isn't there?" Her friend's eyes were serious now.

Marylu didn't respond. Didn't want to. Days ago she would have called herself or anyone else four kinds of fool for thinking there would ever be another man to pique her interest. Now she wasn't so sure.

But Chester, a murderer? If nothing else, she wanted to know his story. Mrs.

Burns's wagging tongue did little to convince her that Chester was indeed guilty of taking someone else's life. Besides, she had long ago learned it best not to believe something until she heard it straight from the source.

Jenny picked up the edge of the material and poised to make the first cut. "You know that Mrs. Burns sometimes gets things wrong."

It was as if Jenny had read her mind. Though her friend's words were a much kinder explanation of Mrs. Burns's motive than she would have offered up. "I'll be making sure of the story. You can count on it."

ꙮ

Cooper opened his big trap as soon as Marylu stepped through the door and into the kitchen.

"Heard you've got yourself some butchering to do tonight."

She raised a brow and spun a circle at her ear with an index finger. "You finally gone plumb crazy. What butchering?"

Cooper ran a hand over his close-cropped, more-scalp-than-anything hair. "Hair butchering. Chester was wide-eyed over the idea of coming here this evening. If that boy could talk proper, he'd have been spilling words all afternoon."

She paused to absorb this, secretly pleased but not for a moment going to let it show. She moved aside as Miss Jenny rustled through the door behind her.

Cooper creaked himself vertical and reached out to take Miss Jenny's packages.

"Why thank you, Cooper."

"Why sure. Can't let a pretty gal like yourself tote around heavy things."

Marylu snorted. "You let me do it often enough."

Cooper slapped the package down onto the table. "I said 'pretty gal.' You needin' your hearing checked?"

It only took her a second to yank up the heavy iron skillet and wave it threateningly.

Jenny stepped between them.

"Don't you get in the way, Miss Jenny. I'm going to give him what he has coming."

"Marylu, really. A fine example of Christianity you are."

"I am. The good Lord expects us to fight the devil. Now let me at him."

Cooper doubled up and slapped a hand to his thigh.

Jenny shook her head, but the smile broke through. "What would I do without you two to keep me on my toes?"

Marylu lowered the skillet. "I can think of a few things I could do without him around."

Cooper folded himself onto the bench and started up coughing.

Jenny sat beside him, a hand on his shoulder. "You need me to call the doctor?"

"I've got some good strong medicine for him," Marylu inserted. "Cure him of every bit of meanness ailing him. 'Course, it would cure him stiff and cold."

"How can you be so mean to me?" Cooper raised his watery eyes to meet hers.

Marylu huffed, admitted that he didn't look too good, and then relented. "I'll get you some tea."

He coughed real hard. "Lots of honey."

"I've made you hundreds of cups of tea in your life, and you're going to sit there and act like I don't know how you like it?" Marylu suspected Miss Jenny would coo over him a bit longer. She had a soft spot for the old man. Marylu set about cutting up roast and chopping vegetables for a stew. When the water for the tea came to a boil, Marylu got down the honey and began fixing three cups.

For all the drama Cooper could drum up, their little ritual of taking tea, and reading the Bible at the end of the workday, never failed to bring its own brand of comfort. They were a mismatched family, to be sure, but they loved each other.

She loved Cooper even more when he was quiet, though she had to admit that cough had her worried. The sound seemed raw, and she pondered the idea of putting some crushed garlic into his tea to ward off any further sickness.

When she set the teacups out, a thick silence settled around the room, disturbed only by the vague crackling of the wood fire fueling the stove. Cooper seemed content to warm his hands around the hot cup, his gaze distant. Jenny stirred her tea absently, as if Marylu hadn't quite worked the sugar into the amber liquid, but she guessed the woman had her mind on business, or a dress or bonnet.

Marylu slipped down on the bench, not realizing until she got still how much her body needed the rest. Muscles seemed to unbunch, and her knee protested being bent after so many hours. She inhaled the steam and wished she'd put a pinch of cinnamon into her cup, but the prospect of rising didn't appeal in the least, so she contented herself with sipping the tea plain.

"Guess we'd best be reading before the night gets away from us." Marylu grunted and reached toward the Bible sitting in its usual place at the end of the table. No dust collecting on this Bible. Not with Cooper to keep in line, a task made all the lighter since he almost always deferred to her and Miss Jenny to do the reading.

The leather cover of the Bible had begun to crack from the years of wear. Marylu ran a finger down the fracture and wondered if the local bookbinder could do something to mend the tear. The Bible had been a gift to them from Jenny's mama and daddy, and she sure and certain wanted to keep it in good repair.

"You gonna read or start to bawling?" Cooper frowned, though his eyes held a mischievous gleam. A cough choked him up, followed by another.

"You just worry about sucking down that tea. You hear?"

Miss Jenny put a hand to Cooper's shoulder. "I really think I should fetch the doctor."

"I'm an old man," he barked, the words punctuated with another cough. "If I gotta go, no doctor's gonna prevent it."

Marylu flipped the pages to Samuel. "And we're surely not going to stand in the way, either."

"Honestly!" Jenny sent Marylu a stern look. "The two of you are just terrible."

Cooper balled a fist and pressed it to his lips as if to stifle another cough. Marylu saw the gesture for what it was worth, a ploy to cover his amusement. The man's dark, watery eyes met hers long enough to deliver a wink, before another cough yanked at his chest.

Jenny didn't notice the exchange, unconsciously patting the man on the back as the coughing fit continued.

Such a straying of attention made Marylu hold her finger underneath the verse she'd been about to read and frown. Miss Jenny's stare wasn't directed at the cookstove in an I-need-to-get-a-new-one kind of way. No, her eyes were focused on something Marylu couldn't see, and she had a feeling she knew what had her employer and friend so distracted. What *man* had her so distracted, to be exact.

Marylu ran her finger down the Bible passage they were to read that evening and wondered how best to approach the subject of Aaron Walck. The man had captured Miss Jenny's fancy soon after the death of his wife, and it seemed, to Marylu's mind, that Jenny's interest hadn't waned a bit.

"Are you going to begin, Marylu?" Miss Jenny asked.

"Got it right here. First Samuel 18." As she read out loud, the verses became mere words, so caught up was she in trying to make sense of Miss Jenny's preoccupation.

"This is such a sad story. Saul started out with such promise and slid away into such bitterness," Jenny murmured.

Marylu gave an absent nod. "Spirit gets hold of a person and don't let go."

"He made bad choices," Jenny added.

"Reminds me of that young Zedikiah. He best be getting some sense in that head of his before his brains shrink up." Marylu opened her mouth to add something more to the statement but closed it.

Miss Jenny's gaze had sought out Cooper's and something passed between them. Cooper wasted no time in starting up a coughing fit, but Marylu knew she'd missed some silent message. A message that looked much like a gentle rebuke.

Chapter 5

For the next hour they ate and talked about Saul. Miss Jenny seemed inclined to have her say about the man's change of heart and his ability to sire a young man like Jonathan, who had a soft heart despite his father. And all the while, Marylu listened to Miss Jenny's soliloquy with rising suspicion.

Cooper seemed bent on studying the ingredients of the stew and the rim of his bowl. She wanted to stop her friend and ask what was going on but thought it best to hold her tongue.

It wasn't long after Cooper had shuffled his empty bowl to the counter that Miss Jenny seemed satisfied and closed the subject.

When Jenny left to work on some mending for Cooper, Marylu whirled on him. "What was that all about? I saw her giving you messages with her eyes."

"To know me is to love me."

"That's not the kind of eyeballing she was giving you, and you know it."

Cooper's shoulders slumped, and a sigh further deflated his frame. "It's an old problem."

"I'm listening."

The old man didn't raise his face or even twitch. Marylu's stomach twisted. She could remember only a handful of times ever seeing Cooper cry, and they were always like this. He'd get real quiet and still and then haul the handkerchief from his back pocket and take a swipe at his eyes and snort into the cloth. All the signs tears were there.

He crammed the kerchief back into his pocket and finally raised his face to her. "You think you know all 'bout me, but you don't. Sometimes a body's done too many wrongs and ain't nothing no one can do to help."

Whatever it was, it had to be bad. She twisted it over in her head how it was that Jenny knew something about old Cooper she didn't. The revelation seemed a recent one, making it all the more mysterious. Cooper hardly ever went anywhere or did anything out of his routine.

She turned her back on the man and set to work on the dishes. A light knock on the door broke the rhythm of swishing her rag around the plate. She glanced over her shoulder to make sure Cooper would break from his doldrums to open the door.

"Good to have some man-company for a change," she heard Cooper greet their visitor.

Marylu set aside the clean dish. "I'll get my shears out in a minute. Let me finish up these dishes. You had yourself some supper, Chester?"

Not only did she not expect an answer, she didn't wait for one. Plucking a bowl from the open cabinet, she ladled stew into it. No bachelor she knew would cook for himself unless held at gunpoint.

When she turned, bowl in hand, she met Chester's gaze. He stood at the closed door as if afraid to enter the room, or unsure of himself, though his eyes held the light of a man full of sass.

Marylu's hair prickled along her scalp. She slid the bowl down the table, careful not to spill any, and motioned Chester to take his seat. "Got more where that came from if you've a mind for it."

Chester took a hesitant step toward the bench, then stopped and lifted an eyebrow first to Cooper then to her.

"We already ate." She pointed at the open Bible. "We were spending some time in the Word. You be sure not to splash on the pages."

She didn't stay to watch him eat, afraid the sight might be more than she could handle. Mrs. Burns's words came back to her. Yet Chester's soft eyes that held such fascination for her seemed incapable of hatred. She might as well just admit that he had a way about him that she found appealing.

Marylu stretched upward and retrieved the scissors she used to cut cloth and snip hair off Cooper when she couldn't stand looking at the bush on his head a minute longer. Though hair on that man's head hadn't been a problem for the last ten years or so. It fell out faster than it grew.

When she returned to the table, Cooper sat chatting in a low voice to Chester, telling him of life in the area since the great battle at Gettysburg. Chester listened with interest, his bowl not nearly as empty as she expected. She forced herself to watch him spoon some into his mouth. Nothing drooled out the sides. He seemed to take a bit longer to chew and work things around, but other than that, nothing out of the ordinary. She almost sighed her relief then wondered why it mattered so much.

She worked the scissors in her right hand, the sharp snap gaining the attention of both men. Smile lines appeared beside Chester's eyes as he chewed.

"You sharpen these like I asked you?" She directed the question at Cooper.

"Sure did. Sharpened them real good."

She nodded, and with nothing left to do but wait, she sat herself down across from the two men and pulled the Bible close to read more about Saul. And to give herself some time to gather her wits before putting her fingers in the hair of the man who had captured her interest so easily.

ɞ

Chester did his best to keep his eyes on his stew or on Cooper's face, but every time Marylu moved from one place to another, he knew he must be giving himself away. Cooper didn't seem inclined to tease him none, but Chester didn't want to let down his guard.

She captivated him. He imagined he could see the nobility of her character in the fine shape of her nose and the squareness of her jaw. Tendrils of hair popped out from beneath the kerchief she wore on her head and got him to wondering what it would be like to see her without the covering. Was her hair tinged with gray? Would it be curly and short or longer and pulled back?

He didn't miss the fine stitching of the dress she wore or the little details that spoke of a woman good with a needle and with access to fine materials. At least finer than most of the women he knew.

He dipped his spoon and stirred the savory stew, inhaling deeply of the rich scent of beef and potatoes. The woman could cook, though he'd never doubted it for a minute with all the stories of her he'd heard.

When she snipped the scissors and questioned Cooper, he allowed himself the opportunity to savor every bit of her appearance without the worry of Cooper seeing his admiration. He swallowed the bite of potato he'd been working on and wondered what she thought of him. Did she see a strong man or a coward?

He fastened his attention on spooning up another morsel of stew. It didn't matter what she saw. He knew the truth. A woman like Marylu could never admire a man like him, and probably the rumors of his past had reached her by now, swollen with speculation and rife with inconsistencies, but the basic truth was there.

The very thought clenched his stomach, and he knew the tremors would prevent him from taking another bite. He fisted his hands and dug them into his lap, willing the trembling to stop before it started.

He stabbed a quick glance across the table at Marylu, relieved to see her attention on the Bible in front of her. But Cooper noticed, the old eyes probing deeply into his. They sat, gazes clenched, for minutes before Cooper moved his head in a slow nod. Chester didn't know what the gesture meant, but the old man braced his hand and rose slowly from the table.

"I think Chester's ready for those scissors."

Marylu's head snapped up. "You stay put, and I'll work you over, too."

Cooper shook his head. "Not me. I've got myself a project to work on." He ran a hand over his grizzled hair and favored Chester with a smile that looked more like a grimace. "Don't let her get too much of your scalp."

"You get out of here," Marylu spat. "I've shorn more old goats like you than sheep. Chester at least won't give me any lip."

Cooper's dry chuckle was punctuated by a stale cough as he opened the door.

"You shouldn't be out in that night air with that cough."

Cooper didn't reply. The door shut, leaving only a cold draft of air to wash over Chester.

Marylu shivered. "Don't know why that man can't listen to me for once." She stood in profile to him, lost in thought, gaze on the door that Cooper had disappeared through, unconsciously opening and closing the scissors she held.

Chester rubbed at his chin. Honestly, he couldn't imagine it either. For a moment he lost himself in what it would feel like to be looked after by a woman. Any woman. But especially Marylu.

Another snap of the scissors and she startled from her reverie and turned toward him. "You sit still now and I'll get to work. No use me worrying over that man. He sure doesn't worry himself over his body's needs."

Chester nodded and figured it better to agree. At least while she held a pair of scissors.

Chapter 6

Cooper's doings shrank away as Marylu set about snipping at Chester's head. She brushed his hair back with her fingers to gauge the evenness of her cuts then trimmed some more. The mostly black hair fell at her feet, looking like miniature balls of coarse yarn.

He sensed the way he needed to turn his head to accommodate her cutting, which pleased Marylu. When she ran her fingers through the ever-shortening mop, she became more aware of the intimacy of the gesture and all she had missed being unmarried. She swallowed hard over the swell of grief.

If things had worked out all those years ago, she might very well be cutting the hair of her own man instead of every stray Cooper brought in. Rather than allow that line of thinking to distract her, she grasped for some subject to chat about, but the notion shattered when the question burned through her mind, *So, did you really kill someone?* If he said yes, she just might go down on her knees and take to crying. And her knees hurt too much already for that to happen. If only there was some way to communicate with him.

She froze mid-snip. Her gaze fell on the cupboard above the bucket of water. If Chester wondered why the steady snipping motion stopped, he didn't react.

Marylu slipped the scissors into her pocket and crossed the room. Yanking open the cupboard door, she lifted onto her toes and slid her hand along the rough wood of the top shelf. Her fingertips grazed a cool, smooth surface, and she withdrew the object and faced Chester, holding the board up for him to see.

His head tilted at her, brow lowered in concentration. It was a reaction she hadn't expected.

She stroked the smooth surface of the slate and guessed the answer to her next question, but asked it anyhow. "Do you know how to write?"

Chester lowered his gaze to his hands, as if the answer lay somewhere within the rough cuticles and broken nails. It was a reaction she had seen often in the generation that had sampled the poison of slavery.

"Then I'll teach you."

His head popped up.

Marylu witnessed the doubt that shifted into a glimmer of hope. She nodded. "I've done it before. Many times in fact. Miss Jenny made sure my family could read and cipher. I pass that on when and where I can."

ᘓ

Chester felt a gentle hand squeeze his heart. Conviction shone from Marylu's eyes, turning them soft and gentle. He basked in what he saw reflected there, a surge of gratefulness carrying with it a flow of peace that washed over his heart and through his mind.

She brought the slate with her and passed it across to him. "You take that and use this to write with." She skirted the table and bent down, her face inches from his, though her full attention was on the slate.

His heart raced as her profile was silhouetted against the lantern farther down the table. He could see the texture of her skin, smooth and soft. Warmth emanated from her, enveloping him and lighting his imagination with what it would be like to hold her close.

"What you need to do first," her voice flowed over him, "is you need to learn how to hold this here pencil." She stroked her hand over the length of his and flattened it against the table, not for a moment realizing the effect her touch had on his senses. She cupped her hand around the pencil and showed him how the tool was moved by the fingers. "It's very simple, but I don't care how you hold it as long as you can make the letters right." She pulled his hand off the table and pressed the pencil into his palm. "Now it's your turn."

He mimicked what he'd seen her do. Her praise boosted his desire to try harder. When she showed him the motions of a letter she called A, he watched closely and repeated her bold strokes. She beamed a smile down on him that reminded him of sun-warmed Spanish moss twisting in a breeze.

She rained down a steady stream of praise as they progressed through the alphabet. Marylu sang the entire stream of letters he had just practiced writing. She pronounced each one, over and over, as she finished trimming his hair, and he worked the pencil on the slate to form the last of the vowels.

"Sharp as one of Miss Jenny's straight pins. You'll be writing books before too long."

She brushed off his shoulder, then moved across the room and replaced the shears in the cabinet. She untied her long apron and draped it across the bench seat before taking her place beside it.

Clearly, they were done. He had no more reason to stay, and it was late. He could feel the exhaustion in his bones, but his mind, too, felt the weight of all that he had accomplished.

"You take that on home with you and practice in whatever spare time you can find."

Her gaze met his. Before he could talk himself out of the gesture, he reached to cover her hand that she had rested on the table. The contact buzzed pulses of pleasure along his nerves.

She seemed startled. Eyes wide. She stared down at his hand, back at him, then jolted to her feet so fast the bench fell backward.

An immediate lump formed in his throat and swelled. He had panicked her. Her smile now became one plastered by politeness as she hovered near the door.

Chester didn't understand her reaction but knew it best to leave. He nodded his appreciation while pointing to his shortened hair and hurried out into the night, the prospect of returning to his small room leaving him hollow.

Chapter 7

It had been the first time a man had touched Marylu with tenderness since Walter's lips had pressed a kiss against her hand. In her mind she could still see Walter's dark head bent over her fingers. Feel the softness of his lips. But scratching out those tender moments was the moment he had taken a step backward and disappeared into the moonless night. Never to return.

Chester's hand, his touch, had startled her, sure, but her own reaction, that rush of exhilaration, left her afraid. She could have discounted the gesture as one of gratefulness for what they'd accomplished, for he'd been obviously enthusiastic about his progress, but it had been the dark softness in his gaze that told the truth. And she'd felt that same warmth from him the first day in the shop when he'd dared to defy her clean floors with his muddy feet.

She pulled the lantern closer and raised the glass to blow out the flame, when the door opened and Cooper slipped into the circle of lamplight.

He seemed startled by her presence.

"Just like you to sneak in like an errant schoolboy."

Cooper shrugged and melted onto the seat as if every last ounce of strength went from him in that second.

Marylu's expert ears picked up on his labored breathing. "Should be in bed, snugged up warm, not traipsing around in the cool night air with a cough like you've got. I told you that."

No response.

She moved around the table and felt his forehead. He was burning up with fever. She wished for Chester's presence and strength now to help lift the old man to bed. "Up with you. I'll raise up Miss Jenny and send her to fetch the doctor."

"No need," his voice, thick with sickness, scared her more than anything. "I'll be fine come morning." He coughed.

"You won't be fine, because if that fever don't kill you, I might be tempted."

She put a hand on Cooper's arm and lifted, signaling he should raise himself.

He struggled to his feet and shuffled toward the back door.

"Now you get over to your little room quick-like and snuggle up in that bed. I'll bring you something hot and have Miss Jenny get the doctor."

"Doctor Kermit, not that other doctor. Old Kermit don't mind looking after us darkies so much." Cooper closed the door behind him.

She left to heat water and rustle around for some honey and the cinnamon she hoarded for special bakings and sickness. As she set about preparing the herbal tea, her mind turned again to Chester's touch then to Walter. Tears burned, but she widened her eyes and refused to release them. She lifted the cup and inhaled the cinnamon sweetness. The clutch of a memory, long buried, grabbed at her mind. Walter's fever. The way she had nursed him back to full health.

A rustling startled her, and she half-turned.

Miss Jenny stood in the doorway to the kitchen, worry etched in the lines beside her eyes. "I heard you down here mumbling to someone. Cooper?"

Marylu faced her friend, the cup in her hands.

Jenny's eyes dipped to the mug of tea she held. "He's worse?"

"Best fetch Doc Kermit. Or you can stay with him and I will. I told him to get himself to bed."

"I'll go. Bring some water to boil and make a tent. I'll leave immediately." Miss Jenny spun on her heel, but she held out a hand to stop her momentum. "He just got back?"

"Not ten minutes ago. Came in looking like a beat puppy."

"Was he alone?"

The question rattled around in Marylu's head and raised a whole new set of questions. "He courting someone?"

"No. No, not at all. I just. . .wondered."

☙

Chester couldn't help but grin at his progress. Despite Marylu's withdrawal from him at the end of the evening, he had felt her pride in his accomplishments. He had worked over the alphabet on his slate most of the night, the slate pencil screeching with every carefully formed line and curve, until his eyes became heavy.

Indirect moonlight lit his room, and he pushed himself down deep under the covers. He wondered if Marylu lay sound asleep, or if late nights were spent in some sort of needlework, or maybe she read more from her Bible. After the long days she worked, sleep would come easy for her, he was sure. Nothing to haunt her nights, being raised up in a family that cared about the people under their roof.

He squeezed his eyes tighter and shifted position, willing away the thoughts that always invaded his mind when he lay down to sleep. An endless litany of harrowing moments spent on the run. Fearing capture. Of the cold nights and the pain of an empty belly.

Stop it!

A light scratch brought him alert. He lay still and tense. He hated mice and dreaded not only the thought of the little critters but also the bigger threat of their cousins. He tried to console himself that he'd not seen any of the furry vermin during the day.

Another scratch, followed by a muffled curse.

His mind flew. His small room was closest to the back door of Mr. Shillito's hotel. He drove back the covers and made short work of pulling his trousers on and snapping suspenders into place over his nightshirt. He opened the door of his room and peeked through the crack. He didn't need to see anyone to know the back door of the hotel gaped. A cold draft of air shot through the hallway and blew around his bare ankles.

A dark shadow leaned against the wall. Weak light indicated the outline of a slender man.

Chester caught the scent of alcohol. He moved slowly, unsure if the man posed a threat or simply couldn't function as a result of his inebriation. He would need to get the man to his room. At least this drunk was too soused to tear up things.

Chester took two steps in the man's direction before the shadow sunk down the wall and landed in a heap. Snuffles indicated the first stirrings of slumber that would, Chester had no doubt, lead to an all-out snore session. He poked the heap with his bare foot. Nothing. He reached down and grabbed the man's arm, startled to realize the form was that of a black boy. His mind flew over the possibilities. He stooped to wedge his shoulder beneath the boy's armpit and guide him to his feet.

The stranger must have woken long enough to understand what was being asked of him, as his movements became independent. Chester limped with the semiconscious man to his door, shoved it open with his toe, and barely got the boy through it before he lost his grip. He tried to catch his breath and hoped all the while that the noise he'd made didn't waken the only patron present on that floor this evening. Thank goodness they were in the room at the end of the hallway.

Chester took the time to light the two candles at either end of his room. He pulled the candleholder closer to the boy's face. He couldn't have been more than sixteen. Chester knelt beside the young man and slapped him lightly on the cheeks. He didn't get a response and really hadn't expected one. He rose and grabbed his shirt, balling it up to make a pillow for his visitor's head. Sleep would be the best thing for now.

Chester sat on the edge of his bed and stared at the too-thin form and the pants frayed around the hem. He blew out the candles, more bothered than he wanted to be by the still form of a drunken youth whose weakness for drink had him wandering around alone.

Chapter 8

"You're looking tired." Marylu swept Chester from head to foot the next morning as they worked in the same room, Chester bent over a drawer that tended to stick. "You must have stayed up working on your alphabet."

He nodded, eyes brightening, and held up a finger. He turned the drawer upside down and used his index finger as a pencil to write the letter A, followed by the rest of the alphabet.

Marylu watched his progress with satisfaction. When he got stuck on Q, she spoke the consonant and wrote it on the drawer bottom. Chester tried to imitate her. When he lifted his face, she shook her head. "Remember, the stick goes this way at the end. The other way makes the letter a G."

He tried again, more diligent in his determination than any other person she had ever tried to teach. When he kept writing the stick in the wrong direction, she shifted to stand behind him. She placed her hand over his, her index finger pressing against his to show the direction of the tail of the Q.

His face was inches from hers. A sudden wave of heat gripped her and made her yank her hand away and stand straight. He seemed not to notice her quick retreat. Again he made the circle of the letter and began the line, pausing at the bottom in uncertainty.

Pulling air into her lungs, she leaned forward, doing her best to maintain more distance between them. "Now over to the right and up."

He nodded and finished the letter. He repeated it then went on to finish the alphabet again, but Marylu stopped watching the letters and focused on his hands. His face. The curious little scar over his right eye.

He reminded her of Walter. Not in looks, but in the fact that he was needy. Walter had needed care and the courage to continue what he'd started. He had been near death when Miss Jenny's family had freed him, along with the others. With Marylu's knee strained, and a bone in her ankle broken by the horse, she had determined to keep a vigil by Walter's bed in the hidden room, surrounded by all she needed to care for him through the day. And as their bodies healed, their hearts became knit together.

Likewise, she knew the close proximity to Chester, night after night of teaching him to read and cipher as she planned, would do the same. Over the years of teaching others, she had seen the emotion, almost near worship, that her pupils often lauded her with. In their minds, she had given them a wondrous gift. But despite that, none of the handful of men she had taught had been one she could love, so she had shrugged off their adoration. Chester was a man she could love. Maturity would make her take the path slower than she had with Walter, and with more thought, but first she must choose whether or not to take the path at all. She must not forget the stain of murder was upon him.

When Chester waved a hand in front of her face, she realized she had not only missed his command performance but she'd also been staring at him, lost in her thoughts. Again, she felt the heat rise up her neck and suffuse her cheeks. She took a step back, suddenly confused and afraid.

Chester's soft expression went quizzical and tense. He rose to his feet, a head taller than she. He opened his mouth then closed it.

"I–It's time we be getting back to work." She willed her voice to have some steel. The soft brown orbs stared down at her. Through her. "That drawer's not going to finish sanding itself." A foolish thing to say, and she regretted the rebuke in her tone.

ଓ

Chester knew fear when he saw it. He saw it in front of him now. Every line of Marylu's face spoke of uncertainty and doubt. Words pushed to his tongue and demanded release, but he could only make noise, so he sought to alleviate her panic with his hands.

Not even her firm rebuke about the drawer deterred him. He advanced on her, and she shrank back a step. He raised his hand slowly and touched hers, the one she held to her cheek. He pulled her hand away, spread his fingers, and pressed it to his chest, where he knew she would feel the strong beat of his heart. His free hand rose to caress her cheek, drawing from courage born of his newfound abilities and the certainty of his feelings.

She did not pull back at his touch. Her eyes slid shut, and her lower lip trembled. He saw the tension rise in her shoulders, and her eyes snapped open, glassy with unshed tears. "I don't even know you. You don't know me."

He let his hand fall away and shrugged his shoulders to transmit his unconcern.

She shook her head, and a single tear spilled down her cheek. She swiped it away and bolted for the door and out of the room, leaving him to stand alone and wonder if the failure had been his for revealing his feelings too soon or hers for allowing whatever dark fear she held to separate her from the courage to love.

Somewhere, somehow, she had been hurt. He was certain of it. And if he hoped to love her, he must prove himself worthy of that love. For the first time in a long time, he thought he might have the courage to do just that.

☙

Marylu avoided the room where Chester worked the rest of the morning. She moved as fast as she could from room to room, complete with her cleaning in record time, except for the room where Chester still sat, the frame of the chest of drawers lying on its side, his dark hands running over the wood in search of rough spots to sand.

She turned from the open doorway, thankful he had not noticed her. She brushed her hand across her brow, the gesture bringing Cooper to mind. She needed to check on him and today, this moment, welcomed the diversion. Anything to take her mind off Chester and the raw emotion that had swelled inside her breast at his touch.

She was too old for love, she decided. Besides, she couldn't get attached to someone who might be a murderer. Marylu pressed a hand to her stomach and wondered, though, what it would be like to love and be loved. To have the children she'd always dreamed of.

She chided herself for such fanciful imaginations. She was Miss Jenny's friend and she could never leave her friend alone.

Chapter 9

Chester finished work on the chest of drawers before putting away the tools and sweeping the floor clean of wood dust. In his head, he planned out how to approach making the table Mr. Shillito had asked him to create. He needed more nails to complete the job.

Standing the broom in a corner, he bent to collect the debris, inhaling deeply of the wood dust and shavings, a scent he never tired of. He had worked with wood for years. Even on the plantation, he'd preferred the feel of the warm wood to the labor of picking cotton. His master had seen his skill and taken him from the fields to work with Sam, a boy not much older than his own seventeen years.

Stroking the smooth surface of the completed chairs brought back the good memories of Sam. The days they'd worked together as friends. Before Sam's jealousy had sucked dry the fountain of friendship.

Chester allowed himself the briefest moment to grieve for the bond of brotherhood they had shared. Or he had thought they shared. He should have seen Sam's weakness in the way his friend talked of others, and known it would be the way he would talk about him behind his back. Or even in the way Sam's face had grown dark when the master's wife praised Chester's creations more than Samuel's.

But he hadn't seen it until it was too late and the knife of betrayal had not only stabbed him in the back but also cost him the loss of his tongue.

The euphoria of confidence he'd felt the previous evening crashed. With heavy steps, he crossed to the trash receptacle and dumped the debris. Brushing his hands together, he decided to take a walk. Maybe he'd head over to Hostetter & Sons' Grocer, where he had first discovered Cooper, to see if the man's cough had cleared up.

He kept his eyes to the ground. Wagons rattled past on the road, and he kept close to the right side. When he shuffled into the town's square, he raised his eyes to the tall clock tower on top of the bank. It touched the underbelly of dark clouds scuttling through the sky.

"You looking for that lazy, no-account Cooper?" Chester shifted his gaze to find Cooper's friend, Russell, wrestling a huge crate to the edge of a wagon bed. "I reckon he's at home playing 'possum for Miss Jenny."

Chester arched his brows in question.

"Miss Jenny says to me this morning that he's got himself a cough. She was picking up tea for him. Can you believe that?" Russell steadied the crate, not showing the least discomfort at having several hundred pounds balancing on his shoulder. "Prob'ly got those women waiting on him like he some king."

He might have talked tough, but Chester also saw the worried frown that wiped away the sting of the words. Cooper had told Chester Russell was one of the men on the wagon that night. They'd been good friends for years, and from what Chester had observed that first week of his arrival as Cooper took him around town, the two harped at each other every chance they got.

Chester widened his eyes, then clutched at his chest and pretended to drop over.

The black man hunched down a bit, distributing the weight of the crate onto his back. He chuckled. "Yeah. It'd be just like him to leave on out of this world so's I have to handle these crates by myself."

Chester grinned and waved at the man, his spirit bolstered by Russell's bent toward having fun at Cooper's expense. He followed the train tracks along Carlisle Street, bracketed by residences and businesses that must have had their share of rattling windows and train whistles. He couldn't imagine living so close to such a racket.

He made a left onto Madison, and Miss Jenny's house came into view. It would be good to visit with Cooper. But for all the man's chatter, Chester often sensed a hollowed-out sadness deep down in the man's spirit. Or maybe that was just a reflection of his own sadness.

Chester kept his eyes averted from those along the road, mentally practicing the letters Marylu had taught him. He moved his lips to form each one. His ragged tongue lifted and curled over each letter, though he never tried to give voice, knowing they would be little more than guttural murmurs. Sounds that felt, and sounded, so foreign and ugly.

ௐ

Marylu hustled west on Baltimore Street toward Greencastle's Square with the intention of checking on Cooper before heading over to help Miss Jenny at the dress shop. She sure needed help. Real bad. Orders were pouring in. No surprise there, what with the wedding season coming up and the variety show over at Town Hall just around the corner.

She murmured greetings to the handful of people lounging in storefronts. At Hostetter & Sons', on the corner of the square, Russell, the grocer's stock boy, talked to a man driving a box wagon. Marylu stopped and backpedaled as Russell raised his hand toward her.

"You tell Cooper he better get himself over here quick. 'Bout near put out my back unloading a shipment from Baltimore this morning."

"I'm going to check on him now. He has himself a nasty cough."

"So I hear." He bent double to lift a small box and waved at the man he'd been talking to. "That Cooper'll get soft with so much attention on him over a cough."

"What you talking about?"

"Miss Jenny was here buying tea for Cooper this morning. Then Chester came by here earlier." He scratched the side of his face against his shoulder. "He went off up Carlisle. Figured he was going to check on him, too."

Marylu squinted up the street as if she would be able to verify Chester's presence right then and there. She debated whether to turn back to the dress shop and leave Cooper in Chester's care. Seemed to her he might not have gone to check on Cooper anyhow. Lots of places and people in town. Who knew where Chester was headed? She better make sure.

Russell was headed toward the doorway of the store but threw a last jibe over his shoulder. "Haven't missed Cooper's talking. Gets me to do the work while he jaws."

Despite his words, she could hear the smile in his voice.

"Tell him I said that, Queenie. It'll put a spring in his step."

Marylu chuckled, embarrassed at his use of her nickname. "I'll tell him you missed him something awful."

Russell set the box down just inside the doorway of the store and popped back out. "You finally meet Chester?"

"Sure did."

"You ask me, I think he's sweet on you."

"Cooper?"

Russell's grin faded. "Him, too, but I was talking 'bout Chester." He hefted another box and headed back toward the store. "Can't talk. Got to get that pile inside before it rains again."

She watched Russell hold the front door open with his foot as he released the box just inside the door then come back out for another one. He remained quiet this time. Dark eyes brooding like a puppy caught in the grain bin. Probably miffed over Cooper being sick and leaving him with the extra work. But, no, that didn't seem right. If there was one thing Russell wasn't afraid of it was work.

She left the man to finish his job and thanked the good Lord again for the special blessing working for Miss Jenny afforded her and Cooper. Some people who had black servants fired them for the least thing, like that Mrs. Burns east of town. But the McGrearys had grown a bond with her mama and daddy. When Miss Jenny came along, she began helping out by keeping an eye on the child. The McGrearys treated her like family, and she and Miss Jenny became fast friends as they grew up together.

When Marylu shoved open the door on Cooper's little house in the

McGrearys' backyard, the first thing she smelled was the scent of chicken.

Jenny sat beside Cooper as he sipped from a mug. "That you, Marylu?"

"Sure is. Heard Cooper might be getting too much attention." Cooper grinned and continued to sip. "I see you got some chicken broth down him. Thought you'd be at the store."

"I was going to open up this morning after you left here," Jenny said, "but I was afraid to leave him. I did get out to purchase a tin of tea. . ."

"Heard about it from Russell." Marylu rolled her eyes and motioned to Cooper. "You baby him like he was an infant." She went around to the other side of the bed and pressed her hand against Cooper's forehead. "He still has a fever."

Cooper glared at her and swelled up to cough.

Quick as a wink, she pulled the cup of broth from his hand before the sharp movements of his coughing fit spilled the broth everywhere. She handed the mug to Jenny, eyes still on Cooper. "Reckon we should get to calling the undertaker."

He slid his hand across his mouth and narrowed his eyes at her.

"Honestly." Miss Jenny shook her head.

Marylu turned and motioned for Jenny to follow her outside. She waited while her friend handed the mug back to Cooper and told him to finish it off. When she closed the door behind them, the two huddled, speaking in low tones. Marylu said, "He's still got the fever, and I don't think it'll be gone tonight either."

"I gave him the quinine the doctor left," Jenny said.

"The cough's what worries me most."

"Dr. Kermit didn't seem troubled by it."

"In my experience it's the cough that kills them."

"Marylu!"

"It's the truth."

Jenny drew in a breath and cast a glance toward Cooper's cabin room. "Mrs. Levy is coming in today for those dresses." She turned her blue eyes on Marylu, her tone beseeching. "Stay here with him this afternoon while I tend the shop. He needs someone."

Marylu nodded, touched by the woman's devotion. "I'll do that for you."

"Thank you, Marylu. And there is chicken on the stove—"

"Already smelled it and got plans to make a nice pie. You go along and leave things to me."

Miss Jenny tied on her best bonnet, trimmed with a feather that looked more like a bird's wing. "Oh, that reminds me. Chester stopped by about an hour ago."

Her heart pounded harder. "Russell mentioned seeing him."

Jenny's smile widened, and she winked. "I think he was looking for you more than Cooper. I invited him to come back tonight."

Chapter 10

The pie dough got too stiff, and Marylu dribbled buttermilk into the bowl to loosen up the lump. Whatever edginess she felt, she took out on the crust as she slapped and dabbed, then rolled and folded. When she finally placed the crust into the pie pan and trimmed it up, she felt better. Something about her conversation with Russell, followed by Jenny's assumption that she was interested in seeing Chester. . . It would be a wonder if the piecrust wasn't ruined by her rough handling.

"You done thumping around in there?"

Marylu brushed her hands together. Clouds of loose flour lifted upward. She smiled. She'd moved him inside where she could get some work done and still keep an eye on him. Seemed to her the patient might be feeling perkier. "You hush your hollering, Cooper, or you won't be getting any of this here chicken potpie."

"Thought you were slaughtering a pig in there. Pie, you—" the last bit got lost as he coughed.

Marylu beat a path to the little room meant for a nursery beside her own. A good spot to hear him holler but far enough away that he could rest. She pulled him upright as he struggled to catch his breath. His body felt cooler. Something to be grateful for, but she still didn't like that cough.

When Cooper finally quieted, she lit into him. "What you doin' hollering at me through the walls? You need to stay still and shut your mouth, or you'll give yourself another fit." She lowered him to the bed and pressed her hand to his face. "Least your fever seems to have broke."

"How long I been sleeping?" he asked.

"Long enough for me to clean this here house from cellar to attic." She didn't like the way the coughing fit seemed to drain him or how he looked so thin and frail.

"Gotta get up." Again the cough seized him.

Marylu placed her hand on his shoulder. "You'll do nothing of the sort. Rest."

His gaze locked on her, and he raised his hand as if to touch her cheek. For a fleeting moment, she thought she saw something soft in his eyes. But the next second his hand fell away and his eyes shut. His breathing evened out.

Not used to his going quiet so suddenly, Marylu steeled herself not to panic.

She reached out and touched his cheek. Fear gripped her hard as she imagined the grim possibility that Cooper might not make it through this sickness. She'd miss him. Sorely miss him. Miss Jenny, too, would grieve mightily over the loss.

Marylu got to her feet and stretched her back. She needed to set the kettle to singing and put together some tea. She made short work of filling the crust with chunks of chicken, carrots, and potatoes and covering it with another crust. Tea steeped in a mug for Cooper, and she crushed a clove of garlic to spin around in the amber liquid and hopefully take the edge off that cough. As the garlic steeped, she got down the Bible and set it in its place of honor. If Chester got here soon enough, he could read with them.

Miss Jenny chose that moment to open the door.

Marylu formed the words of a cheery greeting as she turned that direction, but the sight of tears streaking her friend's cheeks froze Marylu's feet flat to the floor and her tongue to the roof of her mouth.

Jenny sniffed and forced a smile as she untied her bonnet and removed it. "I expect I look a sight."

"You look like someone sat on your prettiest bonnet."

"I'm being silly." Jenny brushed at her cheeks and smoothed a hand down the front of her dress. "That pie smells wonderful. And tea's ready! Thank you so much."

Marylu wasn't fooled. "You done gushing? You know I always have tea waiting for you, and that pie hasn't even gotten hot yet."

Jenny sighed and Marylu wasted no time in crossing the room and bringing her friend into the circle of her arms. "You tell Marylu what's got you crying."

For a minute she wondered if Jenny would reply. She didn't let go, forcing the woman to relax in her embrace. Marylu had held Jenny McGreary and calmed her tears and fears since the first time she'd scraped her knee on a nail and thought she was gonna bleed to death.

Finally, Jenny rested her head on Marylu's shoulder and released a sigh. "Sally Worth came into the store."

Marylu pulled back but maintained a hold on Jenny's upper arms. "What's she doing in there? She always gets her dresses done over at—" Marylu sucked in a breath. It made sense. And knowing Sally the way she did. . . "She's wanting you to make her a dress for some special occasion she's sharing with Aaron Walck."

It was Jenny's turn to gasp. "How could you have known that?"

Marylu whirled away. "It's just the kind of person she is. She wouldn't come to McGreary's Dress Shop unless it was to gloat about some bit of favor she'd gained with Mr. Walck." As she poured tea into a cup for Miss Jenny, another thing became certain that she had only suspected before. She set the steaming cup in front of her friend. "You really care for him." Sure she had known Miss Jenny thought the man's plight a sad thing, that she felt deeply for the ache of his loss. His late wife had been one of Jenny's favorite customers.

The love between the Walcks had been witnessed by the entire town. Just as the sorrow in Aaron's eyes when she died had been witnessed. Marylu especially recalled his lost look as his wife's coffin had been lowered into the saturated ground, rain pouring down on the crowd of mourners. Jenny had seemed mesmerized that day by the sight of Aaron's hair plastered to his head, his coat dripping wet. The palpable grief. Even as others filed away, he had stayed. Dazed. Probably afraid to leave the gaping hole in the ground. It had taken Marylu a full five minutes to coax Jenny away from the graveside and out of the rain.

Lord, this child's tender heart deserves to be loved by a man who can love that hard.

ꟹ

Chester bounded up the back step, figuring someone inside would know why his knock on Cooper's cabin door went unanswered. Surely the man hadn't recovered that quick.

He smoothed his newly clipped hair down, pleased with the ease with which he could manage it now, and raised his hand to knock. He heard muffled voices and the sound of steps before the door swung inward to reveal Jenny McGreary. Chester's excitement dwindled a bit, but he nodded at the woman and lowered his gaze. Scents of home cooking with undertones of spice swirled in the air, and he breathed deeply.

"Please, won't you come in, Chester?"

He raised his head and caught Miss Jenny's smile. He did his best to keep his eyes somewhere other than her face, but when she placed her hand along his arm and tugged him inside, he couldn't help but gape up into her blue eyes.

She gave him a soft smile and held up a finger to let him know to wait. She hesitated, looking embarrassed, then laughed. "I forget you can hear just fine. Right?"

Chester nodded.

"Marylu's quite the cook. Would you like something to eat?"

Chester shook his head and set his slate and pencil on the table. He would never be able to reconcile himself to the idea of a white woman serving him.

Marylu burst into the room just then. She paused in the doorway to wipe her hands on her apron.

He basked in her smile and the way it spilled sunshine into the cold corners of his spirit.

"Sure he wants something to eat. You ever known a single man to turn down cookin' that ain't his own?"

Miss Jenny chuckled and scooted out the bench across from him. She settled her skirts around her and sat down. Marylu made for the stove as Miss Jenny slid the Bible closer and opened it up.

The women chatted a bit about their days, and Chester listened, content to be in the home and in Marylu's presence. Before he knew it, she wielded a huge spoon over a hot dish and slipped something with a golden crust and the smell of heaven right in front of him. His stomach rumbled so loudly that Miss Jenny sent him a soft smile. He felt the heat flush into his cheeks and bowed his head.

"Now eat up," Marylu said. "I'm going to take this broth to Cooper."

Chester shook his head and pointed toward the back door. He pantomimed knocking on Cooper's door, then shrugged and shook his head.

Marylu beamed sunshine down on him. "You're right in that. I brought him inside to keep a good eye on him and so I could get some things done."

Chester nodded and picked up his fork. He stole a glance at Miss Jenny. She winked at him and bowed her head. The blessing was short, and the whole idea of his sitting across from her and eating a supper seemed a strange dream that left him feeling both uneasy and confident. She seemed in a world of her own as she worked a carrot onto her fork, and Chester contented himself with cutting his chicken into smaller pieces with the side of his fork. Little bites he could manage, though the whole process of eating took him time.

Through the open doorway he could hear Marylu's voice but could not make out what she was saying to Cooper. The old man's responses were punctuated with deep coughs that even pulled Miss Jenny up straight.

Her worried eyes focused on Chester.

When he caught the worry in Miss Jenny's eyes, he set his fork aside and clasped his hands together to indicate she should pray. His aunt had coughed like that right before she died, two years before he'd left to make his own way.

"Yes, I have. It's just so much easier to worry than to pray." A sigh escaped her lips. "Do you believe, Chester?"

The question took him by surprise. His mother had believed, her rich alto caressing the words of the old hymns she used to sing in the late evening after hours of washing laundry or spent tending the garden, or the hundred other tasks of day-to-day living. His father loved to hear his mother's voice, but he never joined in, and Chester often suspected that somewhere along the line his father's belief had been snuffed out.

Where did that leave him? Did he believe in God? Of course. He never once doubted an omniscient Spirit who created the world and everything in it. But he knew Miss Jenny's question went deeper than that, and he didn't know how to respond. At one time he'd been a good man who tried to respect his mama's God, but Sam's betrayal had shaken him. Watching the master fall, witnessing the blood. . . It had been too easy to hate since that moment.

His hesitation must have answered the unspoken question, but Chester shrugged and pointed to his heart then to the Bible.

"Would you like me to read it to you?"

To read. Wasn't that the world Marylu had promised to open to him by teaching him letters? And now a white woman was willing to read to him?

Marylu bustled back into the room. "That man is the most ornery critter I've ever encountered." She stopped and shot him a glance. "Make that the second orneriest critter I've encountered."

Chester's grin was huge.

"I was getting ready to read the Bible, Marylu. Will you join us?"

"I'm thinking we need to go in to the room with Cooper. Read something about hard hearts or that talking donkey of that Beulah fellow."

"Balaam."

"Him, too."

Jenny rolled her eyes.

Chester swallowed hard on a piece of chicken just before his laughter reached full pitch. Jenny joined in. "Oh, Marylu, what am I going to do with you?"

Chapter 11

Truth be told, Marylu had never felt like she felt sitting next to Chester and watching him drink in every letter and vowel. His quick mind pleased her greatly. Yet she wanted to hear him speak. If he never tried, did that mean he couldn't?

As he bowed his head over the slate and worked on a couple of simple words, she went over the alphabet in her mind, paying close attention to how her tongue curled and worked around every letter. If she could teach him how to use what was left of his tongue, it just might work.

When he lifted his head, she inhaled a deep breath. "Let's work on your speech."

Chester flinched.

"It can be done. Some letters you'll have a harder time with, but the rest you'll catch on to quick-like."

He nodded slowly, and she saw the smear of disbelief tighten his forehead.

She reached out and touched his fingers. "We can do it. Together."

His eyes fell to the place where her fingers covered his. She followed his gaze. Beneath hers, the squareness of his hands dwarfed her own. She imagined the power in those hands from all the sanding and hammering, and she wondered, too, if the pads of his fingers would be rough from working with wood or smooth and. . . She snatched her hand away and cleared her throat. "Best we get started."

Chester's eyes searched hers, and she saw a challenge there. Yet she hardly knew this man and had no right to feel anything other than friendship. Not this soon. He'd come to town, the label of "murderer" hard on his heels, and other than working for Mr. Shillito and knowing Cooper, fixing him some food and cutting his hair, what did she know of him?

Sure, he stirred things in her that had lain dormant since Walter, but circumstances were different now. She had changed. Matured. And she would not give her heart away so easily. Weariness settled over her shoulders. It seemed she often chided herself with the same argument, when it would be so much easier to simply allow the feelings Chester stirred in her heart.

Marylu steeled herself and stared at a point over his shoulder. She said the letter A, then formed it with her tongue in a melodramatic way that allowed him to see how her tongue moved. He tried to imitate. The sound was garbled, but she made him try again, over and over. They worked through the first six letters.

He concentrated hard and worked even harder, doing his best to follow her directions. Seeing his torn tongue made her heart sad, and several times it came to her mind to ask him about the incident. About the rumor that he had murdered. But to watch the fervor with which he worked to regain his speech and to learn to read, she reasoned it had to be the idle talk of a bored woman. Mrs. Burns's reputation as a gossip preceded her. And Chester had no way of defending himself against rumors, whether true or not. One day, when he could communicate better, she would ask him about it. At the quick rate with which he picked up on the alphabet and the few small words, she would not have to wait long.

The arguments, for and against Chester, ran through her head as they worked together over the next hour. And new things were added to the list of sensations and tenderness his presence stirred.

The flicker of the lantern light against his skin, smooth and dark like leather.

The way his eyes squinted when he concentrated.

And when he raised his eyes to hers after a particular triumph, the warm glow in the depths of his maple syrup gaze spilled over her like warm honey.

When they took a break from speech and went back to writing, he couldn't seem to remember the right way to hold the pencil. She demonstrated a new way. When he couldn't quite get his fingers into the right position, she took his hand in hers and curled his long fingers around the instrument, suspecting all along that his forgetfulness had little to do with his mind and everything to do with her touch. And she played along. On those occasions when their eyes did meet, she tried to cover what his gaze stirred by concentrating on the slate or ignoring him, but she couldn't deny it to herself.

☙

Evening after evening, for an entire week, they worked, and when she walked into McGreary's dress shop that bright Friday morning and saw Mrs. Burns standing in front of the mirror for a fitting, Marylu made up her mind to draw out the woman more on the accusation against Chester.

☙

Jenny stood with a mouthful of pins, as was usual for her during a fitting. It came to Marylu in that moment that she would have to do very little to coax Mrs. Burns to speak up about Chester. So she sidled up next to Jenny and prepared to get down on the floor to pin the hem.

Jenny stopped her and took the pins from her mouth. "I'm having trouble on that dress." Jenny jerked her head to indicate the table behind her.

Marylu noticed the striped material of Sally Worth's gown. The one she'd come in to the shop to have Jenny make so she could brag about her "date" with Aaron Walck. As Marylu ran her fingers over the material, she saw the ripped threads, evidence of Jenny's frustration. Probably less over the gown than over the owner.

If Jenny didn't want to mess with the sewing of Sally's dress, she would certainly take over. Anything to help her friend bear the disappointment of Aaron's choice. She took a seat and threaded her needle. The first poke through the striped silk coincided with Mrs. Burns's first question.

"I heard you were helping that deaf boy learn to spell, Marylu. Is it true?"

Behind the woman's back, Marylu raised her eyes from the dress, straight up to the heavens. And grinned.

Jenny jumped in to answer before Marylu could give voice. "She has, Mrs. Burns. Chester's not deaf at all, just unable to express himself very well."

"Yes, I know. He got his tongue cut out for murdering his master. Heard the story from one of our servants."

By "servant," Marylu knew Mrs. Burns meant Gladys, their black house servant. Gladys's tongue was as well-oiled as Mrs. Burns.

"He's a gentle soul that needs attention." Marylu took a stab at the material with her needle. "He's smarter than most and knows how to still his tongue quite nicely. It's one thing I greatly admire in a body."

Jenny cleared her throat and tugged down on the bodice of the dress Mrs. Burns modeled. She released a stream of chatter meant to distract her client from the implication of Marylu's words.

But the burn of the woman's audacity singed along Marylu's arms and feet. She bent her head over her work and prayed God would help her not to break a commandment.

Marylu grunted a silent "amen" to her prayer just as the door to the shop opened again. Sally Worth glided in, and Marylu started praying all over again. She watched as Jenny turned to see who had entered the shop and applauded her friend for not allowing a trace of emotion to give away her true feelings on her rival's presence. Instead, Marylu felt the pain for Jenny. The memory of her tears the week before turned her heart inside out all over again.

She dug her needle deeper into the material and brought the needlework closer to her face. If she buried herself in her work, maybe she could drown out the conversation that she knew, deep in her bones, was coming. Sally would shoot off about something regarding Aaron, trying to get Jenny jealous. Or in tears.

Her hands tightened on the fabric. *Lord, have mercy on my soul. Help the law of kindness to be in my tongue.*

Mrs. Burns and Sally chatted amicably as Jenny, still with pins in her mouth, continued along the hem of the unfinished gown. If not for Miss Jenny being in the middle of the thing, Marylu would have heaved herself right out of the chair and gone out back until everyone left the store, but she had to stay. Had to protect her employer from the barbs that were sure to fly and be a tongue for her friend, since Jenny's mouth was full.

"Well, *Miss* McGreary," Sally's strident voice dripped, "why, you must get so filthy down on that floor all day long. How do you manage to get the stains out of your skirts?"

And here we go. . . Marylu huffed and stared up at Sally's wide-eyed innocence.

Jenny did her best to smile around the pins in her mouth.

"You work so hard," Sally continued.

Mrs. Burns smoothed a hand down the fabric of her gown. "But she does create some lovely things."

Marylu silently patted Mrs. Burns on the back for that bit of niceness.

Jenny rose to her feet in a smooth motion and removed the pins from her lips. "There you go, Mrs. Burns. I'll have everything done by Monday. Would that suit you?"

"That is just fine." The elder woman swished around in her finery a minute then headed to the back room.

Jenny followed the woman.

Marylu kept a sharp eye on Sally, as that one made her way ever closer to the place where Marylu sat working her needle. "I'll be so excited to wear this to the show."

Marylu chose to take the high road. "Yes, Mrs. Burns is correct in that Miss McGreary does fine work. You'll hold your head high wearing this frock."

"Oh, Marylu. I'm not used to servants speaking first." Sally gave a little laugh. "I forget how Jenny coddles you and Cooper." She laced her fingers and a little smile bloomed on her lips. But it wasn't a nice smile. "It won't be the dress so much as the man with me. Mr. Walck is most handsome."

A grunt crawled up her throat, but Marylu squelched it before it squeezed out. Miss Sally would think it most unladylike of her. Not that Marylu regarded herself as a lady, but a woman, of course. Even if regarded by others as a servant who happened to have black skin.

"I know how much his attentions mean to Miss McGreary. It must pain her deeply to watch his attention shift to me."

Marylu took another hard stab at the material and poured out every prayer for grace she could think of. Let the woman blather on about her catch. If Aaron Walck thought Sally Worth worth his time, then he wasn't the one for Jenny.

"The material is so soft and so beautiful and so expensive," she purred. "But daddy told me to get what I wanted."

Marylu had no idea why Sally's daddy would be so keen on his daughter marrying a widower, versus one of the other nice and never-married young men in town. Unless it meant money.

"Daddy thinks his business, combined with Aaron's, could be very prosperous."

Marylu hid the small smile that twitched at her lips. Let people talk long enough and they'll answer all the questions for you.

Sally tapped her foot, and Marylu imagined the woman was getting tired of carrying on a one-sided conversation. "Jenny said the dress would be done this afternoon."

She raised her eyes to the young woman. "Done so that you can try it on but not done for you to take home. Miss McGreary'll want to fit you before finishing the dress." She lowered her eyes again. "I'll be finished basting it up in about fifteen minutes."

The sound of voices carried from the back. Mrs. Burns and Jenny made their way into the room. "I'll send Teddy over to pick up the gowns tomorrow morning."

"That would be fine, Mrs. Burns."

Without further conversation, but a nod to Sally, the elder woman glided toward the door and pulled it open.

Tension seemed to build as Miss Jenny turned to face Sally. The smile on her friend's face flattened at the corners and proved, at least to Marylu, how stressful Sally's presence was.

"I hope Marylu has helped you, Miss Worth."

Marylu watched Sally swell up for her response. Something caught Marylu's eye at the front of the store, where the door never had shut upon Mrs. Burns's exit. Instead, another person entered, tall and handsome. As Sally's voice raised in irritation at Jenny, Marylu nodded to Aaron Walck. He returned the greeting almost absently, his attention hooked on Sally and Jenny and the tirade falling from Sally's lips.

"And it's not even done yet! I've got a busy schedule, and now I'll have to wait until tomorrow. I wanted to wear it to the minstrel show at Town Hall. You better hope it gives me enough time to find new shoes!"

Jenny gave Marylu a sideways glance.

Marylu signaled with her eyes at the tall form standing just inside the door, even as she responded to Sally's words. "Told her I'd be done with the basting in fifteen minutes."

When Jenny caught sight of the newcomer, she gasped.

Sally turned. "Aaron! Did you get what you needed at the hardware store?"

Marylu's stomach soured at the hypocrisy of the woman.

Jenny's expression showed nothing. "If you could wait, Miss Worth, I'm sure Marylu will be as good as her word and have the dress basted for a fitting." There were equal parts steel and politeness in Jenny's voice.

Sally sashayed over to Aaron and took his arm. "We were just talking about my dress for the variety show. Want to see it?"

Aaron stared down at Sally for a full minute before allowing himself to be drawn closer to the spot where Marylu worked over the fabric. She didn't see one bit of warmth in the man's demeanor and hoped that witnessing Sally's tirade might help him realize his mistake.

"As I said," Sally's voice held a forced edge of gentleness as she finally replied to Jenny's suggestion, "I can't wait. Aaron is taking me on a picnic." She gazed up at him with more heat than Marylu thought fitting.

Aaron grimaced. "About that. . ." He fidgeted. "I won't be able to this afternoon. One of the tools I'd ordered came in, and Edgar's man is delivering it this afternoon."

Sally stiffened and drew away from him. She seemed at a loss for words.

Jenny took the chance the silence offered her. "Then you can stay and wait for the dress."

"No," Sally spit out. "I won't be staying. Perhaps I'll just cancel my order if you're not able to keep your end of the bargain."

"That's fine," Jenny allowed.

Sally's chin jutted. "Fine." She hooked her arm back through Aaron's. "Consider my order canceled."

Aaron's eyes darted between Marylu and Jenny, finally settling on Jenny. He looked sorrier than sorry to Marylu's mind but allowed himself to be wheeled around and tugged toward the front door. He held it open as Sally made her exit and sent one last pained look toward Jenny.

As soon as the door shut behind them, Marylu lumbered upward and gathered her friend into her arms. Words of praise died when she felt Jenny's shoulders sag and heard the sharp intake of breath that indicated tears.

Chapter 12

Cooper's recovery was slow. Between Marylu, Miss Jenny, and Chester, they took turns checking on him during the day and through the night.

Marylu and Chester worked on his words and speech. He became even more pleased with his progress when Marylu and Jenny could understand his talking, even if the words were simple and the letters not the ones that gave him trouble.

His presence in the home simultaneously gave him a sense of family and smote him for not getting over to Mercersburg to see his mother and sister. But his hesitation, he realized, stemmed more than anything from his desire to return to his mama whole. Or as whole as he could be with only half his tongue. He wanted her to be proud of the man he had become, but he feared the rumors of his master's death had reached her ears. She would be able to look at him and know he had suffered for it. She would understand how far and how long he had run to escape, not only those who searched for him to kill him for the deed but also the specter of his own failure at being a man of worth.

The failure ate at him. As he entered Cooper's cabin, Chester clutched what was in his pocket and forced his mind to review the instructions Marylu had given him that morning. "Make sure he drinks his tea. And give him some firm slaps on the back to dislodge the mucus in his chest." It was the same thing she'd told him for the last three days.

Chester slipped over to the bed, satisfied to see the man sleeping. He turned to leave when Cooper's voice caught him. "If'n I'm awake, you promise not to force me to swallow that tea Marylu's been having you make?"

Chester grinned, noting that Cooper's voice seemed less hoarse than it had in the past week.

"You're a good friend keeping up with me, Chester." Cooper wiggled himself upright in bed. "Marylu's forced enough of her herbal teas down my throat to heal a tribe of Indians."

Chester nodded. He produced the tin of loose tea he'd bought at Hostetter & Sons' Grocer and held it up for Cooper to see.

The old man groaned. "If the cough don't put me six feet under, the tea sure enough will. You know she makes me drink it with garlic?" Cooper shook his head. "She's something else, that's for sure."

Somehow it didn't seem right to simply smile a response and act like he hadn't noticed Cooper's preoccupation with Marylu. At first he had taken Cooper's flapping over Marylu's care for him as a man not enjoying being sick. Understandable. But then he realized that the old man's griping was more to mask other things. Deeper feelings. Chester had seen it in the way Cooper's rheumy eyes followed her every move, and though his mouth got saucy right back at Marylu, it was those times Chester caught him watching her that spoke the truth.

Chester heaved a sigh and raised his hands. He pointed at Cooper then to his chest to indicate his heart.

Cooper shook his head. "Don't start all that. Talk."

He worked up the courage to say what he'd been about to mime, and the words flew out of his mouth, rough and awkward. "You love Marylu."

The old man blinked and stared. His eyes sharpened and flashed, then he dropped his gaze to his hands, gnarled together in his lap. "She's a good woman. Always been the kind I'd wished I'd settled down with, but she'd never have a man like me. Too old for her anyway. I've always known that."

"She care for you." Chester formed the words with some difficulty.

Cooper paused, obviously taking the time to figure out what Chester had said. He reached behind him and punched the pillow. "It don't matter now anyway. I'm too old." Cooper's gaze went sharp and clear and pierced Chester through. "But not you. She could love you."

Chester opened his mouth to form a protest.

"You need a woman like her."

The statement hung between them. Chester shifted his weight and held up the tin as an excuse to leave.

As he dipped water from the dipping box outside Jenny's kitchen, he warred with himself on what to say to Cooper. On how to act. While he had been picking up on Cooper's affection for Marylu, it seemed Cooper had recognized Chester's feelings for her as well. Yet he knew he could never be worthy of her. He had nothing to offer.

But Cooper's words bolstered him, too. If anyone knew Marylu, it would be him. Perhaps the old man thought Marylu might welcome Chester's love, else why would he suggest such a thing?

The whole exchange gnawed at Chester. Long past his visit with Cooper and into the night when he sat next to Marylu and worked on his words and speech, the conversation drummed a positive beat against the negatives. Every time their hands brushed, his senses sparked. He wondered if she felt it, too, and explored her features, her eyes, for any sign of what she felt.

She demonstrated how her tongue formed the letter L, and he concentrated harder. He found the letter particularly frustrating and worked his tongue over and over to get the flow of it. When the sound rumbled up from his chest, his tongue seemed too weak to carry off the rolling sound and it became the letter W. He tried again and again.

Marylu finally shook her head. "Let's let it rest for now. It's coming out better, but we've got other things to work on."

He picked up the slate and began writing words. When he finished cramming the entire surface with most of what he'd learned, he held it up. The pleased expression on her face brought a wave of satisfaction. And when she didn't look away, something changed. Her gaze became searching. Questioning. Fear etched a mark between her brows.

Chester's heart seemed to slow its rhythm then speed up. He felt a million things in a matter of seconds. And he felt nothing at all. Her eyes reminded him of the dark grain of the walnut wood he used to build his master's bookcases down in the South. He lifted his hand to grab the rag and erase the slate but stopped.

Her hand rested on the table, and he lowered his to hers, slowly, afraid his intentions would bleed through her mind and she would snatch away. Her skin was soft, and she glanced down at their hands with an expression of wonder. He inhaled and could smell the freshness of lye soap mixed with the chicken she'd fried for their meal.

In the hotel room, all those weeks ago, she had seemed panicked by his touch. Even through their evenings together, as his own feelings had built, he had wondered about that moment and what it was that held her aloof from him.

But now, here, this moment, she seemed soft, her eyes showing a gentleness way down deep. For him. He squeezed her hand and smiled.

She always seemed so brave and strong. Sure of herself in a way he'd never been. Her strength drew him, and he wondered if what he felt with her could possibly be the elusive thing he'd longed for all his life.

He breathed deeper, easier breaths, and an urgency to give voice to his feelings rose in him, buoyed by Cooper's observation.

"You need a woman like her."

"I love you." The L didn't come out right at all, but she understood. He could see it in the widening of her eyes and the way her lips parted. He gloried in her expression, the effect of his words, and he never felt anything harder than he did the satisfaction of having those feelings spoken out loud.

☙

Marylu felt every inch the woman caught in a summertime thunderstorm. This one assaulted her, not with water but with a deluge of emotion that rolled her over and over.

Chester's face mapped out the wrinkles of a hard life, but his eyes glowed with hope.

Time stood still. Her breath caught. He loved her. The wonder of the words rolled and spun and skipped through her heart. His warm hand squeezed hers, and the words slipped over her tongue, poised and waiting to be released.

Her gaze fell to the slate between them and all the words crowded there. She was transported back in time to Walter's slate, filled with words. The quick brush of his lips after he had praised her for being such a good teacher.

The shock of memory jolted Marylu, and she suddenly understood the burst of emotion that had caused Chester to utter such a precious phrase.

How easy it had been for Walter to love her when he saw her not as a man should see a woman but as a pupil feels appreciation and tenderness for a teacher. She had seen it in the handful of men she had taught over the years since Walter. Then there was always the hard reality—true love would never have allowed Walter to leave her side, but infatuation was fickle and slippery.

And now another pupil declared his love.

And she had this minute to respond.

No words came. At the point where communication became essential, her tongue, healthy and whole, failed. And the specter of her doubts charged to the fore of her thinking. What she felt for him gripped her hard. Still, even after weeks together, she hardly knew him. With his newfound ability to talk, she could now ask him the question that burned through her every time she felt the softer emotions swirl in her heart. She was afraid to hear his answer, for should it be affirmative, she would be crushed. She could never love a man whose moral character she could not condone. She valued life too much.

The question begged to be asked. So simple to give voice and finally put to rest her own doubts. Simple, yes, but staring into his eyes, so hopeful and vulnerable, made her ashamed to believe the flapping tongue of Mrs. Burns over a man whose sincerity she had witnessed time and again. But she had to ask.

"There is a rumor," she said, her voice low and intense, "that you murdered someone."

His expression shifted ever so slightly. Surprise mingled with something else, and his gaze skittered to the surface of the table.

She closed her eyes and swallowed, recognizing what his averted gaze meant. Not the innocence she had hoped for, but resignation. Even fear.

Chapter 13

Chester clutched the slate that Marylu had placed in his hands right before she opened the door for him to leave. Her question hovered, unanswered, between them. An effective barrier that he didn't know how to cross.

He chided himself for not trying and, instead, allowing Sam's betrayal to win, again, his silence. But Marylu's question had so taken him off-guard. In his head, the words of his defense formed. He could explain the situation in detail, but only with great care would he be able to say the words out loud. Dredging up his past. Reliving the chase. The dogs. Loneliness. Days of hunger followed by nights of cold that froze his bones. The explanation itself proved an obstruction, insurmountable. Yet his silence won him nothing.

He wandered through the night, without thought of where he was or what he wanted to do. Mind blank. Body riddled with hurt and embarrassment and a hundred other painful feelings.

When the terrible shock faded, he thought of heading out to Mercersburg. He could stay with his mama and siblings. Find work. No one in Greencastle would miss him, except Mr. Shillito, but replacing him would not be a problem.

Exhaustion weighted his steps. Finally, he tripped and fell. He lay there, wanting to never get up. Instead, he rolled onto his back. Blackness obscured everything, the moon hanging behind a cloud. Walking in the dark, ten miles to Mercersburg, seemed too daunting a task. But he wanted to go. Needed to run just as he had needed to when his master's head hit that boulder.

Samuel's voice rang in his head. *"Better run hard and fast and hope no one ever catches you for killing the master."*

He got to his feet slowly, straightening with effort, and squinted into the dimness. His path had led him through town and along a vast field of trees lined like soldiers. An orchard. Behind him lay the outline of the town's buildings, and he did an about-face. As he placed one foot in front of another, he laid his plans for leaving. He would rest through the night, talk to Mr. Shillito in the morning, then begin the trek to Mercersburg. Seeing his mother and brothers and sisters again. . . Excitement coiled in his stomach and leaked into his limbs, until he walked at a pace that left him breathless.

Antrim House came into view and he slowed, grateful for his room. He would ask Mr. Shillito if he knew someone in Mercersburg who needed a hired hand and even prayed the man might. It would save him time looking for a job.

A shadow moved in front of Chester. His heart slammed hard, and he tensed. When the form shifted again, Chester relaxed. He recognized the slender outline of Zedikiah. For the last week, Zedikiah had sought him out more and more, even sleeping on the floor in his room two nights in a row, but only one of those nights had he been drunk. The smell of alcohol grew stronger as Chester neared the swaying form. He reached out to touch the boy.

Zedikiah tensed.

"Chester." He said his name to ease the boy's tension.

"I'm sick," Zedikiah whined.

Chester wedged his shoulder underneath the boy's and reached to push open the door to the hotel. Zedikiah stumbled through the doorway under his own steam, and Chester shut the door to the hotel then swung open the door to his room. The boy lurched inside, staggered, and fell into a heap. He lay there, sprawled, not caring, already breathing heavily.

Chester sat down on the edge of his bed and stared at the still form. He had talked with Zedikiah about his woodworking, even showed him a couple of tricks he had learned, but in all his days here in Greencastle, he had never addressed the boy's drinking problem.

He knew little of Zedikiah's past, except that his mama had been dead for a year. Clearly, with no one to guide him, the boy had lost his way.

How well he understood.

Except Chester's mama hadn't died. He had left her, and all he had known, because stubbornness drove him to leave and foolhardy imagination told him he would be able to make it. Those lonely days in the South, when he'd first been captured and sold to a huge plantation in the middle of a country foreign to him, he had known a despair so deep and cutting that he had been lured to taste alcohol. Its numbing qualities eased the hurt, but the aftermath of his binges made the drinking a vile thing. Only the ache of loneliness that plagued him outstripped the vileness, and he had continued to imbibe.

His cure came in the form of a whipping, when one morning the drinking caused him to be late to the fields. The master's son had administered the "cure" by laying his back bare with the whip. The young woman who tended his wounds invited him to go with her and the other slaves to the little church down the road. So, on Sundays, with the rest of his ragtag slave family, he began attending with Lily, the young woman. His soul awakened to the comfort he recalled his mother talking about. And he came to believe that his mama's Lord would help him.

And now, he had a young boy falling prey to the same siren song of drink.

Zedikiah's presence here, tonight, meant he trusted Chester, but it would take more than trust to help the boy. Zedikiah needed love and support and courage.

"Zedikiah." His tongue tripped over the Z. He clenched his fists and tried the boy's name again. He couldn't make his tongue feel the letter and, instead, knelt to shake the boy awake.

Zedikiah's body twitched and his eyes opened briefly, unfocused.

Chester pulled him upward and wedged his shoulder underneath to pull him to a sitting position. "Wake up," he commanded.

His strength didn't match the dead weight of the young man, though, and Zedikiah fell back again. A moan slipped from his lips, and he rolled away and curled into a ball, as if hurt.

Chester frowned at the inert form and yanked the blanket off his bed. He shook it and let it float downward to cover the boy. He stretched out on the mattress, willing sleep to come, half praying, half begging God to send the burden of helping Zedikiah to someone else. After all, he needed to leave town.

ଓ

Guilt burned through Marylu's mind after Chester left. By turns, she chided herself for asking the question and him for not answering. He should understand her need to know the truth. Even if he couldn't talk well, he surely knew she was patient enough to listen as he talked or wrote it out.

She paced and prayed and fretted and grew angrier by the minute. It was too soon for him to tell her he loved her. They weren't youths in the throes of romantic notions. At least she wasn't, nor would she allow herself to be. They were two mature individuals who had seen clearly how love didn't always conquer. And her teaching him to write and read and talk didn't make her a hero. It made her a woman who cared and wanted to help.

There was no fool way she would love a man so quickly again. Not after Walter. There were things about Chester she sure liked, times he made her feel that same giddiness she had felt over Walter, but it had been infatuation then and must also be infatuation now.

"What the world you doing in there?" Cooper's voice broke her reverie.

Marylu pivoted. A board creaked. "You hush and go back to sleep. You'll wake Miss Jenny with your hollering." Not that she, herself, wasn't doing a good job of it.

The telltale shuffle of Cooper's footsteps let her know he was headed her way. She sighed and sat down on the bench at the table.

"I heard that board creak a thousand times." Cooper popped through the doorway and stared hard at her. "Thought I was having a dream until I realized it was you making the racket." He looked around the room, eyebrows arched. "Where's Chester? Thought he'd still be here working on his talking."

"He left."

Cooper's gaze landed on her, searching. "Something happen I should be knowing about?"

How she wished Miss Jenny had been the one to come down the stairs. No use shedding water on the table in front of Cooper. He'd curl into a ball of agony if she sprung a leak.

"Marylu?"

If there was ever a serious bone in Cooper's body, he showed it in the soft question that was her name. His tenderness caught at her, and she waved him into the room. "I'll get you something."

"Just stay put." He pushed away from the door frame and crossed to the chair. "You always fuss over me like I'm some old man that can't do a thing for myself."

"You can't."

"Can too and you know it. And the last thing I want is a cup of your tea. Whoever put garlic in tea anyway?"

"It's good for you. Gives you spunk, and you sure were needing it."

"It gives me bad breath."

"You already had that."

Cooper chuckled and shook his head. "Chester tell you he's sweet on you or some such foolishness?"

The sudden change in conversation brought her up sharp. She narrowed her eyes. "He been talking to you about me?"

"Thinks you're a fine woman."

"I don't hold to you two talking about me behind my back."

Cooper didn't back down. "You think women have a corner on that market? Not gossip talk." He shook his head. "Man-to-man talk."

"Ain't you one man short?"

Cooper snorted. "That's no way to talk about Chester." He cocked his head and stabbed a finger at her. "Now what's got you riled up?"

She wanted to duck that direct question. Her skin burned with the shame of what she'd done. Whether she needed the reassurance or not, her timing for asking the question of Chester couldn't have been worse, and she knew Cooper would tell her so.

"Must be bad if you can't be looking me in the eyes."

Marylu did her best not to break down right there, and so, for the first time in a long time, she dared to tell him exactly what she thought. "Not bad." She pulled in a long, slow breath. "I just wanted to know about the rumor of him murdering someone."

Cooper pursed his lips. "Yup."

She tilted a look at him. "What you mean, 'Yup?'"

"He sure did do something. If you wanted to know, you should have asked me."

"Mrs. Burns said that he killed his master, but I should be able to ask him."

"Well you asked him. Why'd he leave?"

She didn't know. Not really. Why did he leave? Shame? Fear?

Cooper sat up straight, his eyes grave. "Got the story from another black who jumped off the train with Chester. Recognized him from years before. What I got from him was that Chester's friend made it look like he'd stolen from the master. When the master went to punish Chester for the deed by laying stripes along his back then cutting out his tongue for lying about it, Chester, struggling for his freedom, pushed the man, and he slammed his head a good one on a pile of rocks removed from the fields. Broke his neck or something. Master's son chased him with dogs and posted an ad to get him returned, but no one never caught him."

Relief streamed through Marylu's body. Then guilt pinched along her spine. And anger. Why hadn't he just told her?

"You've got poison in your eyes." Cooper raised his brows and rubbed his jaw.

She leveled her gaze on Cooper. Chester had fought back against an unfair deed. She'd known something haunted him. In all her days helping the McGrearys run the "station" on the Underground Railroad, she had heard many stories, but, though compassionate, the cruelty had never quite touched her. Perhaps it had been her youthful naiveté. Walter often told her how good she had it with Miss Jenny's family, and though Russell and many of those who had stayed in Greencastle still called her "Queenie," in honor of her deed, she realized now how that one moment of courage failed to hold a candle to the hours and days and years of suffering the people she had helped had endured.

Cooper's cough tugged her thoughts back to him. His jaw worked, and his lower lip trembled a bit.

"You best get yourself tucked back in bed."

He didn't move. When he lifted his face, she sensed that he had made some kind of decision. One that cost him much. She opened her mouth to put the question to him, but his words cut her off. "He's a good man for you, Marylu. You best not push him away."

She stiffened. "What you mean 'push him away?' I didn't push anyone away."

Cooper's gaze went dark and intense, and she thought she caught a sheen of wetness there, but he put a fist to the table and shoved to his feet faster than she'd seen him move in a long time.

"Cooper?"

He disappeared without answering.

Chapter 14

Chester faced the boy who sat, back up against the wall, beside his bed. He swung his legs over the side and sat up. Zedikiah looked pale in the morning light, and from the stench of him, Chester knew the boy'd already been sick.

"Get cleaned up," Chester admonished as he crossed the room. He splashed water from the basin into the bowl and held out a threadbare towel.

Zedikiah moved really slowly but took the towel and got to work.

"Do your mama proud."

Zedikiah stared at him, towel dripping a stream of water into the basin.

"No drink." He handed the boy the sliver of soap and watched him work it into the towel.

When he finished wiping his face, Chester gestured to him to take off his clothes.

As the morning sun lifted higher in the sky, he scrubbed Zedikiah's clothes out behind the hotel, until the water ran clear. He wrung out the material and strung the shirt and trousers along a fence. All the while a little clock ticked in his head letting him know he had little time before the sun would be high in the sky and the heat would make his hike to Mercersburg miserable.

Chester returned to his room, the coolness there a welcome respite from the humidity swelling with every passing minute.

Zedikiah sat on the bed, the blanket sheathing his slender frame. He lifted his eyes to Chester. "She left me all alone."

He had wondered if the boy would respond to his earlier admonitions.

Sorrow drenched Zedikiah's simple statement. "What am I supposed to do?"

"Not this," Chester said then mimed raising a bottle to his lips. He shook his head and raised a finger toward the ceiling. "See you. She sad." He tried the last word again to make it clearer.

Zedikiah shifted, and his hands came out to cup his head. Sobs rolled out in waves.

Chester went to his knees to hold the boy close. How he wished for a tongue fleet with words to tell the boy his story.

Lord? He sent the silent plea for help and wisdom. How could he make Zedikiah understand?

He gripped the boy's upper arms and held him. When he caught Zedikiah's gaze, he pointed at his heart then at Zedikiah's. "Understand." Again, he mimed lifting a bottle and pressed a hand to his chest.

The boy's eyes went wide with surprise. "You drank, too?"

Chester did his best to convey with hand motions and a few words his entire tale, pleased to see Zedikiah's rapt attention. He ended with the repeated admonition to "Do mama proud."

The slender form lowered his eyes and scuffed his feet against the bare wood floor. "How?" he mumbled.

Chester reached out to place his hand on the boy's shoulder and squeezed. "Be man now. Work hard." As his tongue gave utterance, a swirl of thoughts frenzied his mind. *He* was his own man. Had been since the day he hovered over his father's grave and made the decision to leave home. Through the dark days of slavery, he had longed for his family, sure, and he'd found a measure of comfort in going to church.

People offered him comfort. Lily, who had nursed him back after his first whipping, especially thrilled his heart. She had been a strong woman. Beautiful, but matured beyond her years by the work and conditions. Just when he had thought to love her, she had been sold to someone down in Mississippi.

He'd been devastated and had welcomed the new arrival of another slave and the change in position from field worker to carpenter for the big house. Samuel's presence had felt like an answer to his prayer for a friend. Someone to offer support and a distraction from the long days. Then the knife had been turned in his gut by Sam's betrayal.

Somewhere in his days running, he had learned to blame God for that. And though hunted, he was free. His freedom had been assured not by some fancy document with broad promises but by hiding himself day and night. Stealing what he needed.

Chester bowed his head, troubled by it all, and the clock in his mind ticked louder. He squinted into the sunshine streaming through the window. As soon as Zedikiah's clothes dried, he would leave. First, he would talk to Mr. Shillito. Perhaps the man would be willing to help Zedikiah find work.

☙

"What you mean you're taking his place?" Marylu sputtered. She eyed Zedikiah and frowned. For all appearances, the boy seemed sober, and the usual reek of alcohol didn't saturate his clothes. And he was smiling.

"Chester made it work with Mr. Shillito that I could take his place while he took care of some things."

"He left?"

"Didn't rightly say where he was going."

Marylu stared at Zedikiah. She pressed her hands together to still the trembling. "Did he—" She cleared her throat. "Did he tell you to tell me anything?"

Zedikiah bent to haul a trunk onto his back. The weight didn't allow him to straighten completely. "Nope," he grunted.

Marylu stepped out of his path but followed him down the steps to the first level and out to the road, where he loaded the heavy trunk into the back of a farm wagon. It amazed her to see the young man bending his back to any work after the many times she had heard reports of storekeepers finding him drunk in front of their shops or in alleys. "You're doing his job?"

He passed her, nodding his head as he went. "Yes, Miss Marylu." Zedikiah turned his face away, but she could see the tendons in his jaw jump. "Chester wanted me to have the chance to prove myself. Told me to be my own man. Someone my mama would be proud of." He sniffed and ran a sleeve across his nose. "Aim to do just that."

"Then you'll be needing some help."

He stared at her, his brows lifted in question. "Help?"

The conviction churned deeper in Marylu's heart. She didn't know where Chester was or if he'd ever return, but she felt sure God was telling her to stop chiding this boy and start lifting a hand to help him. She felt the bite of her conscience that she should have stopped chiding him long ago and, instead, offered to help him work out a plan for his future. He was only a boy. A confused and lonely boy.

Why didn't I see that before?

If he refused her help now and laughed in her face for the tongue-lashings she'd handed out to him, not to mention the time she'd dunked him in that water trough, then she would have to work it through his head how sorry she was for being so blind to his needs. "We'll start by getting you some new clothes and some food to eat."

Zedikiah's nostrils flared, and he glanced away and licked his lips.

Emotion swelled in her throat, and she felt the nudging of the Spirit. "I'm sorry, Zedikiah. Should have been helping you all along instead of being so pleased to make a spectacle of you." She invited him for supper and made a mental note to work up a new pair of trousers for him.

But biting at her mind hardest was not Zedikiah's plight but Chester's departure. Had she pushed him away as Cooper suggested?

When she finally crossed over to Jenny's shop and opened the back door, she knew immediately that she needed to talk. Jenny would listen and help her see things clearly. She scooted down the short corridor that led to the main room, the voices of customers muffling her desire to burst in and spill all the details, fears, and frustrations.

It took a minute for the voices to register. A man's voice. Marylu tiptoed and peeked around the corner into the main area of the dress shop.

Jenny sat with a bolt of material in her lap and a smile on her lips as she gazed up into the eyes of Aaron Walck.

Chapter 15

It about killed Marylu to stay out of the main room with Aaron there. She wanted so badly to know why he was setting foot in a dress shop. Alone. A thousand possibilities streamed through her mind. Instead of stewing, she decided to take action.

She slipped into the smaller room that was used for the ladies to change and scanned the board wall for knotholes. She'd studied that wall enough to know the pine boards had them scattered all over. She pushed on each knot to see if any would work loose. The first three she tried didn't budge, but the fourth, far down on the wall, popped out into the room beyond. She held her breath in hopes it wouldn't make a loud sound as it hit the floor.

She bent her left knee first, careful not to lower herself too fast lest the pain be intense, and sunk to the floor. As soon as she caught a glimpse of Jenny and Aaron, she knew that knot could have clattered and clanged up a storm and they wouldn't have noticed. How could two people so right for each other not see it for themselves?

Aaron was handing over some coins, and Jenny was taking them with a grateful, pink-cheeked smile. The man cleared his throat. "I hope you have a good day, Miss McGreary."

"Thank you," Miss Jenny responded in a breathless rush that made Marylu roll her eyes. "You have a good day, too, Mr. Walck."

Vexed at having gone to all the trouble to hear their conversation only to catch the end of it, Marylu got vertical and went out into the main room as fast as her legs could carry her.

Jenny gasped at the sight of her. "Marylu!"

"I saw him, and you're going to tell me every bit the reason why he came over here."

Jenny's eyes went wide, and she covered her pink cheeks with her hands. "I should have known you were spying on us."

"Not spying." She sputtered to an indignant stop and realized that she had been spying. "Well, not at first anyhow. Got here and heard his voice. When I peeked and saw it was him, I. . ."

Jenny looked over her shoulder at the wall behind her and the knothole in the center of the floor. Her eyes smiled up at Marylu. "I thought I heard something fall. I hope you didn't hurt your knees too much."

Marylu crossed her arms.

Jenny giggled and rolled up the dark material she had spread across her lap. "I couldn't believe it when I saw him walk in. But there he was."

"Your cheeks are pinker than I've seen them since you had the fever two years ago."

She pressed a hand to her face. "Yes, I suppose they are."

"So you going to tell me what he was doing here, or am I going to have to go ask *him*?"

Jenny released a sigh, and her expression sobered a bit. "It was nothing, really."

"*Nothing* didn't seem to be what I was seeing."

With the bolt in her arms, Jenny got to her feet and replaced it in its spot against one wall. "He said he felt badly about the dress and offered to pay me for the material."

"Seemed like he said a whole lot more than that in the time he was here."

"Oh, we talked about the show. He asked me if I was going, and I told him no, that I had work to do."

"Did he say if he was going?"

Jenny brushed a hand across the striped material of Sally's dress. "He was. He wanted to see Eddie perform again. He admires the man's singing."

"Just like you do."

"Yes." There was a wistful clip to Jenny's voice that wasn't hard to translate.

"He say if he was going with Sally?"

"No, and I didn't ask since she already said they were going together."

"After he saw the way she treated you, I thought maybe he'd be smart and change his mind."

Jenny shrugged. "Maybe he feels it wouldn't be the gentlemanly thing to do."

Marylu snorted.

Jenny made a face at her, but when she lifted the striped material, a wistful expression bloomed.

"You know how much you enjoy hearing that young Baer fellow sing."

"It's a minstrel show, so it won't be all about him." Mirth played along Jenny's lips. "And what's this I hear about you being riled up over Chester?"

"Cooper been running his mouth again?"

Jenny tilted her head. "Cooper cares about you. He always has. And you're avoiding my question."

"What question?"

"The one that's killing you."

Marylu licked her lips and pulled in a deep breath. "I'm worried about Chester. He left."

"Then go look for him."

"I don't know where he went."

Jenny laid aside the striped material. "Maybe you had better start from the beginning." She picked up another piece of plain navy cotton and shook it out. Settling in front of the Singer sewing machine, she worked to position it under the needle and smoothed wrinkles with her fingers. "I'm listening."

"I thought Cooper filled your ears."

"Oh, he did, but I want to hear it from you."

But something stirred around in Marylu's mind, and she determined to have her say on the matter before launching into the story of Chester. She moved to the wooden table where Jenny had laid the striped material. "Didn't you say Mr. Walck paid you for the dress Sally left?" She picked up the basted dress and held it up. Since Jenny was slight of form and shorter than Sally, her idea would work.

"Yes. He insisted."

"Then why don't we make it up for you? You go to that minstrel show and show Sally Worth a thing or two." Marylu clutched it to herself. "Since it's just basted together, we can try it on you, then I'll hem it and make final adjustments." She smiled at Jenny. "You'll be so beautiful that Aaron Walck will leave Sally Worth's side and come a-runnin'."

Jenny's laughter split the air. "Probably not, but it is lovely material. You've done wonderful work."

"Who do you think it was who sewed all those little dresses for you growing up?"

"My mother, of course."

Marylu chuckled. "You believe that if you want, but I've got enough pinpricks in these here fingers to prove otherwise."

Jenny hesitated. Her eyes met Marylu's. "You really think I should?"

Marylu crossed her arms and grinned. "Sure as Cooper's going bald."

With a wide grin splitting her face, Marylu followed a determined Jenny to the back room. As soon as the dress swirled down around her friend's slim frame, she knew the dress was perfect. Jenny gave a little gasp of excitement when she saw herself in the mirror, and even did a little preening. Her friend looked anything but plain now. With the pink in her cheeks and her eyes bright with unbridled joy, Marylu swelled with pride.

"Yes, ma'am. That Aaron Walck is going to forget Sally Worth right quick when he lays eyes on you." Marylu left Jenny to change and took the material straight to the chair in front of their Model 15 machine and set to work on the seams.

As her fingers guided the material, her mind went to Aaron Walck and the wistful expression on Jenny's face as she talked of the man. Shy or not, Marylu was sure he'd seen something distasteful in Sally, else why would he feel badly enough to offer to pay for the material? Maybe he didn't know how to handle the situation with her. He seemed the sort who would be unsure of himself in such matters, or maybe he just wasn't sure how Jenny felt, whereas half the town knew Sally's feelings.

"Seems to me two people can come right out and tell each other how they feel without all this mooning," she muttered to herself. When she realized what she'd just said, she stopped pedaling and let the machine go silent. *I'm a fool.*

The sound of Jenny's footsteps shattered her private reprimand. She knew what was coming. Sadness gripped her anew. She tugged the material around to begin sewing a new seam and worked the pedal to get the machine going. Jenny would nail her hide to the wall. She knew it for certain and didn't relish the conversation. Being a realist, Jenny could give sympathy, but the moment she felt someone hadn't made the best of a situation, her patience became short. Marylu closed her eyes and wondered if she had truly put off Chester. If he would ever return. Was he even thinking about her? Oh, to rewind time and get a second chance.

Jenny poked her head around the corner. "Marylu, I almost forgot, Lydia Redgrave's order needs to be delivered."

"Thought she was going to come get it."

Jenny disappeared again, and Marylu heard her rustling around in the back, no doubt locating the two dresses of Lydia's order. When she reappeared, box in her arms, Marylu took them from her and noted the sparkle in her friend's eyes. Part of her wanted to bring up Chester, but the other half held back and eventually won out. Let her friend enjoy the moment. They could talk later.

Jenny took Marylu's place at the sewing machine.

"You going to work on that while I'm gone?" Marylu asked.

"Yes." Her head bobbed, and her foot began to pump the pedal.

When Marylu got out into the sunshine, boxes filling her arms, she thought of Sally's boldness and what the young woman would do if she ever discovered Aaron had visited Jenny. As she crossed Baltimore Street, a train whistle rent the air and pulled past the square of Greencastle. And a plan formed in Marylu's head. If Miss Jenny wouldn't come right out and tell Aaron Walck how she felt, then Marylu would take matters into her own two, quite capable, hands.

☙

If Aaron Walck thought it strange to see Marylu at his factory, he didn't let on. If she'd had the choice, she would have gotten Cooper to do this bit of "man-to-man" for her, but his being down nipped that idea in the bud. Besides, some things a woman should handle.

No doubt about it, Aaron Walck was as handsome a white man as Marylu had ever laid eyes on. His dark hair prompted a body to think the man would have dark eyes to match, so when Aaron blinked up at Marylu, his light gray eyes, made even paler in the ribbon of sunshine, were a bit startling. And no Sally hanging on his arm. Which is the other reason Marylu had chosen to come to Aaron's factory instead of meeting him at his house or church or, worst of all, at the Hamlin Wizard Oil Company's minstrel show.

"Good morning, Marylu."

She liked the way the man smiled, as if life were too short for grousing about hard work and long days. Marylu nodded and got straight to the point. "I know you've been hoping for Sally Worth's company at the Town Hall show. She's been singing about it to Miss Jenny for the last week."

Aaron's dark brows drew together when Marylu paused for breath.

"Anyways, I just came here to tell you right out that she is a hard worker and thinks you're a wonderful, kindhearted man. She always had great admiration for what she saw between you and your wife."

Since there was no machinery in this part of the shop, only a desk, a potbellied stove, and a coal bin, every word she said could be heard. She only hoped that the three men busily working on crafting slender pieces of wood, as another measured out some pieces against a pattern drawn on the floor, would keep what they heard to themselves.

Aaron grunted and glanced at the men, then back at Marylu. "You came here to let me know about Miss Worth or about Miss McGreary?"

"I just wanted you to give Miss Jenny a chance."

This time the color flooded Aaron's face, and he cleared his throat as he got to his feet. He motioned Marylu outside.

Sunshine steamed Marylu's skin pretty quickly, and she aimed herself at a copse of trees where they could carry on a conversation in the shade, away from listening ears.

Aaron leaned against a tall oak and crossed his arms, an amused smile curving his lips. "Are you trying to tell me to court Miss McGreary?"

"No, sir. Knowing grief the way I do, I can't tell you who to court or when to court, but if you're ready to be looking, I am suggesting you at least look Miss Jenny's way."

"And you're discouraging me from. . .*courting*," the word came out hard, "Sally Worth."

"Since you say it that way, yes. There are much nicer women."

Aaron looked away and swallowed. Then a chuckle broke loose, followed by another. Before Marylu knew it, the man was laughing as if a comedy act was being performed before him.

She'd always known Aaron Walck to be soft-spoken, so his laughter at a subject so close to her heart miffed Marylu. She planted her hands on her hips.

He caught her gesture and held up a hand. "I'm sorry, Marylu. It's just so. . ."

Marylu grunted.

Aaron straightened, though a smile still played along his lips. "Sally and I are not courting. Not even close. She asked me to the minstrel show."

It was as if a load of bricks had slid off her shoulders and toppled to her feet. "Why, that's right good news."

"I accepted because. . ." He averted his face, but she saw the mischief die and the sudden rush of grief that cinched his features.

"No need to explain," she offered. "I understand loneliness."

He nodded. "My wife thought a great deal of Miss McGreary's talent and counted her as a good friend."

"I'm guessing Sally wasn't on her list."

He looked embarrassed. "She was quite a bit younger than my wife."

"Flighty and immature, if you ask me. And if you're a godly man, you won't be trifling with her."

Aaron ran a hand over the rough bark of the tree, but the red in his cheeks reminded her of summer-ripened tomatoes.

She reckoned she'd had her say and decided it best for her to leave. "That's all I came for. No need to be letting on that we had this conversation. I love Miss Jenny, and, if I might talk so bold, I've seen the way you look at each other, like butter on biscuits. And there's no sense in wasting time with all the preliminaries when you know a person's heart. Miss Jenny is powerful lonely, and you being lonely, too, well, it only seems natural." She wiped her hands down her skirts and turned. "Think on it."

Without waiting for his response, Marylu climbed back into the wagon and got the horse to back up a bit before slapping the reins against the nag's rump to encourage a nice clip.

Chapter 16

Chester walked west of Greencastle toward Mercersburg. It would take a long time for him to reach the town where he was born, about ten miles of hard walking by his best guess. He patted the paper safely tucked away in his pocket. Mr. Shillito's friend in Mercersburg went by a name unfamiliar to him. His mama might know the man though.

At some point that morning, he had managed to jam a splinter of wood into his index finger. As he walked, he rubbed his thumb over the area where the sliver had lodged deep in his skin. The pain provided focus as he walked in a void of confusion and anger, hurt and fear. His muscles tightened and pulled, but he kept a steady pace. One foot in front of the other. His heart beating hard both made him feel alive and reminded him that his heart might burst and shatter.

Any guilt over leaving Zedikiah had eased when Mr. Shillito agreed to allow the boy to work for him. Chester had no doubt the man would be good to Zedikiah. By this time, Marylu would know he had left town, and he wondered if she cared.

Her rejection had hurt. Yet what had he expected? Did it matter? The fact was only he knew the truth. Samuel's betrayal had been complete by the detail with which he set Chester up. And the loss of his tongue had prevented Chester from defending himself.

When the question had left Marylu's lips, he had hesitated, in shock. How long had she known? Other questions had crowded his mind, but the slowness of his tongue left him at a disadvantage, and he had found it much easier to simply rise and leave.

He paused at the enormous bridge crossing the Conococheague. Water poured and splashed over and around the rocks in its path. A wide river named by the Indians. To the west, he imagined what the skyline of Mercersburg would look like, and his heart raced with excitement at the thought of embracing his mama again.

Trees, capped with their glorious crown of leaves, rustled in the light, early evening breeze as he continued his walk. Eventually the light of day gave over to night. Wan moonlight washed across fields showing full stalks of corn and wheat. Before long the heat of summer would try to burn away the green of the crops.

His feet burned, but he dared not stop. Drawing closer to his goal stoked his need to get there without further delay. No one would be awake in Mercersburg. Not this time of night. He might be better off sleeping in one of the barns or in the cemetery.

He smiled as his mind went over his childhood spent wandering the fields edged by the Tuscarora ridge, splashing in the ample creeks that mottled the countryside. He wondered if old Mr. Brooks still scared the black children with his stories of ghosts and coming to haunt those who did not treat him well in life. He would be old now, Chester realized with a twinge of sadness, probably in his late sixties. Still working the livery at the large stone hotel in the square of Mercersburg.

Chester's thoughts never ranged far from the scents of the night, the urgency of his pace, and the coldness in the pit of his stomach that had nothing to do with hunger. He paused only when he finally laid eyes on the pale white stone structures of the cemetery that marked the beginning of town. Opposite the cemetery, a stark structure with white cornerstones that contrasted with the brick and looked much like the backbone of a skeleton. The thought made him shudder. An innocent structure seemed suddenly foreboding. It had been a college at one time, but he could see no sign now through the darkness.

He tucked his chin to his chest and kept walking. His legs ached, and his back began a dull protest that started at the base of his spine. He went the opposite direction from town, up Linden Street and back to the cemetery where the blacks buried their own. The one where his father had been buried. It had been that dark day, watching his father's coffin lowered by ropes into the gaping hole, when he'd made up his mind to leave home and go out on his own. He wanted adventure and knew another mouth to feed, without benefit of a man to help farm, meant hardship. He had promised his mama he'd get work and send money home.

He'd been a fool.

As he neared the cemetery he grew cautious. His father's grave seemed to glow brighter than the others, drawing him closer. Beckoning. He went and knelt at the simple wood cross. His mother would never have the money to afford more, but she had insisted on this. Chester ran his fingers over the rough wood, remembering the grief of carving the shape and lashing the pieces together with rawhide strips. He still remembered the feel of the wood against his fingers as he'd stroked down the length of the cross, tears working their way down his cheeks.

Now his knees felt the cool dampness of the spongy soil as it seeped through his trousers where he knelt. Only now did he understand those things his immature mind couldn't grasp then. Deeper truths that only life can teach. Bitter lessons that his mother had hoped to spare him but his youthful insistence had dragged him into.

He raised his face. In the dark of the night, he saw a slight mound of dirt to the right of his father's grave. His heart bunched in his throat. A new grave. To be expected. A cross marked the head of the mound. No flowers.

His eyes scanned the cemetery. Not a lot of room left in the row. The grave could be one of his sisters or maybe even a brother. A child. He swallowed and pushed a fist against his lips. His gaze fastened, again, on the mound beside his father.

Oh, Sweet Jesus, no.

He inhaled a shuttering breath. He had no way of knowing who had been recently buried. No use fretting. He unclenched his fist and forced himself to relax. He took the first step away from the mound and stopped. When he turned, it was as if he was watching someone else. His heart ached for the poor man who knelt at the pile of smooth, fresh dirt. Whose knees became caked with the mud and whose eyes couldn't help but see that the grass had only just begun to gain a foothold.

So near his father. He couldn't shake the thought. His fist closed around a clump of earth and squeezed.

"Mama."

It came out clear, the strained sound having little to do with his tongue and everything to do with the tightness in his throat. His world shifted, and a strange peace covered him with the certainty that his mama now rested. He would not see her again down here. Ever. And with that came the certainty that he would not see her in heaven.

Murder. Stealing. Running.

His fragile peace shattered into a war of fear and self-retribution. He'd been afraid to come home sooner, and that fear had cost him the opportunity to feel her arms around him one more time.

His shoulders shook beneath the burden of guilt. The boy who had left with so much hope and promise returned with nothing more than a coward's heart and blood on his hands. Shattered beneath his insistence to leave home was the swollen promise of yesterday's dreams. Those dreams were all the things his mama wanted for him. For all her children. To rest. To be happy. To work hard and be kind. To help others and be respectful. To love her Lord.

But how? How could he know how to be all that with all the other terrible deeds?

He didn't know how long he knelt there and allowed himself to grieve, but when he went to rise, he was forced to stand for long minutes and rub the numbness from his legs.

When he could finally stumble along, he picked his way down the path from the cemetery to the section of Mercersburg referred to as Africa. His childhood home would be there. Someone, he hoped, that knew him or his family.

Chapter 17

Marylu knew before she ever went to bed that lying down would not in itself promise sleep. If not for the fact that she'd just checked on Cooper and found him doing logging duty in a thick forest, she would have sat down next to him and talked herself into a stupor in hopes of getting things straight in her head.

At least Cooper seemed to be making a remarkable recovery, enough so that he insisted on getting back to his little cabin for the night. When she'd come home to get the wagon from Zedikiah, she'd caught Cooper helping the boy, and seeming no worse for the work. It had made her proud to see Cooper taking such a shine to the boy.

She turned over in bed and debated on heading into the kitchen, but her knees ached too much to get up. She sighed and fidgeted. The frame released a sharp crack that set her heart to pounding. When her heart slowed its pace, the face of Aaron Walck pierced her conscience. She'd been so sure of visiting him and telling him, straight out, about Jenny. In hindsight, though, she worried. If Jenny ever found out about her little visit. . . If only Aaron weren't so shy and resigned. If Sally Worth wasn't so forward and pretty.

Marylu sighed and rolled to her side. That's when she heard a board creak overhead. Apparently she wasn't the only one struggling to sleep. Energized at the prospect of talking, she whisked back the blanket and padded out of her room. At the foot of the steps, she stared upward and debated the climb, but her knees throbbed a protest, so she let out a long, low whistle.

Sure enough, she heard Jenny's soft steps shuffle across the floor. The bedroom door creaked open, and Jenny poked out her head. "You can't sleep either?"

"My knees won't let me make that climb," Marylu whispered.

Jenny disappeared for a full minute then reappeared in a dressing gown. When she came level with Marylu, she mouthed the word, "Kitchen?"

Marylu shook her head and they headed back to her room. She shut the door and sat on the edge of the bed.

Jenny took the lone chair and tucked her legs beneath her. "I saw Zedikiah with Cooper. He staying there for the night?"

"Cooper even suggested it. Zedikiah worked hard this afternoon."

"He sure ate more than I've seen any man eat before."

"He's young. No mama to cook for him. No daddy to care. Why, a good wind off the mountains would knock him flat." Marylu paused. "Better to see him eat than to drink so much."

Jenny's gaze met hers then flickered away.

Marylu's senses came alert. It was the same feeling she'd gotten the night Jenny and Cooper acted so strange. A secret brewed between those two, she was sure.

"I've been thinking," Jenny said, her words slow, her face averted. "With Cooper so sick, maybe it's not a bad idea if we take in Zedikiah. He could help out and it would give him some structure."

"A family, you mean."

Jenny's eyes snapped to her face, tension in her expression. Marylu recognized the minute her friend made a decision, for the stress in her features eased. "Tell me about Chester." Jenny asked, "Did you find him?"

For a moment, Marylu hesitated, not sure if she should let the subject go that quickly. If Jenny knew something and didn't want to share, it would be unfair of her to push. But her curiosity had deepened all the more as she had watched the two share guilty glances and flash warnings at each other over the last few weeks. She'd had about enough of it.

"Marylu?" Jenny's smile was tenuous. "I asked about Chester."

She raised her chin and met Jenny's gaze head-on. If her friend didn't want to share, then the decision was made, and she would not push. Yet. "I couldn't find him. I went every place I could think of. . .nothing."

"Did he hop a train? Wasn't that the way he got here?"

There it was. Her deepest fear laid bare. If Chester left Greencastle to avoid further questions, it would be the ultimate defeat to her heart. It was too much like Walter's good-bye. A simple, "I love you," then gone the next day.

All thoughts of Cooper and Zedikiah, of the unspoken secret Jenny held so closely, faded beneath the wrench of her frustration. Her anger. She closed her eyes, not realizing she was crying until Jenny moved to sit beside her on the bed.

"Don't cry, Marylu. Please don't cry."

"It's like Walter all over again."

"Shh. I'm sure he's around here somewhere."

But the ring of conviction was not in that statement. Marylu buried her head in her hands and choked on a sob. "What is wrong with me that I can't have no man love me enough to stay?"

ꕥ

"Mama knew you'd come back when you were ready." Chester's youngest sister sat across from him on the rough wooden bench he remembered so well from his childhood, in the kitchen that had changed little over the years. Ruth, now a grown woman, held out her hands.

He settled his, palms up, into hers.

She turned up the lantern and pulled it closer, then squinted hard at the swollen part on his index finger. "It's deep."

He nodded and continued to study his sister's calm demeanor.

No hysterics or tears when she had discovered him in a corner of the porch before the sun came up. She merely led him inside and set about slicing salt pork and tearing off a hunk of cornbread. "Don't need to know your story. You're home. That's all that matters to me, and all that would have mattered to Mama," had been the first words out of her mouth as she slid the plate in front of him.

In his halting voice, he had explained a bit of his journey and the part about the tongue, leaving out the part about Samuel and the murder, but she'd already heard the rumors.

"Broke Mama's heart, but she insisted until she breathed her last that her boy couldn't do such a thing unless riled up."

Shame washed through him. Why had he thought staying away would keep the news from his mama's ears? In morbid fascination, Chester watched as his sister lowered the needle to his finger and started to poke around.

Her talk filled the uncomfortable space between them. "She died about four months ago. In the cold of winter. Snowed the day we put her in the ground."

Snow. How his mama loved her snow. More than anything he suspected she loved the blessing of a warm home and her family close.

His sister pulled out the splinter and held it up. Their gazes held. Guilt pressed a heavy mist in his eyes that blurred her image. The next thing he knew, her arms wrapped around him, and she cradled his head against her shoulder. Sorrow poured through him and spilled out on Ruth's shoulder. A grown man, crying on the slim shoulders of his little sister, he tried to chide himself. But Ruth's arms encouraged him to grieve harder. He stayed there until the distinct sound of small feet brought him upright.

Ruth rose and skirted about with the efficiency of a woman in command of her kitchen.

Two small bodies appeared. When the smallest laid eyes on him, her eyes went wide. The older, taller boy put a hand to the girl's arm and tensed as if ready to defend.

"Get on over here and eat. Your Uncle Chester has come back after a long time. You can talk his ears off for a change."

Chester wondered if a father would appear, but the way Ruth sat down and the little heads immediately joined her in bowing to give thanks told him this was a normal routine.

"Your uncle is a little slow in his speech, so listen close," Ruth admonished her children as she broke off a corner of cornbread. She popped the morsel into her mouth, caught the gaze of the boy, and nodded at him to indicate he should talk.

The boy's hands stilled, and his eyes sunk to his lap. "My name is Daniel," came the small voice. "I'm eleven."

Chester reached out and rubbed his hand over the boy's head. He turned to the little girl and tried his voice. "You five?" His tongue felt thicker than it did in Marylu's presence.

The two children stared at him.

Embarrassed at the sound of his words, he sent a pleading look to Ruth. Her attention was focused on the little girl. "You understand?"

The girl nodded. Her eyes flicked to him then at her mama, who nodded encouragement.

"I'm seven, and I'm Esther."

Conversation picked up around the table as the children began to share more and more, shedding their shyness and waiting patiently as he tried to work his tongue.

Ruth dismissed them to their chores, and Esther's little groan of protest brought a swift reprimand.

Chester asked the question that begged an answer and watched his sister's expression sag into grief.

"Eddy." She wiped at the lone tear on her cheek. "He got real sick. Never the same after that. He died within a month."

So much sadness and grief. As Chester moved to touch his sister's hand, he felt the burden of her hardship shift to his shoulders and wondered if this was why God had brought him home again.

Chapter 18

Through the long night, Jenny had offered what comfort she could, but the words stopped penetrating Marylu's discouragement.

She berated herself over and again as she cleaned rooms at Antrim House for asking the question to Chester in the way she had. She'd known the rumors, and she'd known the man. Nothing else mattered.

Or nothing else *should* matter.

But it did matter. To her. And that was what tied her up in knots. Cooper's explanation justified Chester's deeds but didn't excuse it. Or did it?

But what about those gentle eyes? They told another story. Except the shadows she sometimes saw deep in the depths of Chester's gaze, she might never have guessed his past held such violence or that he was capable of anything more than tender touches and teasing mischief.

A streak of brightness came in the form of Zedikiah. At breakfast, his bright, clear eyes had provided the sliver of encouragement Marylu needed. The boy had eaten like a starving man, and she'd been more than happy to see it. At Antrim House, he had seemed intent on his work and content in his skin.

When she finally left the hotel, her thoughts were no more settled than they had been since she had asked Chester the fateful question. She crossed Baltimore Street to Jenny's shop and skirted around to the back door. Jenny greeted her with a preoccupied smile and returned to her sewing machine. Too restless to sit and sew, Marylu decided to tackle cleaning the floors in the back room. There, in a modicum of silence, she gave voice to song after song. Old hymns from church. It helped keep her mind on something other than Chester.

After Marylu finished cleaning half the floor, Jenny appeared in the doorway. "I needed a break from the close work, and it was lonely in there."

Marylu dipped her brush and continued scrubbing, at a loss for words. Tired.

"You're lost in your own thinking and singing to avoid it all, and that spells trouble," came Jenny's observation.

She couldn't look her friend in the eyes. "Not done much else but think."

"He's around here somewhere, Marylu. I just know it. He'll turn up."

"That's what I'm afraid of."

Jenny's eyes widened. "You're afraid he *is* around?"

Marylu didn't know how to explain. She sat back on her heels and wiped her wet hands together. "Don't know what to think. I do know I best be busy, or my head might explode from all this thinking."

"You're worried."

It wasn't the words but the way Jenny said them that stopped Marylu for the second time and forced her to take a hard look at her friend. "It's like I said last night. It's like Walter all over again." She bit down on the words and swallowed hard.

"It's not the worrying that I find so strange. It's your inaction."

This time Marylu was confused. "Done asked after that man all over town. Don't rightly know what else there is to do but pray and wait."

Jenny's skirts swished over the wet floor.

Marylu shooed her back with her hand. "Gonna drag your hem right through—"

But Jenny knelt right down on the floor beside Marylu and grasped her elbows. "Listen to me, Marylu. You've got a chance, don't you see? He's out there. Somewhere. You don't need to be here scrubbing my floors and trying to help me." Jenny's eyes burned into hers. "You need to find Chester. Whatever fear is stopping you from knocking on every door in this town to find him needs to be put aside."

Marylu didn't know what to say. "I did look. You know that. Couldn't find him anywhere."

"Really? I've never known you to give up so easily, or is it you're afraid to find him?" Jenny squeezed her arms. "Walter hurt you. Real bad. But I've never known you to back down from a challenge, and that's exactly what you're doing now. Walter's going to steal your future, and you're going to let him." Jenny's hands fell away, but her gaze remained firm and steely. "That's not the Marylu I know. That's not the woman who risked her life to set free a wagon full of frightened blacks and helped hundreds get north." Jenny's eyes burned into hers. "Whether he knows it or not, Chester needs you. And you need him."

☙

Chester heaved the ax into the stump. He wiped sweat from his brow and breathed deeply of the warm afternoon air. He'd chopped wood for two hours. Ruth now had a long cord of split logs snugged up against the side of the dilapidated stable that housed the cow and horse in the colder months.

Repairs. So many things needed to be done, and he had spent most of his time splitting logs putting it all into a mental list. Repairing the chicken coop would be next. After that, patching the stable. The log house seemed in good shape. For now. He had no doubt the roof leaked in places, evidenced by the water spots on the floor in the room the children shared, but with summer well in place, a few well-placed pots would buy him some time. He could work for weeks and still not be done. And he needed to look up the man Mr. Shillito knew and secure a paying job.

Chester swallowed over the dryness in his throat, longing for a drink. He wondered how Zedikiah fared under Mr. Shillito's guidance. He hoped the boy stayed sober and that someone else would take interest in him. It tugged on him that he should let Cooper know where he had gone. His friend might worry. He owed him some sort of explanation. Chester flexed his fingers. He could write a letter and send it with someone headed toward Greencastle. Explain about Ruth's need, and that his original intention in coming to Greencastle had been to get to Mercersburg and check on the family he hadn't seen in so many years. Cooper would understand.

It was Marylu who wouldn't understand.

Marylu.

Chester stretched upward to relieve the dull ache in his back and pulled a suspender back into place. He closed his eyes. *Marylu.*

"You've got a lot done," Ruth called from the garden, where she worked the plow deep into the ground. Her gaze raked over him then the pile stacked against the shed. "Not too bad for an old man."

Chester stretched, his legs stiff from last night's long walk, too little sleep, and too much wood chopping.

Ruth left the plow and headed toward the house. She lifted her head. "Daniel! Esther!" Her voice rang out across the yard that separated her from the structure where the children worked inside.

Esther's head poked out from an upstairs window. "Daniel's beating the rug, Mama."

"When he's done, I'm wanting him to plow. Your uncle is needing a drink. Get one for him, little gal."

"Yes, Mama."

Ruth glanced back at him and pointed to the front step, shaded by a huge oak tree.

Sweat trickled down his back, and he gratefully accepted the prospect of the cool spot. As he settled himself on the step, Esther appeared with a tin of cold water. He gulped it down, uncaring of the droplets running down from the corners of his mouth. When he offered the empty tin to Esther, she smiled, took it, and scurried off.

Ruth sat beside him, her face in profile. He recognized that profile, a twin to his mother's, and the reminder was a physical ache. "You going to be moving on or staying?"

He gave the question some thought and realized with a heavy heart that the answer had less to do with him than it did with her. If he left, she would be alone again. If he stayed, she would have someone to help. To trust and depend upon.

Writing a letter would be slow work. He could get to Greencastle and back in short order and still have plenty of daylight to finish up work and get started on his search for a job. He could make sure Cooper's cough was better and that Zedikiah was staying out of trouble. Say good-bye to Marylu. "I need go Greencastle. Horse?"

Ruth's gaze missed nothing. "Something there you need to take care of?"

He nodded.

Her dark eyes flashed. "You been wandering a long time. Mama feared you were dead."

Chester leaned forward and cradled his head in his hands. He had hidden for good reason, she must understand that. Coming home would have brought trouble to his family, and he couldn't bear seeing his mother's face and confessing his deed.

No, he had walked steadily west and north in those days, always on the alert, always afraid. It choked him even now, that icy feeling that at any moment the dogs would be on him and sink their teeth into his flesh, followed by their master. Forcing his mind from the past, he lifted his head to the sky.

"After hearing of the master being slain, she reckoned you were too ashamed to come back."

Chester didn't look at her. The truth laid bare his soul. How his mama had known him.

Ruth's gaze turned soulful. "She wanted me to give you something." She pushed to her feet, the step letting out a moan at the release of the weight upon it.

She left him alone. And he had all the time he needed to consider what it might be that Mama wanted him to have. Her favored possessions had been few and precious and probably things better left for Ruth to give to her children. Her Bible, for one, would be the thing his mama would hold dearest. The legacy for her children and a silent admonition to look to Him for direction on the paths they chose.

He heard Ruth's steps drawing nearer and looked up as she came into view. In her hands she held the Bible. A lump solidified in his throat.

She held it out to him.

He shook his head and pushed its cool leather cover away. "Give to babies."

She grasped his wrist, her rough skin scratching against his, and laid the volume on his palm. "She wanted Daniel to have it, but there is something inside that is for you."

Chester's heart hammered, and he saw, for the first time, the way the cover of the Bible humped over a bulky object pressed within. Curiosity ran parallel to the great sadness that threatened to overwhelm him.

"Open it," Ruth's voice, both soft and hard in tone, admonished him.

He gulped and blinked to relieve the blurriness in his vision. He pushed his finger into the cavity where the bulky object lay and flipped the pages open. His breath stopped. A storm of emotion billowed and blew through him as his trembling hand lifted out the snowy white kerchief, edges laced with delicate embroidery. In slow motion he lifted it to his face as images flashed through his mind.

His mother's face the day he left.

The handkerchief clutched in her hand.

His first step toward the road.

That moment when he'd paused to look over his shoulder.

He had gulped and fought his fourteen-year-old doubts. He had never seen his mother cry. She had stood, stalwart and seemingly immovable, eyes resigned to his decision to leave. He knew then that she would not beg him to stay. Would never resort to hysterics or open displays of grief. She would remain detached, yet attached to his heart always. Still, the little boy in him wanted to see evidence of sorrow.

He had forced his eyes forward and kept them on the road a few more steps, before the urge to look back and freeze her image into his brain for the long days ahead gripped him and he turned. She still stood there, her hands lowered now, her features blurred by the distance between them.

Another step. Then another. At the end of the dirt road, right before it turned to wind out of sight, he had given one last glance over his shoulder, and that's when he had seen her, handkerchief raised to her face. He'd known then how much she loved him and would miss him. He had stopped on the path, torn between running back to the only safe haven he had known and making his own way. Only the need to lessen her burden kept him moving, to make more of himself so he could send money back and help her.

Chester's breath rattled as the memories crashed in, and he stroked the soft material against his cheek. The handkerchief, a symbol of her love for him, of her grief and sorrow, and a hundred other emotions that she never gave voice to but were there. . .and all for him.

Chester clenched his fist around the delicate fabric and struggled against another wave of tears as they burned for release. He shoved himself vertical and took quick steps away from the porch, unconsciously heading down the same path he'd taken that day.

And only then did he release his tears, adding to the cloth the salt of his grief that mirrored the salt of grief his mother had released so many years ago.

Chapter 19

Ruth pushed a cup of hot coffee across to Chester. Rain pattered against the glass of the kitchen window. He wrapped his hands around the tin. His stomach full of warm food, his heart full of the residue of laughter he had shared with his niece and nephew before Ruth had shooed them off to bed, bowls in their hands.

She had paused at the base of the stairs and called up a reminder. "Daniel, you make sure Esther sets her bowl right under the leak."

"Yes, Mama."

Chester felt a grin. Some things never changed. Ruth sounded just like their mama, who had liberally tossed last-minute warnings or reprimands up the staircase after they'd gone up to bed.

He could tell the minute Ruth finally relaxed. Her shoulders slumped forward, and her eyelids became heavier than before. The sight of her exhaustion stirred something within him.

"I take"—he stumbled badly over the hard T—"care of you."

Ruth's gaze snapped to him. "No."

He flinched at the hardness of that single syllable.

"You've your own life to live. I'll not be taking you from that."

He struggled for an answer.

She never gave him the chance. "Daniel will resent you being here. He's used to doing hard work." She held her hand out to him across the table, her expression placating. "You've got to understand, Chester. I'm a woman quite capable of making my own way. Daniel and Esther need to know hard work. If you're around it could get too easy."

He reluctantly took her hand, her way of offering appreciation for his offer. And in some strange way, he understood her fear. She didn't want to become dependent on others. Still, he had to try. He lifted his free hand, pointed to her then to himself. "Family help each other."

"You've got a life ahead of you. Live it."

"Just me, Ruth."

Her eyes shifted over his face, and he felt that same deep-thinking demeanor he had often witnessed in their mother. As if she could read his mind and thoughts. His heart.

"You haven't ever loved?"

He opened his mouth to utter a protest, but his throat closed on the word.

"You spent over a month in Greencastle before getting over here. Why? Why wouldn't a man who's been gone so long get right over to the place where his family was when he got so close?"

"Got some work." But the words fell flat when her gaze continued to burn into his. Demanding the truth.

"That's good. Work's good for a body." She released his gaze and stood to open the door. A breeze shifted through the house. It swirled around him and cooled his skin. He lifted the cup to his lips and frowned. The coffee had cooled to lukewarm.

"Go back to Greencastle and work. You can come visit us sometimes."

"I get job here."

Her gaze lifted to some point over his shoulder. "You could. But you don't need to. I do some work for one of the women in town, and she pays good. Other than splitting wood, I can take care of things. Daniel and Esther and myself. . ."

The way she said it got his attention. Daniel. Esther. Ruth. A complete family, yet he sensed she left something unsaid. Another name that needed to be added to the list. He followed her out onto the porch. A lone man came up the dirt road. He lifted his hand as way of greeting, and Ruth returned the gesture. Chester faced Ruth and lifted his eyebrows and smiled.

She jutted out her chin. "He's a good friend."

He snorted.

She flapped her hand at him. "You get on back to Greencastle."

"I'll come visit."

Ruth's smile went wide. "We'll welcome you."

Chapter 20

Marylu set out toward Mercersburg when all else failed. No one had seen hide nor hair of Chester. Several, including Cooper, had told her heading out to Mercersburg would be the place to find him, with him having kin there and all. So, she guided the old horse west on Baltimore Street, at war with herself over not just what she'd say but what to expect should she find him.

Jenny's admonition stuck in her head. Going after Chester was one thing. Admitting to herself that she was drawn to the man meant letting go of hurts and fears that she'd harbored since Walter's good-bye broke her heart. Too, her rejection might mean that he had moved on in his heart.

Out on the road and past the cemetery and then the raging Conococheague, she trotted the horse, forcing her mind away from the problems and doing some praying. Wouldn't do to not let the Lord know her worries and gain the benefit of the peace He wanted her to have. Only when she felt the peace in her soul did she breathe the air into her lungs and realize the good Lord had full control. If she found Chester, she would rejoice. If she didn't, it wouldn't be for lack of trying.

A mile more up the road, with the sun sinking over the Tuscarora ridge in the distance, Marylu saw the outline of a man on the horizon. Walking. Dark skinned. And she knew in her heart who it must be. She pulled back on the reins and slowed the horse. Uncertainty rose, and even though miles separated them, she panicked anew at the idea of seeing him again.

I'm scared, Lord.

☙

Chester left Mercersburg the same way he got there. On foot. Ruth told him many times to take the horse, but he knew Daniel needed the animal to get back and forth to town, and Ruth needed the animal to help plow the rougher spots.

But he didn't leave without saying good-bye to his mama. Evening shadows cast scary outlines on the gravesites as Chester stood above his mama's grave and repented of his youthful foolishness and his cowardly ways. Still, everything felt twisted up inside him. The load of guilt and fear too much for his shoulders. He longed to be at peace again. If going to church meant peace, he would go. The small church he had gone to in the South, sensing his mama's

God so close to him, had failed him somehow. But his mama's voice, her expression unyielding, would tell her children that God never failed.

He closed his eyes, tired in every sinew and tendon. *Lord, I don't know how to do this. Don't even know what I'm supposed to do or if You hear, but I need to know the answer to this here question of mine.*

He moved on in his silent conversation to his mama. He clutched the slightly yellowed kerchief, and when he finished saying a final good-bye, he tucked the square into the little sack his sister had prepared for him and turned his face toward Greencastle.

For better or for worse, he had to go back and explain to Marylu all that had happened with Samuel. He loved her and wanted to believe she would understand his heart and his fight for freedom.

And Zedikiah needed someone. It dawned on him that the burden in his heart had much to do with his belief that God should send someone else to care for the boy. He needed to care for Zedikiah. To guide and help him, and others like him. To be kind, as his mother had taught, gentle, as she had admonished.

Miles down the road, day giving out to darkness, he saw a wagon on the rise coming from Greencastle. He didn't think much on it. One wagon looked much like another. His feet got to hurting, though, and he stopped to rest, grateful the sun was sinking behind him and hoping for a wagon to come by that was headed either to Greencastle or farther on to Waynesboro. Might be he could hop a ride. He raised his face to the wagon heading his direction and wondered if they might be going into Mercersburg with the intent to head back toward Greencastle in the morning. He could sleep in the fields and wait if they'd agree to take him along. Didn't seem much like the driver was in a hurry to get anywhere, though.

Chester rubbed his knees to ease the ache. It felt good to lean over and stretch his back. The wood cutting only added to his overall misery now. He grinned at his aches and pains. In his days down south, he'd worked long hours in the smoking hot sun and never thought a thing about it. He'd grown soft. His smile sagged into a frown. Soft and aimless.

He sucked in the mint-cool evening air and raised his face to the beautiful rainbow colors streaking the sky. When he craned his neck and checked behind him toward the Tuscarora ridge, the intensity of pink and orange danced like a fire on the mountain range, as familiar to him as Mama's corn bread.

Southern sunsets could be as beautiful, but something about this one tonight seemed heavy with promise. He chuckled at the fanciful thought. No different than any other night. Same sun. Same Lord in heaven painting them. Sometimes He let the colors shine through, and other times He let the clouds hide them.

The jangle of wagon wheels crawled toward him as the vehicle got nearer. He turned his head and raised his hand to stop the driver and ask his question, but his gesture froze solid when he recognized the woman behind the reins.

His hand fell to his side, his gaze fixed on Marylu. She didn't look none too happy to see him. Or was that worry tightening her expression?

"You need a ride?"

Her question hung in the air between them. He hesitated. His eyes scanned over her face and searched for any sign of disgust or pity, softness or warmth. He could discern nothing and took a step closer to the wagon. "Saw sister." He gestured over his shoulder to the west. "My mama died."

"I'm sorry. Sorry for her as much as you. I can't imagine losing a son and not setting eyes on him before breathing my last. It must have been terrible for her. And for you."

Her words hammered at him, but the last three softened the blow, and he saw a flicker in her expression that promised warmth.

"Seems we've a lot of talking to do." She twirled the reins through her fingers, then pulled them loose and speared him with a look. "You going to get in this here wagon and get on back with me, or you walking?"

His smile came slowly, building as her lips twitched then began their own upward curve. "Feet hurt." He chuckled.

"Then get up here, and let's go home."

Home.

Sounded good to him.

Chapter 21

Chester moved as if to vault himself into the wagon's bed, but Marylu would have none of it and stopped him. "You sit up here with me where we can hear each other. No use hollering back and forth."

What she wasn't prepared for was having him so close. The wagon seat seemed to shrink mightily as soon as Chester took his seat. When he grinned down at her, she lifted the reins and pulled on the right one to bring the horse around, as much to get them headed in the right direction as to cover the rush of warmth his smile pulled from her.

She flicked the reins in unison, and the horse plodded along. "You're headed back to Greencastle?" she blurted, immediately regretting the words. It sounded desperate.

From the corner of her eye, she watched for his reaction, but he didn't move other than the swaying that came with the rhythm of the wagon. "For Cooper. For boy's sake. Mine."

She blinked, unsure what to make of the words. "I'm not sure what you mean."

"No more running." He swallowed and coughed lightly, and she reasoned his throat must be dry after walking so far. When his gaze met hers again, his eyes were soft. "I been a fool. Samuel my friend. He told master I stole."

He paused and looked away. His chin trembled, and the muscles in his cheeks rippled. "I stole nothing."

It came out choked and strained, and Marylu could feel the depth of his emotion. More than that, she understood it. His friend had betrayed him just as Walter had betrayed her heart. She should not be surprised to see the tenderness of Chester's heart regarding his friend's betrayal.

Marylu released pent-up breath, relieved that her instincts to trust him had not failed her.

"How'd your tongue come to be. . . ?" The words seemed so harsh, but he picked up on her meaning.

"He make it look like I'd stolen. Like I lied. Try cut out tongue. Samuel held me."

"You escaped." Marylu filled in the blank based on Cooper's version of the story.

Chester nodded. "Pain. I went crazy. So hard. Hurt. When knife make cut, I—"

Marylu studied Chester's profile silhouetted against the fading brilliance of evening sky. The cocoa of his skin and the curve of his nose. The shadows under his eyes, cast there by the waning light of day. She pulled back on the reins and made short work of twisting them around the hand brake.

He glanced at her, surprised. She touched his hand. His gaze locked with hers, and she saw the pain there, brought back by reliving his past.

"You listen here," she began. "It wasn't your fault. If you knocked that man back and he was hurting you, it wasn't your fault. Just 'cuz I've lived up here with Miss Jenny's family doesn't mean I've not heard the stories of cruelty. What that man did wasn't right, and Mr. Lincoln told everyone that. Cooper told me some of your story, but I wanted to hear it from you." She paused to gather her words and thoughts. "You're a hero, Chester. More than me because you and all them slaves who suffered and endured were *there*."

"You helped."

She shook her head and placed her free hand against his cheek. His warm skin eased the chill in her fingers, and she closed her eyes for an instant to absorb the touch. When she opened her eyes, she gave him a gentle smile. "I helped. But I've never known suffering like what I saw and heard about from those we helped. Like what you been through."

Tears welled in his eyes, and he swallowed.

Her lips trembled. "Don't you see? It's one thing to see it and hear about it. It's another to live through it and to survive. *You're* a hero, Chester."

A tear spilled down his face, then another. Slowly he lifted his hand and covered hers where it rested against his face. With infinite tenderness, he pulled her hand to his lips and pressed a gentle kiss against her palm.

cs

Chester lowered Marylu's hand and turned her fingers in toward her palm, cupping the kiss he had just pressed there. His heart rejoiced at this woman. At her bravery and her strength and the beautiful words that made his heart soar and dispersed the dark clouds in his soul.

He'd expressed once before his love for her, and those very words rose to his lips now and demanded release, but he held back. What she offered him was enough.

Marylu ducked her head and messed with the reins, and Chester grinned at her embarrassment. Confidence rose like the sun in his heart. To win this woman, he would need to be a man worthy of her.

As the wagon picked up speed, Chester pursed his lips and wondered about Zedikiah. The boy needed the job at Antrim House much worse than he did. Zedikiah needed to feel a sense of self-worth that came with a job well done. Chester stared down at his hands, at the blister on his middle finger, and he realized that, more than anything, he wanted to work with wood again.

"Furniture maker in town?"

Marylu cast a sideways glance at him. "Furniture?"

He nodded.

"A couple. You looking to leave Zedikiah doing your job at the hotel?"

He realized it meant he wouldn't see Marylu in the mornings.

"Sure do have a way with furniture," Marylu said. "The way you got those repairs done at the hotel. Mr. Shillito was impressed, too. He won't be happy to lose you. Cooper will be glad to see you. And Miss Jenny."

Chester looked hard at her profile.

"Zedikiah would be missing you, too."

When she turned her head, he sent her a knowing smile, and the way she jerked her head forward again, intent on the horse's head and then the scenery that surrounded them, only confirmed that Marylu spoke for everyone but herself. It amused him that she found it so difficult to express her own wants.

He chuckled and stretched his arms up in the air. Then, as casually as possible, he settled his left arm on the back of the wagon. Her back brushed up against him with the swaying of the wagon. If she noticed, she didn't let on a mite.

Chapter 22

Chester insisted on walking to the hotel from Jenny's house since it was dark when they got back to Greencastle, and Marylu finally agreed. From her place at the window, she watched him rub down the horse and give it grain, his body nothing more than flashes of white from his shirt and the horse's white stockings and blaze face glowing in the night. She pressed her forehead against the cool glass, surprised and pleased at the swiftness of the change in him. The Lord's doing, she knew. Change always came about easiest when the soil of a heart is tilled and loosened for planting.

She pressed her hands to her cheek at the memory of his kiss on her palm and the way he'd planted his arm on the wagon bench behind her. She could not deny the protective feeling she received by his gesture. She had savored every moment of the ride home, quiet talk of nothing more than sunsets and mountains, crops and farmers.

When he came close to the window where she stood and raised his hand, she sighed and blew out the lantern, then crept through the house to her room. It didn't take long before she heard a light knock. She smiled. Miss Jenny would have heard her and want to know everything. She answered as the second knock echoed around the room.

Jenny raised her lantern. "A smile is what I'd hoped to see on your face."

Marylu stepped back, and Jenny squeezed by her and set her lantern on the table before sliding into the chair. Marylu turned to her friend, hands on hips. "Can't a body get some sleep before doing the talking?"

Jenny laughed. "You wouldn't sleep a wink, and you know it."

Marylu settled herself on the foot of her bed. "It's true enough."

"So you found him?"

"On the road from Mercersburg. He was walking."

Jenny tilted her head. "And?"

Marylu savored the story, as much to privately relive the surge of hope as to tease her friend. "We talked, and he told me about the murder he was rumored to have committed."

Jenny listened to the entire story without interrupting. When Marylu mentioned the kiss, her friend's eyes rounded in excitement.

Marylu hid a yawn, but Jenny caught the action and matched it with a yawn of her own. They shared a giggle.

Jenny got to her feet and reclaimed the lantern. "I'm so happy for you."

Marylu's mind went back to her conversation with Aaron Walck, and something else, too. "Tomorrow night is the show." She needed to get Jenny's new dress finished up, which meant she would need to work extra hard at the hotel to gain enough time to get the sewing done.

Jenny nodded. "It will be fun."

There lacked the ring of conviction in her voice, and Marylu knew her friend both dreaded the night and looked forward to it. For herself, she had hoped that Aaron Walck would break off with Sally Worth and run to the dress shop to ask Miss Jenny, but Marylu realized he would probably be too much of a gentleman for such a thing.

She allowed her friend to leave with a whispered, "Sweet dreams," before she remembered Zedikiah.

"Jenny," her whisper shot through the dark. "Is Zedikiah with Cooper?"

The lantern in Jenny's hand cast dancing shadows across her face. She raised it. "No. He left right after you took the wagon to go after Chester."

Marylu thought on that as she settled down for the evening. The news took the edge of joy from her day as she imagined the boy back out on a drinking binge.

☙

Chester's feet protested the walk down Carlisle toward the center square of Greencastle, where he turned left. Antrim House seemed a long way up Baltimore Street to his tired body. The ride from Mercersburg had been worth it, though, not only to spare his body the walk but also for the promise his conversation with Marylu held. She thought him brave and courageous. It brought peace to his troubled mind.

And when he had kissed her palm. . .

She'd been pleased. He was sure of it.

When he finally pushed open the door to his old room, he was relieved to find it empty of Zedikiah. Surely the boy wouldn't deny him a couple of nights on the floor, since he'd done the same thing for him. Chester removed his shirt and stretched out on the floor, leaving the bed for its rightful owner. He released a deep, satisfied sigh.

In the dark he smiled. Then frowned as a scratching sound caught his ear. He stilled. Silence ensued. He curled on his side and closed his eyes again.

Another scrape, louder than the last, jerked him upright. Dread churned deep in his stomach. Zedikiah's face filled his mind and with it a sense of guilt. He should have known as soon as he found the room empty that the boy would be out doing something he shouldn't. Being a hotel, though, it could be nothing more than a restless guest. Chester strained his ear in an effort to pinpoint the direction from which the sound originated.

Out in the hallway, he slipped the door to the outside open a crack. The sound of ragged breathing came to him. He could make out the outline of someone. "Zedikiah?"

The image jerked in answer to the whispered question.

Chester swung the door wider. "Who's there?"

"Mr. Chester, that you?"

Chester's heart raced. "Scare me."

"I thought you were going to be gone longer," Zedikiah whispered.

Chester inhaled the air around the young man, gratified that it didn't reek of alcohol. He reached out to grab the boy's arm and ended up with a fistful of his shirt. Didn't matter though. With a sharp jerk, he hauled Zedikiah into the hallway, then his room, and shut the door. "Where been?"

Zedikiah slumped into the chair and leaned forward. Chester left the boy to his silence to strike a match and light the lantern. When he faced him again, Zedikiah held his head in his hands and was rocking silently back and forth.

The sight caught at Chester, and he pressed his hand onto the boy's shoulder. "Zed?"

He stopped his rocking and turned puffy eyes on Chester. "I was over at the cemetery."

Chester raised his eyebrows in silent question.

"Wanted to get a drink. Needed one real bad. So I went to the only place I knew I'd be safe. Knew Mama would be there, somehow, telling me to be strong."

A shiver went through Zedikiah, and Chester tightened his hold on the boy's shoulder. Instinctively, he knew the tremor was not from cold but from his determination not to drink.

"You tired?"

"Came back here so I'd be ready to work as soon as I got up."

Chester nodded at the news and motioned to the floor.

Zedikiah shook his head. "You sleep on the bed. Wouldn't be right having you sleep on the floor. Mama would haunt me for sure."

Chester tried to protest, but Zedikiah dived down on the floor and shot him a grin.

Chester shrugged and threw him the blanket, wishing he had a pillow to offer. He'd get one tomorrow. "You sleep. Work hard."

Zedikiah blinked up at him, his puffy eyes screaming that part of the story that his lips did not form.

Chester felt the depth of the boy's struggle for sobriety as much as he did his grief for a mama that loved him.

❧

Sunlight swept across his closed lids and stirred him to wakefulness. Chester cast an eye over the floor, relieved to see Zedikiah still asleep. His grief must have drained him, just as it had drained Chester the previous day.

After pulling on his shirt, Chester toed Zedikiah's side until the young man stirred and opened his eyes. "Clean up," he admonished the boy.

Zedikiah blinked and sat up. He smoothed a hand down his shirt then over his hair.

"Mr. Shillito want good work," he suggested to the boy.

"You back now. Are you going to take over your job?"

Chester shook his head. "I find other job. Work make strong. You man now."

Chapter 23

Marylu didn't see Chester at all that morning. But the Zedikiah she saw swelled her heart. Though still a bit scruffy and definitely scrawny looking, he wore a keen expression that Marylu had not witnessed in the boy since before his mother's death. "You didn't come home last night," she grunted to him as he worked to patch a hole in the ceiling. "I got worried."

"You thought I was out drinking."

Taken back by his bluntness, she nodded. "I hoped not."

His chuckle came out dry and mirthless. "Guess I have a long way to go."

She didn't answer, the words sucked away by the change in his attitude. "Chester here?"

"Yup." He braced himself on the ladder and pounded a few nails into a board. "And nope."

"You aim to drive me crazy, don't you?"

Zedikiah's smile was wide. "No, just trying to get this done fast. Mr. Shillito's got a mess of chairs that need repairs. Chester stayed long enough to show me what to do to repair this hole and make it good with Mr. Shillito. He said he'd let me stay so long as Chester agreed to help me know how to make the repairs."

"Well, you come on over for supper tonight. You're going to need your strength to fight the demons at your heels."

Zedikiah frowned down at Marylu. "You gonna help me?"

The fact that he questioned for one minute her willingness to help smote her. With renewed conviction she vowed to pay closer attention to the boy's problems. Drawn to the need in his eyes, she nodded. "I am. Cooper and Miss Jenny, too. We'll all help you. Your mama would want it."

"I know. Chester says the same thing."

It pleased Marylu that Chester wanted to help Zedikiah as much as she did. She missed the idea that she worked in the same building as Chester, but Zedikiah's diligence at the job showed such great promise, not to mention a natural talent with wood.

At the dress shop that afternoon, she worked the pedal of the Singer until Miss Jenny's dress was complete. She took out scissors and began to clip stray threads from the seams.

"Got your dress done for tonight," she hollered toward the back room into which Jenny had disappeared minutes ago.

Between taking orders and trying to keep up with cutting out patterns and sewing, Jenny'd barely had time to sit down. Marylu grinned. Probably so excited about the show that evening that Jenny couldn't sit still if she tried.

Jenny appeared, cheeks rosy with color.

Marylu held up the finished product. "Let's get it on you. Tell me, too, what it is that has you so tickled."

Jenny took the dress and held it up to herself. She stared at it in the mirror for a full minute. Her eyes finally locked on Marylu's. "I saw Aaron today. At Ziegler's."

"Eyeing those new shoes?"

"I was."

"Did you get them?"

"He didn't have my size."

Marylu shook her head. "I told you you should have gotten them last week in time for tonight."

Jenny turned from the mirror and shrugged. "It's too late now." She set the gown aside and picked up an old rag. Maybe she had read her friend wrong after all. That she set aside the gown with such ease and the fact that her expression became pinched did not bode well.

"I can do that," Marylu offered. "You just keep talking about your visit with Aaron Walck."

Jenny swept the cloth down the length of the display case with its pretty assortment of buttons and trims tucked inside. "There's nothing to tell."

Marylu hesitated. Jenny's sharp tone held rebuke. She raised her eyes to look at her friend and wondered what was causing such turmoil that Jenny would be so sharp.

Her friend paused the rubbing motion and crumbled the rag in her fist. "I'm sorry, Marylu. That wasn't called for. I know you're trying to help me. I just want to go and have fun and not worry about Sally and Aaron."

What it meant to Marylu was that Jenny's run-in with Aaron had not resulted in his asking her to attend the show with him. She had so hoped he would. The day he bought the material would have been fine timing for him to admit Sally was not the one for him, or even today at the hardware store. She huffed. *Lord, in Your time. Not mine.* Though she sure wished the Lord would hurry up anyway.

"You're just feeling a might nervous, that's all. You don't have to tell me nothing."

Jenny's gaze shifted, and her hand began an unconscious circular motion along the display case. "He was kind to me. Even asked if I'd changed my mind about attending the show."

"And you said yes."

"I told him about the dress and thanked him again."

"And you stood there and stared at each other like the two addle-brained lovers you are."

"Marylu!"

"Well, it's true. Just he can't see it quite clear yet. He will, though, you can be sure of that."

"No." Jenny bowed her head, the rag hung from her fingertips. "I don't think he cares. He's probably trying to be kind."

"Kind don't buy a woman a dress."

"He didn't buy it."

"Might as well have," Marylu argued. "He paid for the material."

"Because he is kindhearted. Nothing more."

Marylu hoped with all her soul that it wasn't because he was kind. No, it couldn't be. Not with the way she had seen him look at Jenny that day in the shop. What he needed was another visit from her. A reminder.

Jenny slumped into the chair next to Marylu and covered her eyes. "Do you think there's any hope for me?"

Her friend's voice seemed so small and uncertain. Marylu stabbed her needle into the material and went to Jenny. She put her arms around the woman. "If he can't see the woman that Sally is and the difference between you and her, then you need to be looking elsewhere anyway. I'll not have your heart hurt by a man who can't tell the difference between a woman and a shrew."

"Marylu!"

"Well, it's true. She doesn't hold a candle to you."

Jenny's arms tightened around Marylu. "Thank you, my friend."

Chapter 24

Chester raised his hand to knock on the door of Jenny McGreary's house.

Zedikiah answered with a huge grin on his face.

Heartened to see the young man's obvious good cheer, Chester returned his smile and sat down at the table across from Cooper. The spark was back in the older man's eyes. Only on rare occasion did he cough.

Zedikiah slipped in beside Chester and pulled the Bible close.

"Read?" Chester asked.

Zedikiah raised his eyes from the pages of the Bible. "My mama taught me. Miss Marylu taught her."

Cooper leaned forward. "His mama was quite a woman. Reminded me some of our Marylu."

Chester's eyes rolled to the older man. Something about the way Cooper said that, about Zedikiah's mother, set his mind to roiling. How was it that Marylu had never picked up on Cooper's love for her?

Even the way Zedikiah tilted his head at the old man said something. "You knew Mama?"

" 'Course," Cooper snapped. "Most everyone know everyone here in town."

Zedikiah lowered his gaze to the pages.

Chester felt for the boy. Cooper's irritability seemed unwarranted and uncharacteristic. Or maybe it was a side of the old man he was just discovering. "What reading?" He asked Zedikiah to change the subject.

"About King David and Absalom. He got into trouble because he betrayed his father."

Words froze in Chester's mind. *Betrayal*, a word he understood so well. "Happened?"

"Haven't finished reading it yet." Zedikiah raised his eyes. Chester caught the quick, cautious glance he shot at Cooper. Like a man eyeing a growling, snapping dog.

"Had friend. He betray me."

Zedikiah didn't seem shocked by the news, and Chester figured the boy had heard bits and pieces of his story over the last few weeks. "If you were my daddy, would you tell me?"

Chester saw the earnestness in the boy's expression and understood where the question, in regard to betrayal, had come from. He nodded and squeezed the boy's shoulder. "Be proud to have son like you." He stumbled over the phrase but felt it important that Zedikiah understand his sincerity.

Zedikiah's face crumbled, and he stared down at the Bible again. Chester happened to glance over at Cooper, shocked when he saw the old man fighting tears.

"Cooper proud, too," he added, tapping Zedikiah's hand and indicating Cooper.

But instead of Cooper agreeing, he got up and shuffled out of the room.

Chester shrugged.

Zedikiah seemed nonplussed. "Maybe he's sick again."

Chester didn't think so. Something ate at the man. An idea swirled in his head. He, too, got to his feet. "Where Marylu?"

Zedikiah pointed at the cookstove, where pots bubbled merrily. "She left out the back door to get something from the garden. Probably cabbage." Zedikiah made a face.

Chester chuckled and pushed to his feet. "I'll go. Help her." He stepped out back and into the cool night air. He knew that the garden lay back a ways, to his right. He'd noticed the first sprigs of greenery a couple of weeks ago and seen Cooper working the ground. Now, in the light of the waning moon, he could just make out the form of someone headed his way from that direction.

"When did you get here?" Marylu's voice washed over him as she stepped into the circle of weak light falling through the window. "It's a right good thing I have plenty cooking up in those pots." She stared down into her apron, where a bountiful supply of greens were piled.

"Collards?" Chester questioned.

She nodded at him. "Got some spinach in here, too. Now if you'll just hold that door for me."

He hopped up the steps and did as she bid him to. She lifted her apron onto the table and dumped her bounty out in front of Zedikiah. "Where'd Cooper go?"

"Room," Chester answered before Zedikiah.

Marylu laid eyes on Zedikiah. "You get back to his room and tell him to help you pick through this pile. Separate the spinach from the collards. Wash them up for me, too." She spun on her heel and headed Chester's way.

He threw open the door all over again. "Help?" he asked, as she passed him.

"I could always use an extra pair of hands."

He followed her down the path and out onto the moist, newly plowed soil and across to the patch that held rows of greens.

Chester watched as she leaned down, her fingers tearing at the leaves. "Cooper's a fine hand at planting winter greens, but it takes a mountain to move his body when it comes to harvesting. Guess he feels he's done his work by that time."

He wanted to say something about Cooper's strange reaction but got distracted at the sight of Marylu. The dusky haze that beckoned nighttime highlighted the white of her apron. He swallowed and bent to the work. When he had his hands full, he straightened.

"Bring them on over here to me."

His feet sunk into the soft earth. When he reached Marylu, her apron already pregnant with greens, he dropped the bundle into the snowy white cloth. He lifted his eyes to her face and studied the cheekbones lined by the lowering sun, the maple syrup of her eyes. The urge to kiss her pulled at him, yet he hesitated. Too late, she lowered her face.

"I'll leave the rest for now," she said and took a step back.

Chester's heart squeezed in his chest. He didn't move, and neither did she, but she didn't look at him either. He wondered if she had felt it too, that pull. The moon brightened and shone down stronger on her shoulders.

She gave him a furtive glance then leaned her head back to look up into the sky. "It's beautiful," Marylu whispered. "Makes me wonder if Miss Jenny is having a good time."

He didn't want to talk about Jenny or Cooper or Zedikiah. He wanted to tell her how her skin glowed with a subtle light and how her patience had grown his confidence. That her kind words swelled his courage and made him feel more worthy than he had felt in a long time. That though she discounted what she had done, she would always be a heroine to him. Driven by the deep longing of his heart, he lifted his hand and cupped her cheek. "You beautiful."

Her eyes glowed, and she did not look away as he'd feared she might. "Only one other person has told me that before."

He wasn't surprised by the revelation. "Tell me."

Her lower lip trembled. She could and would have looked away if he hadn't held her chin. It was obvious to him that what she was about to tell him was painful. He dropped his hand from her cheek and stroked down her arm, only to clasp her fingers and squeeze, willing his strength to be hers.

❧

She wanted so much not to cry. Walter was a long time ago and now she had this man standing in front of her, loving her, and all she could think about was *him*. It wasn't fair to Chester, yet something beckoned her to bare her heart to him as he had to her.

"His name was Walter." She swallowed hard. "He was one of the people we rescued that night. He got hurt in the rescue, and my ankle got busted. I cared for him for three months, and we fell in love." She paused and raised her eyes to the sky, dark and full of stars. "At least *I* fell in love," she whispered.

It pained her to say that, to admit it. And yet it felt so right to say those words to the man who had already declared his love for her. She felt his gentle squeeze on her fingers again and stared into his face, surprised to see the tears on his cheeks. How could she have ever thought this man, this gentle heart, could have murdered another man in cold blood?

"He left me. Said he had to move on while he could." She pressed her lips together. "But I couldn't move on."

With his free hand, Chester pointed to himself. "I no leave."

Her lips trembled, and she bit down hard on the lower one. Tears slid out from under her lids, and she squeezed her eyes tight, willing away the torrent that threatened. The soft pads of his thumbs wiped at the wetness on her cheeks. When she felt the palms of his hands press against the sides of her face, she opened her eyes.

"I'm not Walter." And with that he leaned forward and planted a warm kiss on her forehead.

A creaking sound broke the stillness surrounding them. "Marylu? Me and Zedikiah are awful hungry," Cooper croaked in a voice that probably carried halfway across the town.

Marylu blinked up at Chester. "I guess Zedikiah got him to help after all." She grinned. Then, softer, "We need to be going inside."

Chester looked down toward their feet and chuckled. She followed his gaze, not understanding what he found so funny until she realized all the greens lay in a heap at their feet. In all the emotion of the last few moments, she'd forgotten the greens and released her apron.

"Guess we'd best be picking more, or they might think—"

Chester's laugh barked out. "We kissing?"

Marylu ducked her head and made as if to kneel to collect the leaves, but his hand under her elbow pulled her upright. He put his arm around her shoulder and wheeled her around to face the back of the house. "I don't mind them thinking it. You?" The words came out so clear, so full of conviction. His eyes danced with the mischief he must have felt.

Her shyness melted away. "No. No, I don't mind a bit."

She popped through the doorway first, squinting against the bright lantern light. Cooper had resumed his seat, but she didn't miss his raised brow nor Zedikiah's inquisitive gaze.

"Got all these sorted," the boy said. "Thought you were bringing more."

Chester stepped through the door behind her, and she moved aside.

"Were. They got lost," Chester replied with a grin and a wink. When every eye fell on Marylu, it was more than she could take. She crossed to the cookstove and began stirring.

Zedikiah sidled up beside her and placed the basket of collards beside her and another basket of spinach beside that.

"You go wash up. Supper will be done soon."

Zedikiah nodded and relayed the message to the other men.

She got lost in the final preparations of supper and got everyone fed and the kitchen cleaned up in record time, her ear tuned in to the chatter of the men. As she put away the last plate, her mind buzzed about the minstrel show and Miss Jenny. What made her smile was the image of Sally's face when she set her eyes on Miss Jenny's dress. That should set her back on her heels.

Marylu set the dish towel aside and turned, colliding with a solid chest. Chester's hands clasped her upper arms as her hand groped for something solid to steady herself. She latched onto a chunk of his shirt front. Her cheeks heated, and she released him. "You enjoy flustering me," she shot at him.

His mouth curved upward for a second before he released her and stepped away.

"If I had my dish towel, I'd give you a good swat."

"If you two will stop your lovers' spat," Cooper groused, "we can read the Good Book."

Marylu sent Chester a mock frown and stepped around him. Chester settled down beside her, and she felt the same protected feeling she had felt on the wagon seat. His eyes were not on her, though, but on Cooper.

The old man's expression puzzled her, filled with an emotion she could not discern. It was as if the men warred on a level she could not understand. Cooper looked away first.

If Chester noticed anything amiss, he didn't let on and instead tugged the Bible across the table to himself. "Zed read Absalom and David." He flipped back a few pages. "Read about David's wrongs." He fastened his gaze on Cooper. "Father done wrong first. Hurt others."

Marylu wished she understood what was going on between Chester and Cooper. "David wronged Uriah." Was Chester referring to his friend betraying him again? She couldn't wrap her mind around what it had to do with Cooper, though.

Chester used his finger as he read. She leaned in close to see the verse highlighted by his finger and helped when he struggled to sound out the words of II Samuel 12:15. They took turns reading a scripture, until the Bible went to Cooper. He stumbled over the reading of the eighteenth verse and finally passed the Book back to Chester, the scripture unread.

"You getting sick again?" Marylu asked.

He shrugged and shot out a cough. "I'm fine, just not feeling much like reading."

She didn't believe Cooper for a minute, but something about the mulish glint in his eyes told her not to push. Marylu returned her attention to finishing up the Bible reading through the twenty-first verse. She motioned for Chester to pick up reading.

Zedikiah frowned as Chester finished reading verse twenty-five and closed the book.

"Makes me miss my mama awful bad."

"She want you be good man," Chester admonished in his slow, halting speech. "Work hard."

"It took David awhile to really see how much wrong he'd done," Marylu inserted.

"Did I do wrong?" Zedikiah asked. "Is that why He took my mama?"

Chester shook his head. "No. You young." He stared at Marylu with a pleading look.

"What I think Chester is meaning is this. You have to trust He wants what's best for you, and sometimes it means people we love die sooner than we want. We can learn other lessons then. How to grow up and be strong."

"Chester just found out his own mama died while he was away. Should he blame himself for her dying?"

Zedikiah stared down at his hands. Beside him, Cooper shifted and covered his face. Chester's gaze met Marylu's.

"No. I know lots of people who've died," Zedikiah finally answered.

"God comfort you. Make you strong. He be your God," Chester added.

Marylu nodded her agreement. "And we'll be your family."

The boy's brown eyes held the telltale sheen of tears, and Marylu stretched out her hand, palm up. Zedikiah clasped hers. A deep sob shattered the moment. Cooper's heaving shoulders told the tale.

Chester went to the man and braced a hand on his shoulder. "Cooper?"

But all that could be heard were the sharp intakes of breath, followed by shuddering sobs.

Beside the man, Zedikiah looked scared.

Marylu slipped her hand from his, her gaze bouncing from Chester's to Cooper.

Cooper moaned and rocked on the bench.

"Cooper?" Marylu bounced to her feet. "You're not sick, are you?"

Her only answer was deep, aching moans.

She swung her legs around and went to Cooper's side. "Here," she directed Chester. "You and Zedikiah lift him and lay him out right here."

"No," Cooper snapped and lifted his head. "Just let me be."

Chapter 25

Chester touched Marylu's elbow and gave a sharp shake of his head. Surprised by the silent command, she stood for a minute as he crossed the room and flung open the door. He cast a look back at her that begged her to follow.

"This is becoming a habit. Slamming in and out," she said. The night air held a distinct chill that it hadn't an hour before. "What is it?" she asked as she crossed her arms and rubbed her skin to ward off the cold.

He faced her, eyes searching her face. "He loved you. Long time ago," Chester finished.

Marylu shifted her weight. "He told you that?"

He nodded.

Cooper had been in love with her? She set aside her confusion over the direction the conversation had taken and thought back over the years. Cooper had become a fixture in the McGreary household after being rescued off the wagon with the others. He had known Walter, and when Walter left, he had stayed. But love? She couldn't remember Cooper ever indicating love for her. Sure, they sparred and picked at each other. But love? She shook her head in answer.

Chester's eyes drilled into her. He seemed to be searching for the answer in her face the way his gaze raked over her. "Never fight?"

Restlessness crept over her. "You mean, did we ever fight?" Why wouldn't Chester just say outright what he was after? His tongue might be injured and his speech slow, but surely he knew she would hear him out. She pulled her gaze from his and skimmed along the ground, again pushing herself to remember something, anything.

She remembered once, about a year after Walter left, that Cooper's mood had become surly and she'd gotten fed up with his biting answers and snappish comments. "If you can't say something nice, then get out of here. Take yourself on a long walk and don't come back until you're able to talk nice."

Cooper's eyes had sparked fire. "Maybe I will, and maybe I won't come back. Doesn't seem you'd notice either way."

Marylu recalled the way the back wall had shook from the force of the door slamming behind him. He hadn't returned for two full days and two full nights. She'd worried that the McGrearys would notice his absence and blame her. Only the then-young Jenny had asked about Cooper. Marylu had told her exactly what had happened and recalled how the young woman's eyes filled with tears.

But that had been a long time ago and the biggest argument she could recall having with Cooper.

"What?" Chester's voice urged. "You remember?"

She shrugged. "It was nothing. I told Cooper to leave one time until he could stop being so mean."

Chester's eyes widened. "You young then?"

Her exasperation rose. "What are you getting at? What does this have to do with anything?"

Chester reached out and captured her hand. His eyes begged her to understand. "Be patient."

Marylu heaved a breath. "I was young, yes, about a year after we got everyone out of that wagon."

"Tell me."

She bit down on her impatience and reviewed the incident before relaying it, verbatim, to Chester.

"That's it." Chester nodded and he released her hand, caught up in some mystery that she did not understand.

"But it was a long time ago. Surely he don't still love me now."

Chester licked his lips. "Maybe not. No matter."

"I don't understand. He loved me. Why does it matter now?"

"You not love him back. He left. Two nights." He paused, holding her gaze. "How old is Zedikiah?"

She processed the change in subject and how the two might connect. Dottie, Zedikiah's mother, had come up pregnant. No father had ever been named, and Dottie had never said a word, though she always seemed interested in talking to Cooper when she got the chance. Marylu gasped. "Cooper is Zedikiah's daddy?"

Chester steadied her. "Makes sense. He cry earlier. Zedikiah talk about his daddy."

Her mind tripped along the new path of thinking Chester had paved. "It does make sense." And something else occurred to her. "Jenny. She knows something."

Chester drew his brows together in question.

"Her and Cooper have been keeping something secret. I'm sure of it. And it all came about as talk of Zedikiah's been coming up more and more." Marylu realized if it were true that Cooper had fathered Zedikiah, it had happened, in part, because of her. She closed her eyes and renewed her commitment to help the boy. "I didn't know how he felt, Chester. He never said a word. I mean, never *those* words."

Chester responded with a nod and a gentle caress against her cheek.

"Do you think he's telling Zedikiah right now? Is that why you left?"

"No. Not all."

ᔕ

She had saved him again, and she didn't even know it. A trembling started in his chest, and he pushed aside thoughts of Cooper. What mattered to him now was God. His mama's God.

"You said Zed not blame for mama's death."

Marylu's lips parted. "Why, of course not." He felt her question as their eyes met. "Do you blame yourself?"

He had banked himself in the feeling that bad things happened to him because he somehow was not good enough. While some grew bitter, he had grown distant. But more than that, Marylu's statement to Zedikiah had pulled an answer from him that surprised him. "I always thought God was for my mama. Her God." He swallowed, wondering if she understood what he meant.

"He is your God, too. He can be if you open your heart to Him."

For so long he had thought his religion sufficient. He'd gone to the little church in the South because his mama had gone. It always felt right somehow because he knew his mama's faith was real and figured his would be, too. But it wasn't, he realized. Even over his mama's grave, he had known something was missing from his heart. He understood now. It was as he had said to Zedikiah, "He'll be your God."

Tears rushed down his cheeks.

Marylu held out her hand. "Chester?"

"Want Him." He pulled in a shuddering breath. "In here." He stabbed at his chest then brushed the wetness from his cheeks. He didn't know what to do, so he did what he had seen his mama do. He got down on his knees.

Marylu knelt beside him, her tears mingled with his.

Chapter 26

They walked back toward the house hand-in-hand, spent and exhausted, yet Marylu felt flush with the victory Chester had won. The kitchen remained well lit, and Zedikiah sat at the table alone. The sight of the young man squeezed Marylu's heart anew. "You set yourself down, Chester, and I'll serve up some apple cake."

Zedikiah raised his head. A small smile teased along the edges of his mouth. Chester emphasized his approval by rubbing his stomach. He chose the spot next to Zedikiah that Cooper had vacated at some point. They spoke in low tones, Chester's responses short and slow, Zedikiah's longer and more drawn out.

She cut generous slices of the cake and breathed a prayer for Cooper. If what Chester suspected was true, how could the man have denied his own son? Zedikiah's drunken binges had gone on for months. If Cooper had stepped in after Dottie's death, he could have prevented much of the boy's wildness. She considered the dull edge of the knife in her hand and wondered how hard it would be to penetrate the tough hide of Cooper's conscience. And here he had sat, night after night, listening to God's Word and never letting on.

How was she to know he'd go off and do something so irresponsible? And if she had known, would it have made a difference? Cooper was too old for her now and had been too old for her then.

She set the dishes in front of the men and stared at the clock over their heads. Maybe she should check on Cooper, but no, she was too angry. She decided the best use of her time would be to work with Chester on his reading and speech.

They worked for another hour, with Zedikiah getting into the methods she used to show Chester how to work his tongue. When the front door opened, her concentration shattered. Chester caught her eye, darted a glance at Zedikiah, and then gave her a meaningful look.

She rose from the table with a smile at Zedikiah. "Why don't you work with Chester while I go check on Miss Jenny?"

ଓ

As Zedikiah and Chester worked over the slate, Chester's mind worked on another level entirely. The boy had a gift for teaching and seemed to know quite a bit. Probably something unknown to most since he'd spent most of his nights drunk and a good portion of his days in a drunken stupor. He'd put on weight since eating Marylu's cooking and had begun to lose the sickly hollowness beneath his cheeks.

Chester saw himself in the boy. Lost. No one to guide him along the way, resulting in an indifference to people, and to life and all that it entailed. As Zedikiah looked through the Bible for a passage to work on Chester's reading, he felt a stirring in his spirit. Ruth's admonition to go and make a life for himself joined with the stirring and swelled. This would be his life. Marylu. Zedikiah. Cooper, if the man would allow. Perhaps even Miss Jenny, if she welcomed him into the circle.

Zedikiah pointed to a verse. "Read this."

Chester glanced at the chapter. Luke. He began, stumbling over the harder words but taking Zedikiah's gentle correction and forging ahead. As if from a great distance, he heard the same words falling from the lips of his mother when he was but a child. A Samaritan man who showed mercy to a stranger when other men passed the stranger by without more than a glance.

Zedikiah was that stranger, just as he, himself, had been a stranger before this night, kneeling in the grass beside Marylu. God had brought him back from his wanderings and shown him mercy when all else had failed him. He was to show Zedikiah. Tend to his physical needs and spiritual.

He left after reading the passage, the voices of the women assuring him they had much to talk about and Zedikiah's exhaustion visible in his face. Chester wrestled with the hows of doing what he felt led to do. Zedikiah wasn't his son. He could show the young man some things, but he could not take the place of his real father.

It didn't matter, though, he supposed. God would show him what to do one day at a time.

ꟹ

Marylu heard the men moving around in the kitchen but felt compelled to stay and listen to Jenny's excited chatter about the show. What could have been a dismal evening for her friend had turned into a wonderful experience.

"Then he sang another song, and his voice brought everyone to their feet." Jenny rubbed a hand over her forearm. "It gave me goose pimples to hear him. Oh, I wish you would have come."

"Maybe next time me and Chester will go along. Did you see Mr. Walck and Sally again?"

Jenny nodded. "Abigail Cross made sure to point them out as we made our exit." A faraway look came into her eyes. "They didn't appear very excited to be together. Nothing like the excitement Sally showed at the store."

Marylu wondered if it had anything to do with her visit to Aaron Walck. Good, maybe it had begun to sink in. He was headed for a heap of trouble with Sally clinging to him.

Jenny stretched and covered a huge yawn. "I'll be asleep in no time."

She moved as if to rise, but Marylu caught the material of her skirt and gave a light tug. "There's something I need to ask you."

"Ask away."

"Might want to be sitting."

Jenny sat back down on the chair she'd just vacated. "Now you've got me curious."

Marylu gathered her thoughts and rolled right into the subject. "Cooper's been acting strange. Tonight he started sobbing when we were reading the Word."

"Is he not feeling well?"

"Right as rain. But troubled."

Jenny's expression became grave. "And you think I know what's wrong with him."

Marylu noted that it wasn't a question but a statement. "I haven't missed how the two of you keep communicating with each other in a way that excludes me."

Jenny stared down at her hands. "Was Zedikiah there when you were reading?"

Her heart stumbled and picked up speed. "Sitting right across from Cooper."

A little sigh escaped Jenny's lips. "It's not my secret to tell, Marylu. I promised Cooper I'd be quiet about it, and I can't go back on my word."

Marylu understood the position it put Jenny in and tried another angle. "It seems ridiculous, but Chester is convinced that Cooper was in love with me years ago. Around the time Walter was here."

If she expected Jenny to smile and laugh, it didn't happen. Her friend's reaction solidified Chester's assumption. "I've always known it. The way he watched you and talked about you, but you never seemed to care. He told me one night that your heroism had elevated you to a level he could never hope to reach."

Deep in her stomach, something fisted and froze. "That's plain nonsense. I never acted different. Never took to all those who called me Queenie." Marylu cast about for some explanation. Why would her friend think such a thing?

"I've always thought it was your hurt over Walter that made him feel that way. You were pretty distant after he left."

"You know why."

"Yes"—Jenny reached out to clasp her hand—"I understood that, but. . ." She pressed her lips together. "Let's let Cooper explain."

ω3

Chester stretched and greeted the blue sky. A lone wagon bobbled down the street in front of the hotel, driven by a man encouraging a horse that seemed disinterested in arriving anywhere, at anytime. The sight brought a smile to Chester's lips.

He went north on Washington Street and took a left onto Madison. In the distance, he made out the form of another man headed his way and realized it was Zedikiah. The boy had made it through another night sober. He rejoiced in his heart for the accomplishment and, as they pulled even with each other, offered his hand.

Zedikiah slapped his palm against Chester's, but no smile appeared on his lips.

"Ate Marylu's breakfast, and you're frowning?"

The young man paused before replying, and Chester knew it took him a moment to make out some of the blurrier words he'd spoken aloud. "Mighty good cook, that one. Miss Jenny made biscuits that'll make you miss your mama."

Chester nodded and felt a stir of sadness. "Not hard to miss my mama."

Zedikiah winced.

Chester wanted to ask so much more, to sit down with the young man and talk him through the grief and disappointment, but his hesitant speech held him back.

Zedikiah lowered his head and started down Madison, retracing the steps Chester had just taken.

He let the boy go. They could talk later, when it wouldn't risk Zedikiah being late for work.

As soon as Chester set foot in the kitchen, Marylu slid a plate, heaped with biscuits, butter, and gravy, in front of him.

"Been expecting you." She smiled into his eyes.

He leaned toward her so Miss Jenny wouldn't hear. "Miss me?"

Marylu laughed and swatted at him, casting a wary eye over at her friend, but Miss Jenny didn't seem to notice them at all. "She probably got her head in the clouds over last night's doings."

He slipped onto the bench and pulled the steaming plate of food toward him. "Where's Cooper?"

Miss Jenny turned at that. She shared a look with Marylu, who finally looked back at him and shrugged. "Still sleeping." Marylu set a cup of coffee in front of him. "What you going to do now that you don't have work?"

Chester winked at her and waggled his brows. To his delight, she looked abashed.

Miss Jenny crossed to the table and joined them as Chester stabbed his fork into a piece of biscuit.

Marylu passed Jenny a plate with a biscuit. "Marylu told me you gave up your job for Zedikiah. Did you check down at the railroad?"

Chester bobbed his head and took a small sip of the hot coffee so he wouldn't embarrass himself if it was too hot. He found it easier to handle liquids since he'd been working his tongue more and more. Guessed it was getting stronger after all. "Wanted to work for you," he said to Miss Jenny but, realizing how it sounded, rushed to add, "pay for my meals."

Miss Jenny's soft smile spilled over him. "No need for that, Chester. You're welcome at this table any time. Any day."

"Sure could use help taking up greens, though," Marylu added, a twinkle in her eyes.

Jenny stared at her friend, obviously confused. "You could ask Cooper to help you. Or Zedikiah."

Chester guffawed, and Jenny pursed her lips, her gaze darting between him and Marylu. "I'm guessing this is a secret joke of some sort?"

Marylu joined them at the table. "What I've been wondering is what we're going to do with Zedikiah. Him sleeping over at the hotel means we can't keep an eye on him, and Cooper's place is hardly big enough for *him*."

It was the dilemma Chester had struggled with as well.

Miss Jenny's eyes scanned the kitchen, the doorway that led to the rooms downstairs, and then back to Marylu. "He needs a space of his own."

Chester latched onto the idea. He set his fork aside. "Zedikiah"—he held up a finger—"Marylu"—another finger—"Cooper"—and then the third finger went up—"and Miss Jenny. But three rooms."

"*You* need a place to stay," Marylu reminded him.

He shook his head. "I find somewhere."

"What about the shop?" Miss Jenny brightened. "You and Zedikiah can stay there. There's that big back room that we use for storage, but I think it could be turned into a decent bedroom."

"I work for place," he said, then folded his hands and lay his head against them to indicate he meant a place to sleep. It would work though, he knew. He could keep an eye on Zedikiah, and the boy could help him with his reading and speech.

"And I'll feed us all up real good." Marylu threw out the offer, her expression showing her deep satisfaction at the prospect.

Chester beamed at her, his heart full.

☙

Underlying her happiness, Marylu felt concern for Cooper and Zedikiah. The old man never did come out of his room to eat. At her insistence, Miss Jenny had knocked on his door to make sure he was fine. But Zedikiah, too, had seemed sad, and Marylu hoped it didn't mean the boy was going to seek out the only comfort he'd known for all these years.

As Miss Jenny worked a beautiful blue silk through the sewing machine at the dress shop and Chester worked on hammering together a wall to separate the storage room into two rooms, Marylu put her worry to words. "If that Cooper doesn't show himself tonight, I'm going to drag him out of there."

Jenny's foot stopped pedaling the machine. "Where did that come from?"

Marylu opened her mouth, then pressed her hand to her lips and swallowed hard over the lump there. Through the night and all morning she had dodged the guilt, but now, with the afternoon settling into a slower pace, it came rushing down on her. "I just wish I'd known. Maybe. . ."

Jenny must have sensed her despair, for she stood and came to her. "Cooper made his choice, Marylu. And I'm sure he will talk to us, but give him some time. I think the Lord is dealing with him."

It took Marylu by surprise, but it made sense. Between Cooper's sickness and his strange behavior of late, God's hand and timing had to be acknowledged and respected.

The door to the shop opened, and Marylu raised her head to see Aaron Walck come through.

Behind her, Jenny did a little gasp. She slipped out from behind Marylu and approached the man as she would any other customer. "Can I help you?"

"Yes." His eyes skipped over her face then away. "I—I—" He stared at Marylu a minute.

She nodded at him and raised her brows.

A small smile tugged at his lips, and he inclined his head, cleared his throat, and locked his gaze on Jenny. "I came to talk to you, Miss McGreary."

Chester ambled into the room, holding a fistful of nails, a question in his eyes. When he saw Aaron and Jenny, his mouth curved into a small smile.

Marylu placed a finger against his lips and backed him toward the storage room.

He grinned down at her. "Miss Jenny have caller?"

"Yes, and I'm not about to let you go out there and ask her a question about boards or nails or anything else to mess up what he's come to do."

Chester arched an eyebrow at her. "What he come to do? You know something?"

Marylu ducked her head and wondered how it was the man could so easily read her. It was at once troubling and reassuring. "She's loved him for a long time."

"Widower?"

"Yes. But another woman had her eye on him." She explained about Sally and her own visit to Aaron's store.

Chester chuckled and shook his head.

She pounded him on the arm. "I don't want her to be lonely anymore."

Something shifted in his expression. His gaze went intense. His hand came up to cup her chin. "I don't want to be lonely."

Her heart tripped, and a song rose to her lips that had nothing to do with music or words but joy. Caught in the light of his warm gaze, she shivered and gave her head a little shake. "I don't want to be either."

"Will you be my woman?"

Marylu stiffened, cautious about his use of the term *woman*.

Chester chuckled and pressed his thumb against her lips. "My queen?"

She drew air into her lungs and held her breath as he opened his mouth again.

"My wife?"

Chapter 27

Two skillets, filled with lard, popped and spattered as the batter for doughnuts hit the hot grease. The two women grinned at each other as the implication of the skillets and the hot grease dawned on both of them.

"And I thought you said you'd never pop and spatter like hot grease in a skillet." Jenny's eyes twinkled.

"Seems to me you're spattering, too."

Jenny chuckled. "I can't believe it, Marylu." She put another spoonful of lard into each skillet. "Are you sure you can handle that dress order by yourself Tuesday night?"

It had been a question Jenny had asked three times. "I'm sure as that grease popping."

They burst into giggles.

"Won't they be surprised to find doughnuts for dessert?" Jenny asked. "Do you think it was too forward of me to ask him over for supper tonight?"

"It wasn't your idea. It was mine. Chester said Mr. Walck looked surprised but excited. Probably sick of his own cooking." Marylu ducked to see out the kitchen window. The sun had long ago sunk toward the west, but enough light still lit the sky for her to be able to see into the backyard. No sign of anyone headed toward the door. "I hope Zedikiah gets here soon."

"Chester will probably think to swing by and check in on him. Seems he should have been back from Mr. Walck's shop long before now."

Marylu took down the tin of cinnamon and put two pinches of the spice into the batter. "They did seem to take to each other." She secretly hoped that Mr. Walck would offer Chester a job.

"Aaron—" Jenny's gaze darted to Marylu's. A blush crept over the woman's cheeks. "I mean, Mr. Walck." She cleared her throat and busied herself with gathering plates. "I think he was impressed with Chester's knowledge of wood."

Mr. Walck's departure from the shop had led to a flurry of words and excited squeals between the two women. Jenny had shared the reason for their visitor's appearance. "He told Sally he didn't think it would work out between them and that he couldn't put me out of his mind."

The news swelled Marylu's heart to bursting, and when she told Jenny that Chester had proposed, Jenny wanted all the details. They had chattered throughout the afternoon, even rejoicing over an order for a trousseau that meant steady work.

Marylu sprinkled a light coating of flour on the work surface and began to roll out the dough. "Grease ready?"

Together they made short work of frying the doughnuts. A platter of golden rounds, sprinkled with cinnamon sugar, sat on the table, dead center. Marylu frowned at the door and checked on the chicken she had baked. "If those men don't get here soon, that chicken's going to be tough as an old rooster."

Wagon wheels rattled, and Marylu and Jenny both stilled to listen close. Marylu swung the back door open and squinted into the growing darkness. "No use guessing when we can look for ourselves." But when her eyes adjusted, she saw the wagon pull up and Mr. Walck and Chester helping down a wobbling Zedikiah. "Oh no."

Jenny hurried up beside her, glanced at the situation, then turned and stared at the table. "Where do we put him?"

"He can't lay out on the floor. Put him in my room," Marylu urged the men as they neared. The smell of alcohol was heavy on Zedikiah.

Miss Jenny's nose wrinkled.

Marylu led the way to her room. They settled Zedikiah down onto the bed.

Chester pulled his feet up. He looked at Marylu with sorrowful eyes. "Shouldn't have left him alone."

She recognized his agony, as it mirrored her own spirit. Even though she thought of Zedikiah as a boy, she knew he was a man by most standards. His drinking would destroy him, as she had seen it destroy countless others. "All we can do is pray and keep an eye on him. Does Mr. Shillito know about this?"

Chester nodded, and Mr. Walck spoke up for the first time. "It's why we were late. Apparently Zedikiah left early, before he'd taken care of some repairs on the sagging overhang that the buggies park under to unload. Chester and I stayed to finish up the project."

"Is Mr. Shillito going to fire him?"

Chester shook his head. "No. We told him"—he lifted his hand as if it held a bottle—"that we try to help him."

"He was kind about the situation," Mr. Walck assured. "But we assured Shillito that if he'd give Zedikiah the chance, we would help out should he go out on a binge again. I think he wanted to help the boy as much as we do."

Touched by Aaron's inclusion and Mr. Shillito's compassion, Marylu turned and swallowed to ease the ache in her throat. "Sure appreciate it. Let me get you some coffee."

When Marylu felt her wrist enclosed by a hand, she turned to see Chester's eyes begging her to wait. She caught Mr. Walck's gaze. "You go on ahead to the kitchen. Miss Jenny's in there and most likely got a pot boiling."

☙

Chester berated himself over and over for not talking to Zedikiah that morning. Surely the boy would have opened up about whatever it was that troubled him. As Mr. Walck left him alone with Marylu, he knew what he was about to demand would place a great strain on the household that had taken him in, but his conscience told him he had no choice. "Cooper?" he put the question to Marylu.

"He's not come out all morning."

He tugged on her wrist. "Talk to him."

Marylu stiffened. "I don't know. Shouldn't we wait until he's ready to talk? Miss Jenny thought the Lord might be dealing with him."

Chester shot a look over at the unconscious Zedikiah then back to her. *Lord, what do I do?*

It had become a rote prayer offered up when they found Zedikiah drunk, then again and again as they finished up the work and brought the boy to Jenny's house. It had been easy to blame himself. For a minute, his senses flared with the remembered scent of rain and wet fields. His mind flashed to the image of cotton, rows and rows, all edged by woods. He could feel the grip of Samuel's hands holding one of his arms and Old Bob the other. A light breeze ruffled the shirt, rent beneath the whipping he'd endured, edges encrusted in blood.

He had been made to kneel for this. The final punishment. His master stood over him, knife poised. Samuel had been the one to hold his jaws open as the master, blade in hand, had worked the edge under his tongue. His muscles had bunched, and his arms strained, and he knew he could not let them do this to him. As the blade began the slice, something inside his head had exploded. With a heave, he butted his head upward, into his persecutor's jaw. The master had fallen backward, his head dashed against a large boulder. Samuel and Old Bob were both thrown aside by the force of his upward thrust. He stood over the white man and watched the blood trickle from his mouth. The paleness of the face gone even more pale.

And then the voice. Samuel's. "Look what you done. You better run. Better run hard and fast and hope no one ever catches you for killing the master."

Chester had done just that. Terrified. Fearful of getting caught and put to death. Of hanging. He had run far and hidden himself. Then the lies had begun. Covering his true identity. Cowering in the shadows as law officers closed in.

He felt now as he had felt then. Helpless. Fearful. But this time he felt those traits for a person other than himself.

"Chester?" Marylu's hand tugged at his shirt.

He made a motion toward the door. "Let's see Cooper." Whatever else he was, he would not allow Zedikiah to wallow in his grief. Cooper held the key. He felt it deep inside his spirit.

Chapter 28

Cooper's eyes were swollen almost shut. From crying, by the looks of things. Jenny poured him a cup of hot coffee where he slumped at the end of the familiar kitchen table. It had surprised Marylu that Cooper insisted on having everyone present, as if he knew what was coming and wanted to make things right with everyone present as witnesses.

Cooper started slowly, as if his tongue were heavy and his mind slow. "Miss Jenny has wanted me to tell the truth for a long time. Months." He lifted his head and raised his brows. "I don't know how she found out, but I know it's created a misery in my soul for longer than I want to admit."

Chester ran his finger around the rim of his mug. Next to him, Aaron Walck sipped his coffee and nibbled on half a doughnut. Miss Jenny sat across from him, her gaze fixed on Cooper.

Marylu nudged the plate of doughnuts closer to Chester, encouraging him to eat, but he shook his head. She knew the feeling. Dread filled her stomach, leaving no room for appetite.

"You loved Marylu," Miss Jenny prodded the man.

Cooper nodded, a quirky smile on his lips. "She was the hero. Beautiful. Generous and brave. Most the men I know loved her. Even old Russell had himself a soft spot for her. But she never saw any of us. Except Walter." He pulled in a quick breath and lowered his eyes to the table.

"If only you'd said something," Marylu said.

Cooper laughed. "In your eyes I was an old man. Still am. I was chasing a fool's dream, and part of me knew it. Then I had to watch you and Walter, night after night." His head drooped forward. "It was me that told Walter to leave."

Marylu gasped and felt Miss Jenny's soft hand cup hers.

"I'd saved up a little bit working at Crowell and Davison as he healed up. It was all I had, and I gave it to him and told him to leave and get north. Forget about Marylu. That I would take care of her."

Quick anger stiffened Marylu's back. She wanted to shout a thousand things at Cooper, but only one slipped out. "How could you?"

Cooper didn't meet her eyes. "When you cried after him all those months, I couldn't take it anymore. So I. . ."

The wave of her emotion eased and morphed into resignation. It was a long time ago. Walter's love for her must have been very shallow indeed if he so easily was bought. She pulled in a deep, steadying breath.

"When you didn't love me back, I got mad. Went over to the widow's house. Dottie's." He ducked his head low between his extended arms, and the sounds of his heavy inhalation could be heard. "Zedikiah's my boy." The words came out, at once harsh and feeble. "Been burning a hole in me for a long time. Seeing him take to drink. I knew his mama would hate me for clamming up about being his daddy, but I didn't know how to go about being one, and he's already grown."

"He needs you," Chester said simply.

Cooper bobbed his head once. "I see that now. Don't mean I know what I'm doing, but it's right for me to tell him." He swallowed. "Maybe he'll hate me."

For the first time, Marylu felt his fear, as if it had been Walter leaving her all over again. She pressed her face into her hands and let the emotions burst forth. Cooper's betrayal. His deceit. Where hate should have been stirred to new heights, she could only feel a dull ache. What had happened happened a long time ago. If things hadn't occurred as they had, she might be saddled with a man she would have grown to hate. God only knew.

But was her love so easy to reject?

"Marylu?" Cooper's voice invaded her thoughts. When she raised her head and saw the veil of unshed tears clouding his eyes, she knew it was within her power to ease the man's burden. God would want her to do that. Still, the words came hard, but forgiveness, she knew, boiled down to choice. *Lord, I want to forgive him.* "I do love you, Cooper. You've been one of my best friends. You and Miss Jenny and her parents."

Cooper's shoulders quaked, and like a building made of sticks, his torso seemed to collapse into a heaving mass. His sobs filled the room.

Miss Jenny rose and went to the man. "It's all right, Cooper."

☙

The evening stretched long, the plate of doughnuts finally empty, polished off mostly by Chester and Aaron Walck. It filled Marylu with a quiet joy to see Mr. Walck staying close to Miss Jenny during the meal. When the man finally said his good-byes, Jenny blushed beneath his beaming smile. Her friend seemed wreathed in happiness despite the hard issue of Cooper's confession.

They waited for the moment when Zedikiah would awake and Cooper would spill his news. Marylu urged Cooper to reveal his relationship to Zedikiah in private, but Jenny argued that it might be better if it was done with everyone who loved the two men surrounding them.

Chester grabbed Marylu's hand and pointed to the door. "Go for walk."

She joined him in the cool night air, feeling a strange unreality about her surroundings. Mixed up in her mind less about her choice to forgive Cooper than about her fear that love wasn't meant for her. If Walter left so easily. . .

She cast a sidelong glance at Chester. Perhaps she was a foolish woman for thinking it wouldn't happen again, for allowing herself to marry a man who had left her once already.

Jenny's admonition shot through her mind. She could not let Walter's betrayal shadow what she had with Chester. And hadn't it been Chester who reminded her that he was not Walter?

It was too much, and her head ached with the weariness of suppressed emotion and confusion. She stopped in the middle of the walk, pulling her hand out of Chester's.

He turned toward her and took a step closer. She saw the question lurking in his eyes. "Tired?"

Such a simple question. Answering yes would be a way out, and she could retreat to the quiet of her room to sort through her feelings. "Very tired."

His eyes became searching, and she looked away. "We should head back." She turned away from him, giving movement to her suggestion, and saw his hand reach for hers. She raised her hand to touch her hair to avoid his contact, afraid she would shatter, fearful it meant putting her heart in danger all the more.

When he came even with her, she darted a quick look at him. His bowed head. Hands jammed in his pockets. Her heart ached with the dejection of his silhouette. In order not to be hurt, she hurt in return. Was that fair?

Before they got back to the back door of Miss Jenny's house, his words stopped her.

"I go Mercersburg."

Coldness froze her heart, and her gaze flew to his, but his eyes were in shadow. It burgeoned then, all the weariness and questions.

"I love you."

Emotion balled in her throat. Walter's last "I love you." Would she ever be able to trust those words? Marylu spun around and hurried to the house, ignoring Chester's throaty command to stop. And when she shut the door behind her, she waited for his knock. Hoping he might follow her, and dreading it if he did.

There was no knock.

Zedikiah and Cooper looked up from the table.

Jenny hurried to her. "Marylu?" Her cool hand on Marylu's arm brought an uncontrollable trembling to Marylu's limbs. "Sit down," Jenny directed.

By some unspoken agreement, Cooper disappeared in one direction, Zedikiah the other.

Marylu shook her head when Jenny tried to get her to talk. "Nothing to say."

"Marylu, that's not true, and you know it."

She laid eyes on Jenny's concerned expression. "I was right, Miss Jenny. No one can love me."

ও

Chester stretched out on the floor of Zedikiah's room. The boy had said little since he'd entered, and he guessed that Cooper's revelation had not resulted in warm feelings between them.

As his body relaxed, he thought of Marylu. He didn't think her shrinking away from him had anything to do with him, not in light of all that Cooper had revealed. His love for the woman must have been deep, though selfish. Chester admired her ability to forgive her old friend so easily, but something gnawed at her in spite of the gesture.

He hadn't known what to say, what with his tongue still not able to speak the volumes that lay dormant in his heart. And his timing in announcing his trip to Mercersburg seemed to startle her, but his nephew needed some help, and he would not say no to the boy or his sister. It had been his hope that Marylu would go with him and meet his family, but her taking off as she had left him little choice but to go alone.

Chester closed his eyes and prayed for Marylu and Zedikiah, Cooper and Miss Jenny, even Aaron Walck. But his mind took little rest from the prayer, and he slept restlessly. When he opened his eyes and darkness came through the window, he raised himself on one elbow and ran his hand over his face. He had almost convinced himself of the merit of starting out on the long walk to Mercersburg now, when he heard a sniffle. Then another.

"Zed?"

"Thought you was asleep."

"Was."

As his eyes adjusted to the dim light, Chester could make out the boy's form where he sat on the edge of the bed. He hiked up from the floor and crossed to the young man, placing a hand on his shoulder. "Talk?"

"Nothing to say."

Chester smiled in the darkness, seeing that there was plenty the boy wanted to say, but he just didn't want to form the words. Or didn't know what words to say. It all reminded him so much of himself. Zedikiah's habit of sliding into self-pity mirrored his own past tendencies to do the same. And it always led to drinking.

"Lord worked in his heart." Chester paused. "Got to let the past go. Look forward."

Zedikiah sat still, an occasional sniff the only sound in the room. "Is it that easy?"

Chester got to his feet, grabbed his shirt off a peg on the wall and shrugged into it. The answer to that question seemed riddled with pitfalls. For someone who couldn't see the answer for what it was, the choice to look forward would be difficult. He had tried for years himself, but once he had embraced the forgiveness and peace, he was able to heal. "Can be," he said.

Zedikiah lay back down on the bed and sighed. "Is that what you did?"

Chester stood straight, fingertips working the last buttonhole. He smiled, knowing Zedikiah wouldn't be able to see it in the semidarkness, but it wasn't a smile for Zedikiah. It was one for himself. Proof of his victory. "Yes. And it works. God will help. Let Him."

"I'm not much for church." Zedikiah put his hand on the door and swung it inward.

"Can change that, too."

Chapter 29

In the morning light, Marylu pulled the thick strips of bacon from the skillet.

Cooper sat huddled on the bench, a miserable knot of a man. Jenny, dressed for Sunday church, sat across from him, speaking in low tones.

Marylu set the tin of bacon on the table.

Cooper didn't even raise his face, and when she exchanged a look with Jenny, her friend looked sad beyond words.

"Someone better be eating up this bacon."

"It smells wonderful," Jenny said out loud, her eyes on Cooper.

Without ever looking up, Cooper rose from the table and ambled out the back door.

"He is the most stubborn man," Jenny groused.

"You just now seeing that?"

Jenny nibbled on the bacon and a piece of dry toast before she pushed her plate away. "I'm just not hungry, Marylu."

"Going to see Mr. Walck this morning?"

"Of course. He is always faithful to the services. He sings, too." Twin spots of color showed on the woman's cheeks, and her eyes shone. Her smile faded, though, and Marylu knew what was coming. "I'm sorry about Cooper."

"It's not your fault."

"And what he did isn't your fault either."

Marylu eyed her friend. She let the words sink in, understanding exactly what Jenny meant.

"You wouldn't talk last night, but I figured I knew what was going through your mind. The way you came into the kitchen and how we never saw Chester after that."

Marylu pulled air into her lungs and stared down at the table.

"It's just like you somehow figured you weren't enough for Walter and that's why he left you. And with Cooper's confession, you did something of the same thing."

"He said he was going to Mercersburg."

Jenny tilted her head. "Chester?"

She nodded. "I felt so exhausted, and I guess. . . I guess I let my emotions and fears rattle me."

"He's probably going to see his sister. He got a note from her yesterday at the shop. I gave it to him."

Marylu closed her eyes.

"You thought he meant he was leaving? After he proposed?"

She shrugged.

"Marylu." Jenny's tone held reprimand. She rose from the table. "I guess I'll be walking to church this morning."

"Cooper's probably got the buggy ready."

Jenny shook her head. "No, I'll walk. Seems like that buggy will be headed west this morning. Don't you think?"

She laughed at her friend's less-than-subtle suggestion. "Seems I've done this once before."

"And both times for the right reasons."

ᏣᏣ

Finding Chester didn't take long. He had just made it within sight of Mercersburg when she pulled up beside him. His eyes widened with surprise.

"If you get in, I'll take you into Mercersburg."

The buggy rocked under his weight then settled when he sat beside her. He caught her gaze and held it, his brows raised.

She saw what he was asking. "I'm sorry. I was tired and confused and. . ." She bit down hard to keep from crying.

His hand covered hers.

"When you told me you were coming here, I didn't understand."

"I'm not Walter."

She gave a short laugh. "Yes, I know that. It's me. I just don't want to be hurt again."

He squeezed her fingers, and she raised her face to see the tenderness there in his eyes.

"I not Cooper." He placed a hand over his heart. "I love because you are dear, kind, devoted. You helped heal me. Showed me God."

Tears gathered in her eyes and blurred his features. She blinked and would have turned away, but he tugged on her hand.

"You make me better man. I need you."

She drew in a shuddering breath. "All this time I thought Walter had left me because I wasn't loveable, but now I know that it was Cooper's doing. I don't know. It's like I can't help but be thankful. What kind of man would say he loves me then leave so easily?"

Chester's face remained expressionless.

"Not the kind I want to share my life with, I'll tell you that. It's like God was watching over me the entire time. Answering my prayers even though my heart was breaking." She stopped and stared out over the fields.

All those prayers. All the tears. Yet God had seen them all and bided time in order to bring Chester to her. She turned back toward him and scanned his gentle face, the wrinkles set around his dark eyes, and she knew in her heart that she could love again. Wholly. And that she did love. The wonder of it settled over her shoulders and deep into her heart. She squeezed his fingers until a smile lit his face.

He pulled her hand to his lips and pressed a gentle kiss against her skin.

She leaned toward him and tilted her head up, giving him a saucy smile.

He didn't move.

"Don't you know an invitation for a kiss when you see one?" She breathed.

His smile came slowly. He leaned in toward her and bowed his head over hers until she felt the warmth of his lips.

In that moment, Marylu Biloxi decided popping and crackling over a man wasn't such a bad thing after all.

Epilogue

Chester was my husband for thirty-two years. The good Lord added him to his collection of saints on a cool, autumn day when the leaves were just beginning to fall from the trees. I rejoiced in his rest, being that he had suffered much after a stroke left him weak on his right side and robbed him of his ability to walk. I'm more sure than anything that he's bouncing all over heaven though. We had a good life together. It seemed once we'd cleansed ourselves of all the demons of our youth that life became sweeter. Even more so because it was shared by us together.

We had us a couple of little surprises along the way. Lillian Jennifer Jones was born right after my thirty-second birthday. Our next little one died, a little boy we called William, and was laid in the cemetery with many tears. On my thirty-seventh birthday, I found myself with child again. This boy came into the world screaming for all he was worth and never stopped. Chester Jones, Jr., was our crowning glory, though he about near killed us both with his wild ways before finally settling down at the age of seventeen.

Miss Jenny and Aaron Walck married shortly after me and Chester. They had a whole passel of young ones. Six babies, one almost right after the other. It wore her out, having all those babies close together, which made it a good thing that Chester and me lived in a little cabin right out back of Aaron's home. It was like caring for Miss Jenny all over again.

And Zedikiah? He had a hard road. We worked together to care for him as best we could. After a rough start, he finally settled down in his work and eventually he became Aaron Walck's most trusted craftsman. Cooper played a minor role in his life, I'm sorry to say. Zedikiah never quite took to having him for a father. I'm guessing that sometimes we only get one chance to set things right. Cooper had his chance, and though he cleared his conscience by confessing to Zedikiah, he was never quite able to move beyond the fact that had he made things right sooner, things would have been different. Both for him and Zedikiah.

Still, he died in his son's arms, and Zedikiah visited his grave often. Sad to see. Best to heal rifts when you're alive than after someone is dead and gone. But the world isn't a perfect place, and people aren't perfect either. Only God is perfect. It's up to us to be more like Him, but some come to it later than others, and some not at all.

I lay my pen aside now, hoping that someone might read this love story and realize that you don't have to be young to find true love. Sometimes it's even better to be older, because youthful longings can choose the wrong person.

My heart is content to leave you in His care.

Marylu Jones
December, 1915

PROMISE OF TOMORROW

Dedication

To my mother with love.

Chapter 1

South Fork Fishing and Hunting Club,
Lake Conemaugh, Pennsylvania, May 10, 1889

Jack Kelly stood cloaked in the shadow of a large tree. From this vantage point, his view of the woman he hoped to make his wife remained quite clear.

Alongside the lake, surrounded by veils of white dogwood blooms, the three Hensley children flocked around the skirts of Alaina Morrison's day dress. Her beatific smile beamed down on their heads. Alaina's close friend, Mary, off to the side of the group, laughed at the spectacle created as Alaina held the candy in her hand high above the shorter heads of their charges. Her voice carried to his hiding place. "Not until after supper. I promised your mother."

Jack drank in the scene. As one child, taller than the rest, made a jump for the candy, Alaina leaned into him with her free hand and offered a tickle to his ribs.

Mary calmed the growing frenzy of laughter with a clap of her hands. "We need to be heading home." Mary tapped the heads of two blond twins and an older girl and motioned. "Let's go before supper is declared too cold to eat."

"Do we have to go?" Little Lily Hensley whined to Alaina as she stood, grubby hands full of the pebbles prevalent at the lakeside retreat.

"We got here later than usual." She touched the tip of Lily's nose. "I'll allow five more minutes of playtime. How does that sound?"

Reinvigorated by the news, Lily clapped Alaina around the knees and the two went tumbling into a patch of spring green grass. Alaina sat up and started a tickle attack.

Jack crossed his arms, entranced by the vision before him. Alaina's yellow day dress did not flaunt the latest style. Plain but crisp, the material flattered her dark hair and eyes. The ease with which she laughed and smiled, accepted disappointments, and shared in fun swelled his heart, just as it had since he'd first talked to her at the store where her mother stitched clothing.

He'd seen her before that afternoon, but only at a distance. When she'd dropped three bolts of material at his feet and he'd helped to pick them up, her smile had made his heart pound and his palms sweat. He'd made the trip to the store across the river every spare moment for the past year and a half. At least until it had dawned on him that he loved her. But marriage meant he would need money.

He pushed the thought away as Alaina spread her arms wide. The smallest child of the prominent Hensley family toddled into her arms. She made a great show of allowing the little boy to help her to her feet, so much so that the two older children, Lily and Mark, pitched in to help.

With the light breeze from the lake at his back, and the promise of summer before him, Jack could no longer discount his feelings. For days he had reviewed his proposal, hesitant to say the words out loud, then unsure why he hesitated at all in asking Alaina to be his wife. But hesitate he did, and he hated himself at the end of every day he waited.

Today would be the day.

Alaina guided her small flock up the walkway toward Moorhead cottage, a large home that held little in common with its name. Built on the edge of Lake Conemaugh, the huge Queen Anne–style home, with its rounded end tower, was the summer retreat for any family rich enough to afford the rental price; a privilege Jack hoped to provide for Alaina someday. Of course, they would need to be members of the South Fork Fishing and Hunting Club first. But he held little doubt that as soon as he completed his invention, he would make that dream come true, too.

Jack turned his head and relished the bright sunshine that cast diamonds on the lake. Several boathouses squatted along the shore, waiting for the influx of summer club members to open their creaking doors and indulge in a little boating. Again, the sting of his inability to afford such luxuries stoked his determination.

Pushing his thoughts aside, Jack squinted toward the end of Lake Conemaugh, where a wide road crossed the breast of a tall dam. The view from the dam into the valley was breathtaking, one of Alaina's favorite spots. Satisfied with the location he had chosen, he inhaled to steady his nerves and returned his attention to the dark-haired beauty.

Alaina's steps brought her closer to him. Lily held her left hand, the three-year-old boy her right. Behind her trailed the twelve-year-old, trying to appear aloof from his siblings and "nanny."

Jack grinned. At twelve he would have done the same thing. He stepped out from beneath the tree and into the waning sunlight.

Thomas, the toddler, saw him first. He tugged Alaina's hand, pointing and drawing her attention to where Jack stood.

When she met his gaze, her expression softened, and she gave him a shy smile.

Jack laughed as Lily barreled into his legs. Her small face tilted back. "You bring me candy, Jack?"

"Lillian!" Alaina frowned. "Didn't I just say no more candy?"

"But Robert brings me candy." Lillian pouted.

Alaina's eyes flicked to his. She flinched, then glanced back to Lillian and held out her hand. "And you know how many times I've told Robert not to do that."

Jack tensed as he watched the flush creep up Alaina's neck. Robert. Again. The man's presence drove a thorn into Jack's side. They had worked together for the last year, a silent rivalry that extended from the workplace the moment Robert discovered his relationship with Alaina. He knew Alaina loved him, but sometimes Robert's persistence wore on him, and niggling doubts caused him to wonder if Alaina's gentle spirit somehow encouraged the man. His words came slowly. "Robert's daddy must be very rich to have so much candy."

Lily shook her head. "He doesn't have a daddy."

"Everyone has a daddy, silly," Alaina said.

"Big people don't." Lily's wide eyes beamed up at Jack.

Jack hesitated, the face of his rival flashed in his mind. He squatted down to look Lily in the eyes. "Robert is a big person, huh? How often does he come see you, Lils?" His voice directed the question at Lily, but his eyes flicked to Alaina.

She looked away.

"Lots." Lily tugged his hand. "Do you have a daddy?"

Jack felt the grip of that question as he stood. He shoved his hands into his pockets and forced a smile. "Miss Morrison is right. Everyone has a father."

Mark, the eldest Hensley boy, shot out from behind them and took the steps, two at a time, up to the porch. "We're gonna be late," he shouted from the top step.

Alaina placed Thomas's hand into Lily's and sent them up the steps. "I'll be along shortly. Make sure you wash your hands. Lily, you help Thomas."

The girl mumbled something and tugged her little brother along. On the third step, she paused and twisted around. "I don't have a father. I have a daddy."

"Come on," Mark yelled from the front door.

Jack cocked a brow. "Inquisitive, isn't she?"

"Very."

He waited for Alaina to look at him. She appeared weary, and he knew the subject of Robert, in her mind, was a closed one. "Robert's been pestering you again? Why didn't you tell me?"

"There's nothing to tell." She held his gaze. "He's been here twice, and I always send him away. He does it to antagonize you, you know."

Jack nodded. "I'll say something to him."

She raised a hand. "Don't."

Jack felt the first stab of irritation. "Why not?"

"Because I don't want to feed your animosity. You used to be great friends, remember?"

"Before you and I started seeing each other. A lot of things can change in a year." He saw the silent plea in her eyes and slid his hands into his pockets. If only he could afford a ring to slip onto her finger when he proposed. After he made good on his plans. "What I do, I do for us."

"Then let's put this subject aside for now and enjoy our time together." She lifted the front of her skirts and took the first step in the long flight to Hensley cottage, speaking over her shoulder. "I've got to get the children settled, and I'll be back."

The edge of his anger cooled as Jack watched her ascent.

She stopped halfway up and faced him. "You know, I've never heard you speak of your father before. Maybe—"

"Another subject to set aside." He cleared his throat to dispel the gruffness of his tone and forced a note of lightness into his voice. "Hurry back. I have a surprise for you."

"You do?"

"I do."

Her eyes sparkled. "I'll hurry." She made short work of the remaining steps and waggled her fingers at him before the door closed and blocked her from view.

Jack settled in for the wait. Mrs. Hensley's maid would take care of the children for the evening, but it was up to Alaina to get them settled for their supper before her duties were done. Ten minutes and she would be his.

His heart rate rose with anticipation. He rehearsed the speech he would make before the proposal. Should he kneel? Would she laugh? He patted his breast pocket to be sure he had a handkerchief in case she cried.

He straightened when the front door opened again and Alaina stepped onto the porch. At the top of the steps, she tilted her face toward the sun as if drinking in its energy. Jack's heart slammed against his ribs. He barreled up the steps.

She startled, a delicate hand at her throat. "You're crazy."

"Crazy in love."

She shook her head at him and stroked her hand down his cheek. "What am I going to do with you?"

Marry me. It was on the tip of his tongue to say the words, but he bit them back. He didn't want her memory of his proposal to be the front step of the Hensley rental.

In another burst of exuberance, Jack spanned her waist with his hands and lifted her down to the step even with him. She gasped at his action. When her feet were on solid ground again, he pulled her close.

She tilted her head back and jammed an elbow against his chest. "Really, Jack, I don't know what's gotten into you." Her gaze darted back to the house. "We need to be aware of who might be watching. You know the club doesn't like trespassers."

"You're not a trespasser. You work for them," Jack pointed out, but he gave her some room and satisfied himself with holding her hand.

"True. Neither of us are members, though, and that's what matters most to the owners."

"I'll be a member soon enough." He swelled his chest and winked. "When I get this promotion, I'll be well on my way to the presidency. Then we'll come up here as often as we please."

Jack tugged on her hand and allowed her to precede him down the stairs. As soon as he could, he twined his fingers with hers. He imagined himself a rich magnate and member of the exclusive club out strolling with his beautiful wife. His normal steps became a rolling strut.

She followed his pantomime and pretended to carry a parasol, head tilted at a lofty angle, her steps small but hurried.

At the end of the boardwalk, Jack could contain his laughter no longer.

Alaina's eyes sparkled as she, too, gave vent to the giggles stirred by their outrageous act. "If anyone should see us, they might think we're mocking."

"Oh, my lady, never us," he drawled. "We have lofty goals to attain such status ourselves."

Though her smile stayed, something died in Alaina's eyes. She bent to retrieve a handful of pebbles and tossed them into the mirrorlike surface at the edge of the lake.

Her silence sent gravel churning in his stomach. "Did I say something?" He touched her elbow. "Alaina?"

When she lifted her face, he could see the strain in her expression. "It's nothing, really. I think we've agreed to put aside unpleasant subjects. I don't want to spoil the evening."

Jack studied her profile a moment and then shrugged away his concern. "I brought a wagon from South Fork. I thought we might have our supper there this evening." His suggestion still did not rekindle the light in her eyes. Taking a deep breath, he braced himself and broached the subject he suspected caused her distress. "It's not you I don't trust, Alaina. It's Robert."

She gave him a wan smile. "Yes, but that doesn't end the strain between you two. Is this promotion really worth your friendship, Jack? Is money?"

How many times would he be forced to remind her? "I'm doing it for us."

He saw in her expression the moment she decided to let the argument alone. "Yes. I know."

Jack exhaled long and slow. Good. Still, shades of doubt niggled at his mind. The joy of his surprise seemed to have lessened considerably, and the weight of that made the moment flawed somehow.

As they neared Jack's rented wagon, she paused to fling more rocks into the lake. He took advantage of the opportunity to absorb her carefree attitude. Most young women wouldn't think about flinging dirty rocks, much less picking one up. Alaina had an easy way about her that soothed Jack, and her way with children never failed to delight him. He wanted children. Lots of children.

With her.

He aided her ascent into the buggy and climbed in beside her, still unsure of what to do.

"Look!"

He followed her line of vision to see a heron rise from the lake. Another stood at the water's edge and craned its neck in their direction.

"Regal," he said and directed the wagon onto the road that crossed the dam. "We're coming up on the view."

The horse tugged the wagon along the road, harness jangling. Jack stopped the animal in the dead center of the road and went around to the other side of the wagon to help Alaina down.

Mottled green marked the stretching, yawning new leaves that peppered the trees in the narrow valley. Birds swooped and spun in dizzying patterns.

Jack refocused his attention on Alaina.

Her gentle smile lifted his spirits. Her eyes danced. "It's so beautiful."

For only a moment, he allowed the voice of caution to have sway. *I could ask her tomorrow night.*

As if sensing his stare, Alaina cast him a sidelong glance, brown eyes twinkling with mischief. "So is this my surprise?"

Jack softened and grasped her hand, his carefully rehearsed words scattered. But one thing he knew for certain. "I love you, Alaina Morrison."

☙

Alaina felt the grip of longing burn her throat as she gazed down into the valley toward Johnstown. She wanted to go home. On the other hand, if not for the Hensleys' early arrival, she would still be dodging her mother's not-so-subtle criticisms about women who settle for less than the best. Meaning Jack.

A breeze skimmed her brow and cooled her sun-warmed back. She closed her eyes to absorb the sights and sounds, the smells and feelings. Jack's surprise visit pleased her. She needed this—to be brought here by the man she loved and reminded of God's beauty.

If only the subject of Robert hadn't surfaced.

She became aware of Jack's stare and tilted her head in his direction. He reached to clasp her other hand. His declaration of love seemed so heartfelt. It pleased her to hear the words, as it had always pleased her, but as he tugged her toward him, the last emotion to settle in her heart and erode all others was one of confusion.

"You are beautiful," he whispered.

She cast about for something lighthearted to say and skimmed a finger over his upper lip. "I see that your mustache is coming right along. Very scoundrel-ish."

He raised his brows. "Scoundrel-ish? You said you liked mustaches. I think it makes me look dignified. And older."

"Yes, older." She shoved at him, laughing. "You look like you're fifty. If you had gray hair, I'd hand you a cane."

He laughed and waggled his brows. "I could marry Widow Sanford."

"She wouldn't have you."

He captured her free hand, his eyes suddenly serious and searching. "Would you?"

Alaina's breath halted. A breeze chilled her skin and ruffled his longish blond hair. In the depth of his eyes, she saw the sincerity of his question. She opened her mouth and gulped air, unable to form words.

"I think I'm going about this all wrong." He bent at the knee, never releasing her hands. His thumbs stroked along her knuckles, and he cleared his throat.

Her heart churned, and she glanced around in a fit of nerves. "Jack, people are looking."

"Does it matter?"

"I—" Alaina swallowed and faced him again as his hands tightened on hers.

Jack's eyes twinkled.

"No. You're right. Go ahead."

"Good, because this ground sure is hard."

"Roads usually are packed hard."

"I think I knelt on a rock."

"Then hurry."

"But what about the pretty speech I've rehearsed for the last two weeks?"

"Two weeks?" she gasped.

"Now, let's see. . . . Oh yes." Jack shifted his weight and cleared his throat. "Alaina, you've brought so much light into my life. I mean to make you proud of me. I need you. I want you by my side, to love me and be loved by me. Marry me, Alaina Morrison. Please."

Words wouldn't form on her lips, and she bit back the urge to giggle. What did a woman say when the man she loved asked her to marry him? "Yes" seemed so insufficient. Yet her heart beat so hard that she wasn't at all sure she could vocalize more than that small word. She pulled her hands away and touched Jack's elbows, urging him to his feet. She nodded, and the first tears started down her cheeks.

He produced a handkerchief, looking quite pleased with himself, and dabbed beneath her eyes.

"Yes, Jack. Yes." Not caring what or who was watching, she lunged into his arms. When she tried to pull back, his arms tightened.

His voice came out deep and rich. "Thank you." He released her and frowned a bit. "I wanted to give you a gold band but I—"

"I don't need one of those fancy rings, Jack."

"I'll buy you one as soon as I can set aside some money."

She stifled a sigh, not wanting to remind him that she didn't need expensive trifles to be happy. With great effort, she pushed away her frustration.

He raised her hand to his lips. "Always?"

"Always," she echoed.

After Jack had seen her to the door of Moorhead cottage and the warm glow of the evening had receded, Alaina lay for hours in the dark room, the sounds of Lily's breathing soft against her ear. She wiped away the tears from her cheeks. All the warnings of her mother, all the fears and doubts, came rushing back to her, until she could stand it no longer and slipped to her knees.

Lord, what have I done?

Chapter 2

May 12, 1889

He forgot you again?" Mary Hilton's eyebrows arched high.

Alaina turned toward the sullen lake waters and closed her eyes. She never should have mentioned it to her chatty friend. Blustery clouds and a chill wind promised an afternoon storm, but nothing compared to what Alaina felt in her heart. She bit her lip to hold back the tears as she gathered the food items into the basket. "He's a busy man. An important man, Mary. The company needs him."

Mary made a sound like an indignant snort. "What about you? What is he in love with, you or his job?"

Directly in front of the boardwalk from where they stood, an old rowboat had settled in muddy soil, no longer used for its original purpose but serving as a flowerpot. Spring geraniums, buds in abundance, petunias, and pansies all craned their necks toward the weak sunshine. Damp air rolled from the lake surface and spiraled around the two friends.

Alaina drew strength from God's beauty and waved her hand. "He is doing it for us."

"I think you should give Robert a chance." Mary hefted the picnic basket and called for her young charges. The children came running, jostling each other the whole way. She turned back to Alaina. "He is obviously interested in you. And he'll get the promotion before Jack will. He's been with the company longer."

Mary had her opinion and never shrank from expressing it, but sometimes Alaina wished her friend would bite down a little harder on her quick tongue.

"Robert would do anything for you, even move you away from grim little Johnstown." Mary motioned the children to go ahead of her. "Why, just yesterday he heard a visitor from the Midwest say Johnstown's sunrise began at ten o'clock and ended at two. How dreary is that? I definitely don't want to be stuck living here all my life."

Alaina had to agree with the visitor's description. Nestled between the mountains, Johnstown's sunny day did, indeed, begin later. Still, Alaina loved the place. The small city's bustle never failed to excite her. Even the constant drizzle of rain in the spring months did nothing to diminish her affection. To her, Johnstown held the best of both worlds. For in the moments when life became too stressful, she could always escape to the peaceful mountains.

"That's just it." Alaina faced her friend. "I don't *want* to live anywhere else. I don't long for the big city like you do. Johnstown is my home."

Her friend looked skeptical. "But don't you get tired of it? And Jack is always forgetting you."

"He doesn't forget. He has to work on his plans when he has the chance. When he thinks he's on to something, he prefers not to break his concentration. You know how important this invention is to him. To us. And it's a long way up here from Johnstown."

"I'm happy for you, Lainey. Really." Mary touched her sleeve. "It's just that Jack is so unpredictable. I wonder what kind of husband he'll be."

Alaina felt the peace leak from her heart. She didn't want to answer. How many times had she asked herself that same question? Not wishing to take the conversation any further, she called to Thomas, Lily, and Mark.

"I'm sorry," Mary's voice whispered. "I want you to be happy, and if Jack makes you happy, then I'll say no more about it."

The Hensley children gathered around Alaina. "Go ahead and see your brother and sister home, Mark. I'll be right behind you."

Mark groaned. Lily, ever the little mother, grabbed Thomas's hand and practically pulled him over in her enthusiasm to get home.

"Slow down," Alaina admonished the little girl. "His legs aren't as long."

Mark herded his siblings up the boardwalk as Mary adjusted the picnic basket and shooed the twins ahead of her.

Alaina stole another glance at the sky. Dark clouds gathered on the horizon, and a rain-swept breeze filtered through her hair and caressed her cheek. Rain. Again. She inhaled the damp breeze and closed her eyes.

"You coming?"

Alaina's eyes popped open. She gave one more glance at the ever-darkening sky and hurried to catch up to Mary.

Her friend chuckled. "Woolgathering?"

"It looks like more rain is on the way."

Mary rolled her eyes. "As if we haven't had enough already." She snapped her fingers. "I almost forgot to tell you. The Garrens are only going to be here three more days."

"They're leaving early?"

Mary nodded. "Mrs. Garren said they wouldn't be needing me for as long as they had anticipated." She did a little bounce on the balls of her feet. "I'm really hoping she'll ask me to return with them to Philly as governess. Aren't the Hensleys leaving next week?"

"Yes. I found out yesterday morning." She skimmed the dull surface of the dark blue water. "I believe they're going to visit Mr. Carnegie's home in Cresson for a month. Then they'll return."

"Aren't you going with them to watch the children?"

She shook her head. "The Carnegies are arranging for a woman in Cresson to help with the children during the visit."

Mary's eyes glittered. She sighed. "I wish they would have asked me. I would have jumped at the chance to be inside that rich mansion with all those high society people."

Alaina frowned, disturbed by her friend's preoccupation with all people rich.

Mary tilted her head and winked. "Does Jack know you'll be home next weekend?"

"I was going to surprise him." Last night, she almost said. She had envisioned his joy and the plans they would make to see the opera, go roller-skating, and take long walks in the evenings during her unexpected reprieve from the Hensleys.

"Well," Mary said, her voice a sympathetic whisper, "you've got a whole month to do as you please. Maybe Jack will finally invent whatever he's trying to invent, and you two can settle down and plan your wedding. If he gets the promotion, that'll be icing on the cake. Should satisfy your mother, too."

A dull throb began behind Alaina's eyes. The reality was, her mother was never satisfied.

As they turned onto the walkway leading to Moorhead cottage, Mary gave her a wan smile and squeezed her hand. "Gotta go, Lainey. I enjoyed the picnic. Like old times, right?"

Chapter 3

Cambria Iron Works, Johnstown, Pennsylvania

Jack Kelly skidded into his boss's office. He pulled out a wadded handkerchief and mopped the sweat from his brow. Working in the constant and terrible heat of the blast furnace for twelve hours never failed to renew his determination to be the next shift manager.

Clarence Fulton didn't flinch at Jack's flurried entrance. His heavy brows shadowed his dark eyes, lending him a gaunt, haunted appearance.

"Good afternoon, Mr. Fulton." Jack inclined his head toward the man, stuffed his handkerchief back in his pocket, and held out his hand.

"Same to you, my boy." Fulton ignored Jack's proffered hand. "Sit down and tell me the latest on the progress of your plans."

Jack's finger roved inside his snug collar to release the sudden tightness against his neck. "I'm still working on the process, sir."

Clarence frowned and leaned forward, his chair belching a groan. "We've poured a lot of money into your research, Jack. I hope you are doing all you can to make sure the money is spent wisely. An invention such as you hope to spawn could revolutionize the steel industry."

Jack clasped his hands tight. His future depended on Clarence's patience. For long hours, Jack had studied the open-hearth process of turning iron ore into steel in hopes of inventing a method safer and quicker. He'd made pages and pages of notations whenever a new theory came to him. So far, none had worked. Now Clarence was obviously worried that his money was funneling into a chasm. Jack adjusted his collar again. He couldn't afford to do the research without Mr. Fulton's monetary backing. He forced himself to maintain an outward calm. "What are your fears, Mr. Fulton?"

"Fears? I wouldn't call them fears, Jack. Concerns, yes, but not fears. You come up with the solution to the slow process, one we can implement right here in Johnstown, and you'll be a very wealthy man." His eyes scraped down the length of Jack.

Jack witnessed Clarence's grimace of distaste at his disheveled appearance. He swallowed hard. "Yes, sir."

"I have another project for you." Clarence's palms smacked against the arms of his chair, and he pushed himself to a stand. "I want you to go up to that club and check on that dam. They've got a new civil engineer, I hear. I want to know what he's doing to insure the safety of the towns in line with that dam, Johnstown in particular."

"Mr. Morrell sent someone before and—"

"Daniel Morrell, God rest his soul, allowed those South Fork club snobs to put him off. I won't."

"They don't take kindly to people being there who don't belong," Jack said.

Clarence waved his hand in dismissal. "Not a problem. Your lady friend works up there for one of those fancy families, doesn't she? Go visit her."

Jack winced at the thought of facing Alaina after he ran out of time the previous night and was forced to choose between making the trek to South Fork or using his precious hours to work on his plans. He'd sent a telegram of regret to her, but unless she went to South Fork with the Hensleys, the chances Alaina got his message were slim.

Mr. Fulton crossed his arms and glared at a map of Johnstown on his wall. "The dam won't withstand all the water that club is filling it with for their fishing pleasure. If it crumbles"—he raised his hand, made a fist, and swiped it through the air—"Johnstown will be wiped out."

Jack nodded and leaned back. Every spring of the six years since he had moved to Johnstown, talk swirled among the townspeople about the South Fork Dam that held Lake Conemaugh. The dam hovered more than five hundred feet above Johnstown. Despite her love of the view the dam generated, Alaina, too, had expressed her fear of a breach many times. A break meant the water would sluice down the valley between the mountains and splash into Johnstown to form an enormous, deep, and deadly, puddle. Still, he had to be practical. Many men had examined the dam over the years. "Might I remind you, sir, that the last inspection indicated—"

"The last inspection was almost five years ago, boy." Clarence pinned him with a hard stare. "Between the April snow and all the rain this month, the rivers are already running high. We had bad floods in '85, '87, and last year. All we need is for the South Fork to bust open and we'll all be rowing down the river, whether we want to or not."

"It hasn't burst yet, sir."

"Yet." Fulton plopped down into his chair and tapped his fingers on the armrest. "Much more rain than this and history will be repeated. If we get doused, history, our history, just might end right here."

Jack cast about for a way to turn the conversation back to his research. He needed a little more time. Plans for a new theory for his invention were almost complete. He had a couple more tests to conduct on his working model. But working twelve-hour shifts made it difficult to find the time. And then there was Alaina.

When Mr. Fulton rose from his chair and regarded Jack in silence, he knew the meeting had come to an end. Jack nodded to his employer and scuttled toward the door.

"I like you, Jack. You're a hard worker. Keep working on those plans and report back to me in three days on the dam. Your diligence in this matter will position you well for that promotion, too." Clarence's lips curved in a semblance of a smile. "Hard work will take you far. Very far."

Elated at the implied promise in Clarence's words, Jack made his exit. He lengthened his stride and began to mentally run through his latest theory, checking and rechecking the process for errors.

"Licking the shoes of the bigwig again?"

He raised his head to see Robert Whitfield coming toward him down the hall. Robert's crude words piqued his ire. "Mr. Fulton knows I'm a dedicated worker. He calls on me when there's a job to be done."

"Or a promotion to be had?" Robert shook his head. "Nah. I've got this promotion in the bag, Jackie. Fulton's stringing you along to bleed what he can out of you, hoping you'll make him rich with your so-called invention." Robert's black hair, slicked to his head with sweat from the furnaces, lent his skin a pasty tint.

If not for the man's generous build, Jack would have laughed at his tough talk. He relaxed his fists, not realizing he had clenched them. Anything he said to Robert would filter back to Alaina through the ever-talkative Mary. He exhaled slowly and stepped around the man. "I've got to get back to work."

Jack's nemesis shrugged and continued down the hallway. "And I've got a meeting." He stopped in front of Clarence Fulton's door and sent Jack a sneering grin. "Can't keep Mr. Fulton waiting, can I?" He pitched his voice lower. "Wait until I'm your boss, Jackie. I'll have time for you and lots of it. Alaina won't give you a second glance once I get that promotion."

Something in Jack's chest unclenched at Robert's naive statement, and he found he could breathe again. "Really? Is that why she has agreed to become my wife?"

Chapter 4

"I'll get it!" Five-year-old Lillian Hensley slipped on sock feet toward the front door. She stumbled when her foot caught on the edge of the carpet. Alaina stretched out her arm to stop the inevitable fall. No sooner had Alaina set Lily back on her feet when she shot toward the door. She struggled hard to open the thick oak plank, her tiny hands pushing against the frame to gain leverage. Finally, it cracked open.

"Why, if it's not little Lillian!"

Alaina heard the voice and saw Lily's huge grin. "You have candy?" The child reached up her arms as the man stepped into the foyer and into Alaina's line of vision. Robert Whitfield.

His dark eyes flared upon seeing her. "Good evening, Miss Alaina."

Lily's lip pooched. "I thought you came to see me."

Alaina grasped the doorknob for support and frowned at their guest. "He does come to see you, Lily. Doesn't he always say as much?"

Robert's eyes flicked over her. "I admit, there are others here who attract me as well."

Alaina gripped the doorknob tighter and hoped he would take her reluctance to close the door as a signal for him to leave. "Then you must have forgotten our last conversation, Mr. Whitfield."

"Mr. Whitfield, huh?" He set Lily on the floor and stooped to press a piece of candy into her palm. Three visits to Moorhead cottage and already Lily knew what to expect. Alaina only wished she knew Robert's intentions. Why wouldn't he stay away?

She worried the Hensleys might protest her visitor, though Mrs. Hensley never seemed to mind. In the absence of their housemaid, Alaina often greeted visitors at the door, with Lily as her ever-willing helper. Lily, scamp that she was, seemed to have a sixth sense when Robert was the person on the other side. Or maybe she smelled the candy offering he never failed to bring.

Robert's hand shot out and tugged the door from Alaina's grasp, swinging it closed.

Aware of Lily's wide-eyed stare watching her every move, Alaina placed a hand on the child's head and smiled. "Why don't you go play and let me talk to your friend."

"You won't send him away, will you?"

She met Robert's gaze. "Unless he has come to see your father or mother, yes, Mr. Whitfield will be leaving soon."

Robert leaned down and spoke in a loud whisper. "I'll bring four pieces of candy next time I come."

With obvious relief that her candy supply wouldn't dry up anytime soon, Lily nodded and skipped off down the wide hall.

Robert turned to Alaina, and she could see the hurt in his expression. "At least I have one fan."

Her words had come out more sharply than she had intended. She wanted to believe that Robert's intentions were good, just misdirected. "There are duties I need to tend to, Robert. Say what you have to say and let me get back to my work."

"Ah." He leaned in toward her and raised his brows. "We're back to first names. I like that."

She fumed at his sheer nerve. "What do you want?"

"Jack said you agreed to marry him."

"It's true."

"That's a shame. How can you be so devoted to a man who forgets you so often?"

Mary had obviously shared with Robert about Jack's latest broken promise. She turned toward the door and placed her hand on the doorknob. "I love him."

"Even when he doesn't show up to take you out? How many times has he broken promises to you? Ten? Twenty? Seems a terrible foundation on which to build a marriage."

She felt his presence as he drew nearer, and she stiffened when he touched her elbow.

"Why not give me a chance?"

"Because—" Words died in her mind, and she struggled for a coherent reply. "Robert, please. Leave me alone."

"I'd treat you with the respect you deserve."

His presence disturbed her less than his words. First Mary, now him, expressing the exact fears she tortured herself with daily.

"I love you, Alaina." Robert's words slipped over her shoulder. "You'll be much happier with me."

She twisted the knob and eased the door open.

Robert, his words coming fast now, desperate, seemed to struggle for something to sway her.

"Besides, there's something about Jack you don't know."

"What would that be, Whitfield?"

Alaina gasped. Jack stood there, clearly having overheard Robert's last comment. His scowl smoldered, his blue eyes the color of an angry winter sky. She looked between the two men, afraid of the fire their sparks of anger might ignite.

Robert ignored Jack and slanted her a look. "I believe I'll leave that for you to figure out for yourself. I've quite apparently worn out my welcome. But please, Alaina, know that you have my deepest sympathy should you choose to marry him."

Her gaze flew to Jack's. She put a hand to his sleeve in silent supplication. Beneath her hand, his muscles relaxed.

Robert pressed his way forward. Jack moved aside and then followed the man's path down the steps. Alaina pulled Jack inside. "Your timing is perfect," she quipped to ease the tension.

"This time."

She saw the stress leave his expression in slow degrees as his eyes roved her face and hair.

"What did he have to say?"

"He was interested in finding out about our engagement." She hesitated, embarrassed to admit her own indiscretion. "Mary apparently told him that you didn't show up yesterday."

The recrimination she expected to see in his eyes didn't appear. Instead, Jack's face melted into a look of chagrin. He opened his arms wide. She nestled against him, his breath warm against her hair, the faint smell of lye soap drifting up from his clothes.

"I telegraphed to South Fork but knew you wouldn't get the message up here unless you happened to go down with the Hensleys for dinner or something. I'm sorry I didn't show up."

She closed her eyes. "Again."

He gave a solemn nod. "Yes. Again. Mr. Fulton called me to his office quite unexpectedly."

She brushed coal ash from the train off his sleeve. It smeared and clung. "You have ash all over you."

"Um," he mumbled against her hair.

Her mind jumped back and forth between her need to apologize and her pique at Jack's certainty that an apology was always going to be enough. She drew in a deep breath and swallowed, her words flowing on her exhale. "I should apologize as well. As much as I love Mary, she talks too much and tells Robert everything."

Jack drew away but held on to her hand. He glanced toward the stairs. "You're done for the evening?"

"Yes."

"Let's take a walk before I head back."

"What made you take the train?"

His eyes searched hers. "I knew I needed to get here to make up for yesterday." His finger traced the ridge of her knuckles. "I wanted to be here."

She felt her tension dissipate at his tender touch. "I have good news. The Hensleys are leaving next Wednesday and won't be back for a month."

"A month?"

"A whole month," she said. "I can start planning our wedding."

Jack blinked, the ghost of a frown pulled on his lips.

"Jack?"

"I'll have to test my new theory. I'm really hoping this time it will work. I could have enough money for us to buy a decent home."

"I don't mind living in Cambria City."

"*I* mind." He released her hand.

Alaina watched as he turned his back and crossed to the parlor doorway, hands stuffed in his trouser pockets. This core of determination she often felt in his character was the root cause for his driving himself, she was sure. But other than his oft-told story of being raised by a poor mother after his father left them, she never could glimpse the reason why he was so adamant they not live in Cambria City. He might have been raised poor, but so had she. At first she thought Jack's reasons were based on pride, but Jack never condescended to any of his friends who lived in the small city where employees of Cambria Iron Works rented homes. To remind him she didn't mind being poor would be wasted words. So she waited.

He stared into the parlor for several minutes before he returned to her and raised her left hand so their hands touched, palm to palm. His gaze commanded her attention. "I have to do this, Alaina. For me."

Chapter 5

Johnstown, May 15, 1889

Alaina slipped into her mother's room, drawn by the snuffling snores and the promise of momentary peace her mother's slumber afforded. Charlotte Morrison slept on her back, hair bundled severely into a long braid. Smoothed by sleep, the etched frown lines could not lend her mother the perpetual sour look.

She debated whether to waken her mother and announce her presence. Tired from the day and the hustle of packing the Hensleys off, Alaina decided to wait. She had sent word last week that she would be home tonight. Apparently her mother had forgotten. She blinked back the burn of tears that threatened and released a sigh of pent-up frustration. She skimmed her mother's left hand and saw the slight, unnatural curl of the fingers grown sore from constant needlework.

Oh, Mother.

Alaina ran a gentle finger over her mother's hand and felt the roughness of skin chafed by the yards of material she measured out and sewed every day. "You work so hard," she whispered. Her mother's body flinched, and Alaina withdrew from the room on catlike feet and shut the door. She began to rehearse how to best tell her mother the news of her engagement.

Sleep eluded her. She wished Jack could have seen her home, but his shift at Cambria ended too late. He would stay later than the rest to work on his research and test his latest idea. Alaina raised her head and pounded the pillow. She shuddered and pulled the blanket tighter to her chin. Tears burned behind her eyelids.

Confusion and doubt returned to further torment her exhausted mind. And, beneath it all, the conviction that Robert would never treat their relationship so lightly. He had pursued her to the extreme, but she often wondered if he did so more to anger Jack than out of affection for her.

Robert's face floated through her memory, the way he had watched her as she'd begun to swing open the Hensleys' front door in an effort to hasten his exit. A knot tightened in her stomach. She pressed her hand there and swallowed against the ill feeling.

Something else, too. Something he'd said. . .

Alaina swept back her covers and swung her legs over the edge of the bed. Her mind churned to bring to full light what hid in the shadows.

"There's something about Jack you don't know. . . ."

That was it! But what had Robert meant?

Alaina walked to the window. Next door, a fine home made of brick stood bathed in the light of the full moon. Jack often flung his hand in the direction of that house and repeated his promise that he would buy her one someday. "When I've made my pile."

She shivered when a draft of cold air rushed through the room and forced her to take refuge under her blankets. Finally, sleep came.

When she next opened her eyes, her mother's frown greeted her.

☙

"He's got it out for you, Jack," Big Frank Mills huffed as he shoveled manganese into the ladle full of iron ore. "Watch yourself."

Jack sucked air into his tortured lungs and kept shoveling. Lathered in sweat, he gritted his teeth against the oppressive ache in muscles that begged him to stop. His reply never formed on his dry tongue, as the two men strained together to finish the job. Big Frank finally broke the pace. Jack didn't notice. His arms pumped hard.

"Easy. That's enough," Frank huffed. When Jack stopped, Big Frank passed him a cup of water. "Drink. Then drink again. You'll collapse in this heat."

"Look at you. You're not even sweating."

Frank guffawed and pulled off his thin-soled shoe. Water dripped out in a thin stream. "I reckon I'm all sweated out."

Jack leaned on his shovel and tipped the cup. He drained the contents and held it out for a refill. Frank tilted the bucket until Jack's cup overflowed onto the floor. "What did you mean earlier?"

Frank swiped his hand across his mouth and then ran his saturated handkerchief across his brow. "Our shift is almost over. You going to stay and experiment?"

"Not tonight." Jack let the shovel fall to the floor, relieved to see the greaser moving down the line. "Buddy's on his way to oil the machinery."

"We might as well head home then." Big Frank tilted the bucket and let the water run down his oversized head and shoulders. His teeth gleamed in the flashes of light from the open-hearth furnaces in front of them. "Next shift will have to fill their own bucket."

Jack drained his cup. "You're avoiding my question."

Big Frank lumbered away and gestured for Jack to follow. They emerged into the night air and allowed the breeze to cool their bodies.

"Who's got it out for me, Big Frank?"

Frank swerved his large head in Jack's direction. "You sure have a nose for trouble."

Jack hesitated. He chose his next words carefully. "You've probably heard that Alaina and I are engaged."

The Scot shook his head and delivered a gut-shaking slap on Jack's back. "Hadn't heard. Congratulations."

"Robert was the first to know."

"He's after you, boy," Frank said. "He sure had a hornet chasing him before you got here. Had a couple of the fellas askin' how it was you could be late and the boss didn't notice and did they want that in their new shift manager?"

"He's jealous."

Big Frank's hand sluiced water from his hair. "Old Mike told Robert to shut his trap and get out."

"I was only late by a couple of minutes. I woke up later than I wanted." A twinge of conscience pinched in Jack's gut. He should have guessed his tardiness would allow Robert the fodder he needed to make a case against him. "Mike knows Robert's trouble."

Frank's eyes were grave. "You need to remember something, though. Old Mike is almost done. He's as good as gone. If Robert can cause a big enough stink among the younger men, Fulton might not consider you for Mike's job just because the guys don't like you." He stroked a hand down his jaw. "I wouldn't put it past Robert and his cronies to cause an *accident* to put you out of the way for a while."

Accidents, Jack knew, occurred hourly, more toward the end of the twelve-hour shifts than the beginning. Carelessness ran rampant when the men grew weary. If Robert were to go so far as to do such a thing, he would have a lot of opportunities to pull it off.

Jack's eyes went to the ragged scar along Big Frank's forearm. A piece of slag had hit him and burned. The Scot had been lucky he had been a good distance away from the flying slag, or its velocity could have penetrated and killed him.

"That's part of the reason I want to make these ideas of mine work. We need a better way of doing this, Frank. Safer. The Bessemer is just the beginning." He clenched his fist. "I'll be on my guard for Robert's tricks."

Big Frank's hand clamped down on his shoulder. "And I'll be praying for you. Why don't you and Alaina come over for supper one evening? Missy and Sam would love to see you."

"I'll tell her," he said, though he knew he needed every spare moment to tweak his plans. Success was so close. It seemed to him the shape was the problem. The Bessemer's oval shape worked so well.

A flash of inspiration ran through his head as Jack raised his face to the evening sky. Mentally he reviewed the details of the new idea. Excitement coursed through him and renewed his strength. He would put the idea to the test as soon as his shift was over. Alaina wouldn't be home from South Fork. . . .

Jack ran a hand over his wet hair when he recalled the Hensleys' premature departure and Alaina's expected arrival in Johnstown last evening. His frustration grew. He needed to act on his new design as soon as possible, but Alaina would expect him, too.

Frank turned to head back inside and Jack followed. "You two going to tell her mama about your engagement?"

Jack's step faltered. "Why, yes. Sure. We'll let everyone know."

"Her mama's not going to be happy."

What energy Jack had felt moments before seemed to leak from him. "We're prepared for that."

Frank shouldered his cloth bag, and they left the building's stifling heat and constant noise. Big Frank chuckled. "You're not going to believe this, but Mrs. Morrison is a good woman deep down. A parent wants what they think is best for their child, even if they don't go about it the way they should. Mrs. Morrison's had her share of hurts, and sometimes you have to look beyond a person's hurt to see their heart. I'll be praying for you."

Chapter 6

Clumps of oatmeal stuck in Alaina's throat with every bite. She finally gave up, shoved her bowl back, and pressed her palms together on the scarred wooden kitchen table, determined not to allow her mother's silence to continue. "Will you need my help today?"

Her mother appeared startled at her words. "No. I'm all caught up. I was expecting another order from Mrs. Stephens, so I worked ahead."

A new silence grew between them. Alaina worked her spoon around the small bowl.

"It's good to have you home again," Charlotte offered.

Alaina smiled at her mother's words, knowing that something unpleasant was coming. Her mother never offered loving words without tacking on a controversial issue.

"Your aunt wants to know when to expect you in Pittsburgh. I wrote back that the end of May is likely. It's a good time to look the college over."

Alaina forced herself not to release the pent-up sigh. Charlotte would take it as a show of anger. "I want to marry Jack, Mama."

Her mother's eyes moved over her face, examining.

Alaina placed her hands flat on the surface of the table. She braced herself for the flood of arguments her mother would rain down upon her. Jack was too young. *She* was too young. Jack was flighty and inconsistent. Jack's job wasn't good enough. They would struggle financially. And the one that all the others inevitably led up to—*she* needed to have a sound education before she married, so that if Jack, in his flighty inconsistency, left her alone, she would not live in poverty.

History repeated.

"I know how you feel." She paused, her eyes sweeping over her mother's graying hair. She softened her voice. "We want your blessing."

Charlotte Morrison's dark eyes glinted. "If you marry *him*, you won't have it."

Alaina's stomach clenched. In her mental list, she had forgotten that particular argument. The Robert-is-a-better-choice one. "I can't love a man I don't respect."

"Then why are you engaged to Jack?"

The gasp escaped before Alaina could steel herself. "How did you know?"

"So he did propose. Mary's mama said as much, but I didn't want to believe that you wouldn't tell me first. I knew something was up, though. I haven't seen Robert as much lately. Poor boy must be working hard to get that promotion."

She wanted to point out that Robert came to the apartment to see her, and being that she was in South Fork, it made sense that her mother wouldn't see him here. But stating such a fact would be foolish and mistaken as irreverence. "You think Robert is so perfect, but you don't *know* him like I do, Mama."

Charlotte stood. Frown lines fanned out from her lips and creased her forehead. "You're right, I don't. But if Jack is as wonderful as you think he is, he won't mind waiting for you to get your education first. And you, being the wonderfully obedient daughter you should be, will listen to your mother."

Stung at the verbal assault, Alaina lowered her face and squeezed her eyes shut. "He's not like Daddy, Mother. Why do you have to compare my situation to yours? I know you work hard. I know we struggle. I've tried to help out as much as I can."

Her mother snatched up the bowls and set them on the edge of the dry sink. She squeezed behind Alaina to reach for her sewing apron and tied it on. "I don't have time for this right now. Mrs. Fortney will be in this morning, and I have three dresses that need some finishing touches." Without even so much as a good-bye, her mother slammed the door. Her steps clumped down the outside staircase that led to the back of the general store they lived above and where her mother worked.

Alaina surveyed the small apartment. Besides the dirty dishes, table, and dry sink, the room held only a tattered rag rug and an array of the colorful aprons her mother used to cover her clothes as she sewed. She noted the neat rows of pins stuck all along the skirt of the aprons. Every single one had scads of small, snipped threads clinging to the coarse material.

Two other rooms completed the apartment. Her mother's room was only as big as the grocer's pantry downstairs, and Alaina's room even smaller. But she loved the sunshine that streaked through her window on summer days. She often felt her room the better choice of the two because it had such a luxury. She smiled. And it had a tree. An old maple tree whose branches reached out to scrape the window on windy nights. Or held the weight of a young man who came calling in the night, though Jack hadn't made use of its thick limbs for many weeks.

Alaina crossed to the window and lifted the sash. A gusty breeze swept the room clean of the musty air always present in the wooden building during the rainy season. She inhaled deeply, braced her hands on the windowsill, and listened to the church's clock striking the hour. A layer of dark gray clouds promised more rain to come. Undaunted by the threat of a downpour, Alaina left the window open as she began to make beds and gather laundry.

With every passing year, it seemed Charlotte's expression became more dour, her attitude more bitter. Long ago, when the letters from her father still trickled in on rare occasion, Alaina learned not to ask questions of his whereabouts. And Charlotte had never made it a habit to mention him, her opinion boldly stated when she tossed the unread letter into the cookstove. But despite the veil of uncaring her mother hid behind, the letter stating her father had died had shattered something deep inside Charlotte.

Lord, what can I do? She heaved a sigh. It seemed the prayer had become a litany of late.

Alaina stopped at the open window and rested her hands on top of the broomstick. She rested her chin and closed her eyes. *Why am I so confused one moment and so sure of myself every time I look at Jack's smile or hear his laughter?* She pondered the half prayer and stilled herself to hear God's response.

The jangle of a harness outside the window snapped her to attention. Within seconds, the first drops of rain plinked against the window. Alaina slid the window shut, breathed on the glass, and wrote, *I love you, Jack.*

He had promised to come by after work so they could announce their engagement to her mother together, but the glow of the surprise was dimmed by Mary's tongue souring the secret and by Charlotte's staunch rejection of Jack. For whatever foolish reason, Alaina had thought maybe her mother's opinion of Jack would soften if the engagement became a reality.

Alaina lifted her mother's spare dress from a peg and folded it over her arm. She would try and talk to Charlotte one more time, during supper, before Jack arrived.

☙

Her mother got home later than usual. Splotches of rain dampened her hair and dotted her apron, but Alaina didn't miss her brief look of relief when she smelled supper cooking.

"Supper will be ready soon," Alaina offered unnecessarily.

Charlotte removed her apron and sagged into a kitchen chair. She flexed her fingers back and forth. "Rain always makes them worse."

"Maybe you should soak them tonight. I could run downstairs and buy some salts—"

"No need. I'll live."

And with that comment, Alaina knew her mother's petulance over their morning conversation had been remembered. She busied herself spooning up the beans and biscuits, wishing she had taken the extra time to purchase a chicken for frying. She set the plate in front of her mother and took her seat opposite.

Her mother picked up her fork, stopped, met her gaze, and nodded. "Go ahead."

Alaina said a brief blessing that she suspected her mother forgot altogether when alone. She lifted her fork and tried to drum up a way to approach the subject of Jack without a wall going up between them. That was the trick. But Alaina could see no way to make that happen.

Best to be direct. It was easier. "I wondered if we could talk about Jack." Before her mother could finish chewing and give a caustic remark, she hurried on. "He's coming over tonight to ask permission to marry me, and I'd like for you to grant it." She bit the inside of her lip when she could think of nothing else to say.

Her mother set her fork down and stared at her. Alaina held her breath, waiting for the storm of her mother's emotions to break in with an angry flow of words. Instead, her mother blinked and averted her face. Charlotte's shoulders stooped, and her hands covered her face. Not until Alaina saw her shoulders heave and heard the first faint sniff did she realize what was happening.

Anger she could handle. Her mother's outbursts had become commonplace, but never before had she witnessed her mother's tears. She rounded the table and knelt beside Charlotte's chair. Glints of silver in her mother's hair reminded Alaina that she was the age her mother had been when she'd given birth to her. If only her father hadn't left them.

Her mother jerked to her feet. "I don't wish to be disturbed this evening. Jack Kelly is no longer welcome in this home, Alaina. Not tonight or ever again."

Alaina rocked back on her heels as her mother swept past, and the sound of the bedroom door lock clicking into place echoed deep in her spirit.

ꞓȝ

Jack braced his feet apart and tilted his head way back to mark his target. His fingers jingled the pebbles in his trouser pocket. Alaina's window above the general store proved a challenge. He contemplated the nearby tree, but the lower branch he used to swing up had broken. He would have to think of something else.

He plucked a single pebble from his pocket and held it up between his thumb and forefinger to draw a bead on the window. A flick of his wrist and the pebble sailed through the air and tapped against the wood planks. Jack mentally adjusted his arc and launched another stone that hit the window with a gentle *tap*. Another followed. Then another. He waited in silence for any sign Alaina might have heard.

As he surrendered to the notion he would have to send a few more through the air, a dim light flickered and then flared to life. The window slid open, and Alaina gazed up at the sky, into the tree, then down at the ground. She gasped at the sight of him. "Jack!" She clamped a hand over her mouth, and her face disappeared from the window.

Jack grinned. He had surprised her.

She reappeared.

"Come down," he said in a loud whisper. The sight of her stole his breath. Her long hair tousled around her head. He could almost smell the warm scent of her skin.

Alaina didn't reply but again disappeared. The window whispered shut.

He waited at the base of the large maple, its branches studded with sprigs of small, spring leaves. He slicked a hand over his hair, still damp from his bath, and pursed his lips to whistle a tune before realizing the danger. Midnight was not the time to sing a cheery tune in the middle of the street. He satisfied himself with pacing in front of Heiser's store.

"What are you doing out here in the middle of the night?" Alaina's whisper cut across his thoughts, and he turned. She seemed to float toward him in the moonlight. Tendrils of hair brushed her cheeks and neck, a dark contrast against her creamy skin.

He took a step closer. Words stuck in his throat at the weight of her beauty. He caught her hands and lifted them to his chest. "I knew you would think I'd forgotten, so I wanted to surprise you."

"I knew you must be working on your plans again."

"It came to me tonight at the end of shift. I had to get it down on paper before I forgot. I think this time it's really going to work. You understand, don't you?"

Alaina blinked and stared at the ground.

Her hesitation made him nervous. "Mr. Fulton also asked me to look at the South Fork Dam. He's afraid it'll collapse under all this rain."

She tilted her head back, the slender column of her neck exposed in the pale moonlight. "More rain on the way, I'm afraid." Her voice sounded tremulous.

He grasped her hand and kissed the palm. "I wanted to be here to tell your mother the news, but Mr. Fulton gave me three days to report so I'll need to go tomorrow after shift. I'll come tomorrow evening as soon as I can and we'll tell her then."

Her expression went solemn, and when she opened her mouth to speak, he pressed a finger across her lips. "Wait, I have a surprise." Jack released her hand and plucked something from the ground at the base of the maple.

"A rose," she breathed.

"Mrs. Sanford's first. She'll skin me for cutting it, but I'll tell her it was for you and she'll get that dreamy look and I'll be off the hook."

In awe, he watched her bury her nose into the rose's blush petals. As she breathed in the sweet fragrance, an incredible vulnerability swept over him as he was reminded of his commitment to care for this woman. Slowly, he raised his hand to spiral a tendril of her hair around his finger. He released the coil. It stroked her cheek, and he mirrored the touch with his hand. Dark and luminous, her eyes caught at his heart.

He took a step closer and satisfied himself with brushing his lips against the cool skin of her brow. "When will you marry me?" His voice came out hoarse, and he cleared his throat.

Her gaze seemed fastened on his shirt. In the length of time it took her to answer, his mind tripped over what her hesitation might mean.

He drew away and held her by the shoulders. "Alaina?" Her head sunk lower. He felt the first indication of the depth of her distress in the vibration under his hands. The soft love in his heart bled away under the heat of his rising terror. "Lainie?"

"My mother knows we're engaged. She made a terrible scene this morning and then hardly talked to me after supper. She said—"

Her words choked off, and Jack's heart froze. He gave her a soft shake. "I'm here, Alaina. Tell me."

She raised her face, and he saw the despair in her expression. "She said you were no longer welcome in our home."

He pressed her close and willed himself to breathe as the next logical question begged to be asked. "How?"

Her shoulders quaked. "Mary. It's my fault, Jack."

His anger flared hot but cooled quickly. He couldn't expect Alaina not to share with her friend. She had to talk to someone, and Mary was the logical choice. He just wished the meddling girl would learn to keep a secret.

Alaina became silent in his arms. Her hair was silk under his stroking hand. "What do you want to do?"

"I don't want her to think I'm being obstinate. If I don't do as she asks, she'll accuse me of being an ungrateful daughter."

"You aren't. You know that, don't you?"

She nodded against his chest.

Recalling Big Frank's admonition, some great truth swelled in his heart. "Your mother is just hurt over your father leaving all those years ago. You can't blame her for that." He pulled back from her and tilted her chin upward. "You can't blame her for being afraid for you."

"She thinks you're like my father. Every time I told her you had forgotten a date. . .well, I finally stopped telling her because she would always say you were just like *him*."

"Meaning your daddy."

Her eyes glistened with unshed tears. "I wish I remembered him."

Jack pulled her close and buried his face in her hair. *And I wish I could forget mine.*

Chapter 7

May 17, 1889

Jack's report on the South Fork Dam took longer than he thought. The crinkled, yellow edges of the *Tribune*, dated 1881, reported that two of Johnstown's own men had inspected the dam and felt it stable enough to withstand the pressure of extra water. Those with doubts felt that even if it broke, the water had plenty of room to spread out before it hit Johnstown.

He laid the paper down on the rough tabletop in his small room and steepled his fingers under his chin. Exhaustion filtered through every muscle in his back.

The short, steep train ride up to South Fork after his long shift had given him time to study the terrain in detail and expand on his own personal worry. The valley from Johnstown to South Fork was narrow, meaning the water would be like a huge, tall wall, barreling down the fourteen-foot drop to Johnstown like water in a sluice. Johnstown would be the dumping ground for every drop that came down the mountain. He ran the scenario of such a wall of water over in his mind, and every time he came up with the same answer—it would be devastating.

Jack rubbed at a spot above his eye where a dull throb had begun. He pulled over a stack of letters Fulton had given to him to examine. Correspondence between Morrell and B. F. Ruff, president of the club, read like the chronicles of two men used to having their own way, Morrell at least possessing the kinder tone of the two. Jack made a mental note of Morrell's suggestion that Ruff put in a drainage pipe and his offer to help finance the reconstruction of the dam. He searched through the stack for Ruff's response and didn't find one.

Another newspaper article in the stack reported on Daniel Morrell's acceptance into the South Fork Fishing and Hunting Club. An interesting fact that caused Jack to wonder if the membership had been a bribe on the part of the club. On the other hand, Daniel Morrell might have wanted to get an inside view of the club's doings. Could be that he was fully satisfied the club was doing all within its power to insure the safety of the dam and he simply wanted to be a part of such an organization. They would never know for sure, due to Morrell's death almost four years earlier.

Jack turned over his own ideas of the dam's issues and wrote his concerns on paper. To his eye, the dam buckled in the middle, the very place it needed to be strongest and highest. The drainage pipe was still a concern, and now with the heavy spring rains, if that earthen mound became soaked through. . . Jack wrote on paper his gut instinct—the dam remained unsafe.

He stretched, blew out the lantern, and uncurled from his chair. The dull throb in his head had become a steady ache. As he stripped off his clothes and lay his head down, his thoughts turned to Alaina. Longing swelled his heart. Her tears tore at him, and her mother's constant disapproval of him chipped away at his patience.

He flipped onto his back and lay with his arm across his eyes. Charlotte Morrison had no way of understanding Jack's drive. He sometimes wondered if Alaina understood or just endured. Sleep didn't fold him into its velvety arms as he'd hoped. Drafts floated in from the cracks in the walls and made him shiver. He pulled the blanket tighter around his chin and opened his eyes to the dark, hollow *ping* of rain against the roof.

With a grunt, he swept back the covers, crossed to the old kitchen cabinet hung on one wall, and retrieved a tin can. Even in the dark, he could see the water stain on the wood floor. His toes curled at the cold wood as he set the can beneath the spot where the leak always occurred. He squinted up to where the dull whitewashed ceiling sported a ragged gold ring. The first drop of water hit him on the forehead. Jack moved aside and tugged the can closer to the spot where he had been standing.

He stretched and scratched his chest. The clouds let loose with a tirade, and he waited for the inevitable. A sloppy *ping* let him know the can still lay out of line with the leak. He groaned and gave in, lit the lantern, and brought it back to the dark splotch of water, centering the can directly over the spot.

His landlady, Widow Sanford, had just had a bathroom installed in her home, along with a phone and steam heat, but the small shack Jack rented remained without those amenities. His relief at being left out of the so-called *improvements* was great. The last thing he needed was a rent hike.

He eyed the report on the table and allowed himself to dream about the benefits getting the promotion would give him. He had allowed Alaina to see the outside of his place only once and vowed then and there that he would not marry her unless he could provide better than the one-room shack.

The rhythmic *ping* of the water stripped him of his exhaustion. He went down on his knees beside his narrow cot and pulled out a box. Its top, carved with flowers and hearts, sketched in his mind a vision of his mother's long fingers tracing the same design, a sad smile on her face. He removed the lid and plunged his hand into the box to lift out the Bible. *Her* Bible, now his.

At the table he pulled the lantern close and opened the fine-tooled leather cover. Little notes in the margins, as familiar to him as the scar on the back of his hand, made him feel closer to his mother and, in turn, he felt closer to God.

He turned to his favorite verse and read it, his mind automatically taking on his mother's voice as he repeated the words to himself.

"Thou wilt shew me the path of life: in thy presence is fulness of joy; at thy right hand there are pleasures for evermore."

Psalm 16:11. How many times had he heard his mother quote the scripture to him in his years growing up, even in those gray days after his father's death?

He squeezed his eyes shut, hands clenched tight. He saw Alaina's longing eyes as she expressed her desire to remember her father. Heard the flat sound of his mother's voice after that terrible night when she sat him on her knee and told him the news. Only later did he understand the shame that she had endured when the truth was made known.

Jack swallowed hard. He shut the Bible and noticed an edge of paper sticking out. Thinking to uncrease a bent corner, he traced the place with his finger and discovered a folded paper behind a loose cover flap. Jack tugged at the corner. It caught where the glued edge of the cover flap held it in place. With his finger, he pulled the flap away and tugged out the folded pages. He recognized the handwriting immediately as that of his father. He scanned the contents, realizing his mother must have kept the letter for a very good reason.

Dear Olivia,

You don't deserve this. Maybe your mother was right all along, you should have married Frederick Thomas. I don't know. I do know that you will be better off without me, as will Jack. I haven't touched a drop in over a month, just as I promised you, but another type of failure greeted me this afternoon while you were out—our bank failed. We've lost everything. It's too much for me. You're strong, Livey, much stronger than I. You'll survive and make a better home for Jack alone than you ever would with me in the picture.

I do love you. Please believe me, and when the time is right, tell Jack I love him, too.

Yours,
Don

Jack let the letter flutter from his hands to the floor. He leaned forward as if punched in the gut and pressed his thumbs against his eyes. Flashes from the past sliced through him, the last one from the day he watched his mother lowered into the ground. If not for his remembrance of her favorite verse, he might have been overwhelmed by his grief. Jack sucked in a deep breath and held it.

God, give me strength to forget. To forgive.

He released his breath and felt the tendrils of exhaustion weaving through his body.

Chapter 8

May 18, 1889

Alaina woke from a deep sleep to the touch of her mother's hand on her arm.

"I thought I'd better wake you before I left," her mother said.

She scooted up in bed, fully expecting her mother to turn and leave, surprised when she stayed.

Charlotte stood still, her eyes on the far wall.

Alarmed, Alaina scooted up in bed and noted her mother's puffy, red eyes and pale complexion.

"Mama, are you ill?"

Charlotte's gaze snapped to hers. "I'll be fine." But she still didn't move.

Alaina grasped her mother's arms. "Mother, please, what's the matter?"

Charlotte's eyes filled with tears. Her mother pressed a hand to Alaina's cheek, then spun and left the room.

Alaina skittered on the edge of concern all morning, not at all sure what to make of her mother's unusual behavior. After she dressed, she decided a quick visit to the store after chores might help alleviate her fears. If her mother was truly ill, she needed to know.

Laundry took all day, and it wasn't until early evening that she got the chance to escape to the store. If Jack kept his promise, he would be here this evening. If only she could get her mother to talk to her first.

Through the back door of the store, Alaina could see Charlotte sitting in the corner, stitching on a long gown of tweed brown and gold. Surrounded by needles, pins, and spools of Clark's O.N.T., her mother appeared relaxed and serene, though her eyes still showed tinges of puffiness.

"Miss Morrison."

Alaina's attention flew to the young man coming toward her. Charlotte Morrison raised her head. Young Victor Heiser, the storekeeper's son, grinned at her with a mixture of shyness and longing.

"Good day to you, Victor. How are you?"

He seemed abashed that she answered him and lowered his head. "I'm doing well."

"And is Miss Powers doing well with the Sunday school?"

He peeked at her. "Yes, ma'am. Though you were the best teacher."

Alaina smiled her gratitude. "How kind of you. Give Miss Powers a chance, and I'm sure everyone will love her as much."

"I suppose." Victor's ears reddened and he shrugged. "Your mother asked me if I still remembered my scripture verses. I do. I repeated them all for her. All forty-two."

Alaina felt the edge of surprise that her mother would inquire. In the six months Alaina taught Sunday school, she had endeavored to commit two verses a week to memory and challenged her pupils to do the same. Friday and Saturday nights during the fall and winter, she had repeated them aloud as she went about her chores. Her mother had never shown the least interest. "You are to be commended, Victor. I don't know that I could do such a thing without first brushing up a bit."

"Oh, you could, Miss Alaina. I'm sure of it!"

She laughed at his enthusiasm. "Maybe I should pop into your class this Sunday. We could have a contest."

Mathilde Heiser, Victor's mother, appeared from the front of the store, her expression harried. "Victor, stop dawdling. Your father needs you." Mathilde gestured to the boy and then rolled her eyes over at Alaina. "How that boy does go on about you. I think you've stolen his heart and most of his head. I keep reminding him that he's no competition to Jack."

Alaina tilted her head and laughed. "I'm sure Jack won't feel threatened, Mrs. Heiser. How is your husband doing?"

"Very well. Your mother's skill has really been a draw for the womenfolk. She is very good."

Alaina smiled over at her mother. "Yes, she is."

Charlotte held up the dress she had been working on and shook it out, but Alaina saw the trace of a pleased smile on her lips. "You've both been very kind to me, Mrs. Heiser. Mr. Springer never seemed to appreciate a woman's need for a fine gown." She paused, her eyes lifting to Alaina. "I think it's about time for my daughter to have some new gowns, too. I wouldn't want the ladies to see the daughter of their seamstress in anything less than the best."

Victor rushed over to his mother and tugged on her sleeve. "Father needs us both."

Mrs. Heiser lifted her hand. "Whatever your mother does for you will be lovely."

Unconsciously, Alaina fingered the material of her blue dress. It used to be her best, but after months of wear, it had lost the luster of newness. She wanted to tell her mother not to worry about making her a new gown, but something about the offer stopped her. How long had it been since her mother last made such an offer? Alaina usually made her own gowns during the winter months. Her mother knew that. Something about Charlotte's offer seemed gentle and kind. Different.

Charlotte stuck a pin in her mouth and nodded. "What brought you down here?"

"I wanted to check on you."

The pin in her mother's mouth seemed to tremble, and Alaina thought she detected a sheen of tears in her eyes.

Her conscience pricked, and she whispered the next words. "I'm supposed to meet Jack this evening." Alaina expected to feel the singe of her mother's anger at the mention of Jack.

Instead, Charlotte merely sat down and reorganized the yards of material. "On your way out, tell Victor to come back when he gets the chance. I want to hear him recite those verses again."

Alaina pleaded with her eyes. "Jack will want to say hello."

Her mother's mouth drooped. "Tell him hello for me." Charlotte returned her attention to the material, her needle sliding in and out in impossibly small stitches.

Alaina headed to the front of the store. She stopped in the middle of the room and took in the bright display of candy and soap powder, medicines, and washboards. Unshed tears made everything a blur. She had so wanted to hear her mother acquiesce and welcome the opportunity of seeing Jack.

A hand appeared in front of her face, with a licorice whip dangling from long, calloused fingers. Her heart leaped and almost turned into the embrace of Jack's arms, but conscious of where they were, she took a step back and plucked the licorice from his hand.

"My, my, greedy, aren't we?"

"You tempt me with my favorite candy and you don't expect me to take the bait?"

Jack's expression held mischief. "I wish you were that excited to see me."

Alaina returned his smile. "Don't be silly."

He twined his fingers through hers and pulled her close enough to whisper in her ear. "One piece for you. I thought I'd make a peace offering with the rest."

"Jack." She shook her head and kept her voice low so other patrons wouldn't hear. "Mama told me to tell you hello. I don't think it's a good idea for us to push too hard right now." Though she loved him the more for wanting to try and make peace.

Jack glanced toward the back of the store and then at the bag of licorice in his free hand. He handed it over to her. "Then I'll surrender them to you for delivery. But you have to promise not to eat them all on your way back."

Alaina accepted the bag and gave him a rueful grin. "I'll try not to."

"Are you hungry?"

She held up the bag. "I won't be."

Jack touched the tip of her nose. "Let's go before I storm the back room and demand to marry you on the spot, with or without her blessing."

The lightness being in Jack's presence had brought faded as she retraced her steps back to her mother's corner of the store. Charlotte didn't look up from her sewing.

"Mama?" The bag crinkled in Alaina's hand as she slipped it onto the low table by her mother's stool.

Charlotte glanced at the parcel. "What's this?"

Her throat thickened and she swallowed. "Jack's peace offering." Before she broke into tears, she hurried back to the front of the store. With one glance, Jack must have understood her need, for he offered his arm and led her to the entrance, giving Victor Heiser, his eyes wide upon them, a slap on the back. He whispered something in the young man's ear, then turned and winked at Alaina.

Once outside, she demanded to know what he'd said to the boy.

"I told him the truth. You're too old for him." He leaned in so close she could feel his breath against her face. "Unless, of course, you prefer younger men."

The way he said it, his closeness, it made her heart beat madly. "No, there's only one for me."

His playful expression became serious. His gaze swept her face and caused her stomach to twist. Beneath the luminescent light in his blue eyes, heat rose in her cheeks.

"Well, then"—he took a deliberate step back and returned her hand to his arm—"if you won't marry me tonight, then we could go for a walk or roller-skating."

She laughed but sobered at the thought of her mother's scowl of disapproval upon learning they had married without her knowledge or blessing. Still. . . "Wouldn't it be wonderful to get married and—"

"Until we reached my place and I carried you over the threshold." He gazed at the darkening sky of lead gray. "We could take turns emptying the mug of water from my leaky roof." The smile he sent her didn't reach his eyes. "Not what I want for you. For us."

"Then let's walk around and see the sights. We could go to the park and walk until dark."

Jack winced. "I can't stay too long. I need to finish my report to Mr. Fulton." He placed his hand over hers, where it lay nestled against his arm. "I also need to spend some time this evening working on my plans since church is tomorrow. I think I'm close, Alaina."

He must have sensed her disappointment because he kept talking, giving assurances, reminding her he did it for them, but she scarcely heard him. All the doubts tumbled around in her head and welled in her chest. His invention always seemed first priority, and she couldn't quite shake off the sincerity of her mother's many warnings against Jack.

"He is always chasing after his dream of money. Marry a man who will put you first."

And then there was the one her mother never directly spoke but Alaina felt in every line of sadness on her mother's face.

Your father chased after the dream of money and never returned.

She knew Jack wanted to earn a good living, but how far would he go to do that? Was his need driven by something in his past? Maybe his parents were rich and he had been disinherited.

Alaina slipped a glance over at Jack as he talked. They were engaged. Surely he could tell her about his mother and father. He knew all about hers. She had a right to know. Maybe it would help her understand him better.

She waited for a lull in his words. "Jack, tell me about your parents."

"My parents?"

The sudden shift in topics had taken him off guard. Something like panic seeped into his eyes.

"Yes. You always avoid the subject. I want to know about them. Shouldn't I meet them before we marry? Don't you want to include them in our plans?"

Jack's face set like chiseled stone. She felt the wall of his anger rise with every second, brick by angry brick. "I'm an adult. I don't need their permission."

"Surely your mother would—"

He released her abruptly, his gaze full of pain. "She's dead, Alaina. My mother is dead. She won't care about a thing."

"What? How did it happen? I mean, when?"

A muscle jumped in his jaw. "A long time ago. Before I moved here."

"What about your father?"

His gaze went white-hot. He turned away, fists clenched at his sides. "It's a topic for another time."

She touched his arm and felt the taut bunch of his muscles. "Please, Jack."

He bowed his head and knotted fists rubbed his eyes.

Alaina felt his pain without understanding the reason for it. Shame washed over her at her insistence. "I'm sorry." She ran her hand down his upper arm to his wrist and then lifted his hand to gently uncurl his fingers, all the while silently begging him to look at her. *Please, Lord, take this hurt away.* She wanted so much to erase the entire conversation.

On another level, his reaction to the simple question chilled her. What did it mean? What was in his past that proved so painful it rendered him speechless?

Finally, she felt the tension leave him.

He squeezed his eyes shut and regarded her with a look of profound exhaustion, as if he had fought many demons in the last few minutes. "I've got to go," his voice scraped out.

"I understand."

"I'll walk you back."

"No." She forced a smile. "I'll be fine."

"Alaina. . ." He paused. "I need some time. It's not a topic I—"

"Then I'll wait."

Chapter 9

May 19, 1889

Alaina started upon seeing her mother, dressed and ready for Sunday morning services. She tried to recall the last service her mother had attended and settled on Easter, two years ago, when her aunt had come over from Pittsburgh for a short visit.

"You're dressed," she stated the obvious, then laughed.

The comment pulled a smile from her mother as she smoothed a strand of hair back from her face. "It's time, don't you think?" Her mother gathered the material of her best dress in one hand and frowned at the brown plaid. "I need to start on new dresses for both of us. This material is so thin at the elbows."

Her mother continued to fuss over the dress while Alaina tried to make sense of her question. What did she mean by, "It's time?" Time for what? Time to go? But no, it couldn't be. Jack wouldn't arrive to fetch her for another twenty minutes.

"Alaina?" her mother asked. "Would you fetch my Bible?"

She did as bid, expecting the Book to be collecting dust on the small table her mother used to hold a lamp. To her surprise and satisfaction, she saw that the Bible lay open on the table and rejoiced at the implication. It had been such a long time since Father had left. Perhaps her mother would return to the faith she had once held so dear.

She searched for a way to bring up the topic of her mother's sudden Bible reading and churchgoing when Jack arrived. Upon seeing him, her mother's frown deepened. Alaina feared she might say something harsh, but Charlotte nodded in response to Jack's greeting and allowed him to help her into the hackney with a small smile bestowed on him as his reward.

After Jack found his seat, he caught and held Alaina's gaze for a long, blissful moment. "The great thaw," he quipped in a whisper.

She rolled her eyes and pressed her finger to her lips to shush him from further comment.

Jack engaged her in conversation about the weather, though she noticed he did avoid the usual question of what they would do after service. Charlotte seemed content to make the trip in silence, and Alaina left her to it after her first few attempts to bring her into the conversation failed.

She enjoyed sharing chatter on various subjects with Jack. After the previous night's storm of emotion, he seemed attentive, though circles showed under his eyes. They were engaged in a fiery back-and-forth regarding the chances of the dam breaking when they arrived at the small church.

Frank's children, Missy and Sam, ran up to them.

Jack swung Missy up into his arms and allowed her to perch on his shoulder. "What are you up to this morning, Miss Missy?"

The child giggled at Jack's greeting and beamed at Alaina. "He's silly."

Frank broke through the small crowd, his suspenders worn and his Sunday trousers in sad need of patching. It was on the tip of Alaina's tongue to offer to do the mending when her mother spoke up.

"Frank Mills, what a surprise."

Frank's face lit, and he dipped his head in a shallow bow. "A pleasure to see you, Mrs. Morrison."

"You must bring your mending to me. Missy's dress needs a patch, and I'm sure there is enough material left over from some dresses to make her a new frock."

"And me?" Sam piped up.

Jack scrunched up his face. "You want a dress, Sam?"

Sam cocked his head. "No, why would I want that?"

Jack and Frank guffawed at the boy's confusion.

Charlotte sent them a withering look. "And a pair of pants for you, Sam."

Alaina could only stare at her mother, struck completely dumb, not only by her generous offer but by the interest she showed in the children and Frank. She glanced at Frank and wondered if the big man had captured her mother's fancy. But no, it couldn't be. Charlotte had only met Frank twice before.

Jack let Missy slip to the ground and sidled up next to Alaina as Frank and Charlotte continued their conversation. "Is this the sun coming out?" was Jack's question.

"I—I don't know. I'm as surprised as you are. More so."

Jack chuckled. "Frank's not a bad-looking bloke."

But it didn't explain the sudden change in Charlotte. What had prompted her mother to go from shy and resigned, even bitter, to considerate? Was it simply God's working in her mother's heart? She didn't know, and she wouldn't ask.

When the pastor appeared at the front doors, the group began a mass migration inside.

Jack winked down at Alaina. "I'm going to test the waters. If Frank can be charming, then I can be downright saintly." With that, he strode up to Charlotte.

She glanced his way in time to see his proffered arm. Charlotte hesitated only a moment before accepting, leaving a chagrined Frank standing by himself.

He recovered quickly, though, when his gaze met Alaina's. He copied Jack's gesture and offered his arm, a good-natured grin coloring his cheeks.

She lay her hand lightly on his arm as he tilted his head and whispered, "You watch. Jack's going to win her over."

ঞ

If Jack's restless night hadn't been unsettling enough, then listening to the sermon on Judas's betrayal and Christ's forgiveness stirred the cauldron of his emotions into full boil. Every word the pastor uttered seemed to stir the same question. *How to forgive betrayal?*

His fidgeting caught Alaina's attention, and only a severe frown from her stilled his quaking limbs. He tried to focus on his plans and ignore the nagging of his spirit, but the pastor continued, now extolling Christ's ability to forgive the unforgivable.

Jack rubbed his hands down his trousers. So many years had passed since his father's failure and death. Did he truly have to forgive a dead man? Wasn't moving on enough? Putting the past behind him and striking out on his own hadn't been easy, but he'd done it. And now he was engaged to Alaina, a beautiful, gentle woman. What would she tell him to do?

What would his mother say? Had she forgiven his father before her death? He tried to remember any conversations he'd had with her in regard to his father and couldn't think of one time when she'd spoken a cross word.

His fingers dug into his palm. Hard. He wanted to believe that she had talked, maybe to others, and blamed Don Kelly for her trouble. It would make Jack's anger toward him easier to deal with.

As the notes of the final hymn lingered in the air, Jack squelched the desire to jump over the pews and burst outside. Instead, he did his duty and waited with everyone else for the pastor to greet his parishioners, one by one.

Alaina kept sending him confused looks, as if trying to diagnose his sudden illness, but the symptoms remained a mystery too hard for her to unravel.

The pastor shook Jack's hand but held on to prevent him from moving along. "You're working hard, Jack. Your face shows your weariness. Unless there is something else troubling you?"

Apparently his fidgeting hadn't gone unnoticed. He could feel Alaina's stare. Shame washed over him. "Your message was quite stirring."

A knowing twinkle flashed in the pastor's eyes. No doubt the man understood evasion when he heard it, but he allowed Jack to pass and turned his attention to Alaina.

Jack waited for her, chagrined when she picked up where the pastor had left off.

She placed her hand on his arm and leaned toward him ever so slightly. Jack could see the strain of her concern. For him. "This is not about a sleepless night, is it, Jack? It's about last night."

The arrow of her words hit its target. "Let's put it aside and enjoy our afternoon."

Her eyes flashed. "I won't be put off forever."

"I'm not putting you off." He shifted his weight and tried to keep his voice even. "I just don't have anything to tell you."

"You're troubled. You fidgeted more than a wayward boy of five during Pastor's sermon. I think I have a right to know what's troubling you."

"We can talk tomorrow night when I come to visit."

Her dark eyes snapped. "I'm supposed to share in your troubles."

Irritation pricked. "I'm fine."

Alaina's nostrils flared. "Then I'll leave you alone." She jerked around, head held high, and disappeared into the crowd.

Jack rubbed his hand over his brow. Alaina never pushed back, but she'd pushed back this time, and the experience left him shaken.

"Never seen her quite so fired up."

Jack looked over his shoulder to see Frank. "Me neither."

"You going after her?"

"I don't think she wants me to."

Frank's gaze lifted to something over Jack's shoulder. "Well, if you are, you'd better hurry. She and her mother got themselves a ride."

He didn't run after her. There was no use. How had things gone wrong so quickly? The prospect of returning to his dreary place or poring over his plans for a new angle from which to work all seemed hollow now.

Chapter 10

May 20, 1889

"Our hero," Clarence Fulton boomed when Jack opened the door of his boss's office.

Jack squinted in the midmorning light coming through the window, clutching his report in one hand. "I came by to drop off my findings on the South Fork Dam."

Mr. Fulton resumed his seat and fixed Jack with a stare that made him cautious. "The clouds are breaking up now." Fulton scooted his chair forward. "Without the rain pouring down, the dam doesn't seem like such a great threat. I'll read over your report. However, I'm more interested right now in that process you're working on."

An edge of irritation made Jack clench his teeth. All that work and now the report meant almost nothing. He made himself concentrate on Fulton's enthusiasm on the other project. "I'm on to something with that. I know it. I'll be working on it today."

"Good. Good. You show great promise, young man. Great promise."

The meeting came to a swift end, and for once, Jack felt relieved to step from his boss's office. As he got closer to the huge room of open hearth furnaces, the temperature spiked, and every footfall became a struggle against his exhaustion. In silence, he watched the men on first shift and empathized with the tedious, dangerous routine of the hot work. As the men bent and shoveled, Jack's muscles echoed the tension and misery so familiar to the job. He strained when they strained, and their shouts quickened his pulse.

He pushed through the doors and out into the light and cool air. In a corner of the yards that surrounded Cambria, with clear view of Cambria's own railroad depot, Jack rolled up his long sleeves and settled into deep thought about the entire process of converting iron ore into steel. He ran his hand over the miniature egg-shaped Bessemer converter he had shaped from scrap metal and studied his new theory, paying particular attention to the tuyeres through which air was blown to remove impurities from the molten iron. If blasting too much air removed too much carbon, then the resulting product was negatively affected. His new theory worked to solve this problem. With a surge of excitement, he bent his head over his plans.

The work was an elixir. He fell into the rhythm of trial and error, always reviewing the process and tweaking the amount of air blown into the molten iron. Only when he took a break did he allow himself to once again scrape up the discomfort over Alaina's question about his parents—her demand to share what troubled him about his past.

His father.

Jack stared at his hands and realized, ironically, that as much as he detested what his father became as he got older, he had, to a great degree, followed in his father's footsteps. Even as a five-year-old, he recalled being intrigued by his father's passion for creating solutions to problems around their small farm.

But as Jack had gotten older, things had gone wrong. His father kept inventing new and better ways of doing things, but drinking became his new obsession. It took Jack several years to realize that his father's regular drinking companion seldom drank at all. Instead, the man listened to Jack's father's ideas and cashed in on them. Only when the same man stopped giving Jack's father generous stipends did the situation at home become critical and the nightly rages against him and his mother worsened. In the end, he lost both his father and mother within six months of each other.

His mother's agony, the poverty his father had plunged them into by his poor choices, stirred Jack's agony anew as a veil of tears blinded him to the papers in front of him. The pair of pliers he had been using fell from his hand and clinked against a piece of scrap metal. He clenched his fists and swiped at the wetness on his cheeks, struggling against the familiar and bitter hatred his father's memory always stirred.

Pastor's sermon pounded in his head. A bitter Christ would have been useless in God's plan, yet He could have chosen that route. But Jack realized that Christ's decision to hate Judas would have destroyed His life, and the lives of everyone with life and breath.

For him to choose to cling to his bitterness would destroy him just as certainly. He knew it as sure as he knew he was close to a major discovery in his plans.

But how to forgive? He didn't know.

The sound of the whistle signaling the end of the shift and the beginning of another helped shake Jack back to the project at hand. His hand trembled as he pulled another sheet of paper from the pocket of his trousers and spread it out next to the others. He forced himself to focus on comparing his old notes with his new. After reviewing everything, he decided to tinker with the idea of heating the molten iron longer, lowering the impurities. Then. . .

His blood pumped hard through his veins as a chill shock snapped through him. If he could lower the impurities by heating longer and reintroduce. . .

Jack swallowed hard and made furious notes as the idea unfolded in his mind. Throughout his shift he reviewed the process over and over. By the time he arrived home that night, his excitement had faded into a bone-weary tiredness that made his muscles ache. He bypassed eating and did only as much as necessary to prepare for the next morning, when he would arrive earlier than necessary so he could work on this new angle.

Satisfied, he stretched out on his cot and pulled the blanket up over his shoulders. As he lay there, his mind caught between sleep and wakefulness, Jack remembered Alaina. Her smile, her concern, her anger. . .his promise to see her.

For a minute he hung in a semiconscious state, disgusted at how he could forget so easily. Again. But his weary mind and body pulled him down into a black oblivion he had no strength to fight.

Alaina will understand.

Chapter 11

May 21, 1889

"Don't pour!" Jack's scream rent the air seconds before the molten steel touched the water in the steel mold.

An explosion rocked the men not already undercover back on their heels.

Jack skidded into a low crouch and shielded his face. A blast of strong, hot air choked him and scorched his skin. Chunks of metal shot around the room, and Jack heard the muffled groan of pain next to him that told him Big Frank had been hit.

When the air settled, the factory whistle screamed the news of another accident to all within listening distance. Shouts lifted above the sounds of machinery as other men went to the rescue of those downed by the explosion.

Jack jumped up and hustled over to where Frank lay within a few feet of the mold. Still. Silent.

"God, no. God, please, no." He flipped Big Frank over. His heart plummeted at the sight of blood. Frank's shirt smoked where the heat had singed the material. "Frank? Frank!" He patted his friend's cheek, strangled with dread when Frank remained unresponsive. He lifted his head. "Help! Over here."

Someone appeared at his side, and together they lifted the big man and carried him away from the heat of the open hearth furnaces.

ও

Hospital beds lined both walls of the long room. Frank lay, pale and bandaged, eyes closed, halfway down the long room.

Jack recognized other workers and waved a greeting to those who were awake.

One of the men, Sweeney, as everyone called him, returned Jack's greeting with a grim, "How many this time?"

"Three." Jack stopped and ran a cautious eye over the man's bandaged arm and chest. "Three died. Five injured."

Sweeney rubbed at the bandage on his arm, then grimaced. "Hurt's like fire, but it's a graze."

"You were blessed not to have been killed."

The man leaned back against his pillow and gave a nod.

Jack headed down the row toward Frank and stopped at the foot of his friend's bed. He bowed his head, grateful Frank's life had been spared.

He lifted his face to find Frank's glazed stare upon him. "Not dead, am I? Was thinkin' God had allowed some pretty ugly angels to mess up heaven."

Jack's breath released in a relieved gust. He laughed and moved to the side of the bed. "Hey there. How're you feeling?"

"Like a piece of hot slag got me in the gut."

"And the face." Jack felt the burn of guilt. "If I hadn't left, it would have spared you from doing the pouring and getting hit."

Frank blinked slowly. "God orders the day, son. Haven't you figured that out yet? No amount of guilt is going to change the way things happen."

It took a minute for Jack to gain his voice. He gripped Frank's hand. "What about Missy and Sam?"

Frank seemed to drift off to a faraway place for a moment. Then his eyes fixed on the ceiling. "I don't know. Mrs. Sanford can't keep them. Too old."

"I'll do it. I'll take care of them for you, Frank. Alaina is home from the lake. She can watch them during the day and I'll help her in the evenings."

"You've got work to do, boy. Riches to make. An invention to invent."

Jack could hear the hopeful note behind Frank's playful words. "Then it's settled. Alaina won't mind, I know it. She loves Missy and Sam."

"You've a good heart, Jack."

"You concentrate on getting better."

☙

After Sunday, then forgetting about Alaina the night before, Jack felt every bit the fool for arriving on her doorstep with two children in tow.

She opened the door immediately, and his anxiousness lifted at her look of pleased surprise.

"Why, Missy and Sam, what are you doing here?"

Missy promptly broke into tears, and Sam shushed her.

Alaina met Jack's gaze with a question.

He leaned forward and whispered in her ear.

She gasped in dismay, then stooped to take first Missy's hand and then Sam's and led them inside.

Jack swept the room for any sign of Alaina's mother.

"She's not here. She's downstairs finishing up an order due tomorrow." Alaina pulled young Missy onto her lap and wiped her tears. She cuddled the six-year-old close and smoothed her ruffled hair.

Jack placed his hand on Missy's head. "How about I go downstairs and get some candy?"

Alaina gave him a searching look.

He winked and crouched to whisper into Missy's ear. "I need someone to help me pick. Want to come?"

Missy's solemn, gray gaze stirred something in his heart. "Will my daddy die?"

Jack rasped a hand down his unshaven cheek. Other than his initial fear that Frank had been outright killed, he hadn't considered his friend might die from his injuries. Frank was older than most of the men, at thirty-three years, but his strength would be in his favor. But to offer the child hope and have things take a turn for the worse. . .

Jack picked up Missy's small hand and got eye level with her. "I can't answer that question. No one can. But we can pray and trust and ask God to help us as we wait. Would you like to do that with me?"

"And Sam and Miss Alaina?"

"Sure."

Missy scrambled off Alaina's lap and dropped to her knees. Sam joined her. Jack and Alaina shared an amused look over the small heads. Missy tucked her hands together and looked at the ceiling. Jack got the feeling the child saw far beyond the stained plaster. Maybe even into the heart of God.

"Do you want to pray, Missy?"

She shook her head and pointed to him.

The words came easily to Jack. When he said, "Amen," he took the little girl into his arms, where her confidence failed her and she sobbed.

Sam stood nearby, tears trailing a silver streak down his pudgy face. Alaina settled a hand on the boy's shoulder.

"Will Mrs. Sanford watch us until Daddy is better?" Missy's words muffled against his shirt.

Jack swallowed hard. "I was hoping Miss Alaina might spend some time with you while your father recovers." His eyes pleaded with Alaina. "Your father said Mrs. Sanford was too old to watch you both full time."

He hesitated under Alaina's steady gaze, ashamed to be asking her for a favor when so much still stood between them. *I'm sorry,* he mouthed to her.

She didn't smile, but her eyes traced along Missy's back then over Sam's head and down to his shoes. Her expression softened. "We can make a place for you two on the floor in my room."

Sam hugged her legs, and Missy smiled shyly up at her.

Jack got to his feet. "Why don't the two of you head down to the store and check out that candy display."

"You want to kiss her?" Missy wanted to know. Her nose wrinkled as if the thought disgusted her.

Jack laughed. "You think that's so bad?"

"Daddy kissed Mommy a whole lot," she continued. "He loved her." With that, she turned and headed down the steps.

"Hold on to the railing," Alaina called after them.

He caught her gaze. "Maybe a better question is, would Miss Alaina even allow me to kiss her?"

Chapter 12

The weight of Jack's question caused her to hesitate. Always she was so quick to forgive him for breaking his word to her. What had it earned her? "I don't know, Jack." She couldn't bear to return his stare or to see the hurt in his eyes and stared down after Missy and Sam instead. "We'd better go after the children."

"Alaina, wait." His hand encased her wrist, but she refused to turn. He rested his hands lightly on her shoulders, his words placating. "I got another idea for the converter and began work on it. I lost track of the time. I'm sorry."

She felt the warmth of his breath against her cheek.

"I thought you would understand."

Her throat grew thick, and she stared at him as tears collected in her eyes. "Why don't you try to understand how *I* feel for a change? How it feels to be forgotten by the man who says he loves you and wants to marry you. Not once, Jack. Not twice—" The tears rolled, and her voice caught. "Try ten times. Maybe twenty. You always say it's for us, for *me*. But I don't care about money, don't you see? It's you, Jack. Money is *your* issue, not mine. I'm *happy* being poor. *People* are more important than things. And then, when I want to help you, to reach out to the man I love and share what is obviously troubling him, I'm turned away."

His hands slid down her arms then released her.

Unable to stand it any longer, she hurried down the steps, drying her eyes as she went, not wanting her mother to have further reason to be upset with Jack. As she stepped through the back door of the store, her mother glanced up.

Charlotte set her sewing aside and rubbed her eyes. "I saw the children come in from the back door. Is Big Frank visiting?"

"You should stop for the night, Mother. It's not good for your eyes to work such long hours."

Charlotte waved a hand in dismissal of her concern. "I'm paid well to have these gowns done quickly. The money is worth the long hours." She stretched her neck from side to side, her eyes flicking toward the entrance that led to the front of the store. "Now how did those two come to be here?"

"Jack brought them over." Her mother's lips curved down into a frown, and Alaina hastened to continue. "Cambria had an accident today. Frank's in the hospital."

Charlotte's face drained of color. "Oh no."

"The children need a place to stay, so Jack thought I could watch them during the day while he's at work."

Her mother's mouth tightened. "Did he think to *ask* first?"

"It happened so suddenly—"

Charlotte's eyes flashed. "Stop it, Alaina. Stop defending him. I can't stand to see you hurt by him."

The door behind Alaina creaked open, and she knew without looking that it was Jack.

"Good evening, Mrs. Morrison."

Charlotte tilted her head in acknowledgment of Jack's greeting, but her lips remained pressed into a grim line.

Alaina nodded toward the front of the store. "Why don't you check on the children, Jack?"

Charlotte resumed her seat and repositioned the material around her legs. "I've got to get this dress finished."

Jack remained glued to the spot. "Since I have to work, I wanted to know if it would be all right for Sam and Missy to spend the day with Alaina. There was a bad accident today. Frank got hit real bad."

Charlotte jammed her needle into the material and pulled through the other side. "So Alaina tells me. But it's not my decision. It's up to Alaina."

"Mother, Jack's trying to be polite."

"I would consider it polite if he didn't bother me with questions that don't need my answer."

Jack flinched. "I don't know what I've done to deserve your hostility, Mrs. Morrison, but whatever it is, I'm sorry."

Charlotte's head shot up. "Just like you're sorry for all those times you haven't shown up to take Alaina on a picnic, or roller-skating, or for a stroll? That kind of sorry is a word with no meaning."

A muscle jumped in Jack's jaw. "I can understand how you must feel that way, but I assure you, Mrs. Morrison, that I work very hard only in hopes of providing for Alaina in a way befitting to the woman I hope to marry." He turned toward Alaina, as if seeking some measure of support.

It was there on her tongue to assure her mother that she understood and didn't hold it against Jack, but it struck her that putting voice to such sentiments would be a lie. A lie she had perpetrated to give Jack peace, all the while allowing her own to slip away.

"You want to believe that, Jack Kelly. But I've been where Alaina is now. You cannot blame me for instilling in her a need for caution against marrying you, when you mistreat her as much as you do."

Jack's face flushed, and Alaina, afraid of drawing attention to themselves should Jack choose to continue the argument, grabbed his hand and tugged.

"Let's leave. Now."

To her relief, Jack acknowledged her request with a stiff nod but turned once more toward her mother. "I know you are right in many ways, but I have seen the other side of poverty and know the strain it puts on a person's mind. I want to avoid putting that kind of strain on my wife."

Charlotte did not respond, though the quick stab at the material let Alaina know her mother had indeed heard.

☙

Jack called to Missy and Sam as he followed Alaina to the front of the store. The children bolted toward him and held up the candy sticks. Peppermint for both Missy and Sam. He smiled and feigned interest in their chatter, not hearing much more than the ring of first Alaina's and then Charlotte's verbal attacks.

The children sucked happily as they went up the big steps.

Jack held back. "I'll wait here."

Alaina followed the children upstairs. "I'll settle them and be back down."

Beside the big maple tree, Jack rehearsed what he would tell Alaina. It would cheer her to learn that he'd be turning in his final papers to Mr. Fulton soon, freeing him to spend more time with her and the children. It would put her fears to rest. And Charlotte's.

The streetlamps flickered in the dark, and drops of rain forced Jack to take shelter under the maple's spreading branches. No matter what he did, it never seemed right.

"Jack?"

When he faced her, she stood in the shadow of the branches. He captured her hand and turned her until the lamplight highlighted her expression. Strain and worry marked the areas around her eyes and mouth.

Shame washed over him, and his heart twisted for the pain Alaina's eyes reflected. "I've made a mess of things."

Alaina stayed silent, and her silence put a weight in his stomach. "I should have told your mother that I'd be turning in the papers to Mr. Fulton in only a few days. Then I'll be done."

"That is good news." Her voice lacked conviction.

"It'll mean we can spend more time together. It's only that I've been so distracted by everything. You know how much it means to me to take good care of you, Alaina."

"Jack. . ."

He barely heard her as the feeling that she was slipping away from him grew. Panic surged and he clasped her hand tighter, begging with his words as much as his heart for her to understand.

She pulled her hand away. "What happens when something else 'distracts' you? Is this why you're so angry with your father? Did he do this to you?"

"He was an inventor, yes. But we can talk about him some other time."

"No. No, Jack. I want you to tell me about your father."

The gentle command slashed through his fears and stabbed coldness into his heart, and Jack understood, in that moment, both the depth of his bitterness toward Don Kelly and how much he needed to forgive his father. He gulped air. "He's dead."

Alaina flattened her hand against his until their palms met. He watched as she traced the outline of his fingers with her own.

The motion soothed him. Seconds stretched into minutes and Jack grew calmer, more clearheaded.

When she finally met his gaze, her smile was beatific and gentle. "He hurt you."

He closed his eyes as the emotion welled up again, threatening to drown him.

"Tell me, Jack."

With a hard exhale, he made up his mind. Riding the crest of his anger and frustration, grief and sorrow, he told Alaina about his father. And his mother. The farm. The drinking. The lack of money. His father's death. . .

"He was sick?" she asked.

Jack pressed his lips together to stop the trembling.

"Jack?" She moved in close to him and peered up into his face.

He could not look away from those eyes. Didn't want to.

"How did your father die?"

He struggled to draw air into his lungs. "Mama found him." He closed his eyes against the image that greeted them that morning in the barn. His mother had been out before him, then had come racing back to get him, eyes wild. Hair mussed. Out of breath.

Jack took a step away from Alaina. Then another. Until his back touched the tall maple tree.

"Oh, Jack," he heard Alaina's words through a haze of pain and anguish.

In his mind he saw again the flash of light against the blade of the knife as it winked before he cut through the rope that held the weight of his father's body.

God, help me.

Jack's legs went weak, and he felt himself plunging downward, his shirt catching on the rough bark of the maple.

And Alaina was there beside him. Holding him tight.

"He hung himself, Lainey. He. . ."

Her hand stroked his head as the tears streamed down his face.

Chapter 13

May 23, 1889

In the weak morning light filtering through her window, Alaina felt the pull of a thousand emotions. She lay as still as possible, praying the children wouldn't wake so she might have time to sort through her feelings before helping them get dressed for the day. She focused on a spot on the ceiling and sank into prayer, laying all her struggles at God's feet. Silent tears slipped from her eyes as she reviewed everything that had occurred in the last few days and the terrible secret Jack had revealed. She prayed God would heal his heart.

Learning of Don Kelly's death had left her breathless with hurt for Jack. Her admiration of him had gone up a notch, just as the knowledge of all that he'd faced as an orphan had sketched a greater empathy for him in her heart. It had cost him so much to share with her his private shame, for she knew that his father's suicide had been a wrenching grief that wouldn't heal.

When Jack's tears had finally stopped, she had helped him to his feet and scrambled for something to say, but Sam had chosen that moment to open the door and holler down for her. She'd been torn then, wanting to give Jack the reassurance he so needed, but the sound of Missy's crying forced her to choose.

Jack's gentle shove and his whispered, "I've got to get back anyway," had helped.

She'd hesitated long enough to rise on her toes and touch her lips to his cheek before rushing up the steps, saddened to see the slump of his shoulders as his steps took him away from her.

That had been two days ago.

She worried over his extended absence yet knew instinctively that he would drive himself to finish his work for Mr. Fulton until it was completed. But it wasn't fair to Missy and Sam. They were growing restless and worried about their father.

She couldn't help but see that it was one more time when people meant less to Jack than his drive to have money. Now, though, she understood the basis for his drive to succeed. On one hand, she still felt slighted by him, but on the other, she understood how growing up poor and watching his father lose everything, drink by drink, had scarred him.

Alaina wanted so much for God to give her peace about her relationship with Jack. His approval. It seemed like all opposition had been unleashed on them since their engagement. An involuntary shiver made her teeth click. She wiped the moisture from her face and tried to dissolve the gripping knot of fear in the pit of her stomach. More than God's direct answer, she feared His silence.

Sam stirred and bounced to his feet, balled fists working at the sleep in his eyes.

Alaina had to smile at his display of enthusiasm for the day. "Good morning, Sam. Did you sleep well?"

He blinked around the room, his gaze settling on her. He gave her a solemn nod and poked at Missy. The girl grunted. Her hair spilled out behind her along the pillow next to Alaina. By the looks of the curls, it would take quite a while to get the tangles worked free.

Within minutes, Missy, too, bounded to her feet and began a stream of chatter as she dressed.

"Missy, stand still so I can button you," Alaina admonished the girl.

"I have to go out," Sam said. "*Now.*"

Freed from Alaina's ministrations, Missy reached to snap Sam's suspenders into place. "I'm ready."

Alaina showed the children from her room and pulled on her day dress. They made short work of the trip to the outhouse and reentered to find her mother working on breakfast. Alaina leaned in to plant a kiss on her mother's cheek.

"Miss Alaina," Missy popped around her elbow. "Sam has dirt all around."

"Well, it sounds like Sam needs to wash up. Let me get some water heated."

"I can take care of myself!" Sam stormed at his sister. "Stop bossing, Missy."

Alaina silenced Missy's reply, "Let's try not to fight." She put Missy to work setting the table as the water heated.

Charlotte served up the oatmeal with a grim smile for each of the children and a kiss on the top of Alaina's head.

"I want some syrup," Missy declared.

Alaina fetched the can and allowed each a spoonful of brown sugar and a dollop of syrup. The scent of the maple and the velvet texture of the oatmeal soothed Alaina and helped her focus.

"Why hasn't Jack told us about Daddy?" Missy asked.

Alaina gestured for the girl to eat and shook her head. "Jack has to work, just like your father would have to work if he were feeling better."

Missy scooped up another spoonful and aimed it at her mouth, but one more question slipped out. "Will Daddy lose his job? Mark Rosenfelt's daddy lost his job after he hurt his hand."

"I don't know, Missy. Why don't we make it a matter of prayer?"

Charlotte remained quiet through the meal but spoke up as Missy scraped the last of the oatmeal from her bowl. "Why don't you help me, Sam, while Miss Alaina helps Missy get cleaned up?"

The boy nodded and shoveled in the last bite.

Alaina smiled her gratitude at her mother and took Missy to her room. She brushed the gnarls out of the long, wheat-colored hair and braided it to prevent further tangles.

"My mother used to do the same thing." Missy yawned into her hand.

Alaina's fingers stilled. It was too easy to forget how much grief Missy and Sam had already experienced in their young lives. She closed her eyes and forced away the last vestiges of her own melancholy, remembering an oft-stated phrase of her old Sunday school teacher.

"Those who too often look inward, seldom look upward."

No matter the problems she might have, Sam and Missy needed her full attention.

ꟹ

Jack stopped at his place long enough to clean up before heading over to Alaina's. They had reason to celebrate. He'd pulled a lot of long hours between his job, working to prove his theory, and checking on Frank, but his burden had lifted considerably when he'd passed his plans to Mr. Fulton during a break in his shift.

Clarence Fulton had stroked his face as he read over the papers, and when he'd raised his eyes to Jack's, his smile had been huge. "I think you're on to something. Let me pass these up to someone who would know more about such things, and we'll get back to you." Clarence squinted at the calendar on his desk. "We should hear something back by the end of the month, I'd say. How does that sound?"

Elation had carried Jack through the rest of the long, hot shift and all the way home. As he splashed water onto his face to soothe his hot skin, he felt buoyed by thoughts of the time he would get to spend with Alaina. And Sam and Missy, of course. He combed his hair in the small mirror over his shaving stand, noting his need for a trim, then snapped his suspenders into place.

When he arrived at the dispensary to check on Frank's condition, the edge of his happiness faded somewhat. Frank's skin was flushed with fever.

When Frank saw Jack, he waved him over. "Miss the mites. They behaving themselves?"

Jack grinned. "Hello to you, too."

Frank grunted. "You have any idea what it's like lying flat on your back like this?"

"I wish I did."

Frank frowned. "Don't talk foolish."

Jack hitched his chair closer to the edge of Frank's bedside. "I see you're not feeling well."

"Doc says the fever could kill me or make me better. Sobering words." Frank's jaw worked, and his Adam's apple bobbed. "I'm all Sam and Missy have, Jack."

"You'll pull through this. Only the good die young."

His friend scowled. "Then you'll surely outlive me by a few centuries."

Jack laughed.

The levity shattered Frank's scowl and seemed to improve his temperament. "I really appreciate Alaina watching Missy and Sam for me."

"You know how much she loves children."

Frank threw off his thin blanket. "You'd better make that woman yours soon, or someone else is liable to claim her."

Jack clamped his hands together. "Sooner rather than later, I'm hoping. If I get this promotion, we'll be set."

"Promotion or not..." Frank's brows lowered. "Why you looking so smug?"

"Congratulate me. I just turned in the papers stating my theory to Mr. Fulton. I'm on to something, Frank. It's really going to work."

Instead of words of praise, Frank gave him a hard look. "You're not listening to me, boy. Get your head off invention. Lying here's made me think about a whole lot. You included. And I'm telling you, you'd be better off with Alaina than with anything a promotion or that invention will get you." Frank shifted and winced, his face losing some color, his voice roughened from pain. "Be glad when the burns heal up and these ribs let me draw in a decent breath."

"I'll bring Missy and Sam by. They'll be glad to see you."

"How long's it been since you saw them?"

Frank's question brought a surge of anger. "Awhile. I had some work to do and—"

"Tell them I miss them and I love them."

Jack could see the tension in Frank's face and body and knew his friend must be in a great deal more pain than he allowed others to see, but it didn't give him a right to try and tell him what to do.

Frank grimaced. "Even Alaina?"

"Alaina what?"

"Tell her you love her. Daily, Jack. Time's too short."

Jack winced at the sharp edge of rebuke in Frank's tone.

"She's too precious to be ignored."

"I don't ignore her."

Frank's eyes burned into his. "You mean, you don't think you do."

Chapter 14

Jack bounded up the steps to Alaina's. Laughter spilled through the closed door, putting a smile on his lips. He almost hated to knock and interrupt the flow of joy. A high-pitched squeal rent the air, followed by another, and he imagined Alaina chasing Sam and Missy, as he had witnessed her play with the Hensley children so many times. Longing to be a part of the scene, he knocked, and the door opened to reveal the wide smile of Charlotte Morrison. "Mrs. Morrison," he nodded and held his breath as he watched her smile wither and her eyes lose the luster of joy.

"You're here for the children?" She neither opened the door in invitation nor slammed it in his face.

He exhaled. "I thought Alaina might walk with me for a bit."

Charlotte stared back over her shoulder, then retreated enough for him to see Alaina crossing the room as she worked to untie her apron. He didn't miss the warning glance Alaina gave her mother. For her part, Mrs. Morrison seemed resigned, more than angered, by Jack's arrival.

"I'll ready the children and meet you outside," Alaina directed him. She yanked the apron over her head and brushed back a few tendrils of hair that had pulled loose.

He retreated a step and nodded. "I'll be here."

It only took a few minutes before she appeared with the children. She had changed from her work dress into her best blue, worn patches evident around the elbows and cuffs. How he wanted to purchase an entire new wardrobe for her for a wedding gift. Alaina's eyes would shine with excitement and delight over the materials. She could have all the ruffles and frills, bustles and trains she wanted.

The children ran straight to the maple tree and began to give chase. When Alaina came level with him on the last step, he captured her hand in his. The coolness of her skin sent a spark of awareness through him.

"I have good news. I turned in the papers to Mr. Fulton today."

They turned when Missy squealed. Sam jumped out at his sister again, and Missy screamed with fright.

Alaina laughed, her eyes on the children, but Jack couldn't take his eyes off her. When she caught his gaze, something flared in the depths of her burgundy-brown eyes. "They're as happy to play as I am to hear your good news. We can set a date."

"Mr. Fulton said I should know by the end of the month, and I'm sure the announcement about the promotion will be soon. We'll set a date after I know more. We'll be financially secure."

The spark in her eyes lost its luster. "Of course. We'll wait."

Jack released a frustrated breath at the flat tone in her voice.

Missy chose that moment to barrel into Alaina. The child pressed her face into the folds of Alaina's skirts. Missy remained there only a few seconds before beckoned by her brother to play chase again.

Alaina watched the children circle the maple. "I think Mother is actually enjoying their presence," she murmured. "You should have seen the way she carried on with them before you arrived."

"Perhaps grandchildren will endear her to me if nothing else will." Jack tried to keep his tone light.

Alaina gasped and glanced at him, then away. Fire flamed in her cheeks.

Maybe he was playing the fool thinking he could wait to marry Alaina. She often said how content she would be to be poor. . . . But when his mind skittered to the leaky roof and mice in his sad shack to his mother's final days, surrounded by dirt and filth and wearing rags, he knew he would have to bide his time. He lifted his face to the sun and tried to reabsorb the lightheartedness he'd felt upon arrival. "Why don't we go for a picnic in the mountains?"

"A picnic?" Missy, closest to them, stopped so fast she slipped on the rain-soaked grass.

Sam stooped to help her up. "A picnic?" But his expression was anxious.

Jack didn't understand Sam's reaction and lifted an eyebrow at Alaina.

Alaina held his gaze. "Isn't there somewhere else we should go?"

He caught the direction of her thoughts and gave Sam's hair a tousle. "Sure. We'll eat, and then we'll go by and see your papa. How's that sound?"

But Sam didn't respond. He stared off into the distance. Missy drew closer to her brother.

"I think we should save the picnic for later," Alaina suggested. *They're worried,* she mouthed to him.

Jack acquiesced. "To the hospital then."

ଓ

When they arrived, they were told Frank was sleeping and they could not visit. A nurse did tell Jack that Frank's fever had broken. A good sign, she had assured them.

Missy and Sam sagged in disappointment at not being able to see their father.

Alaina hoped the picnic would put a sparkle back into their eyes.

Jack, seeming to sense the importance of diverting Missy's and Sam's attention, grabbed their hands and began chattering about visiting the grocer to buy candy. "But first. . ." Jack's hand snaked out and tousled Sam's hair. He withdrew and, quick as a wink, lunged back into a boxer's crouch, hands fisted.

The boy responded to the fun immediately and let out a flailing, sloppy right hook that Jack easily blocked.

Alaina watched the fun with amusement.

Missy rolled her eyes and planted her little hands on nonexistent hips. "I'm hungry."

Jack dove in toward Sam and caught the boy around his waist. He raised the boy over his shoulder and winked at Alaina. "Well, now that Sam is out of the way, I guess there'll be more for us to eat. Right, Missy?"

Sam squawked and began to kick his feet in protest.

Jack laughed and let the boy slide to the ground.

Nothing could hide the shine of joy in Sam's eyes, and Alaina was reminded, again, how much she loved Jack's fun side. If only she could lift the burden of his need for the promotion or to make the invention that would line his pockets with the money he so desperately wanted to lavish on her. No matter how many times she stated her contentment, it seemed to fall on deaf ears.

Alaina combed her fingers through Sam's mussed hair, but the boy grimaced and pulled back.

"Best let her spiff you up, Sam. Women like to do that sort of thing."

Alaina cocked an eyebrow at him. "Oh?" She let her gaze slide over Jack's hair. A sudden longing to straighten the lock flopped on his forehead brought immediate heat to her cheeks.

He noticed. "Do I need spiffing?"

She raised her chin. "I'm sure you do, but I'll not be the one doing it."

Jack leaned in close to her ear. "A shame. I'll make sure not to be spiffed when we marry. Then you can spend the day getting me straightened out."

She gasped and felt the receding heat of her previous blush flare back full force. But she couldn't quite quell the tingle of excitement his outrageous comment stirred. To be his wife. Her heart raced with the thrill of it.

Her gaze caught his and held. She felt herself wrapped in the warmth of his blue eyes. A small smile crooked the corners of his mouth. His hand closed over her forearm and slipped down to cradle hers. When he lowered his head a fraction, she tilted her head back even more. The touch of his lips brought a sigh to her throat.

"Yuck!"

Alaina's eyes flew open.

Jack's face, so close to hers, split into a huge grin, and he turned toward a disgruntled Sam. "Oh yes, little man, you should try it sometime," Jack admonished Sam with a playful swipe at the boy's shoulder.

"When you're much older," Alaina added, sending a warning look at Jack.

Jack's head jerked back, and he released a stream of hearty laughter.

Alaina stamped her foot and crossed her arms. "Jack Kelly, you're incorrigible."

He brushed the hair from his forehead and shrugged. "Got to teach him what courting a beautiful woman is all about."

Missy pulled on Jack's free hand. "Momma used to do that to Papa. It makes me miss her."

"I didn't mean to make you sad, Missy." He squinted up at the sky. "Why don't we get to picnicking before it rains again?"

Chapter 15

Taking Alaina out always filled Jack with great satisfaction. They visited the grocer, and he dipped into his hoarded fund of coins to purchase candy for the children and apples, cheese, and a bit of bread for everyone.

He watched how Alaina interacted with others they met along the walk to the hill, both strangers and friends, and never failed to find himself endeared to her all the more for her kindness and gentleness of spirit. He found himself wondering how Charlotte Morrison could raise a child with a temperament so contrary to her own. But he knew life's disappointments had dealt a blow to Charlotte that had shaped the person she'd become. Frank had been right. He must keep that in mind, though sometimes it was hard. Even harder to comprehend was the idea that Alaina might suffer a disappointment because of him. End up poor and miserable. He clenched his jaw. Not if he could help it.

When they settled the blanket on the ground, she spread out the meager meal, and Jack felt hot shame. There should be more food. More candy for the children. Alaina should have better clothes. . . .

She sent him a questioning look from her place next to young Missy, and Jack felt the sudden pressure of time being wasted. Perhaps he should go over his notes again. Though he'd turned his theory over to Mr. Fulton, he couldn't keep at bay the nagging fear that he'd forgotten something. By the slant of the sun, he knew he had little time left in the day to review his plans before his shift started. He swept to his feet, threw his apple core far out into the tall grass, and stretched.

Missy helped Alaina gather the remaining scraps of bread. She showed Missy how to tear the pieces into smaller bits and then scatter them for the birds. The child watched in wide-eyed wonder as a single cardinal floated down and hopped closer and closer, his bright little eyes on a good-sized crumb.

Jack couldn't help but smile at the child's delight.

Alaina sidled close and whispered, "I'm worried about Sam."

The boy was nowhere to be seen. "Where'd he go?" Jack asked.

She pointed to the edge of the woods, where Jack caught a glimpse of Sam's dark head among a thicket of tall grass. "I think he's worried about his father."

Jack rubbed his forehead. He could well understand the boy's concern and felt the claw of doubt scratch at his own mind when he considered Frank's condition. "I'll go talk to him, but I have to get back to town." He caught Alaina's gaze. "I can't stop this feeling that I overlooked something in my notes."

He held his breath, hoping for her understanding. A sharp chill shot through him when Alaina, instead, turned away, back ramrod straight. He reached out a hand to turn her toward him but let it drop back to his side when his tongue found no words to console.

He stepped around her and focused on retrieving Sam, but every footfall fanned the embers of his anger. Why couldn't she understand? Didn't his time with her this afternoon show how much he cared? The tender kiss and the smoky look in her eyes had seemed so full of promise for their future. Yet every time he mentioned the project, it seemed to build a wall between them.

When Jack reached the spot where he'd last seen Sam, he stopped and squinted into the tall grass. The boy sat far away from his original location, feet dangling just above the shorter grass under the fallen log upon which he had perched.

"Sam? It's time to go. We've got to head back to town."

Sam didn't raise his face, though a curt nod of his head acknowledged he'd heard. He slipped off the log, feet dragging with every step.

When he got within reach, Jack pulled the boy close. He pressed the back of Sam's head against his side and swallowed hard over the knot of emotion swelling in his own throat. Under his hand, he felt the first shudder of the boy's narrow shoulders. He knelt in the tall grass to get eye level with Sam. "You're afraid for your father?"

A small, quiet sob shook the boy's chest. "Will he—" Sam sucked in a shuddering breath. "Will he go away like Momma?"

How much Jack wished he could give the boy solid reassurance, but he understood the extent of Frank's injuries and knew the days ahead would play heavily on whether or not Sam's father would recover. Yet Sam wanted someone to tell him no. To drive away the merciless bats of fear beating their wings against his fragile peace of mind.

Jack dragged in a deep breath and grasped the boy's heaving shoulders. "I don't know, Sam. I do know that your father is badly hurt but that he's strong and wants to live so he can take care of you and Missy."

"He said Momma dying was for the best. Does God think taking him will be for the best, too?"

Jack's eyes squeezed shut at the rawness of that question. He pulled Sam into his embrace and spread his hand on the boy's small back, while the memory of himself as a young boy being embraced by his father after a fall washed over him. Jack swallowed hard and, for the first time, let himself grieve for that part of his father that he'd loved and trusted.

Sam tugged on his sleeve. "Are you sad about Papa?"

Jack ran the back of his hand across the wetness on his cheeks. "Yes. Very. He is my friend, Sam. A very good friend."

Chapter 16

May 29, 1889

"Well, Jack-o, guess you'll have to get used to calling me 'sir' now." Robert Whitfield's triumphant expression came into sharp focus.

Jack's spine stiffened. Rage began a slow boil.

The promotion.

After all the grunt work he'd done for Fulton. . .all his plans and hopes dashed.

"No worries, though." Robert bared his teeth. "I'll be a good shift manager. The boss has a lot of confidence in me. More than in others."

Jack saw the bait dangled before him. Robert clamped a hand on Jack's shoulder, outwardly looking like a friendly gesture, but Jack felt the unnecessary pressure and schooled his features not to show any pain.

"I'll look forward to working as your boss. But I warn you now. . .I don't tolerate those who don't do their jobs."

Jack clenched his fists, hoping his glare would stab a hole in Robert's cockiness. His thoughts splintered. How could he tell Alaina the news? He would never be able to afford marriage now. He would be forced to break their engagement. But how could he do that?

Robert took a step back. "Since I get off before you, I'll deliver the good news to Alaina. She'll want to know, right?"

Jack forced himself not to react as Robert gave his shoulder a pat and sauntered off. He had no doubt the man would be on Alaina's doorstep within an hour, gloating, and he could do nothing about it.

He worked fast and hard during his shift. Images of Robert arriving on Alaina's doorstep haunted him. He picked up his pace and shoveled harder. Faster.

"You're gonna kill yourself, Jack." He heard Frank's voice in his head.

Thoughts of his friend's condition, of his inability to care for his family, helped bring perspective to Jack's problems. At least he could still earn a wage. He was unharmed and strong, and he could still hope Mr. Fulton found his theory worthy.

When the greaser came along to oil the machinery, Jack breathed in relief and made his way through the room to the outside. Rain sprinkled down on his face, cooling his body.

More rain. Little Conemaugh bore none of a resemblance to its name now. It raged and slurped at the banks, barely containing its swelling girth. Jack considered what the constant rain was doing to the South Fork Dam. If the Little Conemaugh roared like this, the streams feeding into Lake Conemaugh would be swollen as well, in turn pushing the lake higher and higher toward the crest of the dam.

Only a handful of people seemed worried about the structure. Too many years of crying wolf had cauterized most of Johnstown's population's ability to see the dam as a real threat.

But the knowledge he'd gleaned in his research for Mr. Fulton weighed on him. His already exhausted limbs stiffened with fear. *God, if that dam goes, we're all dead.*

Losing Alaina would be devastating, whether losing her to Robert or to floodwaters. He couldn't let either happen.

When he opened the door to his room, a thin, steady stream of water cascaded from the roof. He emptied the smaller pot of its store of rainwater and placed a bigger pot underneath the growing hole in the roof.

What he needed most was a bath. He smiled at the absurdity of taking a bath when all he needed to do was stand outside with a bar of soap to get the job done. But mirth fizzled when Robert's leering grin popped into his head.

☙

"You'd be happier with him."

Alaina pressed the palms of her hands against her eyes. No matter what she did or said, her mother's words kept pecking at her love for Jack. Robert's visit, though short and to the point, hadn't helped matters, and her mother overhearing Robert's news that he'd received the promotion instead of Jack only added fuel to her argument.

"Robert is the kind of man that will do something with his life. If you're not careful, you'll lose him to Mary. You can bet she has her eyes on him."

"Mary is my friend," Alaina reminded her mother.

"Friend or not..."

Alaina felt the tension stretch along her nerves. She knew what her mother's next attack would be.

"At least go to Pittsburgh and look the college over. Give yourself some time away from here to clear your head."

Alaina let her hands fall to the table. "Meaning, away from Jack."

Charlotte's lips tightened into a firm line, and she squinted harder at the needle poking through the hem of the gown she had been working on all evening. "Away from Jack is not a bad place to be."

"Why do you hate Jack so much?" There, she'd asked the question that had nagged at her for so long.

Charlotte set aside her sewing, her expression stricken. "It's not that I hate him, Alaina. Jack's a nice young man. But why can't you wait awhile to marry? Consider going to college. If he wants to marry you, won't he wait? Doesn't he want what's best for you?"

Missy appeared at Alaina's elbow, hair mussed and tears welling in her eyes. "Sam pulled my hair."

Welcoming the intrusion, Alaina went to where Sam sat on the floor rolling an empty spool back and forth between his hands. She sank to the floor, her skirt billowing out around her, and slipped an arm across Sam's shoulders. "Why did you pull Missy's hair?"

She felt the rise and fall of Sam's shoulders as he released a sigh. Missy sniffed.

"Sam?"

His voice came to her sounding small and scared. "I want my pa."

Alaina pulled the boy closer just as Missy burst into tears. The creak of the boards let her know Charlotte was coming to offer some assistance. They shared a look over the little girl's head. Alaina's mother touched Missy's shoulder. The child spun around and flung herself into Charlotte's arms, rocking the older woman off balance. Regaining her position, Charlotte pulled the child close and stroked her hair.

Alaina couldn't deny the children their need to see their father. If Jack showed up on the doorstep in the next few minutes, he could come along, but waiting for him, never knowing if he would forget or not, was not an option with Sam and Missy so obviously upset.

Alaina stood tall and stabbed a glance out the window. At least the rain had let up. She hated the idea of wading through the water standing in the streets from the constant downpours, but she had no choice. "Missy, Sam, let's get you bundled up and over to see your father."

Missy rubbed at her eyes and straightened in Charlotte's arms. "Really?"

Sam jumped to his feet. It was as if a great load had lifted from the boy's shoulders. "Will Jack come, too?"

"I don't know." Would this be what it was like to be married to Jack? He wouldn't come home to his family, always placing work above her? She might be able to endure the slights, as she had in the past, but for her to knowingly subject any children they might have together to the same thing seemed irresponsible. Or maybe she wasn't being fair to him. She hugged herself, not knowing what to think or feel. A shiver quaked through her.

"Alaina? Are you catching a chill?"

It had been easy to discount her mother's worries. Perhaps too easy. Her mother's expression was pinched with concern. For her.

"I'm fine, just. . ." She pressed her lips together as they began to form the words she knew would put sunshine on her mother's face. Words she was afraid to say because it meant part of a dream was dying. She drew in a slow breath. "When we get back, I'll help you with that dress. Then I'll cut out a new one—"

Her voice faltered the slightest bit. She braced herself mentally and met her mother's direct gaze. "Maybe I can have it done before I make the trip to Pittsburgh."

Chapter 17

Something sour churned Jack's gut at the dark windows and silence that met his many knocks on the door of Alaina's home. He feared Robert had already arrived to sweep Alaina away to some theater show and dinner, regaling her with stories of his new promotion and—

Jack heaved a sigh and shook his head. Alaina loved him. He loved her. Still, he had hoped to tell her the news himself, to wrest from her the promise that she would wait and to hear the words he so needed to believe—*I love you.*

Instead he turned and slogged his way back through the flooded streets. Water funneled and poured, his already wet shoes becoming saturated. He stopped long enough to stare up at the spire of the Presbyterian church, its stone face cold yet solid.

With nothing left to do but wander the streets, an idea that did not appeal to him in the least, Jack meandered back toward Cambria City. The evening stretched before him, long and dark. Robert's face, a smirk on his lips, loomed in Jack's mind. Taunting.

When he arrived at his house, he emptied the tin mug of its collection of water and set it back in place. At the small table, he glanced over the notes he'd made while writing his report on the dam and the theory he'd turned in to Fulton. They seemed nothing more than dry, cold facts. Sadness gripped Jack. For all the work he had put into his theory and the report on the dam, in trying to prove himself a good worker to Fulton, success meant nothing if he did not have Alaina by his side.

☙

To Alaina's way of thinking, Frank looked worse than the previous day. He appeared unfocused and acknowledged the children with wan joy. If Sam and Missy noticed their pa's decline, they didn't express their dismay.

Worry nibbled at the edges of Alaina's mind. What if Frank didn't live? She could hardly leave the children in an orphanage. Jack would know Frank's wishes and whether he had relatives or not, but gazing upon the sweet faces as they clung to their father's hands, she knew her own heart would struggle at the idea of saying good-bye.

"When are you coming home?" Missy asked.

Frank turned his head on the pillow, his face flushed.

Alaina worried the fever had returned.

"They had me up just before you got here, Missy. Wore me out. But I'm gettin' stronger."

His words brought a measure of relief. If he'd walked around, that explained his flushed face and the exhaustion. Alaina caught her mother's gesture and followed the flick of her hand that indicated a cane leaning against the wall. "What a beautiful cane, Frank. Did you make it?"

He blinked his eyes, and a slow smile curved his mouth. "One of the fellas carved it for himself when he got in an accident. He gave it to me yesterday before he left."

Missy grabbed up the cane and began to swing it around. Charlotte shook her head, and Missy set it back against the wall.

"You're feeling stronger then?" Alaina asked.

"Still have a bit of weakness, but doctor says the wounds are healing well."

Missy resumed her post next to her father as he admonished them to be good and motioned the children, one by one, to lean in for a kiss.

Alaina made feeble attempts to converse with the children on the way home. Water in the streets made it necessary for her to carry Missy, while Sam clung to her mother's hand. The children appeared relieved by their visit and happier in spirit, splashing in puddles and laughing.

Though they grimaced at having to change out of their wet clothes, Alaina's promise of something hot to drink motivated them. Charlotte helped Sam peel off his sodden trousers as Alaina knelt to help Missy undress and pull a nightgown over her head, then ran a towel over her saturated locks to absorb excess water.

"Of all the times not to have hot cocoa," Charlotte fretted.

"Can I have tea?" Missy chirped. "And honey?"

Sam slipped onto the bench and swung his legs. Missy scampered over to her brother, damp hair already forming ringlets that framed her face.

Alaina pulled on the drenched fabric of her skirt to release her legs so she could stand. "I'll get the honey."

"Regular little angels." Charlotte smiled at the children. "You go change, Alaina. I'll get them their tea."

Grateful to be free of the saturated dress, Alaina pulled on a dry winter gown of worn brown wool to stave off further chill and hung her wet clothes over a metal tub to drip dry. She paused to stare out her window, unable to see much for the rain and darkening skies but well aware that her heart felt as dark and heavy as the fabric she'd just hung up. Having made the decision to sew a new dress locked her into going to Pittsburgh. Her mother would not let her back down from her promise now.

When she returned to the small kitchen, the first things she noticed were the drooping heads of both Sam and Missy.

She shared a smile with her mother, who mouthed, "*Bedtime.*"

Alaina pressed a hand against Missy's back. "Why don't I tuck you two in for the night?"

"Are you going to read us a story?" Missy asked.

"Not tonight. I don't think you could stay awake to hear it all."

Missy pooched her lip but said no more.

Sam slid off his chair and followed without protest. It took very little time to settle the two into the makeshift bed and say prayers. Missy dropped off sometime during Sam's prayer for their father and that the rains would stop, and then he stretched out beside his sister.

"I love you, Alaina," he said, his voice thick with exhaustion.

"I love you, too, Sam. Sleep well."

Missy stirred, sighed, and curled closer to her brother's side. Their heads were close together.

Alaina pulled the blanket up around their shoulders and cast another glance outside, her mind suddenly full of the many times she'd heard the rumor of the Lake Conemaugh Dam bursting open. Her mother never seemed bothered by the prospect, but Alaina knew if it did happen things would be bad for Johnstown. It nibbled at her that she couldn't leave her mother here, alone, with that threat looming large. Only the knowledge that her mother would discount the notion of the dam bursting flushed the idea from her mind.

She sighed. A dull headache gathered strength behind her eyes, and she rubbed the spot to ease the pressure.

"Alaina?" She turned to see the outline of her mother in the doorway. "There's got to be an inch of mud in the store, so I promised Mr. Heiser I'd clean it up this evening."

She nodded and swiped her hands down the skirt of her dress. "Why don't you let me do it?"

"If we work together, it'll go faster." Her mother's gaze slipped to the window behind Alaina. "Seems this rain will never stop."

"I was just thinking of that dam."

"It makes me glad we're not on the ground floor," Charlotte responded. She took a step closer to the doorway and paused. "Alaina, there's something I need to say to you."

The words glued Alaina to the spot. She braced for a verbal assault.

But her mother's expression softened. "I want you to understand why I'm so"—Charlotte squeezed her eyes shut—"so hard on you."

"You don't have to explain."

"I just don't want you to have to struggle. To have your heart broken by a man who can't keep his promises. Jack is so like your father."

"Why didn't you go West, too?" The question slipped out before Alaina gave it thought. In all the years since her father had left, she'd never ventured to ask, afraid of the response. She opened her mouth to apologize and take back the words.

Charlotte flinched but recovered quickly. Tears gathered in her eyes.

Alaina reached to offer some measure of comfort. When her mother turned and left the room, she followed, as if drawn by an invisible cord.

Her mother sat at the kitchen table and gestured for her to sit as well. "It's good that you ask, though the telling isn't easy." She pressed her lips together as great tears welled.

"Momma, you don't have—"

Charlotte gave her head a firm shake. "No. It's a question that needs answering. One that God has Himself been asking me. You see, your father did ask me." She clamped her hands together and squeezed her eyes shut. "I didn't want to go. It was hard for me to think of leaving Johnstown. He wouldn't budge either and told me he'd go ahead and send for us when he got settled."

"So he didn't abandon us?" Shock rolled over Alaina.

Her mother didn't respond for a long time as she sobbed into her hands.

The part of Alaina that wanted to comfort her mother dried up and blew away. Anger reared its ugly head. "How could you let me believe all these years that he left without ever looking back? He wanted us to go with him."

Charlotte nodded and smeared back the tears with the back of her hand. "I didn't realize you thought that. When he wrote letters, he never asked me again. I guess I took that as his way of saying he didn't want us."

That statement cut through Alaina's anger. She could understand her mother's reasoning. "Why did he stop writing?"

Charlotte shrugged. "I wish I knew. Between him not asking for us to join him and not writing, I've allowed myself to become"—she stared at the scarred tabletop—"bitter."

It made sense now. Her mother going back to church. The softening. Her reactions to Jack. Her bitterness. "But one thing you must understand, Momma, is that Jack is not Father. He wants to provide for me and make sure we're well taken care of."

"But that's no excuse for the way he forgets you."

Alaina nodded. "Yes, I know, but you've got to see him apart from Father. He's his own man."

Her mother stared at her for several minutes. "Yes, you're right. I've known that. Deep down inside, I've known that, but I still say you should be cautious. No man should treat you as Jack has." Charlotte reached out and laid a hand on Alaina's arm. "I have a surprise for you. I've been sewing dresses for you from scraps and leftover yardage my customers didn't care about."

"You have?"

"I saw the way you looked at him. At Jack. And I knew you would want to marry. I didn't want you to start out in rags. And I always hoped you might change your mind and go to college. To Pittsburgh. So I've got two dresses for you in my room."

Alaina understood the pleading in her mother's eyes and knew that she was being asked a question. She swallowed. "I'll try them on."

"Good, we can get you on the train west tomorrow morning." With that her mother left the room.

Alaina's head whirled with the generosity and suddenness of the gift, but something else, too—for the opportunity to see a side of her mother that she'd never seen before and for the knowledge that her father had not abandoned them. That was the most important of all the gifts she'd received.

Chapter 18

May 30, 1889

Jack breathed in the taste of freedom. Memorial Day meant a holiday. It meant festivities and banners and a nice tribute to the veterans of the Civil War. As he emerged from his shack and waved a hand at his landlady, who was busy herding her grandchildren indoors, he rubbed at the spot above his eyes where a dull ache had started to build after his restless night.

The fact that Robert had received *his* promotion burned in his mind. His anger flared and tasted hot on his tongue. After all he had done for Fulton, the man gave the position to Robert. Jack grunted and squeezed his eyes shut. Robert would continue to rub it in his face, he had no doubt, but he would have to take it. If he protested too loudly, Fulton just might fire him, and if he got fired, there would be no way he could ever afford to get married. Besides, he still had his plans.

Jack opened his eyes. Fulton's willingness to finance Jack's foray into inventing a better method of turning iron ore into steel still meant he had confidence in Jack's ability. And if the plans were accepted, it could mean a promotion to something far above Robert's new position. The very idea made Jack want to laugh. Oh, to see the expression on Robert's face then. And Alaina would be so proud of him.

In his mind, he could see the twinkle of pride in Alaina's dark eyes. He imagined her mane of hair, pulled back into ringlets, and her petite form gowned in the latest fashion. His heart pounded, and he lengthened his stride.

As he passed over the Little Conemaugh, he took note of the swollen, raging waters and how the water rose far above its normal level. He stabbed a glance at the pouting sky and made a mental note to take the train up to South Fork and check on the dam for himself.

Water stood knee-deep in some of the streets. He wondered what James Quinn of Foster and Quinn, a general store, thought of all the rain. He was one of the few citizens Jack knew who worried over the dam breaking.

"Hallo!"

Jack stopped in a deep puddle and waved as a hack pulled up beside him, the animal's back dark with water and sweat. "Ben, doing the business today, right?"

"Sure enough." Ben halted his horse right beside Jack. "The ladies especially aren't wanting to get their feet wet."

"I'd think on a day like this most would want to stay dry. The wet only adds to the chill in the bones."

"Ah, but there's something about Memorial Day that lightens the spirit." His grin turned knowing. "Steady stream heading to the depot. If you hop in, I'll get you there before she leaves."

Jack studied his friend's expression and wide grin and felt the first squeeze of dread. "Before she leaves?"

Ben's smile wilted. "Why, sure." The man glanced over Jack's shoulder and scratched his chin with the edge of the reins in his hands. "Took her, her momma, and the children over there for the ten fifteen to Pittsburgh. Want a ride?"

"Pittsburgh?" He tried to make sense of the news being dumped on him. Tried to understand why Alaina would be headed to Pittsburgh. Or maybe. . . "Her mother must be headed out to visit."

Ben raised his eyebrows. "From the chatter and the way she was dressed, Alaina's the one traveling."

Jack took a giant step forward and swung himself into the hack. "Hurry then." The jerk of forward motion slammed Jack against the seat. He closed his eyes, unable to understand Alaina's trip to Pittsburgh or her lack of communication on the matter. What about Sam and Missy? He dared not jump to conclusions without talking to her.

A church clock struck the hour of ten as the horse pulled up in front of the B&O station.

Jack pressed a coin into Ben's hand and spun toward the station. People lined the platform. A pile of trunks and boxes waited to be loaded.

He scanned the crowds until his eyes focused on two familiar faces. Sam and Missy each held one of Charlotte Morrison's hands. When Alaina's mother caught his gaze, her lips pressed together.

But the woman who stood up beside Missy, her back to him, hair pulled back in ringlets and wearing a gown of rich material cut in the latest style, was what set Jack's heart to beating. It was as if the mental image he'd had of her on his walk to Johnstown had materialized.

Alaina's mother nodded his direction.

Jack took a step closer.

Alaina turned, her eyes solemn, but the soberness faded into something else as he drew nearer.

He searched her face, the burgundy of her eyes, and tried to put meaning to the question he didn't know how to form.

"Jack." She lifted a hand and he caught it and brought it to his chest.

"Jack!" Missy's mouth curved into a smile.

He lifted his hand in a wave and forced a grin, all he could muster, then faced Alaina. "Ben told me you were here. Pittsburgh?"

"She's going to see the school like I've told her she should from the first," Charlotte offered.

Alaina turned. "Momma, please."

"Give my girl a chance. Some space. That's all I ask." Charlotte's no-nonsense tone held a note of desperation.

Jack felt dumbstruck by her words and the strange reality of Alaina's obvious decision to leave.

"The train is coming, Alaina," Charlotte murmured and shrank back with Sam and Missy. "Don't take long."

☙

She was a coward. She knew that now, facing Jack, seeing the anguish on his face.

Her mother had encouraged her to leave as soon as possible, and now she understood why. When she sat to write a letter to Jack, her mother insisted she hurry and pack. When she had paused from work with the intention of asking Victor Heiser if he'd carry the letter to Jack, Charlotte waved the idea away. "You've no time for that. He's had no time for you." And she'd allowed her mother to have sway over her.

But now, facing Jack, she knew she should have sought him out as her heart had told her to. "I've got to go, Jack. I've got to see what's out there for me."

"The college?"

"Momma has always wanted me to go. To see for myself. You know that."

"But what about us?"

Tears burned her eyes. Frustration mingled with love, but the frustration took firmer hold on her emotions. "Us?" She stared down at their joined hands and felt the well of all the forgotten plans and the excuses that followed. "I don't know. There never seemed to be any us. Just you and your determination to get rich. To invent whatever it is you—"

"Is it so wrong to want more for you than what you have now?"

It was the same old argument. She knew she would never get him to see that she needed *him* more than she needed *wealth*, and for the first time she recognized that she could not change him. She could not alter his drive. Only God could do that.

Her mother had been right all along. Marrying a man with such fierce focus meant she would be ignored. Was being ignored. In his bid to become rich, he'd become as fierce as his father, not in temper but in attitude.

The train came pounding into the station, leaving them suspended in pained silence as the vibration and noise drowned out any attempts at words.

His thumb stroked along the back of her hand. His tender touch impaled her heart and brought a wave of fresh tears to her eyes. He became a distorted image. When she raised her free hand to wipe the wetness from her cheeks, Jack produced a handkerchief in a swift motion.

The train settled into place, and people began to churn into action around them.

Alaina couldn't speak.

"Please don't leave," Jack whispered.

"I've got to do this." She wanted to say, "For me," but recognized how it seemed to reek of selfishness. Was she being selfish? Wasn't he? Marriage meant unselfish commitment. Not this. She had to release him.

"I lost the promotion. Is that why you're leaving?"

"No."

"You didn't know, then?"

Her lower lip trembled. "Robert told me."

"We'll make something work out."

"Why didn't you come over last night?"

"I did. You weren't home. I thought you might be out with Robert."

Stung by the veiled accusation, she caught her trembling lip between her teeth.

His free hand captured hers and he squeezed. "When you come back, we'll set a date. I can still work at Cambria, and if my plans go through. . ." The words tumbled from him like the raging waters of the Little Conemaugh. "Maybe we'll have enough money."

She shook her head, and his hands squeezed harder.

His eyes pleaded. "A trip away will help settle your mind. It'll be good for you to get away. They say distance makes love stronger."

"I can't—" Her voice caught on a sob. "Jack, please. Listen to me."

"The plans will work, and I'll have enough to marry you. We'll set the date for the end of June. If Fulton doesn't think the idea will take, then I'll work on another."

"Jack, listen!"

"All aboard!" the conductor called out.

"It's time, Alaina." Her mother hovered at her elbow like an anxious bird. "Your bag is aboard."

"Mother, please." Her tears fell freely now, and she faced Jack again.

His eyes held a wet sheen that beckoned her own tears.

Charlotte retreated as the conductor shouted out another call.

"I've tried, Jack." She licked her lips and tasted salt. "I've tried, but I can't do this. I can't marry you."

His chest rose sharply, and he pulled her into his arms, where the scent of his damp shirt filled her nostrils and made her close her eyes against the desire to take back what she'd just said.

"Alaina, don't leave me," he whispered in her ear. "Don't leave me."

"People are more important than things, Jack."

"You are important to me."

"When you think of me."

"But I do, Alaina. All the time. I do it for—"

She couldn't bear to hear him say it yet again. She wrenched herself from his grasp just as the conductor gave his last warning and the train whistle rent the air.

Jack reached to grab one of her hands, but she took a retreating step out of his reach. She took another step, shaking her head, unable to meet her mother's gaze, only able to see the rawness of emotion slashing sorrow into the angles of Jack's face.

She pressed a hand to her mouth and finally turned toward the train to run the final steps. The train started forward as she slid into her seat, alternately waving to her mother and grieving over the slumped shoulders and bowed head of the man she still loved. Her breath fogged the glass, and she resisted the urge to write the words "I'm so sorry, Jack" in the dew, but she felt them deep in her heart and soul.

Chapter 19

"You're a fool, Jack Kelly. A young, arrogant fool."

Jack sluiced a hand over his wet head and glared at his friend. "I came for some measure of comfort, and I get condemnation?"

Frank sat up in bed, propped by no fewer than four pillows, and pursed his lips. "Being near death helps give one new insight. You've treated that girl like a new hat. You don't give it the time of day unless it's a special holiday. Then you're glad to wear it."

He bit back the angry defense of his actions and said the words that had echoed through his mind ever since Alaina had disappeared onto the train. "I loved her."

He had wandered for hours, barely acknowledging the greetings from store owners and the barber. Not even the jokes about the high water or the sight of a man in a boat paddling down one road freed him from the chains of his remorse and grief. He loved her.

"Aye, boy-o, you loved her. As much as a pigheaded scrap of a man can love anyone."

His head snapped up. "You—"

Frank raised his hand and poked a finger into Jack's chest. Even from the hospital bed, Jack felt the sheer strength of the man in that one gesture. And something else. He saw the fury. "Wake up! How many times did you promise her you'd see her and not show up?"

Jack firmed his jaw. "She knew I had to work on my plans and—"

"How long you been feeding yourself that line, boy? How long you been ignoring what's important? Where's your faith, man? God Himself tells us to love a woman more than we love ourselves."

"I know that verse. It's for the married."

"And you were planning on treating her good only then?"

"You know what I mean."

Frank rose up. "It doesn't matter now, does it? You ignored her in favor of gain, and now you've lost everything."

With great effort, Jack stamped back the tirade of words that perched on his tongue.

Frank must have seen his struggle, only he didn't hold back. "Your money will keep you warm. But will it give you the companionship and love that a woman can give? Wake *up*, Jack!"

"I can see"—he sucked in a ragged breath—"that I made a mistake seeking you out. I thought you might help bolster a fella in his time of need."

"You thought I'd give you sympathy and soothe your pride. Pride isn't meant to be soothed, boy. It's meant to be repented of."

"I grew up poor, Frank. Remember? No one could ever be more humbled by that than me."

"It's become a pride to you to gain riches and overcome your past. You want what you didn't think you had as a boy and what you now think is owed you." Frank rubbed the back of his neck, and Jack caught the wince of pain that the simple movement caused him. "How many times has Alaina told you she doesn't need to be the wife of a rich man?"

Jack froze. Had he talked to Alaina? He ran his fingers along the rim of his damp hat, regarding the roughness of the material.

Alaina's face filled his mind. Her pleading words echoed to him. *"I don't need to be rich, Jack."* He pounded his hat back on his head and spun. "I'll leave you to your own company then."

"Jack."

He spun around as Frank relaxed back, deep into the pillows, and closed his eyes. "Do us all a favor and keep your eye on that dam. Heard there's more rain on the way. That thing's not going to hold forever."

ᘓ

As the train picked up speed, Alaina struggled against the burn in her throat and the even worse hole where her heart had been. She rested her forehead against the window and prayed for strength and wisdom. . .and Jack. Always for Jack.

Releasing him had been the hardest thing. On so many levels she knew it was the answer, the right thing to do, but the pain consumed her like fire.

The conductor asked for her ticket just as the tears began staining her cheeks all over again. His kindly face smiled down at her. "If there's anything you need, ma'am. . ."

"Thank you," she croaked out, but the show of sympathy unraveled what little composure she'd managed to hold on to. Turning back to the window, she buried her face in her hands and let loose the torrent in a series of soft sobs that made her grateful the train didn't travel with a full car of passengers.

She seemed to move in a haze, partially aware of her mother's sister meeting her and the ride to the small, but richly furnished home. Her aunt's stream of chatter, so contrary to her mother's quiet nature, relieved her of the need to keep a constant dialogue going, and though sunshine spilled down in Pittsburgh, Alaina felt grateful for the warmth of the new, heavy dress material.

When her Aunt Joanne, or Aunt Jo as she preferred, took her on a hackney ride up Eighth Street to the college, the immenseness of the building overwhelmed her senses.

"I'm so excited to have you move here and attend," her aunt chattered on. "You've kept up your studies? Knowing your mother, I'm sure you have." The older woman twisted on her seat and shaded her eyes to squint at the building. A deep sigh escaped her. "Oh, how lovely. Brings a thrill to my heart every time I think of women in higher education. We'll give those men something to think about, right, dear?"

Her aunt seldom required a response, and Alaina allowed her to continue the one-sided conversation. She needed to say something. Wanted to say quite a lot, really, but not about college or Latin or anything else related to life outside of Johnstown. It felt too much like acknowledging a life without Jack.

Oh, God, what have I done? Am I in Your will now, here, or in Johnstown?

Chapter 20

The long ride up from Johnstown had accomplished a diversion, though he couldn't remember what he'd been thinking about or getting on and off the train. He recalled the crash of the raging Little Conemaugh River that followed the trail fourteen miles up from Johnstown to the South Fork Fishing and Hunting Club. When he disembarked in South Fork and found a horse, he rode straight up to the dam.

Frank's words had spooked him. All the talk of the dam breaking. Yet it looked firm and solid and unyielding to him as he sat astride the horse. He spent an hour riding by the spillway stream and remembering the picnic he and Alaina had taken beside the beautiful fall of water. And at the crest of the dam, where the water lay a mere four feet from the top, he recalled the proposal. The sun in her hair. The smile that lifted his spirits and set his heart into a gallop.

Every memory they'd shared seemed to rip at him until he felt heavy and realized the light was fading from the sky. He finally kicked the horse into a gallop and took the short trip back down to South Fork.

There he had the horse looked after and crossed to a small restaurant, where he ordered the special and listened to the people talk about the rain. As he speared a chunk of roast and lifted it to his lips, he knew he needed rest and wondered if he would be able to sleep at all. He stared down at his nearly full plate and felt the food he had eaten ball up in his stomach. He pushed the plate away and scrubbed a hand over his hair and down his neck.

An older man entered the restaurant and, seeing the vacant chair across from Jack, headed straight for it. Tom Hennesey was a talker who often hauled club members up to the lake, including Alaina, which was how they'd come to know each other. Jack inclined his head as the man straddled the chair, then laid a hand on the seat and pulled it closer to the table. "Hear Johnstown's a swimming hole."

Jack couldn't help but grin at the man's choice of words. "Saw a rowboat going down a street on the west side."

Tom spit out a laugh. "You'd think old Johnstown would learn a thing or two 'bout being in a floodplain. Guess they liken themselves as ducks. Me, I'm getting myself to higher ground. If any more rain's a-coming, you won't see me swimming for my life. Nope. I'll be standing atop the mountain laughing."

"You think it's going to break?"

"You know these mountains, son. Thunder gusts happen all the time. And this weather"—he scratched at his chest—"been all over the place this month. Makes my bones weary and worries my mind something fierce."

Jack pushed his plate in the man's direction. "I'm done if you want to finish off what's there."

Tom guffawed, one gnarled hand clamping the edge of the dish and pulling it his way. "Don't mind if I do. Shame to see good food go to waste." His eyes traced over Jack's face from beneath bushy brows. "You so lovesick you can't eat? Heading up to see your girl?"

A knot swelled in Jack's throat. "She's not up there. Her family pulled out early."

"Seems strange. What you doing up here then?"

Jack's conscience pulled at him. His tongue held the explanation as if the saying of it would somehow dispel his sense of unreality. After all, Alaina could change her mind. He really had meant that the time away would be good for her. For them. But despite his conviction, the thought did little to ease the pain.

Tom stopped chewing and craned his neck, eyes more alert than Jack wanted. Jack scraped his chair back just as Tom handed down his verdict. "You got yourself girl trouble."

Jack tried to shake off the comment.

But Tom waved him to stay put. "Got a thing or two to tell you about women. Now don't look that way. I ain't spilling anything I shouldn't be. Was married myself once. She died a few years back of the diptheria that swept through here in '79. You'd've been too young to remember much of it. Lot of children died, but got me real shook when my wife came down sick." Tom's brows beetled, and he tore off a corner of a biscuit and sopped up the juice from the roast before popping it into his mouth. "She was my life."

Jack edged his seat closer. "You mean your wife?"

"Nope. Said it just like I meant it. She was my life. Took real good care of each other. When she died, I thought I'd 'bout near shrivel up and blow away." Tom paused long enough to tear off another piece of biscuit.

"Why are you telling me this?"

Tom's head snapped up. "So's you can make good and sure to listen to what it is she's trying to tell you."

"Trying to tell me. . . ?"

"Woman doesn't free a man up unless she's got rock-solid good reason. I've met your girl. She's a good one. Good heart. Gentle. Not hard to see that, even for an old one like me. Reminded me of my Rebecca. That's the kind of woman a man needs most." Tom paused. It seemed the man was working up to something else.

Already Jack had been surprised by Tom's candor. Most men joked and lamented being married, especially as the family grew. One of the reasons Jack wanted so much to be free from poverty before marrying. So many men had struggled to put food on the table, working twelve-hour shifts, six days a week. It wearied him to think of struggling like that the rest of his life.

"What about the kind of man a woman wants?" The words slipped out. Embarrassed by the question, Jack moved to rise.

"Reckon a woman's wants aren't so much different from a man's. Someone to share life with. To love on and be loved by. All the other stuff is just leaves on the tree."

Pain swelled in Jack's heart as he stared down at Tom and allowed his words to sink in. They chipped at him. Could it be that his need to make a comfortable living was more for him than Alaina? She'd told him so often enough. He wondered how it would feel to live with her as husband and wife and struggle as the other men struggled. Jack swiped a hand over his damp hair. "I need to go."

"Go?" Tom chuckled. "Where you planning on going this time of night? You needing a place to stay, I reckon you can bunk at my place."

☙

Dear Jack. . .

Those were the only words Alaina had managed to write in the hour since she'd retired to her room. She had escaped after convincing her Aunt Jo that her quietness stemmed from nothing more than exhaustion. Truer words she would never speak.

She cradled her head in the palm of her hand and stared at the paper and those two words. Tomorrow she would begin a tour of the college and look into requirements and tuition needs.

Her aunt had promised, many times, to help along those lines. "Regis left me quite comfortable, and I made a vow to your mother that I would help if you chose to attend. Your being here would be company for me, too. You might even meet some nice young man during your time here."

If she had suspected her mother and her aunt had been in close communication, that statement assured her of it. She could just imagine her mother's long dissertation to her aunt about Jack's perceived inadequacies.

Alaina squeezed her eyes shut. *I don't want to be here, God. I want to be back in Johnstown. With Jack.*

But she knew Jack needed to see her in a different light. Breaking the engagement had been the right thing to do. She felt it deep in her spirit, even if the shadow in Jack's blue eyes drained her of joy.

How can I cause such hurt yet know I'm right in my decision?

The question brought the story of Christ to her mind. And Abraham and Isaac. The widow who sacrificed not just her life but the life of her only son for a man she didn't know. Of God's sacrifice in watching His only Son suffer and die. Such pain. Beauty for ashes.

Instead of continuing the letter, she slipped the sheet of paper from the surface and crumpled it into a tight ball as a tear splashed onto the wood of the small writing desk.

Chapter 21

May 31, 1889

Jack woke with a rush of anxiousness that left him with a dull headache. A form moved through the shadows. Disoriented, he sprang to his feet.

He heard the strike of a match, and a sudden flare of light brought Tom's face into clear view.

Jack relaxed.

"You hear that?" Tom asked.

That's when he understood why he'd awoken so quickly. "Rain."

"That's not rain, son. That's the worst mess of water rushing down from the sky that I've ever heard. We just might find ourselves riding down this mountain on a mud slide." Tom brought the lantern to the table close to the one small window on the front of his house.

Jack narrowed his eyes to see outside, but nothing except the glint of light off a sheet of water met his vision. The deluge sounded like a live thing trying to crush the house flat. "We should check on things," Jack spat. "Make sure everyone is safe."

Tom considered a moment and then shook his head. "It's eleven thirty. Decent folk are sound asleep. This might not last long anyhow. You know how quick the storms can be through here." He lifted the chimney and blew out the light. "Best get some rest. Tomorrow might be a long day."

Jack lay back down on the hard floor and pulled the thin blanket over his shoulders. Sleep wouldn't come. Instead, his mind labored under the idea of what it would be like to lose Alaina. She might never return. The idea left him hollow and scared, and for the first time, Jack knew no amount of money was worth being alone.

Through the night he lay awake reviewing the string of events, missed dates, broken promises, and Alaina's adamant, "I don't need to be rich," over and over. And every moment was underscored by Frank's observations of his selfishness and pride. His friend's words bruised him.

He swallowed and rolled to his side, then punched at the rolled-up blanket he used as a pillow. The threadbare blanket encompassed everything he felt about being poor. It made him feel fragile and weak. Vulnerable.

A picture of her smiling face flashed into his mind and froze there. *Alaina.* She would laugh at the prospect of threadbare blankets and a leaky roof. It would become an adventure for her to figure out a way to make things better. Even the small apartment she shared with her mother lacked the dreariness he would expect from someone poor. Perhaps because Alaina and Charlotte took time to make it look cozy and warm.

Jack rolled to his back and blinked up at the thin ceiling, where the sound of rain had grown more vicious. Alaina radiated a peace and contentment he didn't have. It drew him to her and was one of the reasons he felt it so easy to break promises. He knew she would always be there. Loving. Kind. Content.

Well, she's not here now, Jack, old boy.

While her faith had grown, his had shrunk. Frank was right, though it pained him to admit it. He'd become selfish. In his pursuit of what he wanted, what he thought was best for *them*, he'd tuned out Alaina.

A tug at his conscience shed light on his cluttered thoughts. He'd tuned out God as well. The balancing factor in his life. The One who never failed to show him how to love others first and himself last had faded into the background along with Alaina. No—he squeezed his eyes shut—no, he had shoved them into the background, rejecting them because he thought accepting them meant he would be forced to accept being poor. And humble. And vulnerable.

And because he'd been unable to forgive his father.

"People are more important than things."

Could he forgive his father his weaknesses? Or would he allow his private bitterness against Don Kelly to destroy him? How could he forgive?

That dark night so many days ago when he'd agonized over his plans and Pastor's sermon, he recalled asking the same question. How could he choose to forgive? Except now he knew the answer. It was simply that: a choice.

He closed his eyes. It would not be easy, but it would be a start.

God, I've been so full of myself, the prayer began, as he drew in a ragged breath and exhaled his confession. *So full of myself and so scared. . .*

ଓ

"Get up! We gotta get out of here."

Jack bolted upright at Tom's frantic voice. He stared out the window into gray light. Jack rubbed at his right temple, where a dull ache reminded him of his rough night, but the memory also brought something else, a peace that he hadn't felt in a long time. "What's going on? Is it still raining?"

Tom didn't answer but jabbed a finger at a skillet with a lone pancake. "Grab it and let's go. I wanna know about that dam. Water's running high all up and down South Fork. It must be at the crest of that dam, and I don't want to be anywhere near here when it goes."

"I'll get the horses."

"Already got them. Was out this morning and down to Stineman's supply." Tom finally turned, his eyes tripping over Jack's face. "They was saying how everything was fine. That the dam was going to hold."

"Who?"

"Boyer and the fella from the club. Beedwell, I think his name was."

"You don't believe them?"

"All's I'm saying is, this weather isn't helping. Look at the Little Conemaugh. It's a raging beast." Tom paused and pressed his lips together. "I've seen a lot of things that are unnatural, and I'm not much of a praying man, but I pray God have mercy on me today because if that dam goes. . ."

Tom dashed outside as Jack pulled on his shirt and leapt to follow before Tom left him behind. Their horses splashed up Railroad Street, where a small crowd clustered in front of George Stineman's general store.

"That's that Parke fella," Jack heard Tom mumble. "If he's here, things must be bad."

Before he could ask who the "Parke" fella was, Tom kicked his horse and took off up Lake Street toward the dam. Jack matched the pace but eased his horse some when he saw just how badly the road to South Fork had deteriorated because of the rain.

The road forked, and Tom swerved to the right where the trees parted. When the old man pulled his horse up tight, the animal almost sat down in the road. Jack came abreast of the slack-jawed man. He snapped his head to follow Tom's line of vision and felt dread shoot down his spine. A bunch of men, looking small from the distance, raced along the breast of the dam, seemingly at the command of a man on horseback.

"They're trying to raise the height of the dam." Tom's words came hard and fast. "There's no way they'll have time. No way."

Jack didn't wait to hear more. He nudged his horse hard toward the breast of the dam, shocked when he saw that the water was nearly level with the road.

Tom came up beside him and reached out his hand to grab the bridle of Jack's horse. "Don't go out there. It's too dangerous."

☙

"Your heart isn't here, is it, dear?"

Alaina realized she'd been staring at the food on her plate, lulled into silence by her aunt's continuous chatter. "I'm sorry, Auntie. I guess I'm not that hungry after all."

"I expect this has to do with that boy your mother is so desperate to get you away from."

Alaina gasped. "She told you about Jack?"

"Of course. Charlotte tells me a great many of her fears. It's what sisters do, you know. Oh, for a while she never told me anything, mostly when I was married to Regis, but I believe that was because she was embarrassed. She felt that I was far above her socially. How absurd is that? It's not as if I'm better than her at all. She's my sister and I love her, but she loved your father. His silence has hurt her very badly."

Alaina opened her mouth but could think of nothing to say.

"Your mother simply doesn't want to see you hurt like she was hurt."

"Yes, I know. She told me about refusing to go West. Why didn't she go, Auntie?"

"Why, indeed. She's stubborn. Would rather nurse her wound to him than acknowledge the wound she inflicted." Her aunt shoved her plate back. "Now I want to hear about this Jack fellow from you."

"I—" Alaina gulped and locked her hands together under the table. "Jack wants what's best for us." She expected her aunt to charge into the conversation to dispute that, but she remained silent. "He works for Cambria Iron but has a great mind for inventing. He keeps trying to come up with a better way to make iron into steel, but his ideas haven't worked so far."

Her aunt nodded. "He is a decent sort?"

"He's a very hard worker."

"Alaina"—her aunt's gaze became direct—"why do I sense a hesitancy in you regarding this young man?"

The young maid appeared to refill Alaina's juice glass. She crossed to fill Aunt Jo's glass as well.

"Thank you, Tia," Aunt Jo said.

"My pleasure, ma'am."

Aunt Jo sipped her juice and relaxed back in her chair. "I fear being alone has relaxed my manners. I'm not nearly so strict as other ladies, but then I don't really care to be." She gave the young maid a kind smile that Tia returned before disappearing. "She wants to go to the college."

Alaina tilted her head. "Tia?"

"Yes." She lowered her voice. "I agreed to pay her twice what other maids earn if she would promise to save half for the first year of tuition."

Warmth for her aunt's kindness flooded through Alaina. How different her mother seemed from her Aunt Jo. But the thought shamed her when she remembered her mother's surprise and fingered the excellent material of her stylish new dress.

"Now, your young man. Your mother seems to worry ever so much about your marrying him. Too much, in my mind, but then I never had children to worry and fret over, so I'm sure I don't understand."

Alaina ordered her thoughts before she spoke, relieved when her aunt didn't press her to hurry or distract her with more questions. She took a bite of the now-cold pancakes and a long swallow of the orange juice. "Jack is handsome and fun." Her heart swelled at the thought of his antics, and she pressed the napkin to her lips to cover the smile.

"No need to go all prim and proper. I've been in love, too, and well know the giggling foolery of a smitten woman. Regis was a trickster, he was, and he made me laugh on many occasions when I would have cried. That is a priceless attribute."

"Yes." Alaina nodded. "He loves children and. . .and. . ." Words suddenly failed her, and she stared down at the congealed food on her plate.

"Then why are you here?"

Aunt Jo's soft question beckoned forth the only answer Alaina could give. "Because Momma wanted me to come so badly."

"My sister is blind to your needs. In her effort to protect you, she is unable to see your love for this young man."

"There is more to it, though, Aunt Jo. Sometimes Jack. . .forgets me."

"Excuse me?"

Alaina put some steel in her voice. "I said, sometimes he forgets me."

"I thought that's what I heard you say. But please, forgets you how?"

She explained about the missed dates and watched her aunt's expression for signs of disgust or outrage, as she often saw on her mother's face.

"It seems to me you have a young man who is hardworking and diligent. Not bad traits at all. But"—Aunt Jo let the silence grow—"I think there are some things he needs to realize. To start off, he needs to see what a treasure he has in you, that it's not in the hope of getting rich."

"How will he see that?"

Aunt Jo's smile grew slowly. "That, my dear, is something the Good Lord will have to impress upon him. If the two of you are meant to be together, then nothing can separate you."

Chapter 22

Jack heaved the pickax. His muscles bunched as he pulled it to his shoulder and swung downward again with every bit of strength he could muster. The tight group of men around him worked like a machine, each man's cuts with pickax or shovel in perfect synchronization with the next man's. But Jack knew, even as his swing came down seconds before that of the man across from him, that it would never work.

"It's no use. We can't cut through," someone shouted through the rain.

Jack's hands slipped on the wet handle, and he adjusted his grip before raising the tool for another plunge into the rocky slope. He flipped the pickax to the side with the point midswing, but even the point did little more than make an inch-deep indentation.

"Clear out! Clear out! It's going over." The tight ball of men working on carving out another spillway to relieve the pressure of the water building behind the dam scattered.

Jack raised his head to see a sheen of water eat away at the dirt and rock that had been thrown up in the middle of the dam to increase its height.

"Jack!" Tom yanked on his sleeve and got him moving. When the two men stopped on the far end of the dam, the water had begun the slide over the top and dropped in a silvery sheet. "It's soaked through and won't hold much longer," Tom hollered.

Jack jerked. "Warn them!"

Tom's hand held him firm. "It's been done. The line from here isn't working yet. They sent someone down to South Fork."

Jack's mind churned. "I need to get to Johnstown."

Tom faced him, the man's hands clenching his shoulders with a strength Jack would have never guessed him to possess. "Word is, roads are washed out. If you go out now, you could get caught in it."

Even as Tom's words penetrated, the water sluicing over the dam grew in volume, like an insatiable beast that had tasted the sweetness of liberty and wanted more.

"I've got to go."

Tom shook his head. "It's no use. They sent another boy down to South Fork just minutes ago and another man went to clear his family out. I let them have our horses."

Tension grew in Jack's stomach, clenching it hard and churning the cold pancake he'd eaten into acid.

☙

"It seems to me you were rushed to get out of there. He is no doubt devastated and confused, perhaps even angry."

Alaina stared out the window at the street and recognized the train depot. "Auntie, I thought we were headed back to the college."

Aunt Jo's eyes twinkled. "So *you* thought. But I thought to myself, *If I were Alaina, I'd want to head back to Johnstown as soon as possible and talk to my young man.*"

"But if I leave, Momma will be so unhappy."

Aunt Jo's chin tilted to a stubborn angle. "Leave Charlotte to me." The carriage pulled up in front of the station, and her aunt waited for the driver to offer his hand before descending. "Have your say with Jack and bring him and your mother with you back here." Her eyes sparkled. "That will give me a chance to help your mother see reason. Maybe she'll even swallow her stubborn pride and move back here to live with me like I've offered a thousand times."

Excitement and nervousness clawed at Alaina as she crossed the station and perused the length of the train.

"Looks like Mr. Pitcairn is traveling today." Aunt Jo's long finger pointed. "That's his private car right there. Oh, but they're calling for boarding. Have a nice trip and come back if Jack doesn't see the light. Pittsburgh has some quite handsome single young men."

Alaina waved to her aunt until the woman faded to a speck and the train's momentum made looking back a stomach-churning experience. Ash from the engine flew through the window and smeared on Alaina's dress when she brushed at it. She pushed the window up and settled in to work out what she would say, both to her mother and to Jack.

Jack.

An urgency to pray gripped her. Pray for whom? For Jack? Her heartbeat picked up speed, and she bowed her head and closed her eyes, but her mind blanked. *Lord?* Her mind filled with the view of the valley from the Lake Conemaugh Dam. *Lord, have mercy. I don't know what this means, but protect Momma and Jack, Frank and—*

A raindrop splashed through an open window onto her hand, and Alaina wiped it away as a sickening dread filled her. Rain. The dam. All the rumors of the dam breaking and the water sweeping through the valley. Dread choked her throat. She prayed fervently for what seemed like hours and then raised her head to see the landscape blurred by gray rain. In places she glimpsed the high water pooling in lowlands. And all the time, she breathed the same prayer, the urgency not lessening, but her own fear growing until the tension in her body churned an ache in her head.

Chapter 23

Jack kept the horse at a gallop as much as possible during the fourteen-mile ride down to Johnstown from South Fork. The animal he'd borrowed in South Fork seemed game for the journey and displayed fine spirit despite the drizzle, raging water, and washed-out roads.

At places along the route, Jack had to stop and pick his way over a washout, but the horse never hesitated when Jack dug his heels deep in the animal's sides. Just as the valley came into view and the terrain flattened, the horse's strides became more sure, but a deep-throated rumble brought Jack's attention around. He spurred the animal, sure he knew what danger caused the sound. The water would have cut through by now.

Jack crossed the bridge into Johnstown when another rumble swelled through the air. He dared a glance over his left shoulder and saw a black mist and a yellow wall of water. His heart jumped and pounded. Cold sweat popped up along his back and forehead. He pulled the horse up hard and vaulted to the ground. Turning, he gave the animal a hard smack on the rump, and it took off.

Jack flung open the door of a tall building and raced up the steps. His mind absorbed details as he went. The banister and rails, the doors with numbers lining the hall. A hotel. As he raced up the second flight of steps, he heard voices, frantic and high-pitched, underscored by the deeper tones of a man's voice. And over that a deep rumbling that built into a deafening roar. A gust of wind sucked up the steps. Jack's legs burned.

On the third-floor landing, he saw a man at the window and a huddle of people crouching in a corner. Shadows held the people captive, but the deafening roar, growing louder by the second, had etched lines of terror in their faces.

"Is there an attic?" he yelled above the roar.

The man at the window ran toward them, arms waving. "Get up the steps. All the way up!"

As one, the group rose. Jack's eyes darted around the room, but he saw no stairway until the man flung open a narrow door to reveal an equally narrow flight of steps. The house shuddered hard. Water shot through the glass of the windows, sending shards across the room as water poured through the new opening. Beneath their feet, the floor rose like a raft, carrying them to the ceiling. Jack crouched and lay flat to avoid becoming crushed against the ceiling. He rolled over, and the floor disintegrated beneath him. Screams and shouts rent the air around him as people were set adrift in the raging, swirling waters.

Jack struck out. He gasped at the cold water, spat at the wetness invading his nostrils and pushing into his mouth. More cries and screams came to his ears, moans, all sifted through the roar and crash of water, the tearing of wood and rip of nails popping. Lifting and tumbling, the water swelled and churned until the building itself simply disappeared. Jack fought the pull of the undercurrent, shocked to see the menacing pewter of the sky.

A hard shove brought pain to his shoulder. Water filled his ears, and something grabbed his leg. A hand? He bent in two to feel for whatever it might be, but the grip released. A huge piece of debris barreled toward him, a man and woman huddled together. Jack saw the woman's mouth open. . .then she was gone. The water rolled him. When he braced his body, he sank lower, so he relaxed, exhausted. His hand touched something hard, and he squeezed his eyes shut to clear water. A board floated away and then shot back toward him, taunting him with its nearness.

He moved that direction, arms leaden, legs limp. Every movement brought him closer to the board. The board shifted direction and flowed away as if sucked by a gaping mouth toward a distant point. With the last bit of strength he could muster, he made a grab for the piece of wood as it began to twist away again. Jagged pain raced up his arms as his hands slid over the rough wood and he pulled himself partially onto the surface.

Jack's nerves burned. He floated, pulled by the current. Afraid to raise his head and see more terrible sights, he knew the sounds were enough.

When he'd rested and his vision cleared, he lifted his head to take in his surroundings. Rooftops. Boards. A dead horse. As he watched, a tall building, of which only the top floor was visible, swayed and plunged beneath the surface. He began to paddle toward the distant mountain.

"People are more important than things." Through a fog of exhausted uncaring, he saw Alaina's smile. The smile dimmed into a frown and her arms stretched out. *"You can do it, Jack."*

The icy water began to work its brand of paralysis. Moving became more difficult. Jack clung to the words he heard in his mind, Alaina's image having long faded. Something moved around his legs. Water began to swirl around his body and pull at him. He tightened his hold on the board.

Oh, God, was all he had time for before another wave engulfed him.

ꞯ

"What is it? Why have we stopped?" Alaina put the questions to the conductor.

"Everything is fine, I'm sure, miss. We'll move along shortly."

Left with little to do but wait, Alaina watched the muddy, swollen river rush by not far from where they sat.

A woman farther up in the car gasped, and the man behind her shot from his seat and pushed his face against the window. His expletive accompanied a man surging into view on the swift river, clinging to a board. More debris swirled and tossed in the angry waters, and another person shot by.

Everyone on the train seemed frozen to the spot. Then the men in Alaina's car seemed to come alive all at once. More exclamations, more shuffling of feet, then they started getting off, one by one. The women hovered at the windows and watched in terror as a house crashed into a clot of debris.

Within minutes the men had found makeshift poles or anchored each other in an effort to catch people. A young man cinched a cord around his waist and struck out toward the house caught in the trees. Alaina watched the man's struggle with bated breath. He twisted and turned every which way, at last arriving at the shattered house. When he emerged, he held something close.

"He's got a baby!" one of the women next to Alaina exclaimed.

"Where is this coming from?" A woman threw the question out to no one in particular.

Alaina collected the words, then spoke them out loud, her lips dry and her eyes burning. "Johnstown. It's from Johnstown. The dam must have broken."

"True. There's too much water for it to be a simple flood," someone else replied.

"Do you know someone from there?" a dark-haired woman asked the question of Alaina.

"My mother and fian—" Her voice broke. "Fiancé are there."

"Oh, how terrible for you."

Genuine sympathy oozed from the woman and broke down every ounce of Alaina's composure. Her legs became weak, and she folded herself onto the seat, buried her face, and allowed the sobs she'd held back to break free. Jack's expression at the train station filled her mind and made her despair that much harder to bear.

Momma. Jack. Missy and Sam.

The list of names marched across her mind and further deepened the well of her cries. She felt the pressure of two arms cradle her close and cared not who it was who offered the comfort. She clung to the person as if she herself had been set adrift in the wildly raging river.

"Look!" she heard one of the women say.

The person holding her tensed, and Alaina could feel her benefactor's body shift position, though her arms remained around her. Alaina kept her eyes closed.

"He's going back."

"No!"

Alaina raised her head then, and the raven-haired woman smiled down at her and stroked her cheek. Then she, too, rose and crossed to the windows.

"He is going back."

"One of us should tend that baby."

"There's a new mother in the next car. Perhaps she could care for the wee one."

The conversation between the women swirled around Alaina. She felt detached and afraid. A deep coldness clenched down on her spine and made her shiver, and still they talked.

"He's bringing out someone else."

"He must be exhausted."

"Oh, the child won't be all alone then. Thank the Good Lord."

She never understood where the strength to rise came from or what drew her to the window, but when she saw the rescued woman come closer, carried by one of the men, her dress little more than rags around her, Alaina felt the shock shedding from her mind and body. She took a step back as the man carrying the woman answered the frantic waving of her fellow passengers and brought the rescued woman on board. She sucked in a breath and went to the place where the man settled the shivering, wet form onto a seat. "Mrs. Newton!" Alaina knelt, her skirts billowing around her.

The woman's gaze landed on her, dull and unfocused.

"You know her. That's good. Keep talking to her while we get her warm." Alaina's benevolent companion turned away and raised her voice to be heard. "I need any spare clothing you can offer. Hurry now! Someone run over and check on the babe. The news will help her."

Alaina remained where she was and took the cold, pale hand in her own. "I'm the daughter of your dressmaker, Mrs. Newton. I remember you well. My mother worked from Heiser's store."

Mrs. Newton's pale eyes ran over Alaina's face. She blinked slowly, and a shiver shook her slender form. "It's all gone," she whispered.

Alaina strained to hear the words and swallowed as comprehension dawned. *All gone?* She pressed the back of her hand to her mouth and gulped. *All. Gone. Momma? Jack?*

She never knew if she fell back or was pushed aside as the women began to bundle the woman in the spare clothing, but as Alaina regained her balance and rose to her feet, she knew she could not stay, stranded in Sang Hollow, four miles from Johnstown. Determination stiffened her spine, and she slipped off the car and into the rain.

Chapter 24

Jack clung to the board, wrapping his arms around it to give his muscles some relief. He wanted to crawl on top of it, but his strength vanished. Blood trickled down his neck, and he dared not touch the spot where the water had slammed him into the brick wall of a building.

A hoarse scream for help, a man's voice, came quietly and then more loudly as Jack's raft floated closer to a home, only the attic visible and the lone man on top. With what little strength he could muster, he paddled closer. The current tried to drag him back, but he kept on. One hand. Then the other. One leg. Then the other. The man quieted as Jack drew closer.

"Jump!" Jack screamed. "Jump, and I'll come to you."

The man twisted on the rooftop, back and forth, as if he searched for some other means of escape. In the dim light, Jack felt the familiarity of that profile, of that form. He dug deep into the violent gray waters to push himself closer to the distraught man.

"Help me!"

"Here!" Jack yelled. The man's eyes landed on Jack. A jolt of surprise ripped through him. *Robert.*

"You going to save me, Kelly?" The question was both wistful and arrogant.

A quiver vibrated through the water, and Jack saw the house shift ever so slightly. "You've got to get off there. Now. Jump before it goes under."

Robert scrambled closer. "Playing the hero?"

The waters shifted direction again. Jack's struggle to get closer to the house morphed into an all-out fight to keep from being crushed against it. He threw out one hand to brace himself even as he fought to retain his grip on the board. Too late, the water jerked the wood from his grasp. He lunged and caught it, just as the water drove him back and slammed his head against the corner of the brick. He heard a scream but didn't know if it was from his own lips or not. Pain slid up his neck, and his vision dimmed.

When his sight cleared, he lessened his grip and felt the water begin to tear at him again, this time in the opposite direction. He tightened his hug on the board and squinted up at the roof, trying to make sense of things. Warmth on his neck let him know the extent of his injury.

Cool water surged upward and engulfed his body. Jack struggled to hold his place close to the roof, to think what had brought him here.

"People. . .more important. . .than things." Alaina's voice.

The words stoked his mind, and the mist over his thinking rolled back. The cry came again, like that of a hurt animal. Close. He looked up and blinked, trying to focus. Robert's form became clear, and Jack's mind flooded with what had become his mission. He sucked air into his lungs and tried to pull strength from somewhere deep inside him.

No. He didn't have to do this. Robert's weight on the board could sink them both. No one would blame him. No one would know.

Air flowed around him, and he blinked slowly. Robert stood for all he had wanted and lost, and the man had rubbed his victory in Jack's face.

Did it mean anything now? Could he doom the man to death without trying to save his life?

God, help me.

He lifted his head. "Robert." No. His voice didn't carry over the noise of the water, of distant screams and crashing. Of Robert's own panicked cries. Jack swallowed and raised his head higher. "Robert! Robert, I can't stay here. The building's going to go. Jump!"

Robert stilled. His head tilted as if he heard something Jack did not.

Like an invisible hand, Jack felt a shove that sent him surging backward, away from the rooftop. Even as the distance between them grew, Jack saw the building sway. Desperate, he tried one more time. "Robert, jump!"

Another shift of the house seemed to jerk Robert back to reality. He ran up the roof, slipped, caught himself, and began a desperate crawl to the ridge.

The house shuddered, and Jack tasted terror for the man. "No!"

When Robert reached the tip, the house twisted and rose, then collapsed inward. Brick crumbled, puffs of smoke and mist sprayed outward, and then the roof disappeared.

Chapter 25

Jack felt the bite of Alaina's admonition as he drifted, aimlessly, helplessly, pulled by currents he couldn't see that had rendered him too weak to fight. He relived Robert's plunge into the monstrous body of water. His pitiful wails, even his taunting remarks, he understood. Eyes squeezed shut, he reviewed his foolish pride. His neglect. Hadn't Alaina told him all along she didn't need to be rich? How his pride had hurt her. He would listen now, if given another chance. He would hear her and marry her and love her.

Now, in the midst of disaster, houses didn't matter. Stoves and sewing machines and fancy clothes and *money*. Nothing mattered more than knowing those you loved were safe and well and whole.

He allowed himself the sobs when he considered he might not get another chance. He had to try, to fight as much as he could. First, he must rest. His eyes felt heavy, and he floated, numb to his surroundings and the sounds and the awful swirl of water that dragged him around.

When he finally raised his head, he thought he heard voices. He floated close to a building. People hung out the windows, arms outstretched and beckoning him. It penetrated slowly that they were calling to him.

"Over here!"

He blinked away the dullness and started to kick his feet. A familiar face came into focus, but he couldn't put a name to the man. "Hurry before you crash."

Then he felt it. A current. Sucking him out. Away from the man and his hand and the hope of a solid place to lay his head and rest. He moved his feet, and the muscles in his legs cramped. He ground his teeth against the pain and moved them anyway, wanting so much to rest, to slide away.

You can do it, Jack.

He moved his head, kicked as hard as he could. A stab of pain shot through his brain. Then hands were reaching for his board and pulling him close. He heard the grunts and groans of men, felt himself lifted.

"Bad gash on his head. Get the doc."

In what seemed minutes, someone leaned over him and said, "I'm Dr. William Matthews."

Jack closed his eyes, secure in the knowledge he was out of the waters. He breathed a heartfelt *Thank You, Lord*, and allowed himself to slip away.

ᏣᏰ

When Jack woke in the dark of night, he found himself in a room full of people. Some lay on the ground, moaning, their snippets of prayers punctuated by the cries of children in the high-ceilinged room. Close to the front windows as he was, Jack could see those around him, while those farther into the room were shadowed in dark gray. But the reason for the light in the pitch dark of night sickened him—fires had broken out.

He sat up and touched the single strand of cotton circling his head. A dull ache throbbed at the base of his skull. A high-pitched scream rent the air and then faded, but the sound brought Jack to his feet and made his scalp crawl.

"She's giving birth. Babies do not wait for convenient times to be born. Just as death does not rely on convenience to schedule its grim appointment. We must be ready."

It took Jack a moment to put a face to the voice. A little woman sat in a corner, her clothes in tatters. She shook in the chill air, folded her head onto her drawn-up knees, and went silent, as if the explanation wrenched the last of her strength.

Another scream rose. This one lingered long before it faded back, and within moments, the pitiful wail of a baby joined the jumble of shrieks and prayers.

Jack went to the window and tried to piece together where he was and what had happened. Not knowing where Frank was. Or Missy and Sam. Or Charlotte.

"You're awake."

Jack turned, the quick action rewarded with a roll of dull pain that clenched his stomach.

"Take it easy, son. Jack, isn't it?"

Jack could make out the outline of the man who had helped him earlier. "Dr. Matthews."

"Yes." The man inhaled deeply, and his face contorted as if in pain. "Yes. Did our newest baby wake you?"

"No. No, I just woke up."

"Rest did you good. Why don't you stay here and keep a lookout for anyone who might need help. There are still a few people out there like yourself. We fear the building might go at any time, but we can hardly ignore the needs of others."

Jack touched the bandage around his head.

"Quite a gash. I have little to help you with, but I did try to wrap the bandage and stop the flow of blood."

"Thank you. I'll help any way I can, of course."

Dr. Matthews patted his shoulder. "We'll need you, I've no doubt. It will be a long, dark night."

Chapter 26

June 1, 1889

In the strange silence of morning, Jack realized the blow to his head had affected his vision. Where he could see clearly before his injury, now everything seemed cocooned in a dark haze.

Dr. Matthews checked his head again and tore a strip from a shirt left to dry overnight. "Think you can help us get everyone out?"

Jack started to nod, but the gesture sent pain into his head. "Sure."

Together, the men organized a way to get people to safety and toiled the rest of the morning lowering those he'd spent the night with through the window and out onto a pile of debris. From there another man took over guiding them from one stack of debris to another, closer to the mountains and safety.

By the time Jack had helped the last person through, his head throbbed and he felt too sick to notice the rumble of hunger his stomach sent out. He sank to the floor of the building and leaned his head on the windowsill.

"Let's get you out of here."

He gulped against the rising bile. "I can make it fine."

"You're in worse shape than most of those you helped," Dr. Matthews insisted. "There's a place over on Prospect that's rumored to have food."

Jack felt pressure on the back of his head as the doctor removed the bandage and probed the wound. "We need to get this cleaned out. Hopefully some medical supplies are on the way."

"What about you? Don't have to be a doctor to know you're hurt, too."

"I think I bruised a couple of ribs." Dr. Matthews winced. "It only hurts to breathe."

Jack allowed himself a small smile at the man's attempt at levity.

The doctor pulled Jack to his feet. "Come on."

They picked their way across the piles of wood two and three stories tall and places where water still stood.

"You have family here?" Matthews asked.

"My parents have been dead a long time, but I was engaged." He winced at the choice of words. "Her name's Alaina Morrison. She and her mother lived above Heiser's store."

The doctor shook his head. "It's all gone, Jack. Most of Washington Street just. . .washed away."

Jack inhaled the sordid, heavy air, feeling the unfairness of his life amongst so much destruction. If he stopped, if he allowed himself to think long and hard, he would break down. He had to find out about Charlotte. If she'd had warning, maybe she, too, had floated away, alive somewhere on one of the hills surrounding Johnstown. If so, he needed to find her. To learn about Missy and Sam. And Frank.

The only bright spot was his knowledge that Alaina had been spared. Now if only he could have another chance to make things right and love her as she deserved to be loved. He slipped his eyes closed and pressed his fingers against the lids as a crushing pain stabbed behind the sockets.

"Jack?"

Dr. Matthews's grip tightened his hold across Jack's shoulders. Jack felt his arm lifted and Dr. Matthews's shoulder wedged beneath his armpit as the stabbing pain receded and he fell into unconsciousness.

☙

Alaina allowed the man to cover her with a blanket.

"You'll be warmer now, Miss Morrison."

She nibbled at the piece of bread she held and shivered as much from shock as from the chill in the air. Still, God had provided her traveling companions in the form of two gentlemen, journalists determined to get to Johnstown by foot, just as she was.

Through the night, on their four-mile trek across the mountain, they peppered her with questions on the layout of Johnstown and its surrounding towns. When they arrived on the hillside in the early morning hours, and she had first laid eyes on the destruction, the chills began, sending her protectors on a mission to build a fire and find a blanket.

Her friend crouched beside her. "News is starting to trickle in, but Clarence and I will check on you when we can."

She couldn't respond, her mind unable to grasp anything more than the frightful knowledge that she might have lost everyone. *Jack. Momma. Frank. Missy. Sam.* Her head ached, and her throat burned with a fire unquenched by her tears.

Lord God. . .Jack. . . Please, God. . .Momma, Missy. . .so many. . .

She tried to touch the thought of life without Jack, of her mother caught somewhere in one of the few buildings left standing or, worse, in the acres of debris at the bridge that burned and burned and burned. When she finally broke through the shock, she had wandered along the edges of the great puddle that was now Johnstown, to help with those who'd been rescued.

She sat quietly by one man whose leg was obviously broken and tried to keep him warm. A parade of men and women passed her as she held vigil. Searching. Everyone seemed to be searching for someone. Sobs and pitiful wailing became a constant drone in Alaina's ears.

Into the evening she sat with the man, until a wagon came down to take those who were wounded to higher ground.

"There's a camp up a ways," said the farmer who stopped in front of her. "I'll take him up there."

In the fading light of early evening, Alaina saw the deep sadness carved into the lines around the farmer's eyes. "Will you take me, too?"

He nodded and waved to a man nearby. "Help me load him up."

She learned in the short trip up the hill that the farmer, Mr. Fry, lived on the crest and had seen the wave slam into Johnstown.

"Woodvale is gone. Heard say that South Fork was mostly spared, being most of the town is on the hill." She felt his stare. "You looking for your folks?"

She exhaled and pulled a tress of hair back from her face. "My mother and—" *Jack.* The name came to her tongue, but she couldn't say it out loud. Her throat closed painfully.

"You'll find them soon. No sense in thinking the worst yet. It'll freeze you up inside. These ladies up here, they might know someone, or your people might even be there."

After stepping out of the wagon, Alaina realized the short trip had caused her limbs to stiffen. She moved slowly, giving herself time to process the scene.

The shrouded shapes lay in rows a few feet away from those who sipped from tins of milk or chewed on crusts of bread. One woman, a bloody, torn bandage on her head, sobbed uncontrollably. There were so many who needed help or comfort. Most needed both.

Alaina thanked the farmer and left him to unload his passenger. As she drew nearer, she scanned faces for those of her mother or Jack. She crossed her arms and rubbed along flesh pimpled from the chill air.

One of the women saw her and met her halfway. "We have some food if you're hungry."

"No." She shook her head. "I—I came to help." She swallowed. "And to find my mother, my. . .friends."

The woman's eyes went soft. "I'm Liza. We welcome the help." She motioned toward the shrouded forms. "Would you like me to come with you?"

Alaina curled into a ball and rested her head on her knees. She felt the stress of the day in every part of her body and wanted only to blink and have Johnstown return to its previous splendor. To have her mother safely beside her, piecing patterns together and basting material for a fitting. She wanted to see Mary and hear her chatter about the big city and to run in the fields with Missy and Sam.

The men were bringing another body up the hill.

Alaina swiped at the myriad of tendrils clinging to her neck and face and rose to help unload supplies from the back of Mr. Fry's wagon.

One of the women squinted up at the old farmer standing in the back of his wagon. "We can never thank you enough, Mr. Fry."

The man gave a nod. His eyes strayed out toward Johnstown, then back. "It is the very least I can do, Miss Mandy. The people of Brownstown are opening up their homes. Send them our way for the night. We'll feed 'em and make sure they have dry places to sleep and blankets against the cold. Got more of that milk there, too. And ham. Got some bread. Our women are baking up more." As he talked, he bent his back to the work of unloading the goods he'd brought down.

When the wagon was empty, they began to sort the provisions.

The farmer rolled off, promising to return.

The same woman who'd thanked the farmer worked alongside Alaina. "You find your family?"

Alaina pressed her lips together. "No." She blinked and a single tear streamed down her cheek.

"I'm sorry. I tend to speak without thinking. I came down from the farm up there this morning. Seen a lot in my life, but never so much as this."

"My mother is all I have. I was to be married, but I—"

The woman placed a gentle hand on Alaina's shoulder. "Please don't explain. Rest a bit while we finish here."

She shook her head. "It's best for me to keep moving."

"Suit yourself. I surely welcome the help. Looks like more people are heading this way. Word is getting out that we have food."

Alaina's sorrow overflowed as she stared out at Johnstown. "We realize how very little we truly need to survive at times like this."

Chapter 27

June 2, 1889

Alaina wiped her eyes, the weariness and smoke causing them to water. Not to mention the stream of grief that she witnessed as loved ones identified the bodies of their mothers, fathers, children. . .and friends. She bit her lip hard and forced away the memory of Mary's serene expression. The girl's body had been brought in late afternoon, and the reality of her friend's death had chipped away at the last bits of strength that kept her functioning. She'd been grateful then for Mandy's embrace that not only held her upright but also helped take the edge off her grief.

A new stream of people moved into the campsite, while men worked to build shelters for families who needed them. Still, the long line of those sick and hurt had continued to grow with no end in sight.

"The men are getting together to see what's to be done. We can't function under these circumstances for much longer. I did hear we've finally got contact and a train brought in supplies. If we can just. . ." Mandy's words faded, and Alaina knew her friend saw what she had seen, the new stream of people headed their way.

She pressed her friend's hand and forced a smile. "We'll make it. I know we will."

"Oh!" Mandy pressed her hand to her chest.

Alaina followed her friend's gaze and saw nothing to incite such a reaction. The line of limping, wet, bedraggled people hadn't changed.

"It's Dr. Matthews. He came to see my sister when she was so sick and"—she clasped her hands together—"I know he'll be such a help to those who are ill."

Alaina, still unsure which man was the doctor, moved to help with the new wave of hurt and hungry.

Mandy passed her and went toward Dr. Matthews and his companion, one helping the other.

Alaina's attention was diverted by the crying of a naked child and the swollen eyes of a mother, dressed in rags and shivering. "Let me take the child," she admonished the woman. She helped the lady to a spot on the ground, near a fire that a young boy of ten had diligently fed all through the long night. Alaina knelt next to the woman and child, at a loss for helping her other than to offer the meager bread and a tin of milk. "I'll try to find something to bundle the child in and get you some bread and milk."

The woman reached for her baby, then curled her body around the child in a silent offer to share what little body heat she had. If she couldn't get him covered soon, the child would catch pneumonia.

Lord, please send us blankets soon.

Alaina pulled at her skirts as she rose to avoid tripping over the hem and turned to find Mandy behind her.

"Dr. Matthews is going to do what he can for those here."

Alaina glanced behind Mandy and saw the doctor leaning over the man he'd helped in. His shirt was little more than a strip of cloth across his chest. The strip around the man's head was dirty and caked with blood. Their supply of well water had dwindled to nothing in little time, but Mr. Fry had assured them other wagons were headed their way. As soon as she could, she would tend to the man's wound.

That's when Alaina caught the profile of the doctor's companion. Her heart beat hard as the man raised his head. The hair. The shape of his nose. His silhouette against the lightness of the sky. . .

"Jack!"

His head jerked her way, but he didn't move.

She stumbled over the young mother's foot and almost plunged straight into Mandy, but she kept going. "Jack!"

Within a few steps of him, she stopped. Her throat closed over a tight wad of tears.

In one swift motion, he swept to his feet. He blinked, then blinked again. The shine of tears in his eyes. "Alaina?"

She went into his arms then and felt his strong arms press her to him.

"Alaina?"

"I'm here, Jack."

He buried his face in her hair, and she felt his chest jerk before the first sob, a harsh, almost animal-like wail, grated against her ear and brought her own tears to the surface.

☙

Robert's plea for help and his inability to rescue him in time. The gash on his head and the long, terrible night that followed. All of it seemed to fade away as Jack held Alaina close. Her softness took the edge off hard reality and sent a breath of relief through every tension-filled limb.

Her tears mingled with his as he stroked her hair.

In the minutes that passed, he absorbed her presence like the starving man he had become since the water had wiped out Johnstown. He pulled back, wanting so much to see her face. Needing to trace the outline of her nose and see the dark eyes he so loved. But her face wouldn't come into focus.

She grasped his elbows. "You're hurt."

"But I'm alive."

He felt the quiver of her body, and fresh tears were falling. "I was so scared. Momma?"

He shook his head. "I don't know. The entire street was wiped out. Everything. It could be days before we know."

She went into his arms again, and he cradled her head against his chest. He wanted to say something comforting, but the words didn't come. He satisfied himself with the knowledge that Alaina was safe. She was here, and hope filled him anew.

But eventually, his injury took its toll, and weakness gripped him. He pulled away from her.

"Jack?"

He lowered himself to the ground and leaned his arms on bent knees. "Just need to. . .sit." Bile rose hot in his throat, and he leaned over. He felt the tug on the bandage around his head and heard Alaina's words, but she seemed to be talking from a great distance. He strained to make sense of everything, but he couldn't.

"I'll take care of you," Alaina's voice reassured.

Jack gave in to her ministrations, knowing he would be safe now.

Chapter 28

Through the day, Alaina sat beside Jack as much as she could. Though Mandy insisted she stay near him, Alaina knew the women were pushed to their limits offering comfort and the little bit of food they could. Besides, Jack remained unconscious, and rather than worry about the implications of his unresponsiveness, she was determined to keep busy.

When she had the chance to grab a few minutes to talk to Mandy, the news was better than she'd hoped.

"The train got through this morning, and people are arriving to help us out." Mandy ran a hand over her flat hair and swiped at her left cheek, leaving a smudge of dirt.

"We'll have help soon. Blankets and water and food."

"Yes." Mandy closed her eyes. "Dr. Matthews and Dr. Lowman are setting up a temporary hospital on Bedford. They'll want to take the worst cases over at some point."

As Jack slept on, Alaina's worry mounted. Knowing the doctors were pressed for time and that there were far too many to care for between the two of them, she did her best to help prepare the patients to be moved. When she came to a lone woman, her hand clutching a scrap of material, Alaina felt a deep sorrow. Almost forty-eight hours since the flood and the lady's arrival in the camp and she still could not be coaxed to say a word or take food and drink. She bent close to the woman and held the mug out. "Would you take a drink for me?"

The only response was a gentle caressing of the fabric.

Alaina set the tin mug aside and placed a gentle hand on the thin forearm. "Could I see the lovely material?" When those words were out, she cast about for something more to add. "It must mean a great deal to you. My mother was"—she steeled herself against the unconscious use of that word and continued—"*is* a seamstress and loves material and making dresses."

Still nothing.

Ever so slowly, Alaina reached out and unfolded the tiny corner of the material to see the subtle pattern of small flowers against a dirty azure background. She processed the tattered edge, as if it had been torn. "It's a beautiful shade of blue. Did you have it made into a dress or do it up yourself?" She realized the color of the lady's dress, although blue, did not match that of the scrap she held. Her heart clenched in compassion, and she raised a hand to stroke the strands of hair back out of the woman's dark brown eyes. "One day I'd like to have a dress made of that color. Blue always makes me think of sunshine and birds. I suspect a lot of people enjoy blue."

The woman shifted a bit on the hard ground.

Alaina picked up the tin. "Would you like a drink? Mr. Fry brought it down from his farm. He's going to try and bring more bread and blankets. If I find one with the color blue in it, I'll be sure to bring it to you. Would you like that?"

No response.

With a sigh, Alaina rose from her spot next to the woman and groped for something more to say to draw out the shattered soul. Alaina turned to check on the next person when she heard the slightest whisper.

"Bluebirds."

She turned back and stared down at the woman. Only when she knelt beside her did Alaina see the stream of wetness along the woman's cheek.

She released her clutch on the material and raised it to her cheek. "Bluebirds."

"What did you say to her?" Mandy's voice floated over Alaina's shoulder. She tilted her head to see her friend.

"I'm not sure. I mentioned the color blue and how it reminded me of birds." Alaina leaned toward the woman and again tried to press her to take a drink.

To her surprise the woman parted her lips and drank deeply, though she turned her head away after one swallow.

Satisfied, Alaina patted the woman's shoulder and got to her feet. In the waning daylight, the chill of the gray day would give way to another cold night. She hated to see the people struggling to stay warm while dealing with such chaos and deep loss.

She stepped over the inert forms of the injured and reached Jack's side. A sigh escaped as she sank to the ground next to him. With gentle fingers, she picked up his hand and twined her fingers with his. She'd left him to pursue her mother's dream for her. She understood now that her mother's dream could not be hers. But her mother had been right in one very important way—she could not promise to marry a man who thought more of wealth than he did of her. She recalled all the broken promises and empty evenings when Jack's promised visit turned out to be another study in loneliness for her. As much as she hated how she had broken the engagement, she would do it again. For her own sake. And if he was the man she thought he was, he would understand that decision.

Watching the rise and fall of his chest, and the stroke of his lashes against his unshaven cheeks, desperation rose in her. It would be so easy to ignore her common sense and marry him, if for no other reason than he was all she seemed to have.

Where was her mother? How would she find her in all this? Alaina's stomach churned.

God, how do I find Momma? Where do I look? And Missy and Sam. Frank.

It was all so confusing, yet she thanked Him for the miracle of Jack's life, and as she did, she squeezed his hand to her breast, then kissed the tips of his chilled fingers.

Chapter 29

June 3, 1889

Jack knew he should open his eyes. The angel that sat next to him kept saying his name and stroking a soft hand along his brow, but his head hurt so much. Pain so bad he knew any light would grind the ache in his head to a sharper point. So he kept his eyes shut.

"You know, Jack, I think it's time you woke up and stopped giving this young woman of yours so much grief."

In his mind, he smiled. Dr. Matthews's voice. He squeezed the small hand nestled in his and decided if he couldn't open his eyes, at least he could talk. "Hurts too much."

"A big, tough guy such as yourself is afraid of a little headache?"

Jack pursed his lips. He heard the quiet challenge and felt the soft poke of the man's words. Just as he had worked up the courage to pry his eyes open, another voice, more gravelly than the first, called Dr. Matthews away.

"Jack?"

He turned his head toward Alaina's voice. "Hey."

"Do you need a drink?"

"Yes." Within minutes he felt the press of a cup to his lips, but the strain of sitting up caused his head to pound harder and brought a wave of nausea with it. He relaxed back and rolled with the pain, swallowing convulsively over the urge to throw up.

Alaina dabbed his head with a cool cloth.

He wanted so much to ask her to put one at the base of his skull where the pain was most acute. He pulled air into his lungs and let it out long and slow.

"Dr. Lowman sewed up the gash in the back of your head."

He didn't remember it. A good thing, he was sure. "How long?"

"You've been unconscious for two days. The doctors established a temporary hospital on Bedford Street, so that's where you are now."

A question swirled in his brain. Something he wanted to ask, but the more he tried to bring it into focus, the more it eluded him, until he finally surrendered to the fog permeating his mind and fell asleep.

June 5, 1889

Joy surged through Alaina as she embraced young Sam despite the awkwardness of his position on the bed. "Sam, look who is here."

Behind them, Missy's squeals filled the air. Sam turned his head, and his eyes lit up when he saw his sister in his father's arms.

Alaina heaved a sigh of satisfaction. When Sam and Missy, bedraggled and dirty, and Sam with a badly bruised and broken leg, had been brought into the hospital late Sunday, Alaina had immediately registered their names in case Frank had survived the flood and was looking for them. Then she had prayed. To see him now, here, with his children close, brought a deep, abiding peace to her.

Frank, propped on crutches against the wall, didn't bother to shield the tears of relief that streamed down his cheeks as he clung to Missy. He raised his head and shook it back and forth. "I don't know what to say." The man lowered himself beside Sam and held his son's hand, stroking the hair from the boy's face.

"Joy unspeakable." Alaina smiled.

"With all the suffering. . ." Frank's voice caught and with his free hand he pulled Missy closer and buried his face in her hair.

He didn't have to finish the statement. Alaina understood. Everyone who found a missing loved one understood the ecstasy and the bitterness of realizing others were not so fortunate. It still wrenched her heart to see a woman fling herself across the identified body of a husband or child. She closed her eyes against the vision. Working to care for those in the hospital, she'd seen it too many times.

Sam shifted on the bed. Fever raged hot, turning his skin a bright pink, but the doctor had hope the boy would pull through. And despite his leg trapping him in debris, the workers had done their best to free the limb without inflicting more damage. What he needed most was food and water and rest.

Frank raised his head. "I couldn't lie there not knowing and started searching right away, sure I'd lost them when I heard that Washington Street had pretty much disappeared. I must have passed out, though, because I woke up and was being carried somewhere. I don't remember too much after that. Someone told me to check at the clearinghouse and there they were listed—" His voice choked off.

Alaina understood his emotion. "Sam said my mother got them to the attic and went down for something. Missy wanted to follow her, but Sam jerked her along just as the wave hit them."

"Your mother?" Frank asked.

She could only shake her head.

"I'm sorry, Alaina. I'll check the clearinghouse and post office on Adams and Main. People are registering all the time." The big man's expression radiated compassion. "I'll head there now."

"You can't. You're hurt, too," she protested.

"I'm big and I've had time to heal. Probably the lying around is making me hurt more than the injury."

"Can I go?" Missy piped up.

"I'll need your help." He got to his feet and pulled the crutch close, then reached to tousle Missy's already-mussed hair. "Some of the roads are still hard to get through, though. Think you're up to it?"

The little girl nodded a solemn nod and clung to his outstretched hand. "Will Sam be all right, Pa?"

Only Alaina understood the worry in Frank's gaze as it scanned Sam's face and then drifted to his heavily bandaged leg. "Give him a few days and he'll be chasing you around Green Hill."

Alaina paced down the aisle to catch a breath of fresh air. So much had happened in so few days. Supplies and money had come in from all over, yet still people suffered, though now more in spirit than in body.

Out the window, the bonfires raged on, their acrid scent scorching the air. Though needful, it still sickened Alaina to watch as dead horses and cows were cremated in the hot flames.

"Alaina?"

She turned from the morbid sight to the voice behind her.

A woman she'd not seen before spoke. "The young man is asking for you."

She nodded, and the woman scurried in a different direction. When she got to Jack's side, it pleased her to see his eyes open. At long last.

His blue gaze swept in her direction and settled on her, though a crease in his brow brought Dr. Matthews's warning to mind.

"Are you still having trouble with your vision?" she asked as she scooped his hand into hers.

"Hard to see you clear. Must have hit harder than I thought."

She brushed her fingertips along his brow, glad no fever seemed present. "Does your head still hurt?"

He winced and licked his lips. "Not as much. Bearable."

"Can you eat something?"

"I am hungry." His eyes closed, and he rolled his head away from her, but not before she caught the way his lips twitched and the working of his jaw. His voice came out raspy. "What if my vision doesn't clear?"

"Jack, hush. You're awake. Alive. Do you know what a miracle that is for me? I thought I'd lost everyone."

His sobs were silent, but she felt every one of them reverberate deep in her soul. She understood that his pain reached far beyond his vision. There were a million questions she wanted to ask him about the whole incident, but she held back as she knew she should. He, like so many others she'd helped in the last few days, had endured so much. More than she could comprehend. They needed time to heal on the inside.

Alaina gripped Jack's hand harder and stroked his brow. "I'm here, Jack."

When he quieted, he rolled his head to face her and swiped at the signs of his tears.

Alaina batted his hand away and stroked the shiny paths glistening along his cheeks. "We'll get through this. You've already come so far."

He touched her cheek, his fingertips rough against her skin.

She nuzzled her face against his hand.

"I love you."

The words melted her resolve to be strong, and the warmth in his eyes brought heat to her cheeks. She straightened in the chair and leaned forward, determined to avoid a conversation best left for another time and place. "We'll talk later. Just rest and get better."

She shifted mental gears and told him about Frank, Missy, and Sam. This seemed to lift Jack's spirits, and when he finally closed his eyes again, Alaina found comfort in the fact that she'd given him good news.

Chapter 30

June 8, 1889

Jack pushed himself to sit up. His head didn't pound like it used to, and his vision had cleared, but he still felt fuzzy. Probably from not eating and from lying around for so many days. He made up his mind that he would walk out of the hospital that day.

Across from him, Sam slept on despite the usual noise. The noise. He'd be glad to go to sleep and not be awakened by groans or grunts or the usual hospital cacophony. With great effort, he swung his legs off the edge of the bed and hesitated. His world spun, then settled.

"Taking off?"

Jack tried to focus on the person at the end of his bed. *Frank.* "If they're putting you in here, I am."

"Well, they're not." Frank spread his arms. "And no more crutches."

"Wonderful. Now help me off this bed and out that door."

Frank's chuckle reached Jack's ears. "You think that's wise? Doctors might have something to say about it."

"They won't miss me, and I'm sure they could use the space."

Jack tensed his muscles to push himself up, but Frank's hand clamped down on his shoulder. "You're an idiot, Kelly. You've not been vertical in almost seven days, and you're going to try to just walk out of here. You'll be on the floor so fast you'll—"

Jack tried to shrug his friend's hand off his shoulder and push forward, but whatever Frank was, he wasn't weak.

"You should at least wait for Alaina."

Which Jack translated to mean, *"Maybe she'll say something to penetrate that thick skull."* He chuckled and relaxed. "You win. I'll behave."

"Good. Now, before she gets here—"

"You going to lecture me again about treating her badly? Because I can tell you that being flat on my back, seeing all the destruction, surviving, has taught me a lot. I've been a fool."

Frank pounded his shoulder, though not with his usual force. "You sure have, and I'm glad you've jerked to your senses. But that wasn't what I was going to say."

Jack squeezed his eyes shut. *Oh, brother.*

"I heard someone say there's quite a few people up in Brownstown who haven't registered. I'm headed up there to see if Charlotte might be among them."

Jack hoped for Alaina's sake that she was. Though he and Charlotte seemed at odds, with Alaina caught in the middle, Jack didn't wish anything bad on her, for her sake as well as for Alaina's. Losing her mother would break Alaina's heart.

Though he'd never given much thought to Charlotte's disapproval of him, he saw now what Frank had tried to tell him months ago. People's lives mold their beliefs, just as his father's continual failings and living in poverty had molded his need to succeed. . .to be rich. Even to the exclusion of loving Alaina as he should. God had showed him so much in such a short span of time.

ᏨᏕ

The crude shelter creaked and groaned with the breezes. Alaina pulled her hair back into a low bun to mask the need for a good hair-washing. She stretched and tried to work the soreness from muscles not used to sleeping on hard surfaces. Oh, to soak in a nice tub of water. She'd give anything for the luxury.

As she crossed from Prospect Hill into Johnstown, Alaina's spirits rose. The townspeople, with a lot of help from outsiders, worked hard to remove debris and build temporary housing. Clara Barton had arrived on the fifth of June, and already hotels were being built under her direction, along with Red Cross tents to serve as hospitals. Still, even with the progress brought by relief efforts, the townspeople seemed cloaked in melancholia. *Time heals all.*

She rounded the edge of the temporary hospital as nurses and doctors were readying people for transfer to the Red Cross tents. Down the row, she could see Frank standing beside Jack. Relief tweaked at her mind to see Jack sitting up, yet the sight also became tinged with worry when she recognized the stubborn set of Jack's jaw and the hand Frank had on his shoulder.

As she closed in on the two, she overheard Frank's intentions of going up to Brownstown to search for her mother. She detoured to Sam's bed and found him sound asleep. She pulled the blanket up higher on the boy's chest and smoothed the chestnut hair back from his smooth brow.

Frank caught sight of her first. "Just telling this brute he needed to lay himself down before he slid off onto the floor. He's got it into his head that he can just hop to his feet and walk out of here."

"He's a bully." Jack reached up to grasp her hand. "You'll protect me though, won't you?"

The warmth of his hand sent her heart into a canter. "I'll protect you." She sent a wink to Frank then scowled at Jack. "Now lie down and be a good patient."

Jack groaned and squeezed her hand. "Yes, ma'am. Somehow it's sweeter coming from you."

"Let's see what the doctor says before you try anything heroic. I do think it's a good idea that you sit up more often."

"I want to get out of here and help out."

"Making sure you're strong enough not to fall down face-first would help everyone out a lot," Frank inserted.

Jack glared at Frank.

Alaina laughed. "You two are worse than Missy and Sam."

"I heard that."

Everyone's attention went to the bed next to Jack, where a sleepy-eyed Sam watched the group. Frank went to his son and hugged him. The two fell into quiet chatter that swelled Alaina's heart. She didn't think she could have borne losing Sam or Missy.

"Am I that easily dismissed?"

She laughed down at Jack. "No."

He raised her hand to his chest.

"Not at all."

"Tell me what you've been up to. What it's really like out there."

The warm feeling melted away. "Why don't you concentrate on getting better?"

His thumb caressed her knuckles. "I hear so much. Bits and pieces. I'm stronger now though, and I want to know what I can do to help. How bad is it?"

Her lip quivered, and she willed herself not to cry. All this time and she'd not given herself much chance to grieve, not that she'd had much time with all the work to be done. But now, looking into Jack's soft blue eyes, the core of self-control crumbled, and she choked on a sob.

Chapter 31

Jack saw the warning signals that tears were impending and pushed himself up. He reached to pull her into his embrace, grateful the dizziness had eased. He pressed his cheek to the top of her head and absorbed her emotions. It must have been very bad. Having seen the great swell of water and having fought its current for so long, he should have known, yet he had somehow held hope.

Sam's eyes were round with concern, and Jack gave the boy a smile of reassurance to erase the worry from both Sam and Frank's minds.

Eventually, Alaina pulled back. "I shouldn't be crying. Some have lost everyone in their families."

Jack pressed his finger to her lips. "Worry for your mother is mixed in with those tears." He stroked the hair from her face. "Besides, I'm hanging on to you as much as you're hanging on to me. I admit the world is still a little shaky."

She pressed a hand against his chest. "Lie down. I don't want you to—"

He caught her wrist. "I'm fine, Alaina. I promise."

"But if you make yourself sick, they might—"

"Shh. Listen to me." His words were taut with urgency. "I want to get out of here. Walk with me a bit so I can get my strength up."

She stared into his eyes, and he saw the silent plea in the brown depths. "It's not something you want to see. Johnstown is. . .gone."

"I've already seen some of it, though it was blurry." He wanted her to understand. "I need to feel a part of what's going on out there."

She didn't protest as he slid to the edge of the bed and let his feet dangle and then touch the floor. As soon as his feet made contact, needles of pain shot into his ankles, and he froze his expression so Alaina would not pick up on the pain the effort generated.

When it finally dissipated, he got to his feet. The room spun and dipped. Despite his best efforts, his weakness was evident because Alaina was there in a second, helping to support him. Jack inhaled deeply and let his breath out in a measured exhale.

"Jack, are you sure this is a good idea?"

He pasted on a smile. "If I fall down, just cover me with a blanket."

"How's your head feel?"

"Better than it has." He didn't mention the fact that it throbbed terribly now that he was upright.

At Alaina's insistence, he took small steps, knowing her eyes were glued to his face for any sign of weakness.

Lord, help me to do this so she can stop worrying about me.

When they finally reached the entry, Jack prompted Alaina to keep going. "I'm doing pretty good. Let's get outside." As soon as he emerged into the sunshine, a myriad of odors assaulted his nostrils and almost drove him to his knees.

Alaina immediately jumped into action and directed him toward an empty crate. "Sit."

"It's terrible," he murmured.

"It's worse up on the hills. What you see down here are mostly visitors who have come in to help. Up on the hill where I've been helping, that's where the people—the survivors—are. They're like lost souls, hollow and empty. Some just stare, others cry, but all of them are afraid, constantly searching for those they lost."

"I want to see more." His mind went to Robert. It felt like such a dream. He would never forget Robert's face or the terror of being pulled by an unseen current.

"Are you sure?"

He nodded. "Yes, I'm sure. And there's something else I need to tell you."

☙

Alaina listened as Jack talked. At first she had thought he'd simply felt a need to ease his own mind about the nightmare he'd endured, but then his tone changed, and he visibly tensed.

He talked of his ride through Johnstown on his simple plank of wood, being twisted by the ebb and flow of the water and pounded against objects in his way. He paused for breath.

She touched his cheek. "You can tell me the rest later. It's all over with, Jack. You're safe."

He squeezed his eyes shut, and his breathing became ragged. When he pressed her hand against his cheek, it was with greater force than necessary. "You don't understand, Alaina. It was terrible. And there was someone I tried to save. I tried to get him to jump—" His voice broke, and his free hand clenched into a fist. "I never understood what you meant by *'people mean more than things'* until I saw him."

She froze, mesmerized by the power of his emotion.

"It all came to me. The job, the inventions. Forgetting you. Saving people—" His jaw clenched, and a storm of emotion darkened his eyes.

"Because you couldn't do anything?"

"No. Because I could, would have, but the pull of the water was too strong.

I felt like a rag doll being pulled apart and tossed. I called to him to jump, but he sneered at me. He was afraid. I could hear his fear. Taste it."

Alaina's mind shuffled through a list of people whom Jack considered friends. "One of the men at Cambria?"

"No." His face contorted. "No. Robert. I was trying to save Robert."

Alaina sat stunned. She turned her hand in his and twined them.

"He wouldn't listen. The house moved and it. . .it *twisted.* My head hurt so much, but I knew I had to get Robert off that roof."

Her heart lifted as she began to understand what it was Jack was trying to tell her.

"It sucked me away from him and I—I don't know. I think I yelled at him one more time to jump, but it was gone. He was gone." He released her hand and covered his face. "I floated for a long time, and all I could think was that I'd been so wrong. So dumb. Selfish." He lowered his hands, his red, swollen eyes searching hers. "I knew, then, how much Frank was right."

"Frank?"

For the first time, the semblance of a smile curved Jack's lips. "Yes. He told me I was an idiot. That I was treating you badly. I kept defending myself and everything that I was doing, thinking that was somehow more important. Having money. . ." He lifted his eyes to the devastation. "I see it now."

"Oh, Jack."

He turned to her and cupped her face. "Can you forgive me? For all those times I put riches ahead of your heart?"

"You thought what you were doing was right."

Jack pressed a finger against her lips. "Don't defend me. I hurt you. Not once, not twice, but again and again and again. So determined to have money that I never once listened to what you told me so often. You didn't want to be rich."

She pressed her hand against his. "I still don't."

"Then marry me, Alaina. Marry me, and this time I'll get it right."

Chapter 32

June 9, 1889

After another good night's sleep, Jack accompanied Alaina to the clearinghouse again. They scoured the names for any sign of Charlotte Morrison, but still no one had registered by that name.

Alaina closed her eyes in defeat.

"You left directions where you're staying. Frank'll find you. Give the rescue workers and Frank some more time," Jack murmured.

He was right, of course. She'd made sure a nurse at the temporary hospital and one at the Red Cross hospital knew where to find her, but days had passed, and she was more worried than ever that Frank had lost heart because the news wasn't good.

And then there was Jack's proposal. He had recognized her hesitation and been sensitive to her reasoning in waiting for news of her mother. But his actions went a long way toward proving his sincerity. He sought her out every morning to check on her, then went off to work at the bridge to help clean up the terrible mass of wreckage.

If only she could say "yes" and feel clear, but she didn't.

"You've got that look again," Jack said softly, his eyes shining their concern. "I told you, Alaina, I'll wait for you. You're right to want news of your mother."

She sighed. "It seems so wrong to feel happy in times like these."

Jack's gaze drifted toward the wreckage at the bridge and over to Cambria Iron. She saw his Adam's apple bob and knew he understood.

Even almost a week since the tragedy, there was still so much grief and chaos. Fear of disease ran rampant. The stench in the air was almost unbearable. So many people had come in from other areas of the country that familiar faces were too few and far between.

Unless you went to the morgue or hospital.

Alaina patted Jack's arm. "I need to check on Sam, then get over to the tent."

Jack nodded and touched her cheek briefly. "You know where I'll be."

She smiled at the tenderness in his eyes, and thankfulness washed through her that God had spared Jack. "I know." She paused, then said, "I love you, Jack Kelly."

ଔ

When Jack came to the tent for supper, he took a moment to watch Alaina, as he had watched her all those days ago at the South Fork Fishing and Hunting Club.

She bent next to a small child and tried to coax a smile from the boy's solemn mouth. She plucked bread from the dishpan she carried and set it on the table. The boy nibbled on the edges and continued to watch Alaina as she talked, engaging the small group of children in some story or another.

His day had been long. The dynamite used to blow apart the debris at the bridge had done the job, but the mess had to be hauled away, long, muscle-aching work. He wanted nothing more than to sleep. To make things worse, his head still beat a dull throb against his skull, making every movement that much more painful.

But watching Alaina, he took comfort in her beauty and gentleness, her faith and the fervency with which she worked. Why hadn't he seen it before? She emptied herself to help other people and never expected much in return. She'd done it by loving him, even as he had shunned her.

When Alaina spotted him, she gave him bread, while another woman set a succulent slice of ham in front of him. Yet another lady arrived to ladle coffee into a tin cup.

He caught Alaina's eye. "You'll sit with me, right?"

"I can't. There are so many others who need—"

The woman ladling out the coffee nodded toward another girl. "Liz just came in. Take a break and talk to the nice young man." Her eyes held a twinkle as she stared between Alaina and Jack. "It'll do us all some good to see that life goes on."

Jack took his time eating, the background noise of hammers and axes, whistles and bells, and the crackling of the bonfires a constant reminder of the tragedy. Still, Jack was thankful for the noise and preferred to think of what it meant. Progress. Rebuilding.

He savored every bite and every minute he could be with Alaina. But no matter how comforted he felt in her presence, another harsh reality kept nibbling at him. What would he do? Cambria would be up and running again, he was sure, but did he want to stay here? It seemed right to start over. Fresh. Away from the misery. If Charlotte lived, they could take her with them. If not, it might be even greater wisdom for him to get Alaina away from here.

But where?

"Money is pouring in from all over to help Johnstown rebuild," Alaina offered.

"So I've heard. They're paying the new men two dollars a day."

Alaina shifted in her seat and poked a bite of ham with her fork. "What will it be like after all this? Will Johnstown be the same?"

"I think that's the question on everyone's mind. It's been on mine a lot."

"Do you want to work for Cambria again?"

He thought of the promotion and of Robert's attitude when he got it over Jack. Where hot anger used to consume him at the thought of being passed over, and where once his anger spilled out on Robert, now there seemed nothing but a chasm, devoid of all feeling save one. Sorrow.

It dawned on him then that he didn't know the answers. No one did. But his faith would carry him through each day. One at a time.

"All I know right now is that I want to help. To see people rebuild and get back on their feet. From there, I'll let the Lord lead."

His peripheral vision caught a familiar figure. He turned in time to see Frank duck into the tent and gaze around at the people. Jack raised his hand to indicate to his friend where they sat. He flicked a glance at Alaina and saw the instant strain tighten her lips.

The big man negotiated through the tables and dropped into a chair beside Jack.

"It's about time you showed your face. You've had Alaina worried."

Frank grimaced and rubbed his leg. "It's been a long haul. I stopped to help some along the way, and it delayed me. When I got there, it took me awhile to go 'round and see who of the Johnstown folk was there." His eyes shifted to Alaina. Dark and piercing.

Jack tensed.

"I found your mother."

Alaina gasped and closed her eyes.

Frank rushed on. "But it's not good, Alaina. She's. . ." The big man licked his lips and stabbed a panicked look at Jack.

Alaina opened her eyes. A question hung there.

"She doesn't remember anything, and she doesn't say much. It's like it stole something from her."

Jack reached a hand out to clasp Alaina's, but she pushed to her feet, her face set. "I must go see her. Frank, you'll take me to her. Jack?"

It seemed to him in that moment that she would shatter completely.

"I'll take you there," Frank promised.

Jack rose and rounded the end of the table. He stood close to Alaina and pressed her cold hands between his warm ones. "Seeing you will bring her back. I'm sure of it, sweetheart."

Chapter 33

Despite Jack and Alaina's efforts, her mother remained cloaked in silence. She lowered her hand from her mother's forehead and hugged herself before glancing over at Jack. "Can you think of anything else to try?"

He shook his head. There was an edge of desperation in Alaina's voice that tugged at his heart. He'd been startled by Alaina's mother's appearance. Her once-full figure had thinned to little more than bone.

Mrs. Bledsoe, the farmer's wife who had so kindly cared for Charlotte, could shed little light on her condition. "When she came here, she was like that. Just wandering. Must have been three days ago that Ben found her and brought her here. She's not ate more than a piece of bread, or said two words put together." The woman's brown eyes were solemn. "Seems I've seen the same look on many other faces lately. Such a tragedy."

The woman had left them alone, with Alaina chattering at her mother, sharing details of her trip to Pittsburgh. Seeing Pitcairn's private car. The way the people dressed. The noise of the city. And on and on. But all her efforts failed and now she looked to him.

It struck Jack as a deep irony that Alaina, who knew how much her mother disliked him, would think he might be able to penetrate the wall Charlotte had retreated behind. What could he say? His heart beat hard as he knelt. *Lord, grant me wisdom.*

"Hi, Mrs. Morrison. Alaina and I are going on a picnic and want to take you along. If you don't mind, Frank and Missy will join us. It'll be fun."

That was it. His mind shut down, and he couldn't think of another thing to say, so he swept to his feet and faced Alaina, keeping his voice low. "Would you mind asking Mrs. Bledsoe if she could spare a bit of food?" He fished out a few coins and pressed them into Alaina's palm. "Give these to her. Perhaps they'll help."

"But what good will a picnic do?"

Jack didn't really know. "I thought maybe if we could be together, normal again, maybe it would help her. We'll go out onto the other side of the hill, away from Johnstown, where the view is nice."

Alaina nodded. "Yes. I think it might help. Everything that happened is too much. It's the same sense I got with one of the women I ministered to on the hill."

Jack squeezed her hand, then released it. "Good. And Alaina. . ."

She caught the tender light in his eyes.

"We'll pray."

ᴒ3

The Bledsoes offered Alaina a room to stay with her mother. Upon hearing that Charlotte was a seamstress, it was Mrs. Bledsoe's idea to gather together a few scraps and a needle and put them into Charlotte's fingers. "Make her feel normal again," the farmer's wife reasoned.

At first Alaina noticed little things. Her mother ate a bit more, and she would massage the material between her fingers, and those things gave Alaina hope.

In the evenings, Jack would come up with Frank, Missy, and a mending Sam, and they would help Alaina take her mother to the little section of woods that had become their special spot. They did their best to keep the conversation away from news of Johnstown.

In the wooded spot, surrounded by a giggling Sam and Missy and watching as her mother watched the children, Alaina allowed the worry to erode her confidence.

Jack leaned forward and tapped her head. "You're thinking too much. You've got that worried wrinkle between your eyes."

She leaned back against him, allowing him to support her weight. "Sometimes I wonder if she'll ever smile again. Or laugh. Even do her sewing. Aunt Jo wants me to bring her to Pittsburgh."

"She's a kind woman, but I think you're going to be your mother's best chance of recovery. We should stay together."

"Do you think we should all go out to Pittsburgh? She wouldn't mind."

Jack didn't answer for so long that she finally shifted to look over her shoulder at him. Blue eyes captured hers. A small smile quivered on his lips.

Alaina became aware of the fact they'd spent very little time without being surrounded by her mother or Frank and the children. "Why don't we go for a walk?"

"A most brilliant idea."

Alaina laughed and shifted away from him.

He swept to his feet, steadying her rise and retaining his grip on her hand.

Frank's eyes smiled over at them from where he sat talking to Charlotte.

Jack chuckled and whispered to Alaina, "I think he approves."

They walked in silence. Alaina noted the change in direction, away from the Bledsoes' farm, and wasn't surprised when they came out on the hill overlooking Johnstown. Though still terribly scarred and riddled with debris, progress had been made.

"Will it ever be the same?" she whispered.

"In many ways, no. But change doesn't mean it's better or worse. Only different."

A cool breeze washed by her, and she leaned her head back to stare up at the sky. "It seems so strange that life goes on despite everything."

Jack didn't seem to hear. He walked on a few steps more and stopped, his body silhouetted against the sky.

She studied him and realized his shirt looked new and his suspenders, though frayed, weren't nearly as gnarled as the last pair. Even his trousers were less tattered. People had sent in used clothing from all over. "There must be a terrible need for clothing," she murmured to herself, as an idea dawned. If she could manage to secure some bolts of material, she could, with Mrs. Bledsoe's help, put together clothes for the victims. But her thoughts stopped there only briefly. Jack's posture let her know that something was wrong. "Jack?"

He faced her. "I have something to tell you."

She swallowed. Maybe in the time she'd been so preoccupied with her mother he had found someone else down in Johnstown. But no, it couldn't be. Jack loved her.

He advanced on her with an amused expression. "You've got that worried line again. Why?"

Embarrassed, she looked away. "I thought you were going to tell me you'd found someone else?" But it came out more a question than a statement, and she cringed.

Jack's hand captured her chin and tilted her face back toward him, his blue eyes darkened with disappointment. "How could you think that?"

"We haven't had much time together." She flushed. "Your clothes look new."

Jack stared down at his shirt. "A man gets some clothes from one of the shipments, and you think I'm dressing up for another woman?"

Alaina stamped her foot. "Don't you dare laugh at me."

"I'm not laughing. Really. I know you've been under a lot of stress. Everyone has." He put some distance between them. "There's something that's happened that we need to talk about."

☙

Jack knew he was being vague, but he didn't know how to suggest what he felt God had been nudging him to do. He'd wrestled with the ever-stronger urging of his spirit for two weeks, and he felt exhausted from the mental struggle.

He drew a strengthening breath. "It's ironic, really, everything that has happened in these last few days." He grimaced. "But let me start at the beginning. After the flood, as I worked at the bridge and around Johnstown, I kept wondering if I could go back to Cambria Iron. They're calling some of the men back and trying to get in full swing. Part of me wants to stay here and see Johnstown rebuilt, but then your mother is so ill, and I wondered if it would be wiser to take her away from here."

"I've thought the same thing," Alaina offered.

Hearing that made it easier and lessened Jack's fear. "But then there's you and me. And money." He swallowed. "You see, the plans I turned in right before the flood hit were looked over, and the boss thinks they might work. He called me into a meeting yesterday and gave me a nice sum."

"That's. . .wonderful news." But Alaina's words were wooden, devoid of happiness, and he thought he understood the sudden flicker in her eyes.

He licked his lips. "When I had that money in my hand, I felt such satisfaction, but something else, too. I realized that God had allowed everything to happen to bring me to this point. I had everything I thought meant so much; now what would I do?"

He paused before continuing, "There are still so many who need shelter, and though food isn't nearly the problem it once was, housing is. I could build a huge house and have families come and live there, but I realized it wasn't what I wanted. I want to divide the money between some families who need it."

Alaina's mouth parted. "Are you serious?"

Jack's throat thickened. "I mean it so much it hurts. I've learned my lesson, Alaina. I want to help someone else. I'll still keep a portion for us, but the rest will go to help those in need. To rebuild life for those so shaken by the disaster."

Tears shimmered in her eyes, and Jack felt the rightness of his words in every part of his body. "We'll move away, you, me, and your mother. Frank and Missy and Sam, too, if they want to come. Then we can settle down and make a home."

Alaina brushed her hand across her cheeks. "Where will we go?"

He shrugged. "Wherever you want to go. We'll travel until we find a place. God will show us."

She hugged herself and stared out over Johnstown, and when she finally met his gaze, Jack saw the spark of a smile. "Aren't you forgetting something?"

He chuckled. "I was wondering if you would notice." He closed the distance between them and grasped her by the waist. "I think this is going on the third time I'm going to ask, so I'm hoping for a better answer."

She reached as if to smack his shoulder, but he captured her hand and raised it to his lips. As he stared into her dark eyes, he glimpsed a future of peace and commitment, not only to her but also to God and to his fellow man. "Alaina?"

"I would be most honored to become your wife."